MIXED BLESSINGS

Elvi Rhodes

WINDSOR
PARAGON

First published 2005
by
Bantam Press
This Large Print edition published 2005
by
BBC Audiobooks Ltd by arrangement with
Transworld Publishers

ISBN 1 4056 1201 0   (Windsor Hardcover)
ISBN 1 4056 1202 9   (Paragon Softcover)

British Library Cataloguing in Publication Data available

Printed and bound in Great Britain by
Antony Rowe Ltd., Chippenham, Wiltshire

MIXED BLESSINGS

For Venus Stanton, the attractive young vicar of Thurston, life could not be better. When she first came to this traditional parish, with its beautiful church and conservative congregation, many people found it hard to accept a woman priest. After a tricky start, however, she has now gained the approval of most of her parishioners, even though some people cannot and will not recognize her.

But vicars have their personal lives as well, although many people often forget this, and to the delight and surprise of the parish Venus is to marry Nigel, the doctor from the local practice. Her eleven-year-old daughter Becky, after some misgivings, has got used to the idea and there is a joyous ceremony at the church, after which the happy pair set off for a honeymoon in France. On their return, they try to settle down to their new life, but Venus soon finds that marriage, motherhood and her priestly duties do not always go together . . .

This book is for Fr Martin Morgan who,
over several years, has made me aware of what
a good parish priest is and does.

ACKNOWLEDGEMENTS

I thank the East Sussex Fire Brigade, and in particular Richard Fowler, Station Manager of Roedean Fire Station, Brighton. He gave me detailed information about causes of fire, what the brigade does on the spot, and the aftermath of a large fire. Almost all of it was new to me. I could not have written this episode without his help.

Once again, I thank Olwen Holmes for reading and commenting on my chapters as I went along. It was, as always, a great help.

Yet again, I thank Shirley Hall, my secretary, who has lived through the book with all my re-writes without once losing her cool. She is indispensable.

CHAPTER ONE

Venus was awakened by the June sunlight streaming into her bedroom. She hadn't drawn the curtains last night—she couldn't think why—and the light was falling on to her face. But even before she opened her eyes, while she was still half asleep, she knew this was a special day, and in the same breath it came to her. 'It's my wedding day!' She said the words out loud.

No-one heard her. Why should they? The clock on the bedside table stood at ten past five: probably the whole country was still asleep. Certainly they would be in the Vicarage. Becky would be sleeping the deep sleep of a ten-year-old. She'd been late to bed last night and it would be a couple of hours before she surfaced. Ann, Venus's mother-in-law from her first marriage, might just be awake. In a way, Venus hoped she wasn't. *Her* first thoughts would almost certainly be of that other Saturday morning, almost twelve years ago, when her son had married Venus.

Dear Philip, Venus thought. And wherever he was—being a priest as well as his widow she knew where he was, wasn't believing in the hereafter part of her job description?—she knew he would be wishing her well. She lay still and thought about him for a little while, with nothing but love, and then her thoughts turned to Nigel, who, in a very few hours, she would marry.

There were times when she had thought this day would never come. She seemed to have been waiting for ever, though in fact it was only seven

1

months since she had sought the Bishop's permission to marry Nigel. That, as a priest serving in his diocese, she had had to do. In something as important as marriage he had to give her the go-ahead. He'd been very nice about it, not at all discouraging, but he'd said, 'It is not the fact that your young man is a Roman Catholic, but rather that you have known him only a short time, and as yet I haven't had the pleasure of meeting him at all. So you must be patient. And when the time does come—' he'd added, much to her delight, 'since you're a very busy lady with a parish to run it will come sooner than you think—I myself will marry you!' But then he'd always been kind to her.

'It will have to be in your own church, St Mary's, Thurston,' he'd told her. 'But since your young man is a Roman Catholic, I would expect you to invite Father Seamus to play a prominent part. I know Father Seamus quite well and I'm sure he'd want to do that.'

He'd been right about Father Seamus, Nigel's parish priest. He was most cooperative. He knew there was no prospect at all of him losing Nigel. When it came to Sundays, and any other day of obligation, she and Nigel, though both of them living and worshipping in the village of Thurston, would part company—he to St Patrick's, she to do her job as Vicar of St Mary's. They would take part in almost identical services, say the same prayers, hear the same readings from the gospels—but not together. They both felt strongly about this, that it was wrong—even sinful. It must seem as stupid to God, they'd agreed, as it did to them. But that's how it was and they must accept it.

It was far too early to get up. The wedding

wasn't until noon and she didn't want to be mooning around, getting in everyone's way all morning, so not without difficulty she settled back against the pillows and allowed herself the luxury of simply thinking. Naturally, she thought about Nigel. He would still be in bed, unless he had had any night calls which had taken him out. She hoped he had made an arrangement with Sonia, his partner in the practice, that if there were any calls she would take them. He was to take the inside of a week off from the practice—he hadn't been able to get a locum any more than she had managed to get another priest to take over St Mary's. There was someone for tomorrow but she had to be back in harness by the following Sunday. Mrs Nigel Baines I shall be then, she thought. The Reverend Venus Baines.

And this, she thought now, was the last time in the foreseeable future that she would lie in this bed alone. From today Nigel would lie beside her. When she turned to him he would be there, he would put his arms around her, he would hold her. She looked forward to that so much, indeed, she longed for it. The last six months had not been easy in that respect, but now they were almost over. And of course, the shared bed was not the only change their marriage would bring. There were others. For a start, Nigel would be obliged to move into the Vicarage because as incumbent of the parish this was where she had to live. Nigel didn't mind that. He had a small flat which he would be happy to leave. She had asked him if he was sure he wasn't marrying her just to get better accommodation. He'd said, 'Oh dear, you've seen through me! Actually, I was looking for a place large enough to

3

take my piano in comfort. And my CD collection.' He was a music lover. Their first date had been to a concert in Brampton. Rachmaninov and Sibelius.

And then, of course, they would eat together, shop together, spend their leisure time together—not that, between a doctor and a parish priest, both busy, there would be acres of leisure—and, very important, she thought, we will look after Becky together.

Becky, as well as her best friend, Anna Brent, was to be her bridesmaid. For weeks now she had been wild with excitement about this. It was one of the things, Venus thought, which had reconciled her to me marrying again! Becky had been more or less allowed to choose the dresses. Apricot silk, ankle length, a wreath of small flowers in the hair, silver shoes, small posies to carry, which were to be delivered from the florist later that morning. Anna's mother, Sally, had made the dresses and she would be getting the girls ready. What Becky didn't know was that Nigel had bought each of the girls a slender silver necklace with a pendant heart, as his present to them.

The best man, Angus Macdonald, a Scotsman with whom Nigel had trained, had travelled from the Yorkshire Dales where he and his wife shared a practice. Until yesterday, when he'd arrived in Thurston, though she'd heard a lot about him she'd never met him. She'd taken to him at once. It was a pity, he'd said, that his wife couldn't come with him. For one thing she had to look after the practice in his absence, and for another she had three small children. Angus was staying at the Ewe Lamb, which now had two rooms for letting. He would have stayed with Nigel except that Nigel's

4

mother and his Aunt Veronica were there, having come over from Quilty, in Ireland, where Nigel was born and brought up. Both ladies were wild with excitement, especially Aunt Veronica, who had never crossed the water before. When Venus and Nigel had met them at Gatwick the previous day Veronica had been struck dumb by it all. 'Which won't be for long,' Nigel had said afterwards. 'Aunt Veronica could talk a glass eye to sleep!'

Looking back, she'd been a bit afraid Nigel's mother, when they'd become engaged, might not approve of her, that she wouldn't be happy about her son marrying out of his church. 'Don't worry!' Nigel had assured her. 'She's happy that I'm marrying at all! She thought it would never happen.'

'Why didn't it?' Venus asked him. She could hardly believe that he hadn't been snapped up, and she knew he'd had a relationship though it had been before he'd come to Thurston.

'Because I hadn't met you,' he'd said.

She looked at the clock again. It was still too early to get up. She would like to phone Nigel; ask how he was, tell him how much she loved him. Her mother would be horrified at the thought. It appeared—she had said it in no uncertain terms—that for the bride and groom to have any contact on the day of the wedding before the ceremony took place was to invite the worst possible bad luck. She had recited several instances, known to her, ranging from a broken leg (the groom) to being left at the altar (the bride). I'm not superstitious, Venus told herself, of course she wasn't, she wouldn't believe any of it, but better not risk it, eh? She wouldn't phone. Nor did Nigel phone her. Possibly

5

his mother was of the same persuasion as hers.

She hoped Becky wouldn't waken too soon. It would be all go once she had. And then her mother would arrive and she'd be like a clucking hen with chickens—bless her heart for she meant well. She will drag my protesting father in her wake, Venus thought.

The gentlest knock sounded on the door. If she hadn't already been awake she wouldn't have heard it, but she could guess who it was and she was right. Ann entered, carrying a small tray set with one of the best china cups, a small pot of tea and a thick slice of brown toast with Cooper's Oxford marmalade.

'Good morning, Venus dear! I didn't waken you, did I?' she asked anxiously.

'No, I've been awake a little while now,' Venus said. 'A cup of tea is exactly what I need.'

Ann poured it, no milk, no sugar. Venus sat upright and took it from her. 'Aren't you going to have one yourself?' she enquired.

'I already have,' Ann said.

There was a short silence while Venus sipped the tea, neither of them quite knowing what to say next. It was an unusual situation. Then Venus found her voice.

'I can't thank you enough . . .' she began.

'Whatever for?' Ann said. 'It's only a cup of tea.'

Venus shook her head. 'You know perfectly well I'm not talking about the tea. I meant I can't thank you enough just for being here today. It wouldn't have been the same without you, but I can imagine how you feel. Or think I can. It's a phrase we use so slickly, and it's often not true.'

'It's all right, love,' Ann said. 'I wanted to be

6

here and it was good of you to let me come.'

'I wouldn't have dreamt of doing otherwise,' Venus said.

They talked for a while—about how excited Becky was, about what a lovely, sunny day it looked like being in spite of the weather forecast, which promised otherwise—and then Ann said, 'I'll leave you to it, dear. I'm sure there's no need for you to get up just yet. You have a long day ahead of you.'

That was certainly true, Venus thought. And before it all rushed in on her she must say her Office, which she must do every day, wherever she was. Today she would do it sitting up in bed, propped against her pillows. The psalm, the Old Testament and New Testament readings, all laid down for the day. Today's chosen psalm, however, was full of woe and foreboding, totally inappropriate, since all she wanted to do was to praise God. Then, though she read that dutifully, she chose another to follow it, the very last in the Book of Psalms. That one said it all: 'Praise the Lord . . . Let everything that breathes praise the Lord.'

Now, she thought, I really must get up. She couldn't bear to stay in bed another minute. In any case, Sandra the village hairdresser was coming to do her hair before she opened up her salon, and I must shower, Venus thought, before she can start on it. It was very kind of Sandra to offer because Saturday morning was probably the busiest time of the week for her. Most of the village ladies went to Sandra, though a few took themselves off to Brampton in search of something they reckoned would be more sophisticated—and would certainly cost more.

7

Naturally, she would not be wearing a veil, not for a second marriage. She had bought a hat. In fact, it was so large-brimmed that she wondered how she would receive all the kisses which would come her way. Especially from other large-hatted ladies. But didn't it go wonderfully with her cream silk, long-skirted suit and her beautiful, totally frivolous and fragile high-heeled shoes, on which she had spent more money than she'd ever spent on shoes in her life? They would probably be killing her before the end of the day, she thought.

She moved about stealthily in the silent house—presumably Ann had gone back to bed—and then she decided to take a turn round the garden. Missie had woken up the moment she'd heard Venus on the stairs and she'd already let her out into the garden in case she should disturb Becky. Even so early in the day it was pleasantly warm with the sun already bringing out the scents from the flowers, particularly from the roses. The irises were splendid; so tall, so stately. They thrived in this rather alkaline soil. She had once read somewhere that if one took the trouble to study the varieties and planted them in the right spots it would be possible to have one iris or another in flower on every day of the year. But then, every season had something to offer in the garden and June, perhaps, was the best month of all.

Missie was sniffing around enjoying herself. She was a six-year-old spaniel cross bitch, black-and-white, with drooping spaniel ears, lustrous brown eyes and a beautiful fringed tail. They had had her from the Rescue Centre and she was the light of Becky's life. Helping to plan the wedding, Becky had seriously wanted Missie to be one of the bridesmaids and on this Venus had compromised by saying that she could go to church as long as she was on the lead and in the charge of Grandma, whom she adored. Missie was a well-behaved, obedient little dog and Venus had often taken her to church, especially during the week, so there should be no difficulty about that, she thought. Also, her father would take Missie for a walk over the Downs before the wedding. And in a weak moment, badgered by Becky, she had agreed that she might wear an apricot-coloured bow. Am I mad? Venus asked herself now.

Everything was so peaceful, not a sound anywhere—and then suddenly the peace was shattered. Becky had woken up and was hammering at her bedroom window, and Missie barking with excitement at the sight of her.

From that moment it was rush, rush, rush. Venus insisted that Becky should eat a proper breakfast. 'I shan't let you put on your dress until you've done so,' she threatened. A resigned look on her face, Becky downed a bowl of cereal and most of a boiled egg.

'And you have to eat as well, Mummy,' she said.

Venus ate a slice of toast, reluctantly.

By the time they had eaten, Sandra was there to do Venus's hair. Ann took Becky off. 'I'll look after her until Anna Brent and her mother arrive,' she promised. Then as they were leaving the room, Mrs Foster sailed in, her husband walking a couple of yards behind her, like the Duke of Edinburgh behind the Queen.

'Dad, when are you going to take Missie for her walk?' Venus asked. 'Do you think now—or later?'

'I'll do both, love,' her father said. 'Best be on

the safe side.' The truth was, he'd be glad to be away from all the fuss and palaver. He clipped on Missie's lead and set off for the Downs. 'I'll not hurry back,' he said. 'You don't need me here.'

Becky called after him as he went out of the door, 'Don't let her get all muddy, Grandpa!'

'I won't,' he promised.

'Your hair's come up well,' Sandra said a little later, looking over Venus's shoulder at her reflection in the mirror.

'Yes, I'm pleased with it,' Venus said. Of course it would be mostly hidden under her hat.

While Sandra had been blow-drying her hair—fortunately she was not a hairdresser who talked all the time—she had thought about Nigel, wondered what he was doing at this moment. It wouldn't be long now before they'd be together for ever. She hoped, oh, she did so hope, that she'd be the wife he'd always wanted, that she'd make him happy for the rest of his life. She loved him so much. She had loved Philip to the same degree, of course, and it had never seemed possible, though now it was, that she could do the same again.

And so the morning went. Sally Brent came and looked after the bridesmaids; Venus, after her hair was done, was taken over by Ann. Her mother inspected her father—who had now returned from his walks with Missie—checking that he was properly turned out. She was not actually heard to say 'Have you got a clean handkerchief, Ernest?' but it was certain she would have. Venus had already learnt, from the weddings she had done at St Mary's, that it was the mother of the bride who was all-powerful on these occasions. Nothing was outside her jurisdiction.

Dead on time the cars arrived. Venus had protested all along that it was nonsense to hire limousines to take them the few hundred yards to the church. She would happily have walked, along with her family, but the thought had horrified her mother. 'What would people think?' she'd demanded. 'We don't want it to look as if we were doing things on the cheap, do we?' Then with her usual common sense she'd added, 'Besides, it could be raining cats and dogs—and where would you get a wedding car at short notice?'

Venus took a last, critical look at herself in the long mirror in the hall. I wish I had stuck at it and slimmed down from a size fourteen to a twelve, she thought. I wish I'd had gold highlights in my hair instead of simply a gold rinse—not that it would show in church, but sooner or later the hat would have to come off. She couldn't go to bed in it. She wished she was six inches taller. Five-feet-two was so undistinguished. But the dress was lovely and her shoes were still wonderful and, as yet, not in the least painful.

When the bridesmaids came into the hall she turned away from the mirror to inspect them. They were perfection, the colour of their dresses suited both of them equally, even though Becky was dark-haired and Anna's hair a pale gold.

'I hope the Bishop won't be late!' Mrs Foster said as she saw Venus into the bridal car with Ernest.

'Oh, Mother! Of course he won't be late!' Venus assured her. 'He has to be in church before me. I imagine he's done a few hundred weddings in his time! He knows the drill.' But her mother had said just enough to sow the smallest seed of doubt in

11

her. Supposing his car had broken down on the motorway? Supposing there'd been an accident? And supposing he'd been called to the bedside of a dying VIP in the church? Where would his loyalties lie?

'Don't be so bloody silly, Mavis!' Ernest said to his wife. 'Get yourself and Missie into your car or you'll be the one who's late!' It was a sign of his taut nerves, Venus knew, that he swore at her mother, and of her mother's that she took it without protest.

Missie, not to be outdone, had a fit of temperament and wanted to go in the bridal car instead of with Mrs Foster. She pulled on her lead, and barked. 'It's what comes of tying a fancy bow on a dog, dressing her beyond her station,' Ernest said.

And then at last Venus was walking up the aisle on her father's arm, and there was Nigel waiting. So was the Bishop, but it was Nigel Venus saw first. He half turned around and gave her a loving smile. He looked wonderful in his smart suit, Venus thought, though his reddish hair was still slightly untamed. He should have had it cut, but she was glad he didn't. It made him look himself, and human. She smiled back at him and for a moment there was no-one in the church but the two of them. Venus knew at once, as sure as sure, that everything was going to be all right. Not just for now, but for always.

And then she looked at the Bishop. He had taken off his mitre and it had been placed on the altar by his chaplain (a kind of Lord-in-Waiting, though she always thought of him as a well-trained, rather superior nanny), who had relieved him of his

12

crozier, the bishop's crook. Over a red cassock he wore a rochet, a shortish surplice, which went into the most beautiful bishop's sleeves, gathered in at the wrists and, as if that were not enough, a chimere, a sort of sleeveless coat, in red, open at the front so that his exquisite pectoral cross, set with amethysts and a ruby or two and lying against his breast, was in full view. His abundant white hair shone silver in the sun which streamed in through the window and fell directly on him, as if straight from heaven. Her swift thought was how glad she was that she'd decided against the long dress with bishop's sleeves which she'd at first planned for herself. Sartorially, she would have been totally outshone by him—as indeed she was now; there was no doubt about it. All these wonderful vestments, which in their ceremonial place, as today, she liked, dated from the time of the Roman Empire. They certainly knew how to dress! And as she knew well, they were not worn to enhance the Bishop, they were worn to the glory of God—though they certainly added to the shine of the wedding.

But the words of the service which now began, simple, forthright, intensely moving, saying everything which needed to be said, transcended all the finery, both the Bishop's and hers. They were from the heart, as were the prayers which were said by Father Seamus. Nigel's responses were firm and strong, and his Irish accent more than usually pronounced. She opened her eyes very wide, trying not to let a single tear escape. She had little doubt that by now her mother would be in floods.

Everything, absolutely everything, went without a hitch. The bridesmaids, as well as looking enchanting, behaved impeccably, as in the end did Missie. When the ceremony was over the Bishop, having donned his mitre and been given back his crozier to pronounce the blessing, processed back down the aisle, preceded by the chaplain carrying the beautiful processional cross which, only now did Venus remember, had been given a long time ago by the Frazer family, benefactors of St Mary's over many generations. If the Hon. Miss Amelia Frazer, the last of the line, knew that it was being used at my wedding, Venus thought, she would not be pleased.

She and Nigel (her husband, she reminded herself!) stood outside the church door, greeting people—as did the Bishop. He was, after all, everyone's Father in God, not just hers. One or two guests who knew what was what kissed his splendid episcopal ring, but not many. That was not quite St Mary's, Thurston. And then it was time for the photographs and for these they moved on to the lawn in front of the church, which had been mown within an inch of its life.

When the photographs were over, and they seemed to take forever because not only had the official photographer been hard at it, doing every possible grouping so that no-one was left out, but almost everyone else seemed to have brought a camera to record the event, the guests moved towards the parish hall for the refreshments. As she'd been promised, everything was wonderful: the flowers, the food, there was even music. The Bishop introduced Venus to a pleasant, quietly dressed lady who, it turned out, was his wife. Venus thought she had probably looked the same when she was the wife of a young curate all those years

14

ago, though it was difficult now to think of the Bishop as anything as lowly as that young curate. I daresay, Venus thought, she long ago gave up the struggle to equal him dresswise.

Moving around by Nigel's side, she met Bertha Jowett. Bertha, until the last few months, had lived in the cottage which Venus's parents bought from her when she moved into a home because she could no longer look after herself. She hadn't thought Bertha would want to come to the wedding, but she'd accepted with alacrity, while making it quite clear that church services of any kind were a load of claptrap. From time to time Venus would visit her in The Beeches and the two of them would have a game of Scrabble, which Bertha invariably won. But then, Venus told herself, Bertha was in the front row when brains were given out. She was not one of St Mary's congregation, far from it. The very thought of being taken for such would horrify her because she was an avowed atheist. 'Though she seems quite to like me,' Venus had once told Nigel, 'she thinks I am seriously misguided, but you could say we are good friends.'

'I'm pleased to see you, Bertha,' Venus said now. 'I shall introduce you to the Bishop.'

'He seems a pleasant man,' Bertha said graciously. 'But I am not fazed by bishops. I have met several in my time. Underneath all that fancy dress they're mortal men.'

'You're looking very well, Miss Jowett,' Nigel said.

'And so are you, young man,' she replied, her eyes glinting.

Eventually, everyone took their places at the

15

tables. The food and wine were delicious, the speeches, mercifully short. Angus Macdonald told a few anecdotes about Nigel which went down well. Then, to Venus's great surprise, the Blessed Henry said some rather nice things about her. Henry Nugent had been her senior churchwarden ever since she'd arrived in Thurston; always supportive, always on her side; she didn't know what she would have done without him. The Bishop and his lady ate little, joined in the toasts, and then left. Soon after that Nigel and Venus left, going back to the Vicarage so that she could change. Her shoes had so far stood up to everything nobly, though whether they would have seen her through the dancing which was to follow later was another matter.

And then she and Nigel were driven to the airport to catch the plane for the short trip to Bergerac where they were to stay in a hotel overnight before driving in a hired car to spend their too-short honeymoon in the south of the Dordogne, where Nigel had been lent a house by one of his more affluent friends.

CHAPTER TWO

They arrived at the hotel in Bergerac, having picked up the hire car at the airport, with half-an-hour to spare before dinner and were shown to their room. The hotel had been recommended by Nigel's friend James, the man who was lending them his house. 'It isn't posh, but it's comfortable,' he'd said. 'And it's in the main street so it's handy for everything.'

Venus watched while Nigel signed their names in the register—Doctor and Mrs Nigel Baines—and tried not to look smug. They had not said they were on honeymoon, nor had Nigel ordered a bottle of champagne to be served in the bedroom—a dead giveaway, though whether of a legally married couple or an illicit weekend who could tell? In any case, neither of them needed champagne. Life was heady enough at the moment.

They looked at the huge bed, and then at each other. The question and the longing was there in their eyes. Why not now? Why not? Nigel took Venus into his arms and kissed her. He ran his fingers over the contours of her face as if she were a piece of precious sculpture. Then suddenly he said, 'No! Not now, my darling. We have all night. We have the rest of our lives!'

They went down to the dining room, where they ate a delicious meal, and when the meal was over they went to bed. And there the love they had for each other found satisfaction and rapture beyond anything they had dreamt of.

*   *   *

Next morning, after an early breakfast, they collected the car from the hotel garage, and drove off. Neither of them had ever been in the south-west of France before. The road from Bergerac to Bordeaux was a straight one and even on a Sunday it was busy with *camions* laden with wine for export, but after fifteen miles or so they left it, at a turning signposted 'Calmet'. Calmet had been described in the guidebook as one of the

17

Dordogne's oldest *bastide* towns.

Driving into it Nigel said, 'It certainly looks as though it's been here for ever.' The *place* was bordered on all four sides by wide pavements, half-hidden under massive stone arches. Though the house James had loaned them was on the outskirts of Calmet, they made straight for the town centre because James had told them there was a Sunday Mass at eleven o'clock, which, on what was such a special occasion, they wanted to attend.

Even though Venus was not a Roman Catholic, because at the moment she was not in England she had been told, and chose to believe, that she would be allowed to take communion together with her husband. It was not so in England. Nigel's church would have forbidden him to do so at St Mary's, or Venus at St Patrick's.

The church was crowded and noisy and the Mass took place at the speed of light. The two of them walked up the aisle together and took communion standing side by side. This might be the only occasion for who knew how long that they would be allowed to do this and, especially at the beginning of their marriage, it meant a lot to both of them.

Afterwards they strolled around Calmet, stopped for a glass of wine at a pavement bar, and watched the world, or this lovely part of it, go by. Then they had lunch in a small restaurant, crowded with families of several generations.

'Does no-one in France eat Sunday lunch at home?' Venus asked.

The meal was wonderful. So many courses, but only a little of each. It was four o'clock before Nigel paid their surprisingly modest bill, and they left. After that they bought eggs, milk, bread, fresh

18

from the second baking of the day, cold meats from the *charcuterie*, and a few salad items. Then they picked up the key from the agent and set off to find the house, which was, they were told, three kilometres away up a narrow, climbing road. Blonde cattle, looking incredibly clean, grazed in the fields on one side of the road, and on the other side grew a crop of something Nigel said was maize. The house was a farm cottage, and spaced around it, but not too close, were four smaller houses and one or two barns. There was no sign of life from any of them.

'Well,' Nigel said, 'James did promise it would be peaceful.'

There was a narrow strip of garden—badly in need of attention—at the front of the house. Beyond that the land sloped away for several acres, all of which were close-planted with sunflowers, now in full bloom; huge heads the size of plates, bursting with bright colour, waited to be harvested. Inside the house it felt chilly, but exploring the outhouses they found stores of wood, both sawn logs and kindling, so Nigel soon had a fire going.

It was the start of a wonderful week. In the daytime they walked or drove around the area, though never very far. They took picnics—fresh bread, local cheese, red wine, fruit. After dark, which came early so far south, they walked down to Calmet and ate in one or other of the small restaurants, then strolled back, hand in hand. Just to hold a man's hand again, Venus thought, such a small thing in itself, was so comforting. At night they made love, and then they made love again, and finally fell asleep in each other's arms. And in the mornings, they awoke to the delight of each

19

other and everything renewed.

Not until towards the end of the week did they talk about home, and then it stole slowly back into their speech. Becky, staying with her grandparents, they agreed, would be spoilt rotten. Nigel's mother and Aunt Veronica would be back in Ireland—'Let's go and visit them in the spring,' Venus said.

'And as soon as we get back,' Nigel said, 'I must leave my flat and move everything to the Vicarage.'

'And after that, shall we give a dinner party?' Venus suggested. 'Who shall we invite?'

Nigel shook his head. 'Not too soon. I want you to myself for a bit longer. Later, yes.'

He was right, Venus thought. Between the demands of her job and his there would be too little time together.

Mostly, they talked about themselves: what they did as children, where they went to school, who had been their best friends, what they liked, what they didn't. They were eager to learn everything about each other; nothing was too small or too insignificant. Venus found herself able to talk about Philip and Nigel told her about his former girlfriends. It's OK to do that, Venus thought, because all we want now, all we will ever want, we will find in each other.

'In one way,' she said to Nigel on their last night in Calmet, 'I want this week never to end. In another way I am so looking forward to all the new things waiting for us.'

'But there'll still be the old ones,' Nigel said. 'They won't go away.'

'I know that,' she agreed. 'But we'll be doing them together, or if not actually *doing* them together, at least we can talk about things. Not that

20

you will tell me about your patients, and not that I will tell you what's private to any of my parishioners—though I do remember a girl in a parish where I once lived who thought that after the Vicar had heard confessions he went home and had a cosy chat about them with his wife! "So what do you think Mrs Thompson's been up to now! You'll never guess!"'

In the end, Saturday came, and it was time to go home—and now, for both of them, there was something new, and special, about that word. They were sad to leave, but not unhappy. Back in Thurston would be the real beginning of their new life together.

Early on Saturday morning, they drove to Bergerac and handed back the car at the airport. They had a good flight back and Venus's father, as promised, was there to meet them from the plane. Venus had hoped Becky might be with him but she wasn't.

'She went off with Anna and Sally to an animal sanctuary somewhere or other,' her father told her. 'And she's staying overnight with them. Your Mum would have come with me but we weren't sure how Missie would be in the car so she's stayed behind with her. Did you have a good holiday?'

'Wonderful!' they said in unison. 'Is everything all right in Thurston?' Venus asked.

'Well, I haven't heard anything to the contrary so I expect it is,' Ernest said. That's my Dad, Venus thought. Never trouble trouble till trouble troubles you.

He drove them first to his own home. Her mother must have been watching out of the window for them. She was at the door before they were halfway up the path, Missie at her feet.

'Welcome home!' she said with a beaming smile. Missie ran forward and tried to climb up Venus's leg, which somehow touched her even more than her mother's greeting. The first time I've been away from her, she thought, and she remembers me!

'Is everyone OK here?' Nigel asked. 'Did my mother and Aunty Veronica get off to the airport all right?'

'Of course!' Mrs Foster said. 'Dad took them to Gatwick and stayed with them until they had to go through to the departure lounge. They're two very nice ladies. Your mother's invited us to visit her in Quilty. We think we might go next year. Neither of us has ever been to Ireland. Would you like a cup of tea? The kettle's on.'

'A quick one,' Venus said. 'And then I think we should get back to the Vicarage.' The truth was, she longed to be in her own home, and with Nigel. She had always liked coming home after a holiday, but this was extra-special. She was disappointed that Becky wasn't around to greet them, but then she told herself she was being silly. Why should she have given up a lovely outing with Anna and Sally just to say 'hello' an hour or two earlier?

'Did you go to church on Sunday?' she asked her mother.

'Of course we did, and Becky with us,' her mother said. 'But we didn't go in for coffee.'

That surprised Venus. Her mother loved the coffee bit, the meeting with everyone, exchanging views. Gossip, in fact.

'The Reverend Swinton preached a very good sermon,' Mrs Foster said. 'Are you sure you won't

22

stay for a meal? I've got a nice piece of ham.'

'I'm sure Venus and Nigel have things to do at the Vicarage, Mavis,' her father said firmly. He was good at understanding feelings.

'Very well, then,' his wife said. 'And it's been lovely having Becky. I'll bring her back in the morning, so you can see her before she goes back to school.'

Back at the Vicarage Venus thought how wonderful it was, walking up the path together, both of them belonging there. She handed the keys to Nigel so that he could unlock the door and let them in. She wanted him to feel right from the start that it was as much his place as hers. 'I suppose I should carry you over the threshold,' he said. 'Or perhaps should you carry me as it's your house?'

'It's *our* home,' Venus said firmly. 'Make no mistake about that.'

Everything smelt fresh and clean. Ethel Leigh had been at it with her lavender-scented polish. Venus had first met Ethel when her husband, Ronnie, died and she had buried him. They weren't churchgoers. It was Venus's opinion that Ethel had made her life's work looking after Ronnie and their daughter, Marilyn, who now no longer lived at home. Wanting something to fill in the time after her bereavement, Ethel had gone to help Bertha Jowett move out of her cottage and into The Beeches, sorting diligently and tactfully through half a lifetime's accumulation of goods and chattels without once upsetting Bertha. Then Venus, seeing the magic she'd wrought there, had asked her to give her a hand in the Vicarage. Now she came every Friday morning for three hours. Venus couldn't afford it, but she would rather go short of food than not find the money to pay Ethel. She hated housework. But now, with two incomes going into the pot, it might be possible to have Ethel more often.

Nigel took the suitcases straight upstairs to the bedroom. Venus followed him with smaller bags. When they'd put them down they stood and looked at each other.

'We're going to be oh so happy, my darling!' Nigel said.

'I know!' Venus agreed. 'How could we be otherwise?'

Soon afterwards Nigel set off for his flat to collect his car and bring back his first load of possessions. His piano would have to be moved by experts. They had agreed to decide later exactly where everything would go. Most of the rooms were a good size and Venus hadn't brought a lot of furniture when she first moved to Thurston from Clipton. There would probably be room for whatever Nigel wanted to bring. The Vicarage had been built for a large family.

'I should ring Henry,' Venus said.

Henry had been a pillar of strength to her ever since she'd arrived in Thurston, in spite of the fact that he hadn't wanted her there in the first place. Or, rather, she wouldn't have been his first choice. It was doubtful, Venus had faced the fact, if there were many in St Mary's who had wholeheartedly and honestly wanted her. Their previous vicar, who had been in the post for more than twenty years, had retired because of age and a certain amount of ill health. Nine months after he had left there'd still been no sign of anyone to take his place until she had come along, and brought with her the tremendous drawback of being a woman. She had often thought that the Bishop had leaned on them to have her. Her only value, she had sometimes felt in the beginning, was that she was qualified to perform baptisms, marriages and funerals. But to Henry's great credit, she thought now, once he had given in to the inevitability of having her, he had supported her through thick and thin. Henry was waiting to retire, had been even before she came on the scene. He had been churchwarden at St Mary's for eleven years and they had both agreed that this was too long.

He answered the phone at once.

'Hi, Venus!' he said. 'Nice to have you back!'

'Nice to be back,' Venus replied, though she was not sure that was one hundred per cent true. Just a few more days away would have been welcome.

'Is everything all right?' she enquired. 'How did last Sunday go with George Swinton? My mother said he preached a good sermon.'

'Oh, he did! He did,' Henry said quickly.

'But what?' Venus asked. There was something in his voice, something not quite right.

'It's just that . . . I take it your mother didn't tell you?'

'Tell me what?' she asked.

'So I'd better,' he said. 'If I don't, someone else will. Miss Frazer was there.'

She bit back the words which rose to her lips. They were not suitable for a parish priest to utter. Miss Frazer had not set foot in St Mary's since she had had the letter from the Bishop, more or less warning her off.

'What did she do this time?' Venus asked.

'Nothing,' Henry said. 'Nothing.'

'Oh, come on!' Venus protested. 'She can't just have done nothing! It's not in her to do nothing!' And then it dawned on her. 'Did she take communion?' she asked.

'She did,' Henry admitted.

'You mean she walked up to the altar, took the bread and wine, then walked back to her pew?'

'Exactly that,' Henry said. 'As good as gold. And when the service was over she left the church. Not a word out of her. She didn't go in to coffee.'

This is not the time to think about Miss Frazer, Venus told herself firmly, and I'm not going to do it now. This is a happy day, a happy homecoming which I'm not going to spoil. Sufficient, she thought, to know that if I had been at the altar she would, in whatever spectacular way she could think of, have refused to take communion. And because I am a woman. Clearly, Miss Frazer had found out that Venus wouldn't be in church last Sunday. And that, for the moment, Venus decided, is all I'm going to think about it now. She doubted it would be the end. The repercussions would still go on but she would deal with them as they arose.

'She put a fifty-pound note in the plate,' Henry said. 'I suppose to show us what we're missing.'

'But everything else was all right?' Venus asked.

'Oh yes,' Henry said. 'Well, just the usual. The organ's breaking down again; we had a heavy rainstorm last Tuesday and the water's coming in through the chancel roof. And Mrs Braithwaite fell and broke her ankle because of a pothole in the church path. We shall have to get that mended—I mean the pothole.'

'Much as usual, then,' Venus said.

'Much as usual,' Henry agreed. 'It's nice to have

26

you back!' he repeated.

'It's good to be back,' she told him again.

'Is everything all right?' Nigel asked when she'd put the phone down.

'Oh yes!' she said. 'A few odds and ends, that's all. I expect you'll find some in the practice when you start on Monday. It happens, doesn't it.'

He agreed that it did. She wanted to ask him, though she wouldn't, if Miss Frazer was one of his patients. He had never said she was but she felt sure she wouldn't be on Sonia's list, and there were no other doctors in the village. Though much less reprehensible than women priests, it was likely that, in Miss Frazer's view, women doctors were not quite the thing. And that Nigel was a Catholic Venus was sure she would know. She knew everything in Thurston. And would this put him beyond the pale? Venus doubted that Miss Frazer gave in to illness all that much. In any case, though she knew she and Nigel were here, among other things, for the comfort of one another, she was not going to run to him with all her troubles. He might of course already know about Miss Frazer *versus* the Vicar. Probably most of Thurston did. This was a village; news got around with the speed of a bushfire. She had lost count of how many times she'd been told something *'in strictest confidence'*— though never of earth-shattering importance—and had kept that confidence, only to be told that same thing a day or two afterwards by someone quite different, and also in strictest confidence.

But why had Miss Frazer chosen to come to church last Sunday? Was she suddenly a reformed character? Had she seen the light—a sort of road to Damascus experience? Was this a sign of repentance? It was all unlikely.

While these thoughts were racing through her mind, the doorbell rang, and there on the step stood Sally Brent with Becky.

'I thought you might like to have your daughter back this evening rather than wait until tomorrow. I rang your mother and she told me you were already home.'

All thoughts of Miss Frazer vanished from Venus's mind as she welcomed Becky.

'Have you brought me a present?' Becky asked.

'Several,' Venus told her. 'Did you have a good time while I was away?'

'Fab!' Becky said—and then reeled off a list of the treats she'd had with her grandparents.

*   *   *

The next day was their first Sunday morning as a family, and there were three of them for only the one bathroom. But, Venus decided, since the Mass at St Patrick's started half-an-hour earlier than St Mary's, Nigel must certainly have first turn. Living alone for so long now, she had become used to not having to take turns at anything, so they would have to see how it worked out. Becky, of course, would be more than willing to give up her turn in the bathroom. She would prefer not to have to get out of bed so early on a Sunday morning. None of her friends did, so Venus was regularly informed. And she would willingly skip church altogether. It was a fallacy that all children of the vicarage liked going to church. They didn't. Venus faced the fact that when Becky was older—and what did 'older' mean?—she supposed she must be allowed to

28

choose for herself. Venus did not look forward to the arguments which were certain to arise.

On this occasion Becky was allowed to go last, with instructions about not taking too long because no way would that excuse her going to church. Nigel gave Venus a hug and a kiss and called out his good-byes to Becky. 'I'll be around later to join your lot for coffee in the parish hall,' he promised Venus.

'Please do,' she said. 'Everyone will be wanting to meet my new husband, and in any case I want to show you off.'

'They mostly know me,' Nigel reminded her. 'And I can tell you exactly what will happen. They'll come at me with their symptoms, ask my advice. "Doctor, I keep getting these headaches . . ." It happens wherever I go. Do people come at you in the middle of a party and ask you questions about their spiritual health?'

'On the contrary,' Venus told him. 'They're more likely to shy away in case I should ask *them*! Most people prefer a vicar who isn't what they call "religious". If they say "She's not a bit like a vicar" it's a compliment. Except of course in church. Being religious is OK there, as long as one doesn't go too far. Anyway, off you go or you'll be late.'

It was when he kissed her good-bye again that she remembered her great-grandmother. She had died when Venus was ten years old and now seldom came into her thoughts, but now, suddenly, she did. She used to wear a silver brooch, pinned into her blouse, in the shape of a word. 'MIZPAH'. Venus didn't remember ever seeing her without it. What had become of it?

'Mizpah!' she now said to Nigel.

29

He looked confused. No wonder, she thought.

'Mizpah. It means God keep watch between thee and me while we are absent one from the other.'

He looked at her, then nodded. 'Mizpah,' he said.

* * *

Miss Frazer was not in church. Venus had been at the door since twenty minutes before the service was due to start, greeting people, receiving congratulations on her new state, answering questions about the honeymoon and so on, but all the time watching apprehensively lest Miss Frazer should walk up the path and confront her. She supposed she ought to be pleased if Miss Frazer actually had had a change of heart, the lost sheep returned to the fold, though she considered it unlikely. In any case, anyone less like a sheep than Amelia Frazer was difficult to imagine. A recalcitrant goat or a stubborn mule, more likely.

But for now—though she didn't go so far as to thank God for it—Venus was relieved that the lady seemed not to have returned to give any more trouble. Nor was she mentioned by anyone, though that might have been tact. Apart from the few (mostly women) who had left St Mary's at the same time as, or shortly after, Miss Frazer—and for the same reason, that they couldn't cope with women in the priesthood—the rest of the congregation had not given her trouble. She didn't fool herself that she was approved of; it was more a case of what else could they do and where else would it be convenient to worship?

Blessed Henry gave Venus a conspiratorial nod

30

as she turned to go into church. After which, she set her mind to other things. This was the high point of her week, every week, and she would not let an army of Miss Frazers spoil it.

CHAPTER THREE

At coffee afterwards, for which Nigel turned up in good time, both he and she were made very welcome. Nigel had been popular in the village before ever she had appeared on the scene and she had already gathered that it was seen as quite romantic that the Doctor should marry the Vicar, even though it was a pity that he went to St Patrick's (and possibly vice versa by those who did go to St Patrick's)! It would be no surprise, she thought, if Nigel outshone her. He was tall, good-looking, and full of Irish charm. He had the turquoise blue eyes of some of the western Irish (where did they come from, she wondered) and he spoke with a soft Irish accent. She had brown eyes, which her mother, perhaps wishing to cheer her up, used to describe as 'not brown, Venus love, dark hazel! Much more interesting'. But now, she reminded herself, I am size fourteen, with one or two bulges in the wrong places, though they don't show when I am wearing my cassock. So how could I compete with my husband?

Her mother and father were there, but not Becky, who had gone home. She was excused the coffee bit, which she hated. Sonia had also made one of her occasional appearances, possibly, Venus thought, more to show solidarity with Nigel and

31

herself than from any adherence to God. Sonia had a dislike of institutionalised religion, but Venus loved her just the same. Sonia had been one of her first friends in Thurston—and though she would never say this out loud it was good to have a few friends who were not of the church. It kept her in balance with the world. When Sonia did come to church she usually sat behind a pillar, as she had done this morning, so that she could feel she was observing without being involved.

Rose Barker was there. Rose was the very efficient secretary to the Parochial Church Council. To look at her she was the most unprepossessing person you could ever meet—small and thin, usually dressed in some colourless, shapeless garment which fitted where it touched—but when she opened her mouth and spoke all was transformed. Every word which dropped from her lips sounded like a Shakespearian sonnet. 'Shall I compare thee to a summer's day? Thou art more lovely and more temperate,' Venus heard until she realised that Rose was talking about the central heating system.

Her parents had left a little early to go back to the Vicarage, where her mother would do the last-minute cooking of the lunch. They had been having Sunday lunch there every week since they moved to Thurston and she didn't like to change it now, nor did Nigel wish her to do so. Perhaps, Venus suggested, they might make it less regular as time goes by, but he said 'Don't be silly!'

*   *   *

The rest of Sunday went by much as usual, except,

32

of course, that everything about it was enhanced because Nigel was there. He sat at the head of the table and carved the sirloin of beef, which her mother had cooked to perfection—which is to say Venus had put it in the oven and her mother had taken it out at the right time. Venus gave a thought and a prayer to Ann, who might well be thinking of them, all here together at this time. Before long she must invite her for a weekend, if Ann herself could bear it.

The minute lunch was over her mother jumped to her feet and was straight into the washing-up. There was a perfectly good dishwasher but she didn't trust it to get everything as sparkling clean as she would like. Becky and her father immediately took Missie for a walk—they were always the first to escape at this point—and Nigel took yet another trip back to his flat, this time to collect his CD player and some of his favourite discs, without which he couldn't live for too long. Venus wielded a tea towel.

'There!' her mother said presently. 'That's that lot taken care of! I don't like to see dirty pots hanging around! And now, unless there's anything else, I'll love you and leave you. When your Dad gets back, send him home.'

When the dog walkers returned, her father, as instructed, went home. Becky, followed by Missie, went up to her room, where, Venus well knew, she would watch television, stopping only to come down later and eat a hearty tea, after which she had plans to spend the evening with Anna Brent. It was, after all, several hours since they had last seen each other. Nigel returned with his CD player and set it up. After that, left alone, the two of them sat side by side on the sofa, Nigel's arm around her, her head on his shoulder, and listened to the music. He had chosen Mahler's Fifth, which she found a bit solemn for the occasion, but it was nevertheless very beautiful and in the end it lulled her to sleep, which was probably not what Mahler had intended.

And so the day went. And though they had never spent a day quite like it, it somehow, to Venus, felt warm and familiar, as if they had been doing it for ever.

Later in the evening, Becky now in bed and asleep, they also went to bed. They had been lying down not more than five minutes when the telephone rang. Since it was at Venus's side of the bed, she answered it. 'It's for you,' she said, handing it over to Nigel.

He listened, then said, 'I'm sorry, love! An urgent call!' He got out of bed and dressed hurriedly. 'I'm afraid this is what it's like, being married to a doctor. I should have warned you.'

'I understand,' Venus told him. 'It's also what it's like being married to a priest. If I'm called out to a dying parishioner it's much more likely to be in the middle of the night than in the middle of the day.'

An hour later, during which time she had been lying awake, waiting for his safe return, he crept back into bed.

'Everything OK?' she asked.

'It is now,' he said. 'I got him into hospital. What would happen about Becky if we were both called out at the same time?'

'It's a long shot,' Venus said, 'but if it did happen I'd call for Dad.'

'That's all right then,' Nigel said, holding her close.

It was their first domestic weekday morning, and presumably it was the pattern for what was to follow. There was no lying in bed as if they were still on honeymoon; no leisurely breakfast, talking over what they might do with the rest of the day. Nigel had to leave even before Becky. He and Sonia had an eight-thirty surgery five days of the week. He ate a large dish of Shredded Wheat, drank two cups of tea, kissed Venus goodbye and was off. Venus went upstairs to waken Becky, who was always reluctant to get out of bed, never at her best in the morning. She was glad Nigel would normally leave the house before Becky rose.

'Up you get, sweetheart!' she said pleasantly.

Becky sat up, rubbing the sleep out of her eyes.

'Gran brought me my breakfast in bed when you were away,' she said.

'Well I hope you made the most of it, darling,' Venus said. 'It's downstairs in the kitchen in this house. Come on, you'll be late for school!'

*   *   *

Mondays were when Venus took her day off, though she doubted if she could do so today. There was last week to catch up on and at ten o'clock she was due to meet with her churchwardens in the church for a report on what had been happening in her absence. The other churchwarden was Edward Mason, who had only recently been appointed, taking the place of Richard Proctor, who had vacated the job and gone off to Kingston-upon-

Thames to marry a fellow solicitor. Venus got on well enough with Edward though they hadn't quite got the measure of each other. Furthermore, she would have liked to have taken advantage of Richard's resignation to have chosen a woman churchwarden, but in nine hundred years there had been no such creature in St Mary's and, following on the appointment of a woman priest, she decided it might be too much for the congregation to bear. So she would bide her time. She had no reason to be unhappy with her churchwardens.

As it turned out she did just have time to look around the garden before leaving the Vicarage, and this was something she enjoyed. It made for a good start. It was not a spectacular garden, it never would be. The soil was thin and poor—it could do with a load or two of fertiliser, which so far she had not been able to afford. When her parishioners had tried to sound her out about what she'd like for a wedding present what she wanted to say was 'A load of muck!', but she hadn't had the nerve so she was given a set of quite pretty fruit dishes. A nice thing about the garden, though, was that at the bottom there was a gate in the hedge, opening on to a path which went straight up to the Downs. Sometimes she took that path when she wanted to escape.

She had been in the garden only long enough to see that the weeds had been growing apace while she'd been away when she heard the telephone. She hurried back into the house. It was Cliff Preston of Preston & Son, Funeral Directors, though Cliff was not the son but the grandson of the original owner, the Prestons having been in Thurston as long as anyone could remember. It was a sorrow to Cliff that his own son would not follow him into the business but had instead chosen a career as a representative for an international pharmaceutical company which took him all over the country, and even abroad. Thurston could not compare with that.

'Good morning, Vicar!' Cliff said cheerfully. He was one of the most cheerful men she knew, in spite of his chosen job. 'Everything all right then?'

'As far as I know, though I daresay you're going to tell me otherwise,' she said.

'It's just that old Mrs Minton has died. A stroke.'

'Mrs Minton?'

'You wouldn't know her, I suppose. She was a Thurstoner' (which, Venus had discovered, meant she had lived in the village all her life, and her parents and grandparents most of their lives before her. You had to be third generation to be a true Thurstoner). 'She moved to live with her daughter in Brampton,' Cliff said, 'but she's not a churchgoer, never was. Nor was her family for that matter.'

It was interesting, Venus thought, that so many of the funerals she did were of people who never darkened the door of the church but whose families wouldn't dream of seeing them off anywhere else, and with the full works: music, hymns, prayers, flowers, a suitable, preferably slightly fulsome, eulogy. A sort of last-minute insurance policy. Not that she minded, not in the least, and it was not her place to judge. She tried to give them the same attention as if they had been in church every Sunday for a lifetime.

'Thursday at ten a.m.?' Cliff said. 'That suit you?'

'Fine!' Venus said. 'Give me the daughter's address and I'll pay her a visit.' She wouldn't dream of doing otherwise. It could be a comfort to the family if she could bring in something personal about the departed when she took the service. And in any case, the people of St Mary's parish were her people, whether they went to church or not. They were in her care; she had the care of their souls and she took that seriously. There was an unbreakable bond between herself and them. She didn't expect them to care for her—a priest could not expect to be loved, though it was good when it happened; a priest, however, must always give love. Sometimes she had to remind herself of that.

'Any other news, Cliff? Anyone on the NYD list I ought to know about?' NYD stood for Not Yet Dead—but soon will be. It was useful to know.

'Not right now,' he said. 'It's a bit quiet at the moment, I suppose being June, and good weather and all that. You don't get much pneumonia in June.'

*　　　*　　　*

She was in church ten minutes before she was due to meet with the churchwardens. This was not unintentional. She liked to have time on her own in church. It was then that, as well as thinking about her present congregation, she would sometimes get the feel as she sat there quietly—it was almost tangible—of all those people who had worshipped here—been baptised, married, buried, sought out St Mary's in good times and bad. But not in the church as she saw it now from where she sat, in a pew halfway down the nave. For some of them the nave wouldn't have existed. The tower (four-square and solid, though it was blown down by gales in the twelfth century and had to be rebuilt), and the space to the east of it where the high altar stood, were where it all happened in earlier times. Thurston was a small village then and the tower was large enough to hold its inhabitants. Only as the village grew was the church building enlarged and the nave built, and later the gallery added at the back, plus one or two rooms to be used as a parish office and a vestry, in place of the vestry at the east end. That had become a storeroom for things no longer used which, just possibly, might one day come in handy (though they seldom did). Objects of all kinds were piled up, or leaned against the walls and each other: props from nativity plays, bits of wood—previous use unknown—papers, old hymn books, vestments no longer in use, choir robes when there was no longer a robed choir. One of these days she must really clear it out, but there never seemed to be the time. There were always more urgent things to do.

Until Victorian times, when people began to move out from Brampton to live in the countrified surroundings of Thurston and, coincidentally, the great surge of churchgoing happened, St Mary's had been a long and narrow church, but when the need grew, the south aisle was built on as a straightforward addition to the width of the nave. More pews for more churchgoers. So now, though the chancel and the altar were central to the nave, the south aisle remained a sort of appendage, a bit of a no-man's-land; from an architectural point of view, an afterthought. It certainly was an appendage from her point of view when she was celebrating the Eucharist at the altar. Most of the south aisle was out of her view, which was not helped by the solid pillars which supported it. Her congregation could all be having forty winks in the south aisle and she wouldn't know.

Neither, of course, could she be seen at the altar by those of the congregation who sat in the south aisle. Perhaps that was their choice. She had noticed that there were those who made a beeline for the south aisle when there were plenty of vacant pews in the nave. She thought of them as semi-detached; not quite sure they wanted to be involved, preferring privacy. As every priest knew, there were those who, though they were very nice people faithful in attendance, preferred to worship on their own, in their hearts not joining in with the rest except perhaps for the hymns. One of these days she intended to do something about it, meaning the shape of the church, not the people.

At this point in her thoughts she heard footsteps and voices. Her two churchwardens had arrived together. She moved to greet them and then, on an impulse, she said, 'Will you both go and sit in the south aisle—not together, one near the front and the other perhaps halfway back, while I go and stand at the high altar?'

'What's this then, Venus?' Henry asked.

'You'll see,' she told him. 'Go on, humour me!'

Nice men that they were, they did so without further argument. She walked to the east end and stood in front of the altar.

'Can you both see me?' she called out.

'Of course we can't,' Henry said. 'Well, perhaps a little from time to time.'

'I can't see you at all,' Edward said from the

second row back.

'Right!' Venus said. 'Thank you both. You can come back now!'

'What was that about?' Henry queried.

'Well, if you can't see me how do you know what's going on?' she asked.

'Oh, that's all right, Vicar,' Edward said. 'We'd have the service sheets. And we know the words anyway. We don't actually need to see you.'

'But I'd quite like to see you,' she told them.

'What's this about?' Henry repeated, suspiciously.

'I'd like to abandon the high altar and have a smaller one as near to the front as we could get it,' she said.

This was met at first with silence, then Edward said, 'But the altar has always been up there, below the east window. It's never been anywhere else.'

'I know that. There are three steps from the nave to the tower and a short walk and another three to the altar rail. I watch people going up and down them, some with difficulty, every Sunday.'

'But that's where altars go,' Edward protested.

'It's not the law of the land,' Venus said. 'Why not give it some thought?'

They walked back through the nave to the small room at the back, off the porch, where they were to meet. There were two visitors in the porch, looking at an old map of the church. The porch was small and cramped. If, on a Sunday, two people in or out of their way to church, stopped to have a conversation everyone else was held up. As for the parking of a child's buggy, or a wheelchair . . . ! She would like to re-design the whole area, though how, she'd not yet thought out. It could hardly be

41

more inconvenient than it was at present. However, she was learning to make haste slowly, which was foreign to her nature.

There was not a lot to discuss at the meeting: everything seemed to have gone smoothly in her absence. They discussed what the agenda should be for the Parochial Church Council meeting which took place every two months and was due the following Tuesday. 'I should like my idea about moving the altar on the agenda,' Venus said.

'You'll be up against it,' Henry said, shaking his head.

'Nevertheless!' she persisted. 'I'd like to give it a whirl.'

'So what's your programme for the rest of your day off?' Henry asked her, changing the subject.

'I was thinking of gardening—and I need to go into Brampton to do some shopping, but I also have a bereavement visit—Mrs Minton. Do you know her?'

They both said they did, and that she'd always lived in Thurston but she was never seen in church, except perhaps at the Harvest Festival, or maybe Christmas. 'I think she was once a Sunday School teacher,' Henry said.

*   *   *

Back at home Venus phoned Mrs Minton's daughter about the visit and it was arranged for that afternoon. Since the route to the house took her past The Beeches, Venus decided that afterwards she would call in to see Bertha Jowett. She worried about her. To spend the last part of her life in a residential home, however good it was—and The Beeches was good—was not, she was sure, what Bertha would ever have envisaged. She was fiercely independent, blunt speaking and with a fearsome intelligence not in the least impaired by age and infirmity. What did she do all day? She couldn't read forever, and in any case her eyesight was none too good. Does she stare at the walls, Venus asked herself.

Well, she thought, since my day off seems to have disintegrated there's no reason why I shouldn't spend part of it being soundly beaten in a game of Scrabble with Bertha Jowett. And, of course, as well as getting home for Becky, she thought with pleasure that she might get to see Nigel in between his visits and his evening surgery. They might even have tea together.

*   *   *

Mrs Minton's bereavement visit was, Venus supposed, what one might describe as 'par for the course' or even 'run of the mill', except that she didn't like to use those words because every bereavement was different, and special. People were affected differently. Some wept copiously at the drop of a hat—perhaps they were the fortunate ones—while others were obviously grieving, yet doing their best to bottle it up. This one was different again in that the daughter—her name was Caroline Sidgwick—showed no grief at all; no sense of loss or, indeed, any emotion. She was in her fifties, thin and tired-looking. Perhaps, and maybe with reason, her mother had been a burden to her for a long time. Perhaps she had actively disliked her and had looked after her out of

43

nothing more than a sense of duty? Whatever it was, she had cut short Venus's words of consolation and got down to facts. No, she said, she had no idea what hymns her mother might have wanted, likewise the readings. Could she leave all that to Venus?

'If you wish,' Venus agreed. 'Or rather, I'll give you a few suggestions and you can choose.' At least, she thought, if I am guiding the choice we can miss out on 'The King of Love my Shepherd is'. Not that she disliked it: she just heard it too often at funerals.

'Whatever you say,' Mrs Sidgwick said, shrugging her shoulders. 'I don't know about these things.'

It was to be a short service, followed by cremation. 'And the burial of ashes?' Venus asked. 'In the Garden of Remembrance?'

Mrs Sidgwick sighed deeply. It was her first sign of feeling. 'That would obviously be the least trouble,' she said, 'but then my mother never was one for saving other people trouble. No, she wanted her ashes to be scattered from the end of Brampton pier, and my husband says we have to do that—or rather, he'll do it.'

It was not the first time Venus had met with this particular request. And when the time comes, she thought, I shall be obliged, as politely as I can, to suggest caution. Wait until the tide's in, I shall have to say, or the ashes might fall on whoever's walking beneath the pier. Don't do it in a strong wind or they might blow back into your face.

'Where was your father buried?' she asked.

'At sea,' Mrs Sidgwick said. 'He was in the Navy.' Saved a lot of trouble, her attitude said.

44

Perhaps it was because of her husband that the mother had wanted her ashes to be thrown off the end of the pier, Venus thought. She had been given very few details about the lady, or about her life. It wouldn't be easy to build a eulogy around them and, apparently, there was no-one who was willing to come forward and do this. Poor Mrs Minton— even if she deserved it.

'Well, I'll give you a ring tomorrow,' Venus said. 'I'll let you have my suggestions for hymns and readings. Or I'd be very happy to come and see you again. You might think of something else you want to discuss.'

'Oh, I don't think so!' Mrs Sidgwick said.

'I will need to know if you want an organist,' Venus said. 'Or are you happy for the music to be on CDs? We have quite a selection in the church.'

'Oh, there's no need for an organist!' Mrs Sidgwick said. 'And if you just give me a ring, that'll do. No need to come round again.'

Clearly, I am not wanted, Venus realised. Just needed for the basics.

CHAPTER FOUR

When she reached The Beeches Bertha Jowett had just awakened from her afternoon nap. She gave one of her rare but beautiful smiles as Venus put her head around the door. Her hair, Venus noted, was less like a bird's nest than usual, even though she had been asleep. Someone on the staff must be grooming her—though they hadn't persuaded her to part with the many-coloured butterfly

45

decoration which perched on top, as though it had just alighted there and might take off again any second. Now here's a woman, Venus thought, fresh from her bereavement visit, who, from the little I do know about her, would surely be a splendid subject for a eulogy. But would she even want a church service? Venus doubted it. Around her in the room were displayed a few mementos she had brought with her from her cottage, from the scores which had crowded it. There was a china dog, a retriever of some kind, an exquisite porcelain figurine of a ballet dancer, on her points as if waiting for the music to begin. There were several photographs, in silver frames, including one of what must be her parents, and another of a handsome young man in RAF uniform. Plenty of material for a eulogy if only she would spill the beans. But she had shown no signs of doing that.

'Shall we have a game of Scrabble?' Venus suggested. 'Though we'll have to fix a time limit. I must be in when Becky gets home from school.'

Bertha sighed. 'Everyone seems to be on a time limit,' she complained. 'It's like parking meters. Except me,' she added. 'And that's another paradox. Most of one's life one is battling against the clock—so much to do, so little time—and then, if one lives long enough, or perhaps too long, all the hours in the day are available and there's not enough with which to fill them. However, a game of Scrabble would be most agreeable.'

Bertha's form of gamesmanship, Venus was well aware, was to engage her opponent in conversation at the point when that person was trying to work out how to get the best score from the letters available. Perhaps that was one of the reasons why

46

she usually won?

'The chiropodist came yesterday,' Bertha now said chattily. 'He says I have the feet of a thirty-year-old. "In that case," I asked him, "why don't they work when I want to walk?" He couldn't answer that.'

And then she went on to describe, in detail, the plot of a crime film she'd watched on television the previous evening, which Venus couldn't follow and didn't want to. Then when Bertha had finished that she said, much to Venus's surprise, 'I enjoyed the wedding.'

'Good!' Venus said. 'So did I.'

'They were quite nice people,' Bertha continued. 'Quite intelligent, the ones I talked to—considering they were Christians. You wouldn't think they'd swallow all that stuff.'

Venus tried not to be put off her game. She would have liked to answer back had she not been struggling with seven tiles containing five vowels, a Z and a Q—and no U. Though of course, she told herself, if she thought anything she might say on the subject would have the slightest effect, she would give up the Scrabble at once. But it wouldn't. It was a deliberate distraction on Bertha's part.

'What did you think of the Bishop?' Venus asked presently.

'Oh, very fetching in all his get-up!' Bertha said.

'He's also a very nice man,' Venus said. 'He's been kind to me.'

'I'm glad about that,' Bertha said, sounding more serious. 'You've made the choice to be a minority person, you've flouted the norm, and that can be very lonely. I know that. As I've told you before, I broke away, though in quite the opposite

47

direction from you. I broke away from a family whose whole life was in the church. Not so much in Christianity, but in the church: everything which went on in the building. Every service, every day; every fast, every feast. Nothing mattered outside it. Nothing else must interfere. I felt stifled. My father never forgave me when I left, which I rather thought proved I was right. Come along dear! Hurry up! It's your move.'

Venus threw in her whole hand and picked up a new one, which was slightly better, but before she could sort it, Bertha went out completely, with a cracking score, in her next move.

'Damn!' Venus said. 'Why do you always win? It's a good thing my job isn't a game of Scrabble.'

'I'd be the devil,' Bertha said. 'Waiting to catch you out. Do you reckon the devil always wins?'

Venus shook her head. 'Not in the end. And one of these days I *will* beat you. Anyway, I have to go now.'

'Come again soon,' Bertha said. She was never effusive, but Venus knew the invitation was sincerely meant.

'Of course I will,' she promised.

'And don't worry about being in the minority,' Bertha said. 'You won't be for long. There'll soon be as many women priests as men—though why they should want to be I can't for the life of me imagine.'

'Oh, I don't worry about being in the minority,' Venus assured her. 'It doesn't matter in the least.'

*   *   *

Next day, before he left the house, Nigel said,

48

'What's your programme for today?'

'A Chapter meeting this morning,' Venus told him. 'Odds and ends for the rest of the day.'

'So shall we go to the cinema this evening?' he suggested. Nigel didn't have an evening surgery on Tuesdays, Sonia took it on her own, but he had one in the afternoon. In future, Venus told herself, I shall try to keep Tuesday evenings free of meetings so that we can have regular time off together. Wouldn't that be great.

'I'd like that,' she said. 'We can take Becky, or if she'd rather, she can go to her grandma's. I'm pretty certain she'd prefer that, especially if she's allowed to stay overnight.'

'Whatever,' Nigel said. 'And I'll try to be home in good time so that we can have supper before we go.' He gave her a quick kiss, and was away.

*   *   *

Before the morning was over Venus was inclined to take back what she had said to Bertha Jowett about not minding being in the minority, and this was entirely because of the Chapter meeting. Try as she did, and though she was determined not to let it, it always had this effect on her. The Chapter meeting was when all the clergy in the deanery met together, with the Rural Dean in the chair, and Venus was now, as always, the only woman present. Some of the men went out of their way to be pleasant to her. Whether they approved of her or not, those particular men would still be polite because that was what they were like. Well-mannered. A few men there, only a few, were definitely hostile. They didn't need to use words to

49

show it, they knew just how to exclude her. The ploy was to act as if she was invisible and inaudible. They didn't speak to her, and if she had the temerity to express an opinion it was as if she had not spoken. If they were standing near they would turn their backs on her. Well, I know where I stand with them, she told herself. The rest, that was the majority, were not the least bit rude, they simply appeared not to notice her, they had their own intimates and she would never be one. By now she was used to all this. It was as if she had strayed into the room by mistake and no-one could bring himself to show her the way out. No, she thought, and not for the first time, a Chapter meeting is not where I shall find a bosom pal. It was a sort of Boys' Own Club into which she had blundered. She had opened the wrong door.

That thankfully behind her, in the afternoon she decided to phone Esmé Bickler, ask her how she was getting on. Esmé was the only other woman priest in the diocese—they had trained together—but she served in a different deanery, a few miles away. Esmé had had her ups and downs and though neither of the women would have chosen to be other than what they now were they did manage to bolster each other up from time to time.

'Venus!' Esmé said. 'How lovely! And how is married life suiting you?'

'Down to the ground,' Venus said. 'You should try it.'

'Not me!' Esmé said. Venus knew she had no time for marriage though she adored children. 'How is Becky?'

'She's fine,' Venus said. 'Settled down, I think I can safely say. I had a Chapter meeting this

50

morning.'

'Aha!' Esmé said. 'And how did that go?'

'As usual.' Venus knew she need say no more. Esmé would know what she meant, since hers was the same experience—not that either of them intended to be bowed down by it. What was interesting, and both of them had made the same observation before, was that most of the men involved were really nice when met in other circumstances.

'It was a lovely wedding,' Esmé said. 'You looked gorgeous, Mrs Baines.' And with her words all thoughts of the Chapter meeting vanished from Venus's mind.

'Were there a lot of people from Nigel's church?' Esmé asked. 'I wouldn't know. It's interesting, isn't it, that Anglicans and Roman Catholics look the same from the outside?'

'There were loads,' Venus said. 'And they seemed pretty happy, even though I was taking one of theirs. And me a woman priest, which they don't have.'

'Well, that's the laity for you,' Esmé said. 'I sometimes think they're well ahead of the clergy.'

*   *   *

In the evening Venus and Nigel went into Brampton to the Odeon. Becky, as expected, had elected to stay overnight with her grandparents. 'She will be served with her favourite food and be allowed to stay up well beyond her proper bedtime, so why wouldn't she choose that?' Venus said to Nigel as they sat side by side, chewing some of the nougat they had brought back from France, waiting

51

for the film to start. This was a rare night out.

*   *   *

It was a Saturday morning, six weeks to the day since we were married, Venus thought, and now every day, for me, is a celebration. So how shall I celebrate today? Well, this morning she would be meeting with a group of parishioners in St Mary's, where they were going to set about cleaning the church. She didn't know whether the group would be large or small. She didn't know who would be in it, except that Nigel had volunteered to come along after his surgery. Though it was not his church he intended to support her in every possible way, as she knew she would him in anything they did in St Patrick's. She had put out an appeal, both from the pulpit and in the parish magazine, for anyone who was willing to help with the cleaning to turn up at the church at nine-thirty, bringing cleaning materials with them. And now it was twenty minutes to, so she must hurry. Becky, of course, had opted out entirely. She would spend the morning with Anna and possibly stay there for lunch.

Arriving at the church, Venus walked up the path with Carla Brown and her husband, Walter. When she had first come to St Mary's Carla had informed her that she didn't go to church much—she left that to Walter—but she had come to see what the new vicar was like. Since then she had become a rock; she would do just about anything for Venus or, more likely, she would get Walter to do it. Venus's private name for Walter was 'Fetch and Carry'. He was very nice, though completely in

52

the shadow of his wife, whom he adored. At the moment he was hauling a vacuum cleaner, plus an extended lead which kept getting in the way, and a large canvas bag which contained who knew what?

'A nice day for it,' Carla said. 'Let's hope a lot of us turn up.'

When they went into the church Venus was encouraged by the number of people there, and others were still walking up the path. The Blessed Henry and his wife, Molly, were already inside. Venus hoped they would organise everyone. They knew the church better than most. Elsie Jones, who ran the Brownies, had brought her daughter, Grace, who was herself a Brownie Guide. 'I've reminded Grace,' Elsie said, 'that Brownies always lend a hand.' Grace didn't look enraptured at the thought of lending a hand on a fine Saturday morning. She could think of better things to do. Elsie clearly has more control over her daughter than I have over mine, Venus thought.

Miss Tordoff, member of the Parochial Church Council and probably St Mary's oldest parishioner, was there, ready and willing, but too frail to be very able. Venus reminded herself to find her some useful, sitting-down job to do. Jean Close, through whom she had first met Bertha Jowett, was there, already wearing an overall and her hair tied up in a scarf. There were one or two buckets around, a feather duster, tins of polish, a second vacuum cleaner and a machine to shampoo carpets. 'I thought the chancel carpet was badly in need of a good clean,' Jean Close, the owner, said. 'You'd be amazed what a good job this machine does.'

Under Molly Nugent's guidance—Venus had been right in guessing that Molly had done all this

53

before—everyone set about their allotted tasks: polishing pews, dusting windowsills, vacuuming carpets, sweeping down cobwebs, taking hassocks outside to beat the amazing amount of dust out of them, rubbing up brass, washing stone. Nothing was left undone. Venus was amazed by it all, and yet, she thought, I shouldn't be. She had seen it before in other places. It was as though people were prepared to do anything they thought of as practical, something where the results would show immediately, where they could quantify them. Yet ask them to spend the same amount of time in prayer, and especially in a group, and would they respond so readily? Probably not. There, the results of one's labours were seldom immediately visible. And is a place more holy because it's clean and shining? she wondered. Perhaps it was one kind of an offering to God. On the other hand she was by no means sure that any building should be treated as a shrine. It was what went into them and what was taken away from them which mattered more than the stone and wood and the stained glass.

She was interrupted in these high-flown thoughts, and brought down to earth, by Walter Brown. 'I'm sorry, Vicar,' he said. 'I reckon we'll have to get a plumber to the lavatory. It's well and truly blocked and I can't shift it. Heaven knows what some people put down it!'

They worked all morning, and well into the afternoon. By the time they left, and as far as human hands could make it, the whole church was spick and span. They could all go home with a comfortable feeling of satisfaction.

'Thank you,' Venus said to everyone. 'You've

been wonderful! You really have!'

*   *   *

In the evening she didn't feel too well. There was nothing she could put a finger on. She didn't feel sick, no pain anywhere, she didn't feel she was starting a cold. She was just not herself. She said nothing to Nigel, knowing that, contrary to general belief, if one's husband was a doctor one didn't run to him with every small symptom. It was probably nothing. It might be that her period was overdue.

A little later she was standing in the bathroom, brushing her teeth—Nigel was already in bed and, by the sound of his breathing, asleep—when this feeling of not being herself came over her again, and this time it was intensified. She felt as though something in her inside was gripping her, twisting her innards. She grabbed the edge of the washbasin and clung to it, her eyes tightly closed. And then it passed even more quickly than it had come, and she was herself again. It was definitely her period, about to start. She was sure of it. She finished brushing her teeth and went to bed. Nigel was well and truly asleep.

Next morning she was fine again. She went to her church, Nigel went to his. At one point, standing in the pulpit, she did feel as though she was floating, but it passed quickly. Then, two days later, her period hadn't started, which to say the least was most unusual. She could usually set the clock by it. And then it dawned on her—and why had it taken so long? Was she, could she possibly be, pregnant? Surely not so soon? But of course she could be. It only takes once, as some people

55

know to their cost, she thought. And they were married. And they had made love many times in the last six weeks.

She needed to know. It was imperative. Somehow, though, she didn't want to say anything to Nigel, not yet. She could phone Sonia and arrange to see her, but was it a bit too soon to do that? She pondered on it—and then it came to her. She could do what many women did, some of them dreading pregnancy, which of course she was not. She could go into Brampton, she thought, maybe to Boots, and she could get a pregnancy testing kit. It was not something she could bring herself to do in Thurston, but in Brampton no-one would know her, or think twice about it. She didn't know what the kit consisted of—she'd never needed to know— but she supposed she could follow directions as well as anyone else. So on Monday morning, when Nigel had gone to his surgery and Becky to her school, she got into her car and set off.

*　　　*　　　*

It turned out that a large branch of Superdrug was close to the place where she had parked her car, and that would do nicely. No-one would know her, nor would they be the least bit interested. 'Woman purchases pregnancy kit' hardly merited a headline. (Though 'Vicar of Thurston Pregnant?' in the local paper might just, if only to those who didn't know the vicar was a woman.)

She couldn't find what she wanted on the shelves. Shampoos, tissues, deodorants, nail polish, toothbrushes—a hundred different items were there, but not what she sought, so she was obliged to go to the pharmacy counter, which was staffed, and ask the assistant, a young man.

'Ah yes, madam,' he said. 'There they are.' He pointed to a stack of shelves not more than two yards from where she stood. She thanked him and moved towards them, but he came out from behind his counter and followed her, eager to be of help.

'There's quite a choice,' he said. 'And the cheapest ones are just as good as the more expensive. They're all pretty accurate. Take the test after the first period is missed, and it's best taken in the morning.' He spoke with confidence, as one who knew, though he looked as though he had not long left school. She took him at his word, and bought the cheapest—£8.50—sought the checkout, then left the store without a backward glance.

Next morning, alone in the house, she opened the pack and read the instructions carefully; not that they were complicated, and she would follow them to the letter, though this was something one would definitely not want to do in front of an audience.

Yes, the test said. She was pregnant. The symbols quite clearly showed it. Even so, she would as yet say nothing to Nigel. She would phone Sonia that afternoon when she knew Nigel would be out on visits and she would make an appointment to see her. After all, the testing kit could be wrong, even though it did say it was accurate in 90 per cent of cases. She could be in the other 10 per cent.

'I need to see you,' she told Sonia. 'I don't want Nigel to know. When can I come?'

'Is it urgent?' Sonia asked.

'Yes and no,' Venus said.

'Whatever that means,' Sonia said. 'Well, you

can come around right now if you'd like to.'

It was outside surgery hours, which suited her. She didn't want anyone asking her why she was visiting the doctor. But why on earth not, she argued with herself as she walked the short distance to the surgery. And she knew the reason. It was because it was so soon; they'd been married no time at all. It was a 'what will people say?' situation.

She told Sonia she'd done a pregnancy test and that it was positive. 'Well, they're more often right than wrong,' Sonia said, and then asked all the questions and made an examination. After which she straightened up, with a great big smile on her face.

'Congratulations!' she said. 'You're going to have a baby! Nigel must be thrilled to bits.'

Venus admitted she'd not yet told him anything. Sonia gave her a strange look, raising her eyebrows.

'I wanted to be sure,' Venus said.

Sonia reckoned the baby would be born in early March. 'I'd say a honeymoon baby. And a spring baby. Couldn't be better—all the best weather ahead will give it a good start.'

She gave Venus lots of advice. She must take care of herself, she must eat well, she must take suitable exercise but not overdo it. 'Remember, Venus,' she said, 'you're thirty-five, and although this isn't your first baby it's more than ten years since you had Becky. Of course there are routine tests you must have.'

'But it will be all right, won't it?' Venus asked. She felt suddenly vulnerable and nervous, but at the same time pleased. Oh, so very pleased!

'Of course it will be,' Sonia assured her. 'I'll look after you, you know that. You must just be sensible. Don't get overtired.'

She rose, walked around her desk and gave Venus a big hug. 'It's going to be wonderful, Venus,' she said. Then she handed out a load of leaflets about pregnancy and childbirth, and said, 'I'll see you again shortly—with Nigel—and we'll go into everything. Go home now and tell him. And Becky.'

How will Becky take it? Venus asked herself. What will my mother say? Nigel, she knew, couldn't fail to be thrilled. How soon might he be back from his visits?

CHAPTER FIVE

Nigel came in after his visits, around two o'clock, and had a quick sandwich, standing by the kitchen table. 'I can't stay long,' he said. 'I've some paperwork to do before the five o'clock surgery.'

There was no way Venus could wait until the evening to give him the news. She was bursting with it.

'Sit down for a minute,' she said. 'I have something to tell you.'

Nigel sighed. 'Can it wait, love? I am in a bit of a rush.'

'No, it can't,' Venus said. 'And you'd better sit down.'

He did so, frowning slightly. Venus sat opposite him at the table. Filled with the news, she hardly knew how to begin. Then she took a deep breath, and out it came.

'I'm pregnant! I'm going to have a baby!'

For a second, which seemed like a week, there was complete silence, and then Nigel gave a loud whoop, rushed around the table and pulled Venus to her feet. 'It's wonderful! It's marvellous!' He was ecstatic, searching for further words and not finding them. She had known he would be pleased but she had never realised how much.

'Anyone would think you'd won the lottery!' she said, laughing.

'Sweetheart, it's better than any lottery!' Nigel said. 'This is the best thing that's happened to me in my whole life. Apart from marrying you, of course!' He hugged her again, almost squeezing the breath out of her, and then suddenly let her go as if realising that she was newly fragile.

'It's all right,' she said. 'I won't break. I'm still quite solid!'

'I never thought . . .' he began—and was then lost for words.

It came out, when he regained his breath and was coherent enough to make sense, that he had hardly allowed himself to think, let alone hope, that they might have a child. They'd discussed it, of course they had. They knew it was possible and they wanted a child. 'But at thirty-five,' Nigel had said, wearing his doctor's hat, 'it will be much less likely than if you were in your early twenties.' She had thought at the time that he had said this, unselfishly, to prepare her for disappointment.

'Would you love me any less if this hadn't happened?' she now asked him, though she realised immediately that it was a stupid question.

'Love you less?' he said. 'How can you think

that? Nothing could make me love you less . . .' He paused. '. . . On the other hand, though I wouldn't have thought it was possible—I *do* now love you more than ever.'

'That's all right then,' Venus said.

And then, simultaneously wearing his doctor's and his loving husband's hats, he started to caution her. She must look after herself, she must eat the right things. She mustn't work too hard, she must get enough rest. 'But I expect Sonia has said all this to you,' he said. 'Tell me again exactly what she did say.' So she told him. Not that it will stop him asking Sonia himself, she thought. He would want her professional opinion and he would want to give his own, though whether that would be valid from a man with a vested interest, who knew?

It was almost half-past three and Becky would soon be home from school. They had quickly agreed that they wouldn't say anything to her just yet. Soon, certainly, but at the same time as wanting the whole world to know, they also wanted to have it just to themselves for a little while longer. 'And I must tell my mother before I tell Becky,' Venus said. 'I'm not sure just how Becky will take it, and if she does want to run to someone, the first person she'll choose will be her grandmother. So Mum's got to be ready for it.'

'You're not expecting Becky to be difficult, are you?' Nigel asked.

'I just don't know,' Venus replied. 'She's been the one and only, the apple of my eye, for more than ten years now. She might find it hard to share. I'll have to find the right way to tell her.'

Then he said, 'Come here! I want to hold you in my arms again. I want to hold you both. You and our baby.' And he did so. For a little while they said nothing, nothing at all, then Nigel said, 'I'll have to go, my love. Take care. Have a rest.'

*   *   *

The next morning Venus opened her eyes to see Nigel standing at the side of the bed, in his dressing gown, offering her a cup of tea and a biscuit. This was new. He had not, so far, turned out to be one of those husbands who got up early to make the tea, or bring home flowers or boxes of chocolates. How long would this last?

'How lovely!' she said. 'You *are* spoiling me!'

'I'm going to spoil you every day from now on,' he promised.

'Then I warn you,' Venus said, 'I shall make the most of it.'

*   *   *

The next morning, after Becky had gone off to school and Nigel to his surgery (saying 'Take it easy,' before he left), Venus decided to go to see her mother. She and Nigel had talked it over before they'd gone to sleep the previous night and Venus had said, 'I must tell her or I'll burst.' She knew, also, that he could hardly wait to talk to Sonia.

It should be easy, Venus thought, telling her mother, so why was she apprehensive about it? Why did she feel as though, somewhere, she'd got it wrong? She telephoned. 'Mum, I'm going down to the village,' she said. 'I thought I'd pop in and see you. Will you be in?'

'Of course I will! Where else would I be?' her mother said. 'I'm usually in, aren't I?'

'Well, you do go into Brampton sometimes,' Venus pointed out. It sounded lame, partly because since her parents now lived in the village she'd hardly be going a mile out of her way to see them, and partly because it was not her usual practice to announce that she was about to call. 'Is Dad in?' she enquired.

'He's just going off to golf,' her mother replied. 'Your Dad practically lives on the golf course these days. Not that I mind, of course. A man needs something to do when he's retired, otherwise he gets under the feet. Why? Did you want him for something?'

'No,' Venus said. 'Anyway, I'll see you soon.'

The coffee was ready when she arrived. 'Would you like a scone?' her mother offered.

'No thanks,' Venus said, sitting down. 'Just coffee. I'll have it black.'

Her mother gave her a look. 'Black coffee, no scone. You're not on another diet, are you?' she accused.

'No,' Venus assured her. 'I'm not on a diet.' This was the perfect moment to tell her why, suddenly, she couldn't face milky coffee, or even one of her delicious scones. So why was it so difficult to tell her? In the end, sipping the black coffee, she blurted it out. 'You're going to be a grandmother!'

Her mother looked at her as if she hadn't heard aright. 'I *am* a grandmother,' she said.

'I know. And you're going to be a grandmother again. I'm pregnant!'

With the cup of coffee halfway to her mouth Mrs Foster came to a sudden halt. The cup

63

wobbled and Venus thought it would spill. Her mother's mouth fell open, her eyes widened as if they would fall out of her head. 'You're *what*?' she gasped.

'Pregnant. I'm going to have a baby, next March actually,' Venus said. And then she realised why she'd been uneasy about breaking the news to her mother. Her mother would think it was not quite decent. Then sure enough, her mother came in on cue.

'Oh Venus! It's so *soon*!' she said. 'You've only been married . . .'

'Six weeks,' Venus interrupted. 'And I think I'm about six weeks pregnant. A honeymoon baby, wouldn't you say?'

Her mother found it difficult to say anything at all, which was out of character for her. What does she think people *do* on honeymoon, Venus asked herself crossly. 'Aren't you pleased?' she asked. 'Don't you want Nigel and me to have a baby?'

'Of course I do!' Mrs Foster said, recovering herself, quickly. 'And of course I'm pleased! It's just that it's a bit . . . well, as I said, soon.'

She means she's not quite sure how she'll break it to her friends, Venus thought. And come to that, I'm not sure how—and just when—I'll break it to the parish. That's the trouble with women priests, she could hear some say. They get married and have babies. 'Well, I don't have all that much time to play with,' she said defensively. 'I'm thirty-five.'

'Of course!' her mother said. 'You're right. And I *am* pleased. As for your Dad, he'll be over the moon. He'll be like a dog with two tails. Now, you must look after yourself, love.' She was suddenly all concern. 'You mustn't work too hard. As you said, you're not as young as you were.'

I suppose, Venus thought, I shall hear that several more times, and mostly from well-meaning people—bless their hearts.

'On the other hand,' she said, 'I daresay I could go on having babies for a few more years yet. Some women do.' She knew that was not kind of her. She watched her mother trying not to look horrified at the thought.

'Well,' Mrs Foster said, taking a deep breath, 'I must get my knitting needles out, mustn't I—though I don't know what babies wear these days. Have you told Becky?'

'Not yet,' Venus said. 'I wanted you to know first. Now that you know I might tell her pretty soon. I don't feel as though I can keep it to myself. I'm not at all sure how she'll take it but I know you'll be there for her if you're needed.'

'I will,' Mrs Foster promised. 'And look on the bright side, Venus love. She might be thrilled to bits.'

'She might,' Venus agreed cautiously. It's not quite the same thing as getting a new dog, is it? 'But if she's not, then you'll be here to pick up the pieces.'

*   *   *

Nigel slipped home for a quick look at Venus in between his visits. It was not something he did often but he just wanted, he told her, to make sure she was all right. 'Of course I am!' Venus said. 'Are you going to do this for the next several months—not that it isn't sweet of you?'

'I don't know,' Nigel said. 'Probably not, when I

65

get used to it, but you have to remember I'm new to it, I've never been pregnant before.'

'I've been wondering if I might talk to Becky this afternoon,' Venus said. 'I want to get it over. Also I don't like having secrets.'

'Whatever you think,' Nigel said. 'Then would you like me to be here with you? I could probably manage it.'

Venus shook her head. 'No, I think it's best if it's just the two of us. For the moment, anyway.'

Becky arrived home from school in a happy mood. Clearly the day had gone well. If it had been otherwise, Venus had already decided she would put off the news to another day.

'What would you like for your tea?' she asked Becky. 'You can choose.' She knew that was wrong. Her daughter would, like most children, choose all the wrong, most unhealthy things—chips, crisps, something fried and fattening—and it was her duty, as a mother, to see that she ate healthy food and, moreover, ate what she chose to serve her. But this was a special occasion if ever there was one. It was an open-and-shut case for a bit of bribery. And sure enough, Becky chose pizza, with chips—*no* green vegetables, *please*—and chocolate ice cream to follow. Venus served it all, without demur, hovering around while Becky ate every scrap, and when she asked for another scoop of ice cream Venus couldn't bring herself to refuse it.

When she had scraped the rest of it from the dish Becky said, 'Can I go to Anna's now?'

'You can in a few minutes,' Venus answered. 'In the meantime there's something I want to tell you.'

Becky gave her a suspicious look. 'Is it nice?' she asked. 'I hope it's nice.'

'Well, I think it is—so I hope you will. And it's exciting.'

She perked up at that. 'So what is it?'

Venus didn't know how to get the words out, but in the end they came. 'I want to tell you that you're going to have a new sister or brother!'

Becky sat there, nonplussed, open-mouthed, at first unable to speak, and then she said, 'Why do you want to adopt someone else?'

'Oh no!' Venus said. 'No, not that! I'm not going to adopt anyone. What makes you think that? *I'm going to have a baby!* Nigel and I are going to have a son or a daughter and you are going to have a sister or a brother. Isn't that exciting? Are you pleased?'

'No!' Becky said without hesitation. 'I'm not a bit pleased. I don't like babies and I don't want a sister or a brother.'

I'm not sure I'd expected anything so forthright, Venus thought. 'Oh dear! That's a pity,' she said. 'And I was relying on you to give me a hand with the new baby. I thought you could help me look after her. You're so good at looking after people. Look how clever you are with Missie!'

'Missie is not people,' Becky quite rightly said. 'She's a dog. I'd rather have another dog than a baby.'

'Well, I'm afraid for the moment it's got to be a baby,' Venus said. 'And it will be nice for Nigel to have a son or a daughter, won't it? Not that he doesn't love you just as if you were his very own daughter.'

Becky was silent for a few seconds. Then she looked thoughtful, not altogether happy. 'You and Nigel won't love the new baby more than me?' she asked quietly. 'I mean, just because it's new?'

67

Venus jumped to her feet, rushed around the table and took Becky in her arms. 'Never! Never ever!' she cried. 'You are my first child, which is something very special. And you were your Daddy's little girl. We'll neither of us ever forget that, will we? And I will never love anyone more than you!' How, she wondered, do you tell a child that there's enough love in the world for no-one ever to have to go short of it; that it's all there waiting and all we have to do is take it and then give it? And that the more we do so, the more it will grow, the more there'll be everywhere and for everyone. How could a child believe that?

She tried to explain this to Becky as simply as possible. It *was* simple, and she believed it to be true, but since a great many grown people wouldn't accept it why should she expect her little daughter to do so? And right now she seemed so much younger than her ten-and-a-half years. But, miracle of miracles, she seemed to understand what was being said, even though she would have to test it further.

'And will Nigel love me just the same?' she asked.

'Nigel loves you a great deal,' Venus said. 'You know that, don't you? And he always will. It won't make any difference to the way he loves you. He would like to be your daddy, but he knows he's the second one, not the first. But with me you were the first and no-one will ever take the place that's specially yours.'

'Not even a new baby?' Becky pressed her.

'Not even a new baby!' Venus said. 'Not anyone.'

'Will it be a boy or a girl?' Becky asked.

'I don't know yet,' Venus admitted. 'Which

would you like?'

'A boy,' Becky said, without hesitation. And then, 'Can I tell Anna?'

'Not just yet,' Venus said. 'There are a few people I must tell first, and when I've done that you can tell Anna. You can tell anyone you like. But for a while it's a secret between you, me, Nigel. No-one else, yet. You can keep a secret, can't you?'

'Of course!' Becky said, 'but you will tell Gran and Grandpa?'

'Oh, certainly,' Venus agreed. 'In fact I've already told Gran, and if Grandpa's come back from playing golf I expect she'll have told him. Would you like to go around and see her? You can talk about it to them. But no-one else.'

'OK,' Becky said. 'Where will the baby sleep? Will she sleep in your room?'

'Only for a little while. Perhaps a few weeks. After that he or she will have the bedroom next to yours. You can help me choose things for it.'

Becky nodded agreement. 'And what shall we call it?' she said.

'I haven't thought yet. We can discuss that and you can help to choose.'

'I'll write a list of names,' Becky said. 'Two lists. One for a boy and one for a girl. We could call a girl "Anna".'

'We'll see. You make your lists and we'll choose later.'

Venus felt two stones lighter. It seemed she had suddenly got something right. She would have to tell her churchwardens, the Parochial Church Council, the Bishop, the Rural Dean, and she supposed the Archdeacon unless it would be passed on to him—and of course several members of her congregation, but no need to yet. They would all eventually know whether she told them or not. Before that happened she wanted to work out how she was going to fit in her job in the parish—services, funerals, marriages, meetings, all the usual things plus anything else which cropped up—with being pregnant and—even more mind-boggling—how she would do it once she had a baby in tow. Carrycot by the altar? Changing nappies in the vestry? That was something a male priest would never have to consider. If it were so, his path would somehow be smoothed. His hand would be, metaphorically, held.

And then she pulled herself up short. There was something wrong about all the duties she'd been reciting to herself; something missing. Her attitude was all 'poor little me', and she had missed out from the list two very important parts of her life as a priest; not only important, but essential. And the first one was not to *do*, but to *be*. All the things she had listed in her mind—meetings, church services, funerals and weddings—were necessary, and important, but before any of the doing there was, and always would be, the being. At the heart of everything the priest did was what the priest was and that came way first. She had to *be* the priest. And it was to this being that she had to give time and thought and prayer—all before she started on the doing. What she did, whether it was in the church or in the other parts of her life, could only come out of what she *was*.

And there was something else she had left out of her list of 'duties' (not a word she liked), and it was this. Everything else apart, she had the charge of taking her faith to her people. That was certainly in

70

her job description! And not only the ones who came to church, willing to accept it. She must also take out what she had to those in the rest of her parish. And she could only do that by meeting them where they were.

They might not want her or what she had to offer, but she must make sure they knew it was there. There might be a number of Bertha Jowetts amongst them (though even she was glad of friendship). So she must definitely brighten up her ideas and do more visiting. It was the part of her job she had most neglected, and she must change her ways.

As to how she would find the time, well, that was in God's hands. If she did her bit she'd expect him to do his. Whether, in the circumstances, she would find her bit easy was another matter.

'I'll go round to Gran,' Becky said. 'She can help me with my list.'

*   *   *

And now Venus was thinking of her pregnancy again, and she also had a list for that. Things to do; arrangements to make; information to be gleaned—she had a load of questions to ask Sonia. Also, she must read all about it. It was likely pregnancy had undergone a sea change since she had had Becky, though she was not sure how much birth itself could have changed all that much. So she would do as she did when she was confronted with something she didn't know enough about— she would read a book or two. And because she didn't want to let the village library know too much too soon, she would go to Smith's or Waterstones,

71

or wherever, in Brampton. She would go the next morning. She was so excited at the thought.

*   *   *

Venus was amazed at what was on offer. Aside from the magazine rack, which offered two likely-looking publications devoted to the subject which at the moment filled her mind to the exclusion of everything else, there were two whole shelves on every possible aspect of pregnancy; birth, fertility treatment (cheek by jowl with a hardback on multiple births), one on *Your Baby's First Year* and next to it one entitled *The Terrible Twos*. She couldn't possibly think as far ahead as the last, but apart from that she felt she would like to buy most of the contents of both bookshelves. However, she restricted herself to two books and two magazines, all of which she determined to read from cover to cover. She might even return for more of the same. She would not be found ignorant for want of trying.

She left the bookshop and made straight for the car park. Unfortunately, she had to pass 'Mums and Kids', which was Brampton's answer to Mothercare. There was no way she could pass it. I will slip in just for a minute, she promised herself. Once inside there was no way she could spend just a minute in this temple to fecundity, this tribute to Mother Nature. It was an Aladdin's cave of the jewels of motherhood: tiny garments, cot mobiles, buggies, car seats, disposable nappies, and a reasonable display of maternity wear for expectant mothers ('Ladies-in-Waiting', it called them). She stopped to look at these, though she was unlikely to need one since there could be no better garment

72

for a lady-in-waiting than a clergy cassock. As well as being black it could accommodate all kinds of shapes, from head to foot. She was surprised that no-one had adapted it, in a pretty floral print, for the mother-to-be, and it was while she was considering this that a voice said, 'Hello, Vicar! Now this isn't a place I'd have expected to see you!'

It was Miss Murchison, one of her parishioners, and nor would she have expected to see *her* in 'Mums and Kids'—not because she was a single lady, there were several of those around, but because she was in her late sixties and as far as was known had no family. Venus murmured something about a present for a friend's baby and Miss Murchison nodded.

'I give them all babygros,' she said. 'You can't go wrong with a babygro. Though I think they call them sleep suits these days.'

'What a good idea!' Venus said. 'Thank you!'

'They're just over there,' Miss Murchison said, pointing. So Venus went across and chose one, just in case she was being watched. But not without a small thrill of her own. It was the very first thing she had bought for her baby.

Close by the checkout there was a small book on display, *Name this child!* and she bought a copy. It would keep Becky happy, she thought, and with any luck she will let me have a look at it.

Back at home she unpacked her shopping. What she really wanted to do was to sit down and read all the books, and the magazines, cover to cover—but she kept a tight hold on herself and put them to one side. She flipped through the book of names, but that was really for Becky when the time came, so she didn't actually read it. And then she came to the babygro. She had bought the first size. It was so small, so sweet. She held it for a moment in her hands, squeezing it as if it already had a child in it. And then she decided that she must start a drawer especially for baby things, nothing else allowed in it.

Upstairs, she looked at the contents of the six-drawer chest in her bedroom. Every drawer was crammed full, and, she would have said if she'd been asked a week ago, with things which couldn't possibly be moved, let alone got rid of. But that had been last week, and today was quite different. She had other priorities. The bottom drawer was the deepest, and therefore the most suitable, she reckoned. And then she realised that in a few short months there was no way she would be able to bend down to the bottom drawer. Her bump would get in the way. So she chose the middle one, which was at hand height and would be available to her at every stage. She cleared it of everything, without much thought of where it would all go. Its contents were a mish-mash of all sorts of things: scarves, gloves, sunglasses, keys—to what she didn't any longer know—a pack of cards, a snazzy black camisole which she had given up as lost (how could it have got in here?) and several other assorted items. She turfed them all out, dusted the inside of the drawer, wiped it with a damp cloth, and then lined it with pretty scented paper which she had been given as a Christmas present. It now looked and smelled delicious.

*   *   *

She folded the babygro carefully and placed it in

the drawer, trying not to give way to the tears of thankfulness and pure happiness which she could feel welling up inside her. And then she thought, 'Oh, blow!' and let them run down her face.

CHAPTER SIX

Walking up the church path, on her way to celebrate the Tuesday morning Eucharist, Venus stopped to speak to Joe Hargreaves, who was cutting the grass at the front of the church, manoeuvring the lawnmower as best he could between the graves at the top of the lawn. Joe was the church gardener, and much more besides, since as well as keeping the graves and paths tidy, trimming the shrubs and bushes, sweeping the fallen leaves, in season, from the oaks, the sycamores and other trees which surrounded the churchyard, he was the one who understood the mysteries of the central heating system and the plumbing. He was the one to grumble at if the pipes, which ran down the sides of the pews, were not hot on a winter's morning. Or he would be, except that he'd not be there. Barring Christmas and Easter, Joe gave church services a miss.

St Mary's had a large churchyard, three acres or more. Well, it would be large, wouldn't it, since Thurston people had been buried there for hundreds of years. And the churchyard was Joe's, and don't let anyone forget it.

'Good-morning, Joe!' Venus called out over the noise of the lawnmower. 'Are you all right?'

This was the opening he had been waiting for.

'I'm all right, Vicar,' he said, 'which is more than I can say for this lawnmower! It's seen better days, and those were over long before you came here. It was wonky in the time of the old Vicar, but nothing gets done and it's high time it was.'

He was a small man, no more than five-foot-three, thin as a reed, and in his late seventies. He was reputed to be completely bald under the woolly cap without which few, including Venus, had ever seen him. At the moment, small and insignificant though he was, he had enough temper in him to fill a seven-foot giant.

'It's always the same,' he grumbled. 'The PCC will say "yes" to anything that goes inside the church, but ask them to spend any money on the churchyard and you're up against a brick wall!'

He was partly right, Venus thought, though not entirely—but where would he be without his little moan? 'Very well,' she said. 'I'll bring it up at the next PCC meeting. Though as you know, we're short of money.'

'When weren't we?' he asked. 'But I can't go on pushing this one around for ever, and you'll not get anyone else to do it.' He didn't add 'not for what you pay me' but it hung in the air between them. He wasn't paid much, Venus knew that. She reckoned that advantage was taken of the fact that he had his pension and he owned his small cottage in the village. He lived frugally and had never been known to take a holiday. He could manage.

'We could get one I could sit on,' he suggested. 'It'd make my life a damned sight easier.'

'But would there be room for it to go between the graves?' Venus asked.

'I expect they come in different sizes,' he said. 'I

mean the mowers.'

'Well, Joe, I will mention it,' Venus repeated.

She had been standing talking for too long. Before anyone arrived for the Eucharist she wanted to say her Office, which she had not been able to do at home. In the last week morning sickness had made its unwelcome appearance and it had no sense of time or place. It could last, and sometimes did, until well after lunchtime.

'It is normal,' Sonia had said when Venus complained. 'I expect you had it with Becky.'

'I did,' Venus admitted. 'But it confined itself to reasonable hours and I swear it was less violent.'

'Those things never seem as bad in retrospect.' Sonia had spoken with all the assurance of one who had never been pregnant.

She went to sit in the front pew in the south aisle, her usual place when she said her Office in church. It was out of the way and, moreover, on the wall facing her was a painting of the Virgin Mary, nursing her baby. She had liked it from the beginning but now it had added significance.

A few minutes later she became aware that someone had come in and was moving around at the back of the church. It was not unusual and she didn't look round. He (or more likely she) would not disturb her. She went back to her Office.

The psalm for the day was one of her favourites, full of praise and hope: 'Praise the Lord, O my soul: and all that is within me praise his holy name.' In spite of the sickness, her life at the moment was one of great rejoicing.

When she had come to the end of the readings she knelt down and made her daily intercessions for those, especially in the parish, who needed her

77

prayers: for the sick, the elderly, especially those in nursing homes—particularly Bertha Jowett—for the bereaved and, lastly, she prayed for those in need, not known to her, who had no-one to pray for them by name. This last she had learnt to do from a wise priest she had met during her training. She never omitted it. Then, rising to her feet, she looked round. There was no-one there. Whoever had been in the church had left so quietly that she had not heard them go.

She went and vested for the Eucharist. When she returned to the body of the church half-a-dozen people had drifted in, spreading themselves out in that typically Anglican way so that they didn't have to sit near anyone else unless they wanted to. This was the usual number on a Tuesday morning, though sometimes in bad weather it could drop to four. Two thirds of the number were those who never attended the Sunday Eucharist. They liked their services quiet, and as private and personal as possible; certainly without babies or small children who might make a noise or—*quelle horreur*—cry. Venus was sure it was not that these people didn't like children. It was more likely that they believed that there was a time and a place for them, and it was certainly not in church. She disagreed entirely. On the other hand, she would never limit their choice by cutting out the small services. They were important to the people who attended them.

She felt a sense of restlessness as she walked down the aisle at her usual pace, which was slower than usual because today she was feeling slightly dizzy.

When she reached the front she turned to face

her small congregation.

'The Lord be with you!' she said, holding her arms wide, palms uplifted. And with the words she at once felt calm, and she hoped they did too.

'And also with you,' they replied quietly.

Half-an-hour later found her standing outside the door, in the sunshine, bidding them farewell, having little chats. 'Are you going on holiday this summer?' 'How is your daughter?' There was always one who got away and this morning, not unusually, it was Miss Broome, who scampered off like a frightened mouse. There was also usually one who lingered, and this morning it was Mrs Prendergast. She paused at the door, stood in front of Venus and looked her straight in the eye. 'If I may say so, Vicar,' she said (the weekday attenders never called her Venus), 'you appear a bit peaky. Are you sure you're all right?'

Mrs Prendergast had three daughters and five grandchildren, so she knew what was what. Venus reckoned she was being read like an open book.

'I'm fine, thank you, Mrs Prendergast,' she replied.

'Well I'm glad to hear it,' Mrs Prendergast said. Those were her words, but her look said 'Tell that to the Marines!'

Venus watched her as she walked away down the path, striding with vigour and determination, a woman who knew exactly where she was going and what she was going to do when she got there—but this didn't prevent her stopping to have a word with Joe, who had paused in his grass cutting and was leaning heavily on the mower. Watching them chatting, Venus got the feeling that they knew each other. Joe had lived in Thurston all his life and

79

although she didn't know Mrs P's background—she only knew her as someone who came on Tuesday mornings—she had the feeling that she, too, had been around a long time. It looked as if Joe was spilling out his woes to a sympathetic ear. He wiped the sweat from his brow as he spoke.

Yes, Venus thought, it was a warm day, even for July, and it was going to be even hotter. Becky had chosen the right thing to do. It being the school holidays, she had gone swimming with Anna Brent, the two of them escorted by Anna's mother. It had been suggested that Venus should go with them, that they could make the outing later to fit in with the church, but Venus had bowed out, saying she had things to do. It was not untrue, but the real truth was that she was physically not in the mood for swimming. It required too much effort at the moment. Becky, much to her disappointment, had not yet been allowed to tell Anna about the baby because Venus still hadn't told the other people she thought she should inform first. They would have to wait until she had become a little more used to it herself.

She turned around and went back into the church. It was deliciously cool inside, the sun doing no more than filtering through the stained glass windows, making pools of coloured light on the floor and the pews without letting in the heat. There were one or two jobs she must do. She still felt queasy. She supposed it was a pity not to savour every precious moment of her pregnancy, but the truth was, she would be heartily glad when these first few months were behind her. But, she told herself sternly, she must guard against letting pregnancy take over because she had a full-time job which must not be neglected.

Apart from her regulars there had been three people in the church as she'd walked in to take the service, but now she was alone. The minute she had started the service the strangers had scurried away, as if they might be interrupting. The church had quite a number of visitors in the summer months. Thurston was a picturesque village, not on the coast, but three miles inland, and people who were visiting in the area tended to drop in on the church, since it was old and had an interesting history. If she was around, Venus tried to have a word with visitors. They gave a variety of reasons for being in St Mary's. It was the church in which they'd been married forty years ago; a member of the family had been baptised there; they were just passing and it had started to rain. Whatever the reason, she welcomed them. Visitors were one of the reasons why the church was kept open during the daylight hours, though for Venus it would have been so, visitors or not. She didn't hold with churches being kept locked, even though keeping them open did mean that sometimes things went missing. Small items, usually, though she'd been told, when she'd first requested that the church should be kept open, that a few years ago, before she'd come to Thurston, a pew had been stolen. When the thieves, carrying it out between the two of them with difficulty—it was solid pine—had been challenged by the voluntary verger on duty (there were no longer many of those left), they had said that they were taking it away to be repaired. Vicar's orders! As far as Venus was concerned they could take all the pews. She disliked them.

Walking out into the sunshine again, she decided

to take a look around the churchyard, something she did from time to time to check that everything was more or less in order. She turned right to go around the back of the building, an area out of sight and too often out of mind, neglected because Joe had too much to do. It certainly looked that way today. The grass, in parts, was almost a foot high, encroaching on some of the graves. One day soon, she thought, she would get yet another irate letter from a visitor who had made an infrequent visit to his mother's grave and had not been best pleased with things. It was interesting that none of these letter writers—there had been quite a few of them—ever included a donation for the upkeep of the loved one's grave. People not closely involved with the Church of England tended to think that it was financed by the Government, that they paid for the upkeep of the building and the churchyard through their taxes.

And then she noticed that the grass between two graves, close up against the wall, was well and truly flattened, far more than it would have been by the fox who was a frequent visitor. Moreover, lying on the ground nearby was a screwed-up newspaper, some pieces of plastic—perhaps food wrappers—two empty beer cans and three cigarette ends. Definitely not the fox! Someone had been eating and drinking there and, by the shape and size of the flattened area, more likely than not, sleeping there. It wouldn't be the first time. It was a reasonable place for a tramp to choose in the summer, and she was not without sympathy, but she would have had more for this one if he had cleared away his rubbish.

Cringing, she picked up the debris and took it to

the dustbin, which was no more than a dozen yards away. That done, she went back into the church and washed her hands, scrubbing them thoroughly, then left.

Joe was still working in the front. 'The grass is rather long behind the church,' she said to him. 'I shall be getting letters of complaint.'

'You don't need to tell me,' Joe said truculently. 'But I've only got one pair of hands—and a rotten old mower.'

And she had, she realised, played right into his one pair of hands.

'Well, see what you can do,' she said. 'I know you care as much as I do about the churchyard looking good.' It was not quite true. He cared most (and he had a point there, she thought) about the bits which people regularly saw. Round the back was not in that category.

'Someone's been sleeping there,' she said. 'Have you seen anyone?'

'No,' he said. 'I don't have eyes in the back of my head, Vicar. And I don't have time to look everywhere.'

If he says once more he only has one pair of hands, Venus thought . . . 'Well, I know you do your best, Joe,' she said pacifically. She had always doubted that he liked taking orders from a woman.

*   *   *

She had decided, since she had shopping to do in the village, that she would pop in and see her mother.

'Your father is on the golf course,' her mother greeted her. 'Where else?'

83

She had been baking scones and the smell hit Venus in the stomach. She rushed for the ground-floor loo. What was it about scones? she asked herself as she emerged, her eyes watering. She had always loved them, especially fresh from the oven, thickly buttered and perhaps with a dab of strawberry jam. Was she going to be like this with every food she liked best?

'You can't go on like this, Venus love,' her mother commiserated when Venus went back into the kitchen. 'You've got to keep up your strength! You're supposed to be eating for two!'

'I don't have any option,' Venus said. 'And it's not only scones.'

'What does Doctor Sonia say?' her mother asked. 'Or Nigel? He's a doctor. Can't they do something?'

'They say it will pass,' Venus told her. 'I expect they're right. Anyway, I'm now ravenously hungry. I parted with my breakfast in the church loo. Do you think I could have a slice of dry toast?'

'Of course you can, love!' her mother said. 'Right away.'

The toast was heaven. 'I could eat another slice,' Venus said. 'And hope for the best!'

'Coming up!' her mother said.

'I hope not!' Venus said. 'Did I tell you I go for a scan next Tuesday?'

'You did,' her mother said. 'I sometimes wonder how we managed to have babies in my day. There was nothing like that. We just had to get on with it. Nobody told us much, either.'

'Don't butter the toast,' Venus said. 'Nigel will go with me.'

'I'm pleased about that,' her mother said.

'Though that's another thing. In my day the men didn't concern themselves. When I was in labour with you, your Dad went to the cinema. There was a film he didn't want to miss. He did manage to get back to the nursing home before you were born—not that he was allowed in the labour room.'

'Perhaps he went to the cinema to take his mind off it all, I mean, if he wasn't allowed to do anything,' Venus said. She couldn't picture her father being uncaring.

'I daresay,' her mother said. 'And after I brought you home he was always a good dad. He'd do anything for you. Still will, as you know.'

'I do,' Venus said. 'I've got the best parents in the world. And thank you for the toast.' She bit into it hungrily. 'I feel better already.'

'I'm thinking I might see Doctor Sonia,' Mrs Foster said. 'I'm getting a lot of pain in my leg.'

*   *   *

Sonia had explained the scan to Venus, since it was she who was looking after her in her pregnancy, with Nigel trying, as far as he was able, not to interfere. The first scan, which was now behind her, had checked that certain things were in order, bones, heart and so on, which they had been. It had been too soon to show the sex of the baby, but in any case there would be later scans which would do that. Also, because Venus was in her mid-thirties, she had been offered an amniocentesis scan to follow a few weeks later at which a check would be made for the possibility of any abnormalities for which they would want to be prepared, or which even might cause them to choose to have the

85

pregnancy terminated. Nigel and Venus had discussed this together but, they had agreed, that was something they would not choose to do, therefore she would not take that particular test.

'That doesn't mean,' Venus said to Nigel, 'that I would go as far as saying that abortion was always wrong. I couldn't. For instance, if a very young teenager was attacked and raped by a total stranger, then I might see it differently. But not, I think, if it meant in our case that the baby might turn out to be not quite perfect. But it's a difficult decision and I wouldn't ever like to judge anyone else on it.'

Venus was slightly nervous when they went to the hospital to have the second scan, but Nigel was a bag of nerves, a mass of anxiety. 'Anyone would think they were going to do it to you!' Venus said. 'I promise you won't feel a thing!'

It didn't turn out quite as either of them had expected. Venus, as instructed, lay on her back, facing a screen, the radiologist and Nigel close by. As further instructed, she submitted to her abdomen being spread with a gel and a sort of camera being moved over the area. It was undignified, but at the same time exciting. As the camera contraption was moved around over her abdomen, images appeared on the screen. They were not instantly decipherable either to Venus or to Nigel, but the radiologist clearly knew what was what.

'Aha!' she said presently, excitement rising in her voice as she watched and listened. 'What do we have here? Two images, two heartbeats! It does seem as though we have twins! And it does look as though they might both be boys. They're obligingly facing front and I reckon I can see two little willies! Take a look. See what I mean?'

Neither Venus nor Nigel could see anything as clearly as could the radiologist, though Venus convinced herself that she could. In any case, they were fazed by the news.

'Are you pleased?' the radiologist asked.

It was difficult for either of them to find the words. Nigel had turned pale. Venus felt as though she might faint.

'Are they all right?' Venus asked. 'I mean . . . is everything . . . ?'

'It all looks perfect to me,' the radiologist said.

It was at this point that Nigel, overcome by it all, turned paler than ever, sweat broke out on his brow and he slumped in his chair.

'Oh dear!' the radiologist said, firmly pushing his head down between his knees and holding it there. 'Isn't it always the fathers who flake out, poor souls? It's lucky for the human race they don't have to have the babies or the population would die out!'

She summoned a nurse, who brought a glass of water for Nigel and held it to his lips while he sipped. She didn't actually say 'There, there!' but it was in her face. In the fuss, no-one took any notice of Venus.

'So are you really pleased?' the radiologist asked again.

It was then that Venus allowed the tears, which had been pricking at the back of her eyes, to fall. 'I'm thrilled!' she said. 'Totally thrilled!' She turned to Nigel. 'Tell me you are, darling.'

'Of course I am!' he said in a weak voice. 'It's just that I'm—well—overcome. But it's great. It's marvellous!'

The radiologist said, 'I've got one or two things to do. I'll be back in a minute. Give you time to recover.'

'Are you truly, truly pleased?' Venus asked when she had gone.

'Truly, my darling,' Nigel said. 'It's a miracle.'

CHAPTER SEVEN

It was Wednesday morning. Nigel had already left for the surgery, and Becky for school. The long summer holiday was well and truly over and Becky had moved up into Year 6 for what would be her last year at St Mary's Primary School. This time next year she would be travelling to school in Brampton. Venus was not sure that she herself looked forward to that, though she knew that Becky did. And she had firm friends in school now, Venus reminded herself, so she would be all right.

Usually around this time, when the first rush was over and she was left alone in the house, Venus made herself a cup of coffee. She was walking into the kitchen when the front doorbell rang. She retraced her steps and went to answer it. There on the doorstep stood the Blessed Henry. He hadn't, as she would have thought more likely, telephoned her. Nevertheless, she was pleased to see him because last evening, talking with Nigel, she had made up her mind that it was about time she told Henry about her pregnancy. It would not be right for him to get to know from any other source. After that she would inform all those she thought had a right to know: the Rural Dean (who would presumably tell the Archdeacon), her close friends, and of course the PCC at the next meeting. She would also write a short letter to the Bishop. He had married them and she thought it would be courteous to let him know before he heard it on the grapevine. In no time at all, she was certain, everyone would know. She didn't mind: on the contrary, she would like to shout it from the housetops.

Henry, however, did not look his usual rosy-cheeked, genial self. Quite the reverse. He was rosy-cheeked all right, but it was not so much rosy as fiery red. His heavy brows were drawn together in a rare frown, the corners of his mouth turned down, and his eyes, meeting hers, were angry.

'Why, Henry, this is a surprise,' she said. 'Come through to the kitchen. I was just making coffee.'

He followed her to the kitchen, at the same time saying, 'No coffee for me! I'm not in the mood for coffee!'

'I think I can see that,' Venus said. 'What's wrong? Nothing serious, I hope.' It was a silly thing to say. If it were not serious he wouldn't look as he did, about to explode. He was an equable man. She had never seen him more than slightly ruffled, and even that not often.

'What is it?' she repeated.

'We've been robbed!' he said.

'Oh, my goodness!' Venus cried. 'No wonder you're upset. I know how bad that feels. It's not all that long since I was burgled. Are you all right? Is Molly all right?'

'It isn't my house that's been robbed,' Henry barked. 'It's the church.'

'The church? What on earth would they take from the church?'

'Any number of things,' Henry said tersely. 'In this case a pair of brass candlesticks from the altar.'

She knew the ones he meant. They were part of the scenery. She didn't particularly like them. They were solid, heavy, ornate.

'Oh dear!' she said. 'Were they valuable?'

'They were indeed,' Henry snapped. 'They were solid brass. They were antique. What's more, they were given as a memorial, long before my time.'

'A memorial to whom? Who gave them?'

'They were given by Miss Frazer's father,' Henry said. 'They were in memory of his favourite horse, Roger.'

Venus was taken unawares. Before she knew it she had smiled, then, just as quickly, straightened her face again. In any case, the fact that the candlesticks, like so many other things in St Mary's, were directly linked to the Frazer family was not good news. Miss Frazer had had it in for her since the minute she'd set foot in Thurston and had not hesitated to make that known to all and sundry. It was thanks to Amelia Frazer that St Mary's was financially so much poorer than it had been before Venus's arrival. And some would say that Venus herself was to blame, never mind what she'd done or not done. No way would Miss Frazer give a penny of support to a church which had a woman priest. She was also certain that, though she no longer attended St Mary's, Miss Frazer would certainly get to hear about this.

'It's no laughing matter,' Henry said.

'I know. I'm sorry,' she apologised. 'It was just that . . . well, I've never heard of a horse being remembered by candlesticks on the altar.'

'People were fond of those candlesticks,' Henry said. 'They've stood there for more than sixty years. I remember them from when I was a choirboy. They were polished every month without fail. My mother used to take her turn at it.'

'Oh dear!' Venus said again, inadequately. 'Will we get insurance on them?'

'That's not the point, is it?' Henry said. 'It won't replace them. And in any case, we might not. The insurance company could say, with truth, that they weren't being looked after.'

'But you've just said how well they were looked after,' Venus said.

'Polishing them for sixty years is no use if you're going to leave the church doors unlocked for anyone to walk in and take whatever he can carry.' Henry's voice was sharp, accusing.

Ah, so that was it? Venus felt as though she had been hit, and by Henry of all people! She'd been made well aware that her edict about leaving the church unlocked had never met with all-round approval. It had, in the end, scraped through by the narrowest possible majority of the PCC, and even then reluctantly, with no real satisfaction on either side. Henry had not shown his approval but nor had he been vociferous in his disapproval, and that, she had thought at the time, was because he was trying in every way possible to be supportive of her. She had made what she thought was a strong case for keeping the church open during the daylight hours; that the needs of people who used it were more important than the safety of material objects. And she knew, even now and in full view of the blank places on the altar, that she would do the same again.

'When did it . . .' she began.

'You were in the church yesterday morning. I wasn't,' Henry said. 'Would you have noticed if they weren't there?'

'Of course I would,' Venus said. 'Anyway, they'd have been lit for the Eucharist. Also, there were six other people there, all facing the altar. They would have seen them.'

Henry nodded. 'And it being Tuesday, Joe would be working a long day and would lock the church door only when he left in the evening. As per instructions,' he added bitterly. 'I don't suppose he'd give more than a cursory glance inside.' They both also knew, though neither of them voiced it, that Joe could have been working in any part of the churchyard, out of sight of the door, for most of the time.

'And you unlocked this morning?' Venus asked.

'I did. As you know, I always unlock on a Wednesday because Joe doesn't come in on that day. I do it on my way to my game of bowls, and I always take a look inside; switch the lights on and suchlike,' Henry said. 'And of course I noticed at once.'

He would, Venus thought sadly. He knew and loved every stick and stone of St Mary's, inside and out. If the truth were to be told, she felt more sorry about letting Henry down than about the loss of the candlesticks. But in any case she knew that none of it would change her mind.

'So what do we do now?' Venus asked.

'We call the police,' Henry said. 'Which is not something I would do without consulting you. By rights I should also tell my fellow warden, but, as we know, he's on holiday. I suggest that you ring the police here and now.'

Venus did so. They promised to come around as soon as possible, though the tone of voice of the sergeant to whom she spoke didn't lead her to believe that the situation was of prime importance. 'A pair of brass candlesticks, you say? And you think the theft took place yesterday?' He spoke as someone who was more used to dealing with bloody murder, or as if, even at this minute, he was faced with a large pile-up of wrecked cars and injured bodies in the middle of Brampton. 'Candlesticks,' he repeated. 'Brass.'

'Antique,' Venus added. 'Quite valuable. And there might be other things. We haven't yet had time to look around. Shall we meet you at the church?'

'I'll send a constable,' the sergeant said. 'I can't promise exactly when. We're short-staffed.'

'We'll wait there for him,' Venus said.

'In the meantime,' Henry said to her, 'we'd better check everything. We don't know what else might have gone missing. And we must talk to Joe, ask him if he saw anything suspicious.'

Joe was at home, tending his own garden, when they called at his cottage. 'I saw nothing out of the way,' he said. 'But then I was up in the top bit, about as far away from the front of the church as you can get. I can't be everywhere at once, you know. There's always something to be done up at the top and those graves are just as important as the posh ones.'

If he says he has only one pair of hands I shall scream, Venus thought.

'I've only—' Joe began, but Henry interrupted

him.

'Yes, we know. It's just that the police will want to know the details, anything we can tell them. They should be here in a few minutes.' He looked at his watch. 'Can you come along with us?'

'Not really,' Joe said. 'I've got a lot to do here. They can come and see me if they've a mind to, but I can only tell them what I've told you. I locked up at seven, the clock was just striking. It was broad daylight of course. I popped my head in the church for fear of shutting someone in, but it was empty. So I locked the door and went off home.'

'Very well. That sounds straightforward enough,' Henry said. 'Though I expect the police will want to hear it from your own lips.'

'I shall still be here,' Joe said. 'I've got plenty to do. Of course there's the question of the tramp, if there *was* a tramp,' he added.

'Tramp? What do you mean, a tramp?' Henry asked quickly.

'I never saw him,' Joe said. 'But the Vicar here told me she was sure there'd been a tramp sleeping behind the church. And doing other things besides sleeping, I wouldn't wonder! Dirty devils they are.'

Henry turned to Venus. 'You didn't say anything about a tramp,' he accused her.

'I didn't think of it,' she said. 'I went around to the back of the church after the service, just to see how things were. It's something I do from time to time. There was no-one there then, but it was clear someone had been. The grass was flattened and there was rubbish about. Cigarette ends, a newspaper, beer cans. It's not unusual for a tramp to sleep in a churchyard, is it? I mentioned it to Joe as I was leaving.'

Joe spoke up. 'As the Vicar says, it's not unusual. He wasn't the first and I doubt he'll be the last. I didn't go around the back myself. I was busy. I've only got—'

'Yes, yes!' Henry interrupted. He turned to Venus. 'Well, we'd better get to the church. We wouldn't want the police to be there before us, would we?'

The police were not there. Henry and Venus made a thorough search of the interior of the church but found nothing else out of place. Then they came out and walked around to the back. There was the same area of flattened grass but, as far as Venus could see at a glance, no fresh rubbish since she had tidied it. No cigarette ends, no empty beer can.

'The grass is a bit of a mess,' Henry said. 'I mean the grass around the graves. It needs cutting.'

'I know,' Venus said. 'When I get the next letter of complaint I'll show it to you.'

'I've seen them before,' Henry said.

After another thirty minutes, during which there was no sign of a policeman, Henry said, 'Well, I'll have to go. Molly will wonder what's become of me. We have an appointment in Brampton with our solicitor. It's quite important. Shall you wait here?'

'Yes,' Venus said. 'I'll do that. I'm so sorry about all this, Henry!'

Henry said nothing. He knew that however sorry she might be she would still be adamant about keeping the church open. He couldn't possibly agree with her, and what had happened was proof that he was right—but it wasn't on for the Vicar and the churchwardens to be in open conflict. It could affect the entire congregation. People would

95

take sides, and before you knew where you were, some of them would leave. No, it would have to come up at the next meeting of the PCC, see what happened there.

Aside from this obsession with an open church she was a good vicar and a nice woman, he thought. Of course she also had this thing about wanting to change the whole church around, bring it up-to-date and so on, but that was pie-in-the-sky, it would never happen. Churches were not there to be brought up-to-date. They were there to remain the same, from generation to generation.

Walking down the path, his head full of these thoughts, he almost bumped into the policeman who was walking towards the church door.

'Well!' Henry said. 'You've come at last! I take it you *are* here about the theft?'

'Yes, sir. Police Constable Eddie Barker.' He consulted a piece of paper in his hand. 'The Reverend Venus Stanton?' he said. 'I take it she would be the Vicar?' Venus, he thought. What a name for a reverend.

'She's waiting in the church,' Henry said. 'And she's the Reverend Venus Baines. She re-married not long ago.'

'Re-married?' the policeman said.

'In June. She was a widow,' Henry explained. 'And I'm Henry Nugent, one of the churchwardens. We've been waiting for you—in fact I was just leaving,' he said pointedly.

'Pressure of work, sir,' the policeman said.

'Well, I'd better go back with you,' Henry said. 'But I do have an appointment elsewhere.'

'It shouldn't take long,' the constable told him. 'Just a few facts. I'm afraid burglary's an everyday crime these days.'

'And, I hazard a guess, seldom solved,' Henry said as they walked back into the church.

'We do our best,' the constable said. 'The public could do a lot more to prevent it. They're very careless.'

When the two men came in Venus was sitting in a pew, apparently doing nothing though in fact she was thinking hard about the problem in front of her. She was not blind to what this theft from the church would lead to. The same old arguments, which she had won last time, though largely, she reckoned, because she was the Vicar. A solution acceptable to everyone concerned seemed unlikely and she knew she would find compromise on her part difficult, if not impossible. Hearing the men, she jumped to her feet and went to meet them. There was no-one else in the church, for which she was thankful. The three of them walked together up to the altar.

'This is where the candlesticks were kept?' the constable asked. 'I mean, would someone have moved them temporarily; perhaps someone who was allowed to, and might have forgotten to mention it?'

Henry shook his head. 'Not at all. That was their place, had been for years. The only time they were ever moved was when they were cleaned, and that happened more or less on the spot. The ladies set up a table and cleaned all the brass on the same day. I happen to know they were done last week; my wife took part.'

'And do we know who was the last person to see them there, and when?' the constable asked.

'Apart from whoever stole them,' Venus said, 'I

might well have been. They were in use yesterday morning. It was Mr Nugent who noticed they were missing when he unlocked the church today. Of course . . .' she felt duty bound to add it, '. . . we can't know who would have been in, between me leaving and the gardener locking the church in the evening.'

The policeman looked up from his notes.

'You mean anyone, during the rest of the day, could have come in?' he asked. 'You mean the church wasn't locked?'

'It was not,' Henry said emphatically.

'It's our policy to leave it open during the daylight hours,' Venus said equally firmly.

It might be your policy; it isn't mine, Henry thought. He kept the thought to himself. It wouldn't help to voice it at the moment.

'People like to come into the church for many different reasons,' Venus said. 'Not only to look around, to see the windows and so on. They come to pray, or just to be quiet. One doesn't necessarily know why they come.'

And they come to steal the candlesticks, Constable Barker thought. Or anything else handy. There were one or two nice pictures on the walls; not what he'd want in his living room, but there was no accounting for tastes.

'So,' he said, his pencil poised over his notebook. 'You left the church at . . . ?'

'I suppose about a quarter to eleven,' Venus said. 'I went around to the back of the churchyard, and then on my way out I stopped to talk to Joe, the gardener, but I didn't come in again.'

'And from then until it was locked in the evening, the church was open? Anyone could come and go?'

'Exactly!' Henry said, grimly, his voice expressing his opinion.

The constable sighed—and gave Venus a long look. She felt her colour rise. What could you do with people like this one? he asked himself. They lived on another planet. 'And I don't suppose you have a photograph of the missing candlesticks?' he asked. Of course they wouldn't have.

'We do,' Henry said. 'That's one thing we do have. We had photographs of all our valuables taken a few years ago. At least we keep *them* locked up. If you'd like to come into the vestry I'll show them to you.'

'Right!' the constable said. 'It might help.' Personally, he had little hope of ever finding the stolen goods. They'd most likely be in London by now. But if they hadn't got any further than Brampton there might be a slight chance, with a photograph. Without it, one brass candlestick looked just like another to him. 'And is there anything else missing that you know of?' he asked.

'No,' Henry said. 'The Vicar and I have had a good look around while we were waiting for you. Everything else seems to be in order. The only other thing is, we think there's been a tramp about. The Vicar found signs in the garden behind the church.' He turned to Venus and she told the policeman what she had seen.

'So he could have come in at any time from late morning to early evening?' the constable said.

'He could,' Venus admitted. 'But what good would brass candlesticks be to him?'

Even if the answer to that hadn't immediately occurred to her—which it did—the expression on

99

the constable's face as he wrote it down on his pad would have told her. She had sounded incredibly naïve. She could have kicked herself.

'Good money,' the constable said. 'People like candlesticks. Candles are fashionable. Well, that seems to be it,' he concluded. 'We'll do what we can but it won't be easy. I'd like the gardener's address. I'll go and see him now. And there'll be a Scene-of-Crime officer around to see you. He or she will ring you to let you know when.' He would have liked to have said what he thought about people who made things easy-peasy for burglars, but in this case, he thought, certainly in hers, it would fall on deaf ears. 'Well,' he said, putting away his notebook, 'I'll leave you. Let us know if you think of anything else and if you find anything more missing.'

They watched him walk away, then Venus turned to Henry. 'I'm sorry!' she said. 'I'm really sorry!'

He gave her a steady look. 'What you mean is, you're sorry that it's happened.'

'Yes. That's what I mean,' she said.

'But you're not sorry about leaving the door open? It's not likely to change your mind about locking the church?'

She shook her head. 'I think not.' It hurt her so much to be opposed to Henry, but she couldn't ignore her own deep conviction about keeping the church open. If it came to it, she would fight for that.

'Well,' Henry said. 'I have this appointment. I must go. Obviously we'll have to talk later.'

He left hurriedly, and unsmiling. It had definitely not been the time, Venus thought, to tell him she was pregnant.

She left a little later, not without stopping and looking at the altar, bereft of its candlesticks; not without a stab of pain. There was another pair of candlesticks in a cupboard in the vestry but for the moment she wouldn't put them out, though they would be needed for the Sunday Eucharist. And yes, the vestry *was* kept locked. Was it going to be a case of keeping every precious thing which was moveable in the vestry for safe keeping? She hoped not. She would not be happy, for instance, about removing the cross from its place on the altar. In fact, she was not happy about any aspect of the affair and about the trouble she knew it would cause. Even so, she left the church door open as she set off for the village.

*   *   *

Her first stop was at the newsagent's, where Bob Chester was his usual smiling self. She had a great regard for Bob.

'Good-morning, Vicar!' he said cheerfully. 'Nice morning!'

'Lovely!' she agreed, since they were speaking only of the weather. 'Everything all right with you? I've come to pay for my papers.' Once everyone knows I'm pregnant, which couldn't be long, she thought, then she could order the pregnancy, birth and childcare magazines, in which she was surreptitiously immersing herself, from Bob, instead of having to go into Brampton and buy them at Smith's. But not just yet. At the moment, she felt she was living a sort of secret life.

She paid her bill, and left. Next, she went to Gander's, the bakers in the High Street, and it was while she was standing at the counter that a voice behind her said, 'Hello, Venus! Long time, no see!'

She turned around to face Mark Dover.

'Hello!' she said. 'It's been ages! Where have you been?'

She had first met Mark, not long after she had come to Thurston, at a dinner party given by Sonia. Mark was a painter, reasonably well known and successful. He had, from the beginning, made a play for her and had, in fact, insisted on painting her portrait, which had been exhibited in a well-known London gallery. He had certainly made more than one pass at her but, though she liked him, he was never the man for her. Indeed, she had not been looking for another man. Her memory of Philip, her first husband who had died, was still too fresh in her mind. It had taken Nigel Baines to bring her to life again.

'I've been abroad,' Mark said. 'I've been painting in Spain. Since you turned me down . . .' he was mocking her, '. . . what else would I do?'

She smiled at him. He was always fun. 'You haven't changed,' she said. 'A bit more tanned, but it suits you.'

'Then will you have a cup of coffee with me?' he asked. 'For old times' sake, so to speak. Do you remember we had coffee and their delicious cream cakes here in Gander's when I first knew you? Or being a married woman, are you no longer allowed to do that?'

Oh dear, Venus thought. Coffee and cream cakes? I can't possibly. But he didn't know she was pregnant, nor did she want him to, not ahead of several other people.

'I'd love to,' she said. 'I really would, but I'm in a

102

terrific rush. I have someone coming to see me any minute now.' The last bit was lying through her teeth and she felt awful about it. Also, she would have quite liked to have spent a little time with Mark. It was sometimes good to get away from the church or, rather, from the constraints of being parish priest, and this was one of them. And Mark was fun. 'I'm really sorry,' she said again.

'Ah well,' he said. 'Some other time!'

*   *   *

It was almost bedtime before she had an opportunity to tell Nigel about the theft of the candlesticks. He had had morning surgery, visits which stretched into the afternoon, and evening surgery and then an emergency call-out. He seemed not unduly concerned. 'These things happen,' he said. 'Even when you lock the door, they somehow get in.' Whether that was comfort or not she wasn't quite sure.

CHAPTER EIGHT

The theft of the candlesticks naturally had to be brought up at the meeting of the Parochial Church Council, though in the short interval between the theft and the meeting it seemed that most of the people in St Mary's had somehow learnt all about it and had formed their own opinions. To some it was a regrettable matter, but by no means of great importance: a pair of candlesticks? So? To others it was a loss almost approaching that of the Crown

Jewels. 'And what will Miss Frazer say?' someone asked—to which no-one ventured a reply. It was too awful to contemplate. There was little hope, Venus thought, that though she no longer attended St Mary's, the lady wouldn't hear of the theft. And in between the two extremes of opinion about the loss were many and various theories, all of them reflected and expressed in the views of the twenty members of the PCC, and most of them in the end boiled down to whether the church should or should not be left unlocked, which was hotly debated.

Earlier in the day Venus had seen Henry and had told him she was pregnant. He had, as she had expected, been pleased for her. 'And I must tell the PCC this evening,' she'd said.

Now it was ten-fifteen p.m. The theft of the candlesticks had taken up most of the time without any solution agreeable to all being reached. There had been no opportunity for Venus to make her own personal announcement. The discussion had become centred entirely on the locking, or otherwise, of the church. Venus had stated her case on it, which was already well known since this was not the first time the subject had come up. Henry, unusually grim and not at all enjoying opposing Venus, nevertheless stuck to his guns, as also did Edward Mason, his fellow churchwarden. Rose Barker, the Secretary, was firmly on Venus's side, and so too was the very elderly Miss Tordoff, though in her case it was because she found it difficult to admit to a fault in anyone, even a thief who would steal the candlesticks from an altar. 'After all,' she said, 'it is quite possible that the person who regrettably took them was in dire need:

unemployed; a sick wife, small children . . . one never knows. And who are we to judge?'

'We have a fund for cases like that,' George Phillipson, the Treasurer, said. His was usually the voice of reason. 'If that was so,' he pointed out, 'he could have asked for help. Anyway,' he added, 'I'm against locking the church door except after dark, and it is a fact that some insurance companies, including ones which specialise in insuring churches, actually charge lower premiums to churches which are kept open in the daytime. Less damage is done.'

'That's ridiculous!' someone interrupted.

'It isn't if you think about it,' George said patiently. 'If the thief is stealing from an open church he never knows when someone might walk in on him. So he steals less, takes what's handy, and makes a quick getaway. If the church was locked he's had to break in, possibly damaging a valuable window, and while he's in there he can take things at his leisure, uninterrupted, and make his exit when it suits him. Insurance companies aren't daft!'

'Nevertheless,' a quiet voice spoke up from the back of the room, 'to leave the church open is to put temptation in the way of someone who might never otherwise steal.' It was the voice of Sydney Fairclough. He never missed a PCC meeting, always sat at the back, and Venus had never before heard him utter a sound.

'That is a valid point of view,' Rose Barker said, breaking into the silence which had greeted his remark, feeling that in some way she must applaud his courage in giving voice at all. 'I'm not sure that I go along with it, but it *is* a point of view.'

Edward Mason looked pointedly at his watch.

'And the other fact is,' he said, 'that we've got all these points of view and we're getting nowhere. It's now a quarter-past ten and I don't know about the rest of you but I've not yet had my supper. I came here straight from work. I think we should put it to the vote, and without further ado!'

There was a general murmur of assent. Venus was disappointed. Whatever the outcome, she hated putting things to the vote, but Henry had nodded his agreement at the suggestion, and since it was what both her churchwardens wanted, she said, 'Very well then!'

She was not really surprised that the vote went against her, though she had hoped that the Treasurer's commonsense words about insurance might have influenced more people. It was therefore agreed that the church should be kept locked at all times unless services, including marriages and funerals, were taking place.

'That's that, then,' Henry said. He looked at Venus.

'So be it then,' she said. 'I hope we all realise that by deciding to keep the church locked the criminal has won and the community has lost.'

'Is there any other business?' Rose Barker asked, breaking the short silence which followed Venus's words.

Venus spoke up. 'There is just one thing,' she said. 'And I hope you'll find it pleasing news after this evening's problems. I'm pregnant! Nigel and I are to have a baby! Next spring.'

There was another silence. She felt for a moment as if the world stood still; and then the congratulations broke out.

'Wonderful!'

'How lovely!'

'Great!'

'What a surprise!'

If anyone thought 'How very soon!' it was not expressed.

*   *   *

'So you can now tell anyone you want to in St Patrick's,' she said to Nigel when she reached home. He had already sent the news to his mother and his aunt in Ireland—but he and Venus had decided that the likelihood of twins wouldn't be mentioned just yet. Better to make quite certain, which they would be after the next scan, before telling anyone, even Venus's parents, or Becky. 'And after that Becky can tell Anna—that will make our daughter happy—and I'll be able to tell the whole world, which is what I feel like doing.'

'Do you realise you said "our daughter"?' Nigel asked.

'No, I didn't,' Venus admitted. 'It just came out naturally.'

'Do you think she'll ever think of me like that?' Nigel asked.

Venus touched his hand. 'One day she will,' she said. 'She won't forget Philip but she'll grow to love you for who you are. I'm sure of that.'

'I wouldn't want her to forget him,' Nigel said. 'So, what about the rest of the meeting? Did that go well?'

Venus shook her head. 'Not really, at least not for me. And I'm not really breaking any confidences when I tell you that the PCC voted to keep the church closed outside the times of

107

services. It will be in the parish magazine next week. I'm bitterly disappointed. As you know, it goes against all my thinking on the subject; but I shall have to go along with it, certainly for the time being.'

'I'm sorry, sweetheart,' Nigel said. 'Perhaps, after a while, people will change their minds.'

'I don't see why they would,' Venus said. 'I don't foresee the subject coming up again—unless of course we had another theft in spite of the fact that the church was locked. And that's not something I can actually hope for, is it? I can't put that in my prayers!'

Nigel smiled. 'You're right, honey, you can't. Anyway, it's late. Let's go to bed. You're an expectant mother and you're supposed to get plenty of sleep. Doctor's orders! You go up and I'll bring you a hot drink.'

*   *   *

Two days later, it was ten o'clock in the morning and Venus was alone in the house, attacking a pile of ironing which had been growing ever higher over the last three days, when there was a long, insistent ring at the door. Pausing only to switch off the iron, she went to answer it. As she hurried towards the door the ringing continued without a break. It must surely be an emergency? 'I'm coming!' she called out. 'I'm coming!'

She reached the door and opened it wide; wide enough for the person on the doorstep to rush straight past her, into the hall. It was Amelia Frazer: breathless, red-faced, her grey felt hat askew on her unkempt white hair, her eyes wild.

'How dare you!' she shouted. 'How dare you! You . . . you . . . incompetent impostor!'

Venus took a deep breath and spoke as calmly as she could, though she was far from calm inside. Miss Frazer in a rage, and brandishing a heavy walking stick, was not to be taken lightly.

'Please come and sit down, Miss Frazer,' she said. 'Whatever it is, I'm sure we can discuss it.'

'Whatever it is!' Miss Frazer stormed. 'You know what it is! It is you who have caused it! You and you alone! You have caused my father's precious and valuable candlesticks to be stolen . . . !'

'Please listen to me—' Venus said. But there was no possibility of that happening. She was wasting her breath.

'Those beautiful candlesticks have been on the altar for sixty-two years,' Miss Frazer shouted. 'A gift from my father, a memorial . . .'

If she says to his horse I know I shall laugh out loud, Venus thought. Though it would be from hysterics rather than from mirth.

'. . . Sixty-two years,' Miss Frazer repeated. 'And never come to one moment's harm until you had charge of them! You are not fit to be the custodian of anything; not for candlesticks, not for the faith of the church, and not for this house in which you stand as if you had a right to!'

'But I do have a—' Venus began.

'You have no right! This is a house for the priest. The man who lived here was a good man and true. He was a real priest. I knew this house as if it was my own. Now you have desecrated it. You are not a priest. A woman cannot be a priest. You are an impostor! I will make you pay. I will make you pay for those candlesticks—even though every penny

109

you have in the world would not be recompense for the loss. Nothing will recompense for that.'

'I won't pay,' Venus said. In a strange way she felt calmer now. There was nothing she could do to stop this madwoman but she would not be beaten down by her, she would not even raise her voice. 'The insurance company will pay. We have already reported the theft. And as I've said, I'm very sorry about the candlesticks but I don't take responsibility.'

'How can you not take responsibility?' Miss Frazer shouted. 'It was you who allowed the church to be left open, uncared for. It is entirely your responsibility. Your predecessor, the man in whose house you are falsely camped, would never have done that. And I think you will find, that because of your carelessness, the insurance company will not pay a penny. But I will see that *you* do!'

'I think you might be wrong about the insurance,' Venus said evenly. 'But we shall see. And I repeat, I'm sorry about the candlesticks. And now, Miss Frazer, let me show you to the door. I don't think we have anything more to say to each other.'

Miss Frazer glared, then raised her stick. For a brief moment Venus thought she would strike her, and she tried to work out how she would prevent it, but Miss Frazer banged the stick against the wall with all the strength that her rage had given her, causing a deep crack in the paint. Then she turned and marched out of the door, which Venus only now realised had been wide open on the scene. She wondered who, if anyone, had witnessed it.

She closed the door and went back to her ironing, but now she was shaking. She sat down for a moment to recover, angry with herself for letting Miss Frazer upset her. And would this be the end of it or was there more to come?

After an hour or so she finished the ironing. There was something about running the hot iron over the garments and smoothing out the creases, about the warm smell of washed clothes in her nostrils, which also smoothed her own senses. She could deal with Miss Frazer. Oh yes, she could! She could deal with a dozen Miss Frazers if she had to. And as a small reward to herself she decided that before she went around to the church—there was nothing specific she had to go for, there were no services, but she went every day—she would sit down and telephone all those friends who had not so far heard it, her news of her pregnancy. Now that the PCC were in the picture there was no further reason to wait. And in any case, as she hadn't indicated to the PCC that there was any reason for secrecy about it, it would probably be all over the village already. Good news, in this instance, would travel every bit as quickly as bad.

She made a list. Ann, Philip's mother, must be at the top of it. Ann had never ceased to support her, even when she'd told her she was going to marry Nigel. She must tell Evelyn Sharp, Becky's headmistress, before Becky got in first and told all her schoolfriends. It was good that Becky now had friends. There had been a time, soon after she'd gone to St Mary's Primary School, when she'd been an unhappy little girl, bullied, and had blamed it on Venus for being a vicar. 'Who wants a vicar for a mother?' she'd said. Evelyn Sharp had been a tower of strength in sorting that out. She would also ring Esmé Bickler, and, as a matter of

111

courtesy, the Rural Dean. And for the same reason she would write a short letter to the Bishop. She would get that in the post today.

The phone calls took the rest of the morning. Everyone, it seemed, was pleased for her: surprised, sometimes, but nevertheless pleased. 'It's wonderful news!' Ann said. 'The best! You must look after yourself!' 'I will, I will!' Venus promised her. 'Fantastic!' Esmé Bickler said. 'But rather you than me. Imagine what it'll be like, going to a Chapter meeting in full sail! They won't know what to do with you!'

'I know,' Venus confessed. 'It's an awesome thought.' She had also thought about what it would be like if, at some time in the future, she had to take her twin babies to a Chapter meeting. It was almost inevitable. There wouldn't always be someone with whom she could leave them. But if she steeled herself to doing it, it might be quite fun. It would certainly liven up the meeting! Though I'm jumping well ahead now, she reminded herself.

She put down the phone on Esmé and then rang Evelyn Sharp. 'Becky knows,' she said, 'but now I'm going to tell her she can give the news to her friends. She's bursting to do that and she's been so good at keeping the secret until I'd told other people, including you.'

'That's great!' Evelyn said. 'She'll be a very happy girl.'

By now it was lunchtime. Venus made herself a cheese sandwich. She was very much into cheese. It was somehow, she couldn't think why, an antidote to the sickness which was still plaguing her. How long would that go on? she asked herself yet again. Sonia had said there was no telling.

112

After lunch, she decided, she absolutely must ring the Blessed Henry and tell him about Miss Frazer's visit. She had dealt with it, and as far as she could see there was nothing else to be done, either by herself or by Henry Nugent, but he had a right to know. And was he, in fact, still her Blessed Henry? They had been such good friends ever since she had arrived in Thurston. He had supported her in every possible way, but had the matter of locking the church door now come between them, even though he had won the argument? She hoped not. She was unhappy with the decision but she would go along with it and hope, eventually, for another opportunity to debate it again. So it was with rather less than her usual confidence that she rang his number.

He sounded his usual pleasant self as he answered the phone. Leaving no time to mention last night's meeting, Venus rushed in with her own news.

'I've had Miss Frazer to see me,' she announced. 'Definitely on the warpath! I thought I should let you know.'

'Oh Venus!' Henry said, 'I *am* sorry! What was it about this time?' As if he didn't know, he thought.

'The candlesticks, naturally. She was in a towering rage. I won't go into details, it was the mixture as before, but I really didn't like having her invade my house. And if Becky had been there to witness it I would have been even more upset. I thought I ought to tell you. I don't know what she might do next.'

'There's nothing much she can do,' Henry said. 'At least, nothing practical. They weren't her candlesticks, they belonged to the church. I hate

113

the way people give something to the church and then keep an eye on it ever after. There's too much of that. In any case, she didn't give them; her father did. And they were insured. So don't worry, Venus! And you did quite right to ring me. It's what I'm here for.'

Venus was glad he couldn't see her. Tears filled her eyes at the sound of his kind voice and his reassuring words. He could have added 'Now that the church is to be locked, it won't happen again', but he was too gracious for that. He was her Blessed Henry again.

'Would you like me to go and see her?' he asked. 'I can tell her to back off. Put the fear of the Lord into her—not that I think she has much fear of the Lord. She assumes that he's on her side.'

'No,' Venus assured him. 'That's not necessary. Let's leave it for now. I dealt with her. She might not come back. But thank you, Henry.'

'Then leave me to sort her out if anything else happens,' Henry said.

'Oh, I expect I can deal with her,' Venus said. 'And she wouldn't do it to you. It's me she hates.'

When she had put the phone down she looked at her watch. There was time to write her letter to the Bishop, which she would post on her way to the church, and be back before Becky was home from school. She was half-way down the road from the Vicarage when she remembered that she would need the key to let herself in. She had never needed to do this in the daytime before. It had been the duty of one or other of the churchwardens to lock the church a little while before dusk. But no longer, she reminded herself as she turned back to get the key.

Reaching the church it was clear that no time had been lost in keeping the new rule. The heavy oak door was closed in the face of all comers. Feeling not in the least happy about it, she put her large key in the lock and, with difficulty, turned it, and pushed open the door. Everything seemed particularly dark inside, and perhaps that was partly due to her own feelings. She switched on several lights, and left the door wide open. If someone wanted to come in while she was there, so much the better. There were nearly always visitors around in the village. If they came while she was there it would prove her point and she would welcome them, but for now, she went into the parish office and did some paperwork. Leaving the office door open, she could see who came and went.

She had been working for half-an-hour or so when a woman came into the church. Venus supposed, in keeping with the spirit of keeping things locked, she must leave the office and go into the church; keep an eye on the visitor. It went totally against the grain to do so, nevertheless she went to the back of the nave and started tidying hymn books and leaflets. The visitor was walking around, reading the memorials on the wall, studying the stained glass windows. Then she went to the front pew and knelt to pray. After a while she stood up again and began to make her way out. When she reached Venus she said, 'It's so good to find a church open. I was particularly pleased to do so today because I'm visiting Thurston and this is the church where my parents were married, though a long time ago.'

The two of them exchanged a few more

pleasantries, then the woman said, 'In my church we have a roster of voluntary vergers, so that we can keep the church open most days.'

Venus nodded. 'Yes,' she said. 'When I first came here, so did we, but somehow or other it seems to have fallen apart. People move away, or die, or get too old. And of course, most of them *were* elderly because they were the ones who had the time to spare.'

But surely, she thought to herself, at least something like that could be done again—even a day or two a week would be better than nothing. And perhaps she herself could bring more of her paperwork and do it in the church. She *must* do something.

'What time do you close up?' the visitor asked.

Venus looked at her watch. 'Round about now,' she said. 'I have to be in for my daughter when she comes home from school.'

'Then I mustn't keep you,' the woman said.

Venus left a few minutes later, locking the door behind her and resolving, as she walked home, that as far as she could (and common sense was telling her already that it would not be far) she would somehow be, if necessary, a one-woman church minder. After all, no-one could deny her the right to be in church as much as she chose to be. She was the Vicar! She would not make a song and dance about it, she would just do it.

She had been at home for no more than five minutes when Becky rushed into the house, banged the front door behind her, and banged her satchel down on the kitchen table. She was going through a banging stage.

'I'm starving!' she announced.

116

'Tea coming up in a minute,' Venus said. 'And I have some good news for you!'

'What?' Becky asked, suspiciously. Her mother's ideas of good news were not always the same as her own.

'You can now tell your friends about the baby,' Venus said. 'I've told the PCC and Granny Ann, and a few others on the phone, so now you can tell Anna and one or two other friends if you want to. But not the whole village, of course!'

'Oh, super!' Becky cried. 'Can I go round to Anna's straight away? It doesn't matter about the tea.'

'You can phone her now,' Venus said. 'Then you can have your tea. After that you can go to Anna's.'

'I expect she'll be wanting a baby next,' Becky said complacently.

Venus smiled at her. It was good to see her so happy, and there was more to come for Becky. She would have liked to have told her that it would not be just one baby, but two, and possibly two brothers. But for that she must make certain and wait for the results of the next scan, which would soon be due.

CHAPTER NINE

Within minutes of Becky leaving, Nigel came in.

'I've done most of my visits,' he said. 'Time for a cup of tea and a slice of toast before I go back for surgery. Where's Becky?'

'Gone to give Anna the glad news,' Venus told him. 'Full of importance, she was.' She poured

Nigel's tea and put a slice of bread in the toaster. 'I suppose there's no hope that it won't be around the village in no time at all? I mean with the PCC, and any minute now the school?'

'Does it matter?' Nigel asked. 'I'd be pleased to shout it from the housetop.'

Venus put her arm around his shoulder as he sat at the table. 'You're right, love. Of course it doesn't. And don't think I'm not proud of it. In any case, it's going to show quite soon now.'

He nodded agreement. 'It's just that it still seems unreal.'

'And you a doctor!' Venus said.

'I don't feel like a doctor, not about this,' he said. 'I feel like a prospective, nervous, first-time dad who never thought it would happen to him!'

He ate his toast, drank his tea, and refused a second cup. 'I have to get back,' he said. 'It's going to be a busy surgery. And I have a couple more visits afterwards, so I'll be a bit late home.'

'You work so hard, darling,' Venus said. 'And you're so conscientious about your visits. I wish I could say the same about mine. I don't do nearly enough—though I know it's what a parish priest should be doing.'

'Maybe most of yours don't have the same urgency,' Nigel pointed out. 'Though yes, I know you should do them, and I'm sure you will when you can.'

'I haven't seen Bertha Jowett for ages,' Venus confessed. 'She doesn't even know I'm pregnant. I really must make an effort.'

'Darling, this is *not* the time to be thinking how much more you should do,' Nigel urged. 'You should be thinking how you can cut back on your work. And this *is* your doctor speaking. Anyway, I must be off.' He gave her a quick kiss, and was out through the door.

But he *is* conscientious, Venus thought as she watched him get into his car and drive off down the road. She really ought to take a leaf out of his book—and she'd start by going to see Bertha Jowett tomorrow. Also, it was three days since she'd dropped in on her mother and, even more unusual, her mother hadn't been around to the Vicarage. She didn't worry about her father; he had his own pursuits, but her mother was different.

She picked up the phone, and waited longer than she expected before it was answered.

'Mum! I haven't seen you since Sunday!' Venus said. 'Are you all right?' She waited for the usual 'Of course I am,' but it didn't come.

'Well . . .' Her mother paused.

'You're not ill, are you? Why didn't you let me know?'

'Did I say I was ill?' her mother asked, sounding irritable. 'Of course I'm not ill. It's just that I've been having a bit of pain with my back, and down my leg.'

'You've been having that for weeks now,' Venus pointed out. 'You said you were going to see Sonia. Have you made an appointment?' She ought to know the answer to that. She'd just been too busy with her own affairs.

'Not yet,' Mrs Foster admitted. 'I put it off. I took some aspirin. But I will give her a ring tomorrow. It's getting to be a bit of a nuisance. I can't sleep for it. Anyway, how are you, love? And Becky? I haven't seen Becky this week.'

'I'm fine,' Venus said. 'And so is Becky. She's at

Anna's at the moment. They're practically inseparable. Anyway, I'll pop around and see you in the morning. I would come now, but I must be in when Becky comes home. Nigel has a surgery.'

'No need to fuss!' her mother said.

It isn't quite true that I can't leave the house because I'm waiting in for Becky, Venus thought as she put down the phone. All it needed to sort that out was a call to Sally Brent, who didn't at all mind if Becky stayed a little longer. 'Of course!' Sally said. 'Just give me a ring when you're back.'

But, Venus thought a minute later, was there any sense in rushing around to see her mother immediately, or was she simply wanting to ease her own conscience? She looked at her watch. Five minutes past five, and there was no way Nigel would be home before half-past seven. She had planned fish for supper, which wouldn't take long to cook, so she had time on her hands. She could spend it doing sweet nothing at all, fritter it away—which would be delightful—or, and here her conscience kicked in, if she wasn't going to spend the time with her mother she could go to see Bertha Jowett instead of putting that off until tomorrow.

She dawdled a little longer, scanning the headlines of the *Brampton Echo* which had just been pushed through the letter box. They promised interesting reading for later on, but not for now. For now she was going to The Beeches.

*   *   *

As far as Bertha's face ever lit up—she was not one for showing extravagant feelings—it did so when

Venus walked into the room.

'My goodness!' she said, raising her eyes to the ceiling. 'See what the wind's blown in!'

'I know it's a while since I saw you,' Venus apologised. 'And I'm sorry. I've been busy.' What a feeble excuse that sounds, she thought; but at the same time as feeling guilty, she felt ever so slightly cross with Bertha Jowett. 'Though of course,' she added, 'if it's too much for you, or if you're not in the mood for visitors, then I'll not stay. I'll come back another time.'

'Of course it's not too much for me!' Bertha said quickly, 'I'm perfectly well. And,' she conceded, 'I'm pleased to see you.'

'Good! And I have news for you!' Venus said.

Bertha sat up a little straighter in her chair; her eyes brightened. 'I hope it's good news,' she said.

'Now, Bertha, would I bring it to you if it weren't?' Venus said.

'Well, come on, then,' Bertha said. 'Spit it out!'

'I'm pregnant!' Venus announced.

There was a short, deep silence.

'I'm going to have a baby!'

'I know what pregnant means,' Bertha said. 'And I suppose I shouldn't be surprised. It's one of the hazards of getting married—except that these days it more often happens before.'

'Is that all you can say?' Venus asked. 'Aren't you pleased for me?'

'I am if you are,' Bertha said. 'It makes more sense than being a priest.'

'Oh Bertha!' Venus protested. 'What's wrong with being both?'

'A waste of a good brain,' Bertha said. 'You know what I think about the church—a load of hocus

121

pocus! And when it comes to children, there are far too many anyway. But of course if it's what you want . . .'

'It is,' Venus said firmly. 'I couldn't be more pleased.'

'All right. And I'm sorry!' Bertha said. 'I'm a bad-tempered old woman these days. The truth is, I sit here and wonder if I should ever have given up my little home.'

But she had had to, Venus thought sadly. She couldn't have carried on. And at the time she'd appeared to be quite resigned to it, it had been her own decision, no relatives pushing her into it.

'I suppose the thing is,' Bertha continued, 'that at the moment I don't feel all that perky.'

She didn't look well, Venus thought. Her skin was a yellowish-white, her hair was dull and dank, and hung to her shoulders, in need of cutting. There was no sign of the butterfly ornament. Her hands, clutching the rug over her knees, had scarcely more flesh on them than claws. 'Have you lost weight?' Venus asked.

'I daresay I have,' Bertha replied. 'I don't like the food, for a start. Oh, I'm sure it's healthy stuff, and there's enough of it. It's just not to my taste. And please don't tell me they do their best and it's not easy catering for different people, all of them old, and some of them, like me, cantankerous. I know all that. I've worked that out for myself.'

'I wasn't going to say any of that,' Venus told her, 'though I'm sure it's true they do their best. And it can't be easy for them either. They have to think about cost and nutrition.'

'Nutrition doesn't work if you can't eat what's put in front of you,' Bertha said. 'I usually send mine back.'

Venus sighed. This was not going to be the
easiest visit in the world, Venus thought. She
wished she had time to suggest a game of Scrabble
to take Bertha's mind in another direction, but she
hadn't. 'So what would your ideal meal be?' she
enquired, grabbing at something to say.

'Is this a quiz?' Bertha demanded. 'Or do you
propose to do something about it?'

'I don't know,' Venus confessed. 'I don't know
what you'd choose. If it's caviar, then you're on a
loser.'

'Not caviar,' Bertha said. 'I hate the stuff! Fish
eggs. Disgusting!'

'OK,' Venus said. 'That's settled. No caviar then.
So what?'

Bertha Jowett's face brightened; a look of what
was almost greed swept over it. Good, Venus
thought, she's turned it into a game.

'Well,' Bertha said thoughtfully, 'first of all I'd
like a half-bottle of champagne. Dom Perignon
would be my choice, but a Veuve Clicquot would
do. And a very beautiful crystal flute to drink it
from.' She paused.

'And then?' Venus prompted.

'Don't rush me!' Bertha protested. 'Give me
time to enjoy my champagne. All right then. After
that a little smoked salmon with a squeeze of
lemon . . . and then . . . perhaps half an avocado—
exactly at the correct ripeness, mind you—with a
tangy dressing.'

'You're not doing too badly,' Venus said. 'Will
you be able to eat a pudding?'

'Oh yes, indeed,' Bertha said briskly. 'Nothing
heavy. Strawberries with cream—but proper

clotted cream, not that thin pouring stuff which tastes no better than the top of the milk.'

'Well, you've chosen a nice menu,' Venus said. 'Nothing too heavy; everything delicious.'

'I know that,' Bertha Jowett countered. 'In my time, let me tell you, I've known what it was to eat the best food off the finest china, *and* in the best places. But that's cloud-cuckoo-land, isn't it? When my supper comes in half-an-hour it'll be a beef rissole and tinned fruit salad.'

'I'm sorry,' Venus said. 'I wish—'

'Oh, take no notice,' Bertha interrupted, waving her hands. 'I'm a cross-patch today. I suppose you're right, they do their best. And I know I'm an awkward customer.'

Nevertheless, Venus thought, somehow I'll see she gets that half-bottle of champagne—though it would more likely be a supermarket brand—*and* the smoked salmon.

'Forget it,' Bertha continued. 'What sort of a day have you had?'

'So-so,' Venus admitted. She told her about the problem of keeping the church locked, though perhaps I shouldn't tell her, she thought even as she was saying it. It was still PCC business. But who would Bertha Jowett pass it on to? It was one of her most regular complaints, that there was no-one to talk to.

A pleasant-looking young woman popped her head around the door. 'Supper in twenty minutes, Miss Jowett!' she said.

Bertha looked annoyed. 'Everything has to be done by the clock here,' she said to Venus. 'I was hoping we might have a game of Scrabble.'

'I'm sorry!' Venus said. 'I couldn't, anyway. I

124

have to make supper for Nigel and Becky. But I'll come again before long and we will have a game. Or even two.'

'Very well then,' Bertha said. 'But don't forget!' Then as Venus walked towards the door she called after her. 'And I am pleased about the baby. If it's a girl you could call her Bertha. And look after yourself!'

*   *   *

There was an autumnal chill in the air as Venus walked home from The Beeches, and as if to emphasise it the leaves on the trees had already begun to change colour, and some of them to drop. Scope there, she thought, for Joe only-one-pair-of-hands Hargreaves to have a top-of-the-range grumble when he had to sweep them up in quantity, as would be the case after the first real autumnal winds. Even though it was not on the coast, Thurston was prone to boisterous south-westers, and the churchyard was well-endowed with deciduous trees. It was not yet dark but before long, she thought, when the clocks went back, it would be at this time. She didn't relish the thought; she was not a winter person.

Passing the lych gate, she wondered whether she should walk up the path and check that everything was all right, but since she could see the door was closed (and presumably locked), that there was no-one about and no lights anywhere, she decided not to. She wanted to be home, and the supper under way, before Nigel came in. They tried always— barring emergencies or Becky having hers at the Brents', which was not unusual—to eat supper

125

together. Without formally discussing it, this part of the day had become quality time for the three of them. Venus had stipulated, on first arriving in Thurston, that she would not attend any evening meetings unless they took place at the Vicarage or unless she had a reliable sitter, known to and liked by Becky. She would not leave Becky alone. Things had become easier once her parents had moved into the village. One or the other would sit-in or, which was what her daughter much preferred, Becky would spend the night with them. And now there was Nigel, though he couldn't always be sure of being there; he was often on call.

Venus took her mobile out of her pocket and rang Sally Brent.

'I'm on my way home,' she said. 'It would make sense if I came and picked up Becky. Would that be all right?'

'Of course!' Sally said. 'They have eaten.'

'I'll be about ten minutes,' Venus said.

They were back at the Vicarage well before seven o'clock. Hearing them the moment they set foot on the path, Missie rushed to the door to meet them, barking furiously. Becky was her favourite person in the whole world.

'I'll feed her!' Becky said. 'I expect she's *starving* hungry!'

Missie was the easiest dog ever to feed, Venus thought. She would eat whatever was put before her and thrive on it. No need for champagne and smoked salmon there! But poor Bertha Jowett, she thought a little later as she began to prepare supper for herself and Nigel.

'We had fish fingers and chips,' Becky said. 'Great! And Anna's really pleased about the baby.

126

But of course now she wants one. I told you she would!'

*   *   *

The next morning, as she had promised she would, Venus went to see her mother. She found her sitting in an easy chair, reading the *Brampton Echo*, which was totally unlike her: not the reading of the *Echo*—she did that from cover to cover every week, cutting snippets out for Venus's perusal even though she knew that her daughter read it for herself—but that it was the middle of the morning and she was sitting down, something Venus had rarely seen. Her mother immediately folded the paper, put it on the table at her side, and stood up, though, Venus noted, not without a certain stiffness that was unusual in her.

'I've caught you at it!' Venus said. 'Slacking!'

'It was just a headline, caught my eye,' Mrs Foster said. 'I'll make a cup of coffee.'

'No you won't!' Venus said. 'You'll sit right down again and I'll make us both one. How are you?'

'I'm all right,' her mother said. 'More or less. A bit of rheumatism I reckon.'

'And have you made an appointment to see Sonia?' Venus asked.

'As a matter of fact, I have. On Thursday. She says they're very busy, but I expect you know that. If it was urgent, she said, she'd see me right away, but I told her it wasn't.'

'How long have you had this pain?' Venus asked.

Her mother was vague about it, though when pressed she admitted to 'quite a while'. 'It's in my groin as well. It catches me,' she said.

127

'I'll be glad when you've seen Sonia and she's sorted it out,' Venus said. 'Would you like me to go with you?'

Her mother brushed the suggestion away. 'Not the least bit necessary,' she said. 'I'm sure it's something and nothing. I expect she'll give me some stronger tablets.'

But Venus, going into the kitchen to make the coffee, wasn't sure it was something and nothing. Her mother had the look—unusual for her—of someone who had been, and still was, in pain. It wasn't what she said, it was in the way she moved, and in her voice.

*   *   *

The days went by. A Scene-of-Crime officer had been and gone about the theft of the candlesticks. She was a comely young woman, who looked, impossibly, as if she had not long left school. She had asked pertinent questions about security, or the lack of it, not expressing in words her opinion of that though it showed in her face. She examined several areas, while not saying what she was looking for. 'Actually,' she'd said—it was almost a complaint—'there are far too many different fingerprints around.'

'I'd expect that. It comes of having a sizeable congregation,' Venus had said, a little complacently. 'But when I was burgled last year I was told that thieves seldom left fingerprints. They all now wore Marigolds—rubber gloves.'

'Quite true,' the officer said. 'I didn't know you'd been burgled before.'

'Not here,' Venus had explained. 'It was at the

128

Vicarage. They never caught anyone.'

Nor would they, she had thought then, any more, she still thought, than they would do about the candlesticks. By now the general opinion was that the candlesticks should be permanently replaced with others; the altar didn't look right without them—indeed, they were needed for the services— and the ones in temporary use were simply not good enough. There was no suggestion as to where the money might come from to replace them and Venus herself was loath to use what little money there was to buy expensive new ones. The substitutes in use at the moment were adequate, inoffensive, and fulfilled the purpose, or so *she* thought. The lit candles themselves were the important symbol. If there was any spare money around she would like it to be used for the Sunday School. But it would all have to be debated, probably at length, at the next PCC meeting, and, once again, she would be in the minority.

*   *   *

But what filled her mind most in the following week was the scan, due to take place on Friday, which would show for certain, though even now she had little doubt of it, that, yes, she was expecting twins. It would tell her that they were (or were not) of the same sex, hopefully boys, and that they were, or were not, identical. All these things she longed to know. She had not allowed herself any preconceived ideas of the outcome; she was ready and would be grateful for whatever might be in store. But oh, it would be so wonderful to know!

It was a pity that Nigel would not be able to go

with her—he felt as badly about that as she did—but Sonia would be away for a few days, not returning until the Friday evening, and Nigel would be running the practice single-handed.

'I'm sorry, love,' he said. 'You know I want to be there.'

'Of course I know that,' Venus agreed. 'And if I could have changed the date I would have, but that wasn't possible. But don't worry, I'll tell you every detail!'

And then when Friday came, and she was given the results, they were exactly what she had hoped for. She longed for Nigel to be there to share them with her. It was a moment, she felt, when they should have been together.

'Definitely twins,' the radiologist said, 'but we didn't have much doubt about that, did we? Definitely boys—they were most obliging in facing front again towards the camera! And certainly identical!'

'Which means exactly what?' Venus asked. She felt she knew. She had been reading everything she could lay hands on, and consulting Sonia and Nigel, but she needed confirmation.

'They are one cell which has been split,' she was told. 'They share the one placenta. If the boys each had a placenta they would be fraternal. Identical twins have the same DNA, and they have identical fingerprints and palm prints! And for the record, you—and your babies—seem to be remarkably healthy! But you must take care,' she warned. 'You are carrying two babies, you will have two births to contend with and two babies to feed, so you must keep well, take plenty of rest.'

Nigel was beside himself with joy when Venus

130

gave him the news. 'Having one child was something I hardly dared dream of,' he said. 'But twins!'

'And it's true,' he added. 'You must take care of yourself, my darling. And I shall take care of you, see that you don't overstretch yourself.'

'Oh, Nigel, I shall be fine,' Venus protested. 'I won't be the first person ever to give birth to twins!'

'But you'll be the first person in my life ever to do so,' Nigel said.

'And we must tell Becky,' Venus said. 'We must tell her before anyone else. She'll be thrilled to pieces!'

'Where is she?' Nigel asked.

'At Anna's,' Venus told him. 'Where else? But she'll be home soon. I told her she must be back well before dark.'

Nigel jumped to his feet. 'I'll go and collect her,' he said. 'I don't want her walking home alone, even at dusk.'

'If you like,' Venus said, smiling. 'But Sally wouldn't let her do that. She'd bring her home.'

'No,' Nigel said firmly. 'It's time she was home. I'll fetch her. And I'll take Missie with me, give her an extra walk.'

At the sound of her name, and the word 'walk', Missie went to fetch her lead from the hook.

'You're not to say a word to Becky,' Venus ordered. 'Not a single word. I want the three of us to be together for that.'

'Of course I won't,' Nigel promised, clipping the lead on Missie.

Twenty minutes later the three of them were back.

'We were watching TV,' Becky protested. 'I

131

would have come home before dark.'

'Well, you're here now, honey,' Venus said. 'We have something to tell you. We couldn't wait!'

When she heard the news, Becky screamed. 'Twins!' she cried. 'And boys! Two brothers, all at once! I wouldn't have wanted two sisters, that's for sure! But two brothers!'

'So we take it you're pleased,' Nigel said.

'Of *course* I am!' She paused, then said, 'Anna will be furious! Can I choose both names?'

'As I said, you can help,' Venus told her. Who knew what Becky would come up with? 'But remember, it must be something the boys will be happy with when they're older. Anyway, here's something to help you to choose.' She handed her the book she had bought on her first visit to 'Mums and Kids', when she was newly pregnant.

'*Name This Child*,' Becky read the title aloud.

'You know where those words come from,' Venus said. 'It's what I say in church when I'm baptising a child.' That was one thing she had instigated in her first few months in St Mary's. Unless the parents particularly wished it otherwise, which had only once proved to be the case, baptisms now took place at the Sunday morning Eucharist, with the whole congregation taking part in the questions and answers and in welcoming the child.

'I know!' Becky said.

'So why don't you make a list of names and then the three of us will discuss it,' Venus suggested.

*   *   *

'There'll be all sorts of things to consider,' Venus

132

said after Becky had gone to bed, taking the book of names with her. 'It's not like having one baby, is it? Two of everything they'll wear; double the number of nappies. And what about the pram? A single pram won't do, will it? And the cots. And the—'

'You're going to have the most marvellous time shopping,' Nigel broke in. 'Don't tell me you're not going to enjoy that!'

'Of course I am,' Venus said. 'But . . .' She hesitated.

'But what?'

'I should warn you! It's going to be very expensive!'

'Then I'd better come with you,' Nigel said, smiling. 'Hold you in check.'

The telephone rang and Venus jumped up to answer it. Nigel watched her as she listened. Saw the happy look on her face change quickly to one of horror. 'No!' she said. 'Oh no! I can't believe it! Yes, I'll be right round. Straight away!' She put the phone down.

'What is it?' Nigel asked. 'What's wrong?'

'It's George!' she cried. 'George Phillipson. He's dead! He just . . . he just sat down in his chair, and died.'

'I'll go round at once!' Nigel said.

Venus shook her head. 'His wife said Sonia is already there. But I must go.'

She felt as if she had had a hard, physical blow to the very centre of her body. George Phillipson. He had been far more than the Church Treasurer, he had been a friend to her ever since she'd arrived in Thurston. Whatever had happened, however sticky the situation, he had been on her side. He had

133

been a rock. What would she do without him?

CHAPTER TEN

The Phillipsons lived at the top of a wide, tree-lined road of very pleasant houses which led out of the village and towards the Downs. Venus was ringing the doorbell within ten minutes of receiving the phone call. The door was answered by Sonia, who ushered her into the hall.

'This is dreadful!' Venus said. 'How did it happen?'

'I know very little more than I told you on the phone,' Sonia said. 'They had supper. He didn't eat much, said he felt tired. When it was over he moved to sit in his armchair. His wife cleared some of the dishes into the kitchen, stayed there long enough to make coffee. When she came back she thought he was asleep—and then she realised he was dead. She was beside herself! She can't remember phoning me. Obviously she did. I came immediately.'

'I must go to her at once!' Venus said.

'She's in the sitting room,' Sonia said. 'I persuaded her not to stay in the dining room.'

Connie Phillipson was huddled in a low chair in the bay of the window. The curtains were not drawn, but of the garden outside—a neat, pleasant garden, Venus remembered, from her only previous visit to the house, when George had shown her over it with obvious pride and joy—there was little to be seen now except dim shapes of trees and shrubs. Darkness had fallen quite

134

suddenly. One small table-lamp had been switched on and Connie Phillipson sat in the circle of its light. It did little to illuminate the rest of the room.

She looked terrible. She was a lady of around sixty; tall, plumpish, always smartly turned out, and in normal circumstances attractive. And now, Venus thought, she looked a shrunken old woman. She knew her socially, not intimately, but enough to call her by her first name. She moved towards her, knelt down by the chair and took Connie's hands in hers. They were icy cold. Venus started to chafe them, trying to bring back some warmth.

'Oh, Venus!' Connie cried—though it was more a wail of anguish, as if it might have come from an animal. 'Oh, Venus! What am I going to do?'

'Right now,' Venus said, 'get warm! I'm going to find a blanket to wrap around you, and then you're going to drink some brandy . . .'

'I don't like brandy. Oh my God, what am I going to do?' she repeated.

'Stay just where you are for the moment,' Venus said. 'I'll go and fetch a blanket from one of the bedrooms. I won't be a minute.' She turned to speak to Sonia, who had followed her in. 'I think brandy might be a good idea, don't you?'

Sonia looked doubtful. 'Just a small one, then,' she said, 'or perhaps a cup of tea.'

'I'll leave it with you,' Venus told her.

She went upstairs, took a blanket from one of the beds, found a hot-water bottle in the bathroom, and filled it from the hot tap. Back in the sitting room she wrapped the blanket around Connie, then handed her the hot-water bottle. 'Cuddle that,' she said. 'Hold it close to you. It's not hot enough to burn you and it will warm you up.'

135

Sonia came in with a cup of tea. She gave it to Connie, but Connie's hands were trembling and she couldn't hold it, so Sonia took it back. 'I'll give you a sip from time to time,' she said, 'but try to get it down. You'll feel better for it.'

'I'll try,' Connie said. She raised her head and looked full face at Venus. Her eyes were anguished. 'Oh, Venus,' she cried again, 'what am I going to do?' It seemed it was all she could think of to say. Then she drooped forward again, held her head in her hands. Venus stroked her hair, a liberty she would never have taken had Connie been her normal self.

'Nothing at all, right now,' she said, 'except drink your tea.' The two women sat in silence for a few minutes. Then presently Venus said, 'We must let someone know. One of your family.' She didn't know anything about the Phillipsons' family. Pleasant and friendly though they were, they had never talked a great deal about themselves. She was aware, without knowing quite how she knew, that, before George had retired half-a-dozen years ago, he had been a partner in a firm of accountants in London and that when they bought their house in Thurston George had become involved in the church, though his wife never had, except on the edges.

Connie shook her head. 'We don't have any family,' she said. 'We never had children, and I was an only child and so was George. We . . .' She hesitated, then took a deep breath. 'We lived for each other. Oh, we were quite content. George had the church, and his golf. I had . . .' She faltered again. '. . . Well, I had George. I didn't need anyone else.'

136

'And had you known George was ill?' Venus asked.

'No,' Connie said, her voice rising. 'Not at all. He never said anything.'

Venus looked at Sonia.

'Mr Phillipson wasn't my patient,' Sonia said.

Venus looked confused. 'But Nigel didn't say he was his,' she said.

'I rang Doctor Sonia because she was close,' Connie said. 'We always had her name on the pad, I mean in case of emergency. George's doctor— he's mine too—lives in Brampton. When George first retired we lived in Brampton while we were waiting for this house to be finished. We registered with Doctor Hawkins. We never saw any reason to change.'

'Of course not,' Sonia said. 'He's a very good doctor, I know him well. But I think we must let him know. You'll need to find out if there was anything wrong, if your husband had perhaps been seeing him.'

'But, Doctor Sonia, why wouldn't George have told me?' Connie asked. 'I mean if he wasn't well.'

'Perhaps there was nothing to tell,' Sonia said. But sometimes husbands and wives didn't tell each other everything, she knew that. 'Perhaps you're right and he didn't see Doctor Hawkins. Would you like me to ring him for you?'

Venus knew what she was getting at. Dying so suddenly, if George hadn't seen a doctor for some time there would have to be an inquest. If he had, then at least his wife would be spared that.

'I'll do it the minute I get home,' Sonia promised. 'And I'll ring you back right away. But now, Mrs Phillipson, do you have a friend I could

137

contact, someone who'll stay the night with you? Or you could go to? I don't think you should be on your own.'

Connie hesitated. She hesitated long enough for Venus to realise that she probably didn't have a close friend, or not one she could ask to stay with her.

'Leave that with me, Sonia,' she said. 'I'll sort it out.'

'OK. Well, I must be off,' Sonia said. 'I'll let you know what Doctor Hawkins says.'

Venus saw Sonia out, and then came back to Connie. 'I think we'll have to give Cliff Preston a ring now,' she said. 'Do you know Cliff? The funeral director?'

'I've seen him in the village,' Connie said. 'I don't know him.'

'He's very kind,' Venus told her. 'He'll be a great help to you. Would you like me to do it or would you rather speak to him yourself?'

'I'd be grateful if you would,' Connie said. 'But . . .' She hesitated.

'Yes?'

'It's . . . Well, I don't like leaving George on his own. I just feel . . . well, I think I ought to be with him. Would that be all right?'

'Of course it would,' Venus assured her. 'Whatever you like. Do you want me to stay in the dining room with you or would you rather be on your own with George?'

'I'd like you to be there,' Connie said.

'Then I'll just go and ring Cliff Preston and after that we'll sit with George.'

The telephone was in the hall, but first she went into the dining room, where George was. She

138

wanted to make certain that he looked as good as possible for his wife to see. He had slipped further down in the chair, but not badly so. There was no sign of illness on him, only the pallor of death. She lifted his head and put a cushion beneath it, and crossed his hands. He was already cold to her touch. Dear George, she thought, I am going to miss you so much! After she had rung Cliff, she went to fetch Connie.

Connie seated herself in front of her husband. Venus sat nearby. After a while Connie said, 'Do you think you could say a prayer? You know how much George loved his church. He was far better at that than I was.'

'Of course I will,' Venus agreed.

'And would you say "The Lord is My Shepherd"?'

'I will,' Venus said. 'We can say that together.'

They did so, then Venus said some prayers: evening prayers, prayers for the end of the day and for the end of a life. After that they sat quietly, waiting for Cliff Preston to come.

'Will you stay with me while he's here?' Connie asked. 'I've never had to do anything like this before. I suppose I've been too sheltered, I've been spoilt. But, you see, George was always there, both when his parents . . . and then for mine. He arranged everything. Whatever had to be done, he did it.'

'Of course I'll stay. It's no trouble at all,' Venus said. 'And you'll find Cliff Preston very easy to talk to. In fact,' she added, 'if you'll allow me, I think it would be a good idea if I were to stay the night with you. You know Sonia said you shouldn't be alone. Or perhaps you've thought of someone else you'd like to ask?'

'Oh no!' Connie said quickly. 'No-one at all. No-one I could expect to do that. But really, I don't like to ask you. It doesn't seem fair.'

'You're not asking,' Venus said. 'I'm offering. I would just have to pop back to the Vicarage very briefly to get a few things: nightdress, toothbrush and so on. Nigel can't bring them here because he's looking after Becky. But I'll wait until after Cliff Preston's been.' She had no intention of leaving Connie alone until her husband's body had been removed.

'Of course!' Connie said. 'It's so good of you!'

*   *   *

Cliff Preston did everything that a man in his job could do—and more besides. 'I'm very sorry about this, Mrs Phillipson,' he said. 'What a shock for you! I did know your husband, of course, though not all that well.'

Then without wasting time, though with no show of rushing her, he got down to business, asked the necessary questions. He was sympathetic and respectful, direct and sensible, yet at the same time with a controlled cheerfulness which comforted the bereaved woman and helped her keep her countenance, which was important to her. He rightly guessed she was not a woman who would like to break down in front of a man she hardly knew. And for all his efficiency, not for one moment did he give her the feeling that this was just another funeral which had come his way; that it was all in a day's work.

Venus, observing all this, and marvelling at his

140

skill, thought that there was probably a lot he could teach her, and some other priests she could think of.

In the end he said, 'Well, I won't bother you with anything else tonight. The rest can wait until tomorrow. Could you pop in and see me then, Mrs Phillipson?'

She nodded agreement.

A little later, after Cliff Preston's men had been and gone, taken George, Venus said, 'I'll slip back to the Vicarage. Will you be all right? I shan't be long.'

*   *   *

'Do you have to stay the night?' Nigel queried. 'I wouldn't have thought it was part of your duty.'

'I don't suppose it is,' Venus answered. 'But what would you have me do? Would you expect me to leave her on her own, this first night?'

'I suppose not,' Nigel said. 'What's she going to do the rest of the nights?'

Venus, pushing things into an overnight bag, gave him a sharp look. 'I expect that's a thing many a widow asks herself,' she said. 'Especially an elderly one. She'll do the best she can. I doubt it's ever easy.'

'I suppose not,' Nigel said. 'Is there anyone you want me to inform—I mean about George—or are you leaving that to Connie Phillipson?'

'No,' Venus said. 'But I must ring Henry. In any case I should let him know where I am in case anything else turns up.'

Henry was appalled. 'I had no idea!' he said. 'Not the slightest! He was a wonderful treasurer.

141

What are we going to do without him?'

And more to the point, Venus thought, what is Connie Phillipson going to do without her husband? She did not seem the kind of woman to be able to cope with life on her own.

She had not been back long with Connie Phillipson when Sonia phoned.

'I spoke with Doctor Hawkins,' she said. 'George Phillipson *had* been to see him twice in the last month. It was his heart. Doctor Hawkins warned him that it wasn't good; he put him on medication, told him he wanted to see him again.'

'And George said nothing to his wife!' Venus said. 'How strange! And how very sad.' She could not envisage that either she or Nigel would keep something of that nature from the other. It did seem as though George Phillipson had gone through his married life protecting his wife against everything. That he had done it in love, she didn't doubt, but how much less shocked Connie would be now, how much more capable, if she had known what her husband had known. It wouldn't have lessened her loss, but to have shared his knowledge would surely have been better? How marriages, even happy ones, did differ! That was something she was still learning.

'But at least,' Sonia said, 'there won't be need for an inquest. That's one good thing.'

'But every day knowing about it, not saying anything, taking his medication in secret,' Venus said. 'Poor George!'

'His wife will probably find that he's left his affairs in absolutely apple-pie order, everything done that should be done,' Sonia said.

'Protecting her to the last,' Venus said. But dying

142

with a secret between them, she thought. And of what use is the protection then?

* * *

She stayed the night, finding it difficult to get off to sleep because she missed Nigel's presence so much. She put her arm out, she turned towards him, and he wasn't there. But when she finally fell asleep she knew nothing until she awoke next morning, and for a moment wondered where she was. She put on her dressing gown and went downstairs at once. Connie was already there, sitting at the kitchen table drinking tea, toying with a piece of toast. She still looked terrible. No point in asking if she had slept. Venus poured herself a cup of tea and drank it quickly. 'I'm sorry I'll have to rush off,' she said. 'I have a meeting in the Vicarage at nine o'clock. But I'll see you later today, perhaps later this morning—or this evening, whatever suits you best. There'll be a few things we'll need to discuss: the service and so on. Is that all right?'

Connie nodded. 'And I can't thank you enough for staying,' she said.

* * *

When Venus reached home there was a note from Nigel left for her on the kitchen table. 'Everything OK here. Have seen Becky off to school. We don't like being without you! There's a couple of messages for you by the phone.'

How could I ever keep anything from Nigel, or he from me? Venus thought.

The first message was from Cliff Preston. 'I

143

suggest Thursday afternoon for the funeral,' he said. 'If that's all right with Mrs Phillipson. Will that suit you? Let me know.' Cliff was always courteous, never demanded that she should be there when it suited him. The second was from Henry. 'I reckon we'd better meet—you, me and Edward Mason. There'll be things to discuss. How about this afternoon?'

She phoned Henry back at once. 'Can't all this wait?' she asked. 'If you're talking about a new treasurer, we can't do that in a hurry. Surely it can wait until at least after the funeral?'

'I suppose so,' Henry said reluctantly. 'It depends what's outstanding.'

'Knowing George,' Venus said, 'I reckon everything will be up-to-date. You know how meticulous he was.'

'I do indeed,' Henry said. 'Where are we going to find another treasurer like him?'

For a moment Venus felt that Henry was more concerned about the loss of a treasurer than the loss of the man. But that was unlikely. Henry was the kindest of men. He must be suffering from shock.

'Well, if you and Edward would like to come here around three o'clock, I'll be here,' Venus said. 'But don't come any earlier because I have to go to Brampton.'

To say 'I *have* to go to Brampton' was not entirely true. She was going to Brampton to do some shopping, both for herself and for the babies. Now that it was confirmed that they were twins, and boys, she wanted to buy something specifically for them. Also, it was time to treat herself to something to wear while she was pregnant. All

144

right, her cassock would probably see her through right to the end, but she didn't want to spend her life in it. There would surely be some social occasions when she would want to wear a dress, or perhaps some nice trousers, something worth dressing up for; added to which, everything in her wardrobe was getting too tight and she was aware that her bump was beginning to show. There was also the question of a twin pram, but Nigel had reined her in on that. 'No way,' he'd said, 'is there any need to start thinking about prams at this stage. I know you're nest building, but that's too much and too soon, my love!' he said. 'Anyway,' he'd added, 'where would we put it?'

'Exactly where we'll put it when we've got the babies in it,' Venus had said. 'Probably in the hall.'

'Then no point in bumping into it several months before we need it,' he'd said.

She had felt quite hurt and tearful about that. She'd told him he didn't care about the babies; he'd told her she was being silly. They had almost, but not quite, quarrelled, but at the sight of her in tears he had taken her in his arms and apologised. 'I'm sorry!' he'd said. 'I do care—of course I do. It's just that I'm—well—I'm nervous. I'm afraid of doing too much too soon. I suppose I still can't believe that I'm going to be a father. I don't want to tempt providence.'

At that she had broken down into further floods of tears, but they were happier ones. 'Of course everything's going to be all right!' she'd said. 'I just know it is! You needn't worry, love. I've never been fitter. I'll sail through it. You'll see!' And so they had comforted each other. And now she was about to go to Brampton, and she *would* do some

145

shopping, both for herself and for the babies, but, she had promised, she would not start choosing the pram. She and Nigel would do that together when the time came. Though that, she told herself, didn't mean that she couldn't look at them. Men didn't quite understand.

Her first stop was 'Mums and Kids' and in the end, apart from rushing into the newsagents to buy the latest magazine on pregnancy, it was the only place she did visit. There was so much to see there, all of it tempting. She bought herself a pair of rather smart maternity trousers in black velvet and a silk top in a pale shade of violet. They would see her through some of the social events which would hopefully happen in the months between now and Christmas. In the end, though, she had to leave in a hurry to be back in time for the Blessed Henry and Edward Mason. She had been back in the Vicarage less than five minutes when they arrived.

'This is a terrible thing,' Edward Mason said. 'Why, I was talking to him only last weekend! He seemed as fit as a fiddle then! Was it entirely unexpected?'

'We're not quite sure,' Venus said. 'But certainly it was totally so to his wife, poor woman!'

'Well,' Edward said, 'we must do what we can for her, though what that will be I'm not quite sure. Gwen said she would pop in and see her, but she really doesn't know her all that well. We don't want to seem to intrude, do we?'

'I think she'll need people most after the funeral's over,' Venus said. 'That might be the loneliest time. Learning to live on her own.'

'It's all very sad,' Henry said. 'And we're going to miss George no end in St Mary's. I don't know who can take his place. I can't think of anyone on the PCC who'll come near to filling the bill. He was the best treasurer I ever knew, and I've known a few in my time.'

Edward nodded agreement.

'We must pray about it,' Venus said. 'God will answer our prayers.'

'Not necessarily in the way we want,' Henry said gruffly.

In her heart, Venus agreed with him.

*   *   *

The funeral, on Thursday afternoon, went well, if such a thing can be said about a funeral. It was a damp, sunless autumn day, with a sneaky wind, as they filed out of the church afterwards and gathered around the newly dug grave. It was not all that well attended. There were two or three friends the Phillipsons had made during their time in Brampton. A number of members of the Golf Club came, as Henry had said they would—indeed, Venus suspected him of rounding them up—but the largest number was of parishioners from St Mary's. George, though a quiet man, had been liked and respected there. Venus felt pleased that they had turned up to see him laid to rest.

Connie Phillipson looked worse than she had on the night of George's death, Venus thought. She seemed smaller, buried under a heavy coat and a wide-brimmed black hat. She sought out Venus when the committal was over. 'I'm very grateful,' she said. 'You've been so good to me! George would have appreciated that.'

'I'll pop round and see you, probably tomorrow,'

Venus said. 'And phone me any time you like.' It was all she could do, she thought, and Connie Phillipson was not a woman who would be easy to help. She was too contained.

Most people went across to the Ewe Lamb, where refreshments had been laid on in their usual competent style. Venus wondered how Connie had pulled herself together enough to organise all this and strongly suspected that Cliff Preston had had a kindly hand in it. In the end, and before very long, people drifted away until the only ones left were a man and his wife from Brampton and Venus herself. 'We'll go back home with you,' the Brampton couple said to Connie.

'That's great,' Venus said. 'I have to hurry away now to see my daughter home from school.' She turned to Connie. 'I'll see you some time tomorrow then,' she said. 'I'll give you a ring first.'

*　　　*　　　*

Becky was walking down the road from school as Venus walked up to the Vicarage. They met at the gate.

'Have you had a good day, love?' Venus asked.

'OK,' Becky answered. She was never enthusiastic about school. Then she suddenly perked up. 'I've thought of names for the babies!' she said.

'Really?' Venus said, smiling. 'How nice! And what are they?'

'Alair and Aldo,' Becky announced triumphantly.

'Oh! I see,' Venus said, after a pause. 'Alair and Aldo? Well!' How could she tell Becky, so pleased with herself was she, that they were totally

148

unacceptable? And then it came to her. It was simple, really.

'They're two really original names!' she said gently. 'But I don't think they will *quite* do!'

'Why ever not?' Becky protested. 'I think they're lovely names! I spent a lot of time choosing them. I went right through the book.'

'Well, yes, dear, that was very thorough,' Venus said, 'but, you see, it would mean that both boys would have the same initial. They'd both be A. Baines. And what's more,' she added as an even brighter thought hit her, 'both those names would be shortened to "Al". You know what boys are for shortening names. So there'd be two Al Baineses in the same class at school. Chaos!'

'Oh, all right,' Becky said, reluctantly. 'So that means they've got to have two different initials.'

'I think so, dear,' Venus said. 'And the other thing is . . .' How could she put this tactfully? 'I think nothing too unusual. You know how stuffy boys can be about anything that's a bit different. They might not like it as they grow up. Not like us.' But what am I saying, she asked herself. Haven't I always hated being called 'Venus'?

Becky sighed. 'All right, then. I'll have another think.'

'Why don't we do it together?' Venus suggested. 'Make lists.'

'What about Nigel?' Becky asked.

'Oh, I'm sure he'll be happy with whatever you and I come up with,' Venus said. Or at least he would be if she primed him first.

In the end she and Becky between them—and it took the best part of a week, on and off, but as Venus said, there was no desperate hurry—settled

149

on two names which were agreeable to them both, and also, when he was consulted, to Nigel.

'Anthony and Colin, then,' Venus said. 'I'm sure they'll like those names very much.'

'Anthony means "a man without equal",' Becky said. 'And Colin means "strong".'

Venus nodded agreement. 'That's it then. And Colin does sound a bit Irish, which will please Nigel and Grandma Baines. Of course,' she added, wavering, 'we could have chosen Patrick. That's very Irish.'

'Oh, Mummy,' Becky wailed, 'who wants to be called after a church?' And then she added, 'How will we know which one to call what?'

'Easy!' Venus said. 'They won't be born at exactly the same time, so we'll call the first one Anthony because "A" is the first letter of the alphabet—and the second one Colin.'

CHAPTER ELEVEN

On the following Monday afternoon Venus opened the Vicarage door to her two churchwardens who had arrived to discuss what was to be done about George Phillipson's successor. There was to be a meeting of the PCC on Thursday evening, and they were to report to that.

'Did you and Molly have a nice weekend?' she asked the Blessed Henry as she welcomed them. She knew they had been to the wedding of a niece in Bath.

'Wonderful!' Henry said. 'Quite apart from the wedding, which was splendid, we always like Bath.

We both reckon we could live there happily.'

'Well, please don't,' Venus said. 'What would I do without you?'

That was more or less the end of the small talk. 'We must get down to business,' Edward Mason said as they took their seats in her study. 'Which is the question of where do we find another treasurer to take George's place?'

'It's a small point,' Henry interrupted, 'but I'd rather we didn't say "to take his place". No-one can quite do that. What you mean is "to succeed him".'

'I meant no disrespect,' Edward said. 'I valued George every bit as much as you did. So all right then, to succeed him.' He turned to Venus. 'Henry and I have been speaking to each other about this—'

Henry broke in. He had not missed Venus's raised eyebrows. 'Oh, nothing definite, Venus! We just happened to be on the telephone about something else. Obviously, it's all to be discussed with you . . .'

'And the PCC,' Venus put in.

Henry nodded in agreement. 'Naturally! But they'll turn to the three of us for guidance.'

Venus looked from one to the other. 'And what did you come up with?' she asked.

'David Wainright,' Edward said.

'David Wainright?' Venus made no attempt to hide her surprise. David Wainright had been in the parish hardly any longer than she had—and at once she reminded herself that that was not something to be held against him. He had been on the PCC less than a year, having come to Thurston shortly after his wife had died, in her early fifties, of cancer. When she was alive, so Venus had heard,

151

the two of them visited Thurston regularly and had always planned that one day they would live there. Then when David retired at sixty from his job as an accountant he decided to come on his own. It was what his wife would have wanted, he reckoned. He had attended St Mary's from his very first Sunday and had quickly found himself voted on to the PCC.

'You sound surprised,' Edward said to Venus.

'Do I?' she said. 'Perhaps I thought you'd have thought of someone who'd been at St Mary's rather longer—but that's not a very sensible thing to say, is it?' She turned to Henry. 'So what do you think?'

'Well,' Henry said, 'he's got the right experience. He was on the PCC in his last parish, he was Deputy Treasurer there. Also, no-one else came to mind for the job. I wouldn't say it's a popular one.'

'I suppose that's true,' Venus agreed.

She wasn't totally happy, and she couldn't put a finger on why. He was a decent man, competent; rather quiet, but he seemed to get on well with most people. But—and if she was honest, she knew it was what was at the bottom of her slight reluctance—she had the feeling that he didn't like her. Oh, he was always perfectly polite to her and perhaps, in fact in her own mind she was fairly sure of it, it wasn't so much personal as the fact that he didn't approve of women priests. He had not said so, but she was sure that was true. She wondered, in fact, if he liked any women in positions of authority, at least in the areas he saw as a man's world. Well, if that was the case, and if he was to be considered as Treasurer, he would have to get over it. And so, she reminded herself, would she. She was not without practice, and it was getting easier than it had been in her earlier days. She had been very prickly then. But would it be easy for him?

'And what do you reckon he would think to that?' she asked now. 'Have you any idea?'

'No,' Henry said. 'We wouldn't have mentioned it to him without consulting you first. You *are* the Vicar!'

She smiled at him. Henry was a dear man. He had never made things difficult for her, not even at the very beginning.

'Then let's discuss it further, with David Wainright in mind,' she suggested.

'He won't be exactly like George,' Henry said.

'Nor should we expect him to be,' Edward said.

'Quite right!' Venus agreed.

At the end of their discussion, during which Venus voiced none of her own personal doubts—perhaps they boiled down to prejudice?—she said, 'Then we should ask him if he'll come around here tomorrow evening. We can't hang about. We have to put this to the PCC on Thursday. Henry, I think it would be best if you spoke to him. Shall we say eight o'clock?'

*   *   *

The meeting with David Wainright went surprisingly smoothly, and was quite short. He did not seem at all surprised at being asked to stand for Treasurer. He was polite and agreeable and Venus asked herself why she had ever thought him otherwise. It was agreed that for the first part of the PCC meeting, when he was to be discussed, he would not be present, but would arrive later, after the vote had been taken. 'An hour later at the very most,' Henry said. 'I doubt there'll be a lot of discussion.'

* * *

On the Thursday, Venus went to see her mother. Mrs Foster was pale, her eyes dull. She is losing her sparkle, Venus thought. It was unlike her bright mother, and was a small stab to Venus's heart.

'So what did Sonia say?' she asked nonchalantly. Her mother did not like a fuss.

'I'm all right,' Mrs Foster said. 'Nothing serious. She reckons I probably need a hip replacement. She's making an appointment with a consultant. He'll say for sure.'

'Oh, Mum, I am sorry!' Venus said.

'Oh, it's nothing,' her mother said. 'They do them all the time. I had friends in Clipton who'd had it done. You must remember the Outhwaites? It's not an illness, you know. It's just that it's—well, I admit it—painful, every day, and it never stops. And I'm sick to death of painkillers, they upset my stomach.'

Yes, Venus thought, my mother looks like a woman who's been struggling with pain. And I wonder how long it was before she admitted it. She resolved to have a word with Sonia—though Sonia might well, quite rightly, refuse to discuss her mother's affairs.

'She says I'll be as fit as a fiddle once it's done,' Mrs Foster said. 'She says the pain stops right away. And of course, fortunately for me, as you know, your Dad has his health insurance which covers me as well, so I'll be able to go privately. Otherwise, Doctor Sonia said, you can wait for months on the

154

National Health. Of course you might easily get the same surgeon in the end, whether you went private or not. But never mind me. It's a day or two since we spoke. How are you keeping, love? Can you drink a cup of coffee or are you still off it?'

'I can, and I'd love one,' Venus said. 'I seem to be getting over the sickness, thank goodness. And has Becky told you we've chosen the names?'

'No. I haven't spoken to her for a day or two. She's very taken up with Anna, isn't she? So what are they?'

Venus told her, including Becky's first choice of names. Her mother's face lit up in a genuine smile.

'Alair and Aldo!' Mrs Foster said. 'What a hoot! But I like Anthony and Colin.'

'So do I, so does Nigel,' Venus said. 'Now, is there anything I can do for you while I'm here? Or do you want any shopping doing in the village?'

'Nothing,' Mrs Foster said. 'I have your Dad, and he's very good. I know I go on about him and his golf, but really he's a good man. There's nothing he won't do for me.'

'I know,' Venus agreed. 'But while I'm here . . .'

'Honestly, love, there's nothing. And in any case, you shouldn't be taking on other people's jobs at the moment. You should be looking after yourself.'

'Oh, I am,' Venus said. 'And I don't think I've ever felt better than I have this last week or two. So you look after yourself, never mind me. And do exactly what Sonia tells you to.'

'I will!' her mother said. 'And I feel better for seeing you.'

I must pay more attention to my mother, Venus said to herself as she walked home. It was so easy, without thinking, to neglect one's nearest and dearest, partly because they were less likely to complain.

Back at home, the second post had been and there was a letter from the Bishop:

I am sorry to have been so long in replying to you. I have been at a conference, of which I think there are far too many, and this one wasn't even about my real job, which I reckon is looking after the clergy in my diocese. Thank you for sending me your wonderful news. I do congratulate you and your husband.

You will need some kind of help when the time draws nearer and I will talk with the Archdeacon to sort out what we might best do . . .

Venus felt a glow of pleasure as she read it. What a nice man he was! She had not informed him with any idea of what he might do for her, only as a polite gesture because he had married her, and because she didn't want him to hear first on the diocesan grapevine.

*   *   *

The PCC meeting went smoothly. There was no-one present who had not heard of George Phillipson's death; indeed several members had attended his funeral. Sincere and fulsome tributes, duly noted in the Minutes, were paid to him and it was agreed that a letter of condolence should be sent to his widow.

'But she will need more than that,' Venus said.

156

'She is going to find life very difficult, especially in the early stages, and we must do all we can. We must find ways to support her.' She did not add, 'even though she's not a churchgoer,' but it was implicit.

'And now,' she said, 'while never forgetting George and the wonderful service he has given to St Mary's, we must move on to the question of who will succeed him as Treasurer. I am sure you will have been giving it thought and prayer and if you have any observations to make, then let us all hear them now.'

It did not surprise her in the least that her words were met with complete silence. It was not a post for which she would have expected a rush of people to volunteer either themselves or others.

'Very well,' she said presently. 'And I'm sure it won't surprise you that the churchwardens and I have met together about this and have given it a lot of thought. I will let Henry tell you what we've arrived at.'

'No-one will take George's place,' Henry repeated, 'but we must have a successor. So here are our thoughts, for your consideration.'

As Henry had foretold, the idea of David Wainright as Treasurer seemed acceptable to all, or at least no questions were raised against it, and when it was finally and formally put to the vote there were no abstentions, though Venus did notice that two or three hands were not raised until the last few moments and then, to her mind, reluctantly. But what was the alternative? she thought. There wasn't any.

Shortly afterwards David came in and took the Treasurer's empty chair. He was a much smaller man than George Phillipson, with a pale complexion, grey eyes and rather sparse grey hair. He lacked, Venus thought as she looked at him, the geniality which George had had. Perhaps he thought it not necessary in a treasurer. He thanked the members and said he would do his best to fulfil their confidence. He would need to take all the books and the accounts home with him, he told Henry, and when he had perused them he would very quickly want to have a financial meeting.

The rest of the meeting went as expected. There had been no progress on the matter of the candlesticks. The police had nothing to add. David Wainright confirmed that he would pursue the matter of the insurance further. The tramp seemed to have left, though few doubted he would come back again. 'But at least,' someone said, 'nothing else has gone missing, now that the church is kept locked!' There were nods of approval, amongst which, Venus noted, was David Wainright's. She had not, until now, realised where he stood on this.

'Speaking of locking the church,' she said in a clear voice, 'and you are all well aware that I am against keeping it locked during the daytime, and you know why—I have decided that whenever I can, and naturally when it fits in with my daughter's time at home, I will take as much of my work as is suitable to the church with me, and do it there. Regrettably, we no longer have our Verger rota, but I am happy to be a one-woman guardian whenever I can. So if any of you, or indeed anyone else, wishes to see me, that is where I shall be as much of the time as I can, and, of course, when I'm not needed elsewhere in the parish.'

There was a hush, then Miss Tordoff said, 'But

will you be safe, Vicar?'

'I expect so,' Venus said cheerfully. 'As safe as I would be in most places.'

'I doubt that,' Miss Tordoff said, 'even though I understand you about keeping the church open. I shall pray for your safety.'

'Thank you,' Venus said. 'And of course if any of you wish to join me, or do the odd hour on your own, then that would be welcome.'

The new Treasurer came swiftly in on that.

'Isn't that contrary to what has already been agreed, or at least to the spirit of what we agreed?' he asked.

'I don't think so,' Venus answered. 'It was decided that the church should be kept locked at all times, except when it was occupied by someone in authority. I suppose you could describe me as someone in authority. Or indeed, any one of you, also.' She smiled as she said it. 'Now,' she said, 'this has been a long meeting and I thank you all. Is there any other business?'

*   *   *

'I have to say, I do not enjoy PCC meetings, at least not often,' Venus said to Nigel on arriving home.

'I daresay not,' Nigel said, 'but they're necessary.'

'It's not always easy to see what the agenda really is,' Venus said. 'Sometimes it seems a million miles away from working towards the Kingdom of God. Do you think Jesus had the equivalent of a PCC meeting with the disciples?'

'Yes,' Nigel said. 'They met in an upper room. So come on, out with it! What went wrong?'

159

'I suppose you could say nothing did,' Venus replied. 'But I can't say I'm madly happy about the decision. I mean about the new Treasurer. And I know there's no alternative—anyway it's been agreed. There were no dissensions.'

'Why aren't you happy?' Nigel asked. 'He sounds OK to me.'

'I'm not sure,' Venus said. 'I just feel he doesn't approve of me.'

'Why ever not?'

'Almost certainly because I'm a woman,' Venus said. 'I'm not the right person for the job I'm doing—at least not in his eyes.'

Nigel gave her a straight look. His face was stern. 'My darling,' he said firmly, 'we've been through this sort of thing before. You just have to get it out of your system. I thought you already had.'

'I thought so too,' Venus said. 'But it still crops up. Oh, I know it's no use me thinking the whole world loves me, because it's not true. I still think of those people who left St Mary's because of me. Not only people like Miss Frazer—she's a one-off—but perfectly nice, normal people. I see them around in the village. They say "Hello" to me. Not more than one or two have ever come back. I wouldn't mind so much if I knew they were going elsewhere but I think it's more likely they've left the church altogether. I have to live with that, and it's not easy. David Wainright this evening was just another jab.'

'You do tend to make this woman business the reason why almost anyone might be against you,' Nigel said. 'Why can't it be simply because they have a different opinion on some subjects, nothing to do with gender?'

160

'You don't understand—' Venus began.

'Oh yes I do,' Nigel said. 'And I think you're in danger of having a chip on your shoulder. If someone doesn't agree with you, then you reckon it's because you're a woman, and I'm sure that's not the case. Do you really expect everyone to agree with you on everything? Do you never think you might possibly be wrong, my love?'

'That's not fair! You don't understand.'

'I do,' Nigel said firmly. 'And it's not unfair.'

There was a silence, then Venus said, 'Nigel, we're not quarrelling, are we? I don't want to quarrel with you.'

'We are not quarrelling,' Nigel said patiently. 'I'm trying to be helpful. I don't like to see you worried and unhappy.'

'I'm not unhappy,' Venus said. 'I really am not. It's just that . . . well, I'm not sure what it is. Sometimes I feel as if I'm losing my confidence, and I don't know why. Perhaps it's because I'm pregnant.'

'Perhaps it is,' Nigel agreed. 'But you must do something about it.'

'You never bring your work home with you, do you?' Venus said. 'Don't you ever have bad days?'

'Of course I do! How couldn't I?' Nigel said. 'Sometimes I feel I can do so little. I'm helpless. Right now there's this young man . . .' He broke off. 'I'm sorry,' he said, 'I mustn't talk about patients.'

'You haven't said his name, and I probably wouldn't know him,' Venus pointed out. 'I would never ask you to break a confidence, any more than I ever would with my people.'

'He's not going to recover,' Nigel said. 'He

161

knows it. But he's more honest than I am and I know it would help him if I could just tell the truth.'

'Then perhaps, my love, you should,' Venus said.

She felt ashamed. Here was her husband, perhaps more often than she knew, struggling with matters of life and death, and here she was, getting into a pet because someone didn't agree with her. Moreover, she thought, I am so concerned with myself and my affairs that Nigel sometimes doesn't get a look-in.

'I do love you, Nigel,' she said, 'And I will think about what you've said.'

'I only want you to be happy.' Nigel told her. 'I hate to see you unhappy about anything.'

'Let's go to bed,' she said.

*   *   *

In the morning, the moment she awakened she remembered everything. They had almost quarrelled, but not quite. And it had been her fault. But now she felt stronger than ever. Everything was going to be all right. They could cope with anything. She had never felt so strong and sure.

'Good-morning, my love,' she said.

Nigel opened his eyes and smiled at her. 'Good-morning, sweetheart!' he replied.

*   *   *

When Nigel had gone off to work and Becky to school she said her Office, sitting in her study. As so often, the psalm seemed as though it had been written especially for her. 'He has put into my heart a marvellous love . . . The lot marked out for me is

162

my delight: welcome indeed the heritage that falls to me!' She read it out loud.

Afterwards she rang her mother. 'Have you heard anything from Sonia?' she asked.

'Yes,' Mrs Foster said. 'She's made an appointment for me to see a Mr Conway next Friday. His place is in Brampton. And before that I have to go along to the hospital for X-rays.'

'Good!' Venus said. 'I'm glad you're getting on with it. Would you like me to go with you?'

'Of course not!' her mother said. 'I'm perfectly capable of doing that on my own—though I expect your father will insist on taking me.'

The next call Venus made was to Connie Phillipson.

'How are you?' she asked.

'I'm all right,' Connie said.

She didn't sound it, Venus thought. Her voice was weak and flat, no life in it.

'I wondered if you'd like to come around to the Vicarage for a cup of tea this afternoon,' Venus suggested.

She was surprised to hear herself saying the words. It had been on the spur of the moment. She would meet anyone, almost anywhere, for whatever reason, she would spend as much time with them as they needed, try to help wherever she could, but it was a self-imposed rule that the Vicarage was kept for family and for close friends. Not that someone arriving on the doorstep wouldn't ever be asked in, but she didn't like to impose her work on her family. And now she had just done that, not many minutes before Becky would be coming in from school. But Connie Phillipson had sounded very low. I should have gone around to see her, Venus thought, but wasn't it better to get Connie out of her own house?

There was a pause. When Connie finally answered she sounded hesitant. 'I'm not . . . well, I'm not very good company. And I expect you're busy. I expect you're always busy.' There was a small note of envy in her voice, as from a woman who was seldom busy, and now, Venus thought, less so than ever.

'Not particularly,' she said. 'And I have to be in when Becky comes home. In any case, I usually have a cup of tea around this time. But as you wish.'

'All right,' Connie said. 'I will come. It would be very nice, and thank you for asking me.'

She arrived at half-past three, ten minutes before Becky's arrival with Anna. 'Will you ring Anna's mum and ask her if it's all right for Anna to be here?' Becky said to Venus.

'That's fine, if you're sure you don't mind,' Sally Brent said when asked. 'But she must be home by six o'clock sharp. She has her piano practice to do.'

'I'll see that she is,' Venus promised. 'Would you like me to bring her?'

'No,' Sally said. 'Tell her she's to leave at six sharp and I'll walk down the lane to meet her.'

The two girls went into the kitchen, poured glasses of orange juice, then immediately went up to Becky's room.

'I'll make some tea. Or would you prefer coffee?' Venus said to Connie Phillipson.

'Tea, please,' Connie said. 'Or whatever you're having. I really don't mind.'

'Then come in the kitchen and talk to me while I make it,' Venus suggested.

The talk, Venus soon discovered, had to come from her. There was little to be had from Connie other than monosyllabic replies to whatever Venus said. Poor woman, Venus thought, buttering scones, pouring tea, she looks no more than half alive. They carried the tea and the food into the sitting room. Venus would have stayed in the kitchen but she judged Connie Phillipson to be a woman who liked things done properly.

'How have you been the last few days?' she asked.

'All right, I suppose,' Connie said. 'I haven't been out. The woman who does my housework has been doing my shopping for me.'

'I see. So what have you done?' Venus said.

'I've been sorting through George's things. I'm sending most of them to the Hospice shop.'

'I would have come and given you a hand if you'd mentioned it,' Venus said. 'I know from experience how awful it is to have to sort through your husband's belongings. So many memories, and at the same time it seems so little to look forward to. But it does get better; please believe me. You have to give it time.'

There was another silence, then Connie said, 'I envy you, having your little girl.' It was a surprising remark, Venus thought, because she had appeared to take no notice whatever of Becky and Anna. 'If we'd had children—well, of course they'd be grown up, with children of their own by now, and we'd have had grandchildren, perhaps the same age as your daughter.'

'I'm sorry!' It was all Venus could think of to say. She could have said, if you'd not excluded just about everyone except your husband, life would be different at this moment, but that would be unkind as well as useless. In any case, of what good was hindsight?

They conversed, fitfully, about something and nothing, and then Connie said, 'Perhaps I ought to get a job? But how would I do that? I'm fifty-six.'

'It might not be easy,' Venus allowed. 'But you could do voluntary work. I mean, if you don't have to earn money.'

'I don't,' Connie said. 'George was always a good provider and he looked to the future for both of us, so I don't have any problems there.'

'Well,' Venus said. 'We must look around and see where you could be most useful—which I'm sure you could be. Volunteers are always needed for no end of things.'

'I suppose so,' Connie said. She seemed already to have gone off the idea of taking a job, whether voluntary or not. Her apathy clung around her like a heavy cloak. But I can't judge her, Venus thought, we're two different people.

In the end—she had stayed much longer than Venus had expected her to—Connie said, 'Well, I suppose I'd better be going. I expect your husband will be home soon. It was one of the things I looked forward to most, the sound of George's key in the lock. Always at the same time every working day.'

*   *   *

'I must do something,' Venus said later in the evening to Nigel. 'I don't know what, but I must do something. Otherwise I think she'll just fade away. And another thing: I must think again about keeping the Vicarage simply for family and close

166

friends. That's shutting doors. I mustn't do that.'

CHAPTER TWELVE

Two days later, in the evening—Venus, Nigel and Becky had just finished supper—the phone rang. Nigel answered it, and as he listened his face lit up in a smile.

'Hello there,' he said. 'This is a pleasant surprise!' He turned to Venus. 'It's my mother!' he said. Then he continued with his conversation. 'Yes, Mother, she's fine. And Becky. And your son, should you wish to know. So what about you?' He listened intently to what she was saying, nodding his head from time to time, but continuing to look happy. So everything must be all right, Venus thought.

'Yes. Yes, I'll tell her,' he said. 'In fact I'll put her on in a minute and you can tell her yourself. So how's Aunt Veronica?'

'What does she want to tell me?' Venus mouthed at him. 'Let me listen.'

'Your daughter-in-law is getting impatient,' Nigel said to his mother. 'I'd better hand over. She'll be thrilled to bits. She's been trying to get me moving on the subject but so far without success. I'm too cautious. I thought it was too soon.' He handed the phone to Venus.

'Hello, Eileen!' Venus said. 'How are you? Oh, I'm fine! I seem to have stopped being sick.' Then there was silence in the room while Venus listened intently, at the end of which she gave a cry of pleasure.

167

'Oh, how lovely, Eileen. That's wonderful—and it's very generous. Thank you very much indeed!' She beamed at Nigel as she continued to listen to her mother-in-law. 'Yes! Oh yes! I shall make him go with me; we'll go this very week. And I'll tell you exactly what we've chosen. If I can get a spare leaflet I'll send you one.'

Becky pulled at her sleeve. 'What are you talking about?' she asked. Venus brushed her aside. 'Yes, it was Becky,' she said. 'Would you like a word with her? I'm sure she would with you. So give my love and my thanks to Aunty Veronica. Lots of love to you! Take care!' She handed the phone to Becky, who immediately said, 'Hello, Granny Baines! What were you and Mummy talking about?'

She listened intently, then said, 'Oh good!' After a while she turned to Nigel. 'She'd like another word with you,' she said.

Nigel resumed his conversation with his mother, though for a while, on his side, it was little more than 'Yes! Yes! Right!' Then he said, 'And when are you coming to see us?' He smiled at her reply, and then she rang off.

'What did she say to that?' Venus asked when he had put the phone down.

'She said, "Wait until those two babies are born and there's nothing will keep me away!" '

'I like your mother,' Venus said.

'And she likes you,' Nigel said.

'It's so generous of her to offer to pay for the pram,' Venus said. 'It's going to be quite expensive. And now, my love, I'm going to hold you to coming with me to choose it. No more excuses! After all, you're going to have to push it from time to time. If you think you're going to leave all that to me

168

you've got a lot to learn! So when shall we go?'

'It's not easy—' Nigel began.

'And it's not difficult,' Venus interrupted. 'We just sort out a time when you don't have a surgery and I don't have a service, and we get in the car and head for Brampton. Anyone would think you were going to the dentist for root canal work! I suggest Saturday morning.'

Nigel looked doubtful. 'It will be very busy,' he said. 'You know what Brampton's like on a Saturday.'

'All right then, you pick a time. Bear in mind I have Eucharists on Tuesday and Thursday morning—oh, and a Chapter meeting next Wednesday. And then there are your surgeries. So take your pick from the rest. If it makes it easier, pretend you're going to choose a new car! It's not unlike that, come to think of it, except you're not going to have to pay for it.'

In the end, what with one thing, what with another, it came down to Saturday.

'Then let's get there as early as we can,' Nigel said.

'The moment it opens,' Venus agreed.

*   *   *

On Saturday morning at breakfast, Becky elected not to go. It was a choice between that and going swimming with Anna and Sally Brent. For Becky there was apparently no contest and she left for Anna's immediately after breakfast. Venus was a little disappointed by her choice, and said so to Nigel.

'It seems reasonable enough to me,' he said. 'As

169

well as being something Becky is keen on, the swimming is here and now. A pram, with as yet no babies to put in it, isn't all that exciting.'

Venus was ever so slightly hurt.

'I think it's very exciting,' she said. 'I rather hoped you did.'

'Of course I do, my love,' Nigel assured her. 'We weren't talking about me, we were talking about Becky. You can't expect an eleven-year-old to feel the same as we do.'

Venus shrugged her shoulders. 'I don't see why not,' she said.

Nigel had been reading the newspaper. He folded it very deliberately and turned his full attention to his wife, who was now clearing the table.

'Stop buzzing about,' he said. 'Sit down for a minute.'

'Why?' Venus queried. 'We want to get off to Brampton, don't we? You said you wanted to be there early.'

'Sure,' he said. 'And this won't take long, but I want to be sure you're listening, not stacking the dishwasher.'

She sat down. 'It sounds mysterious,' she said.

'It's not a bit mysterious,' Nigel said. 'It's plain common sense. And I think it's time it was mentioned.'

'What is "it"?' Venus demanded. 'Come on. Say it, whatever it is.'

'It's just that . . .' He hesitated. 'Well, I think perhaps there should be a bit less concentration on the babies and a bit more on Becky . . .'

She looked at him in astonishment.

'Nigel, what *do* you mean? How can you—'

170

He held up his hand. 'Let me finish, darling! I know it's natural that a lot of your thought should go on the babies, and then there's your work, which you can't neglect, but I think now is exactly when you should be giving Becky more attention rather than less. Perhaps we both should, but especially you. As it is, I think she might worry that she's losing you to babies which, for her, are not yet here but are getting a great deal of attention.'

'But that's not true at all!' Venus was indignant. 'You're exaggerating!'

'I don't think so,' Nigel said.

'So tell me, in what way is Becky not getting enough attention?' Venus demanded.

'In small ways, most of them, but adding up to rather a lot of ways. Oh, I'm sure you don't realise it and don't mean it, but why do you think Becky spends so much of her time with the Brents?'

'Because Anna's her best friend, that's why,' Venus said. 'It's simple.'

Nigel shook his head. 'No! It's not just that. She gets a lot of attention there. She's important.'

'She's important to me,' Venus protested. 'Of course she is.'

'Then perhaps she needs to be reassured about that,' Nigel said. 'When did you last take Becky somewhere just for her?'

'I've tried to involve her in everything. She helped to choose the names.'

'Precisely!' Nigel agreed. 'But that was about the babies, wasn't it? And this morning's trip to "Mums and Kids", that's about the babies, isn't it?'

'I thought she'd like to be involved,' Venus said.

'And I'm sure she does. But perhaps she'd like to be involved in something which is just for you and

171

her. You haven't a lot of time left to do that. We know that when the babies are born you'll have to concentrate on them, but if Becky is aware beforehand that she doesn't just come a bad second, or third, then she'll be a happier and more confident girl.'

Venus leaned back in her chair and gave Nigel a long look. 'You amaze me!' she said. 'You know very little of marriage and next to nothing about children but—'

'I just—'

'No!' Venus said. 'Let me finish! You have all this wisdom—and I mean that. If I'm honest—if I think about it, which I probably haven't been doing, then I can recognise the truth in what you say. But how did you come by it?'

Nigel grinned. 'Flattery will get you just about anywhere, my love,' he said. 'But I suppose every doctor, even an everyday GP like me, has to be a bit of a psychologist. And for that matter, surely also every parish priest?'

'True!' Venus agreed. 'Perhaps we practise more of it on other people than on our nearest and dearest. Anyway, we'll do what you suggest. We'll give Becky one or two special treats on her own.'

'No!' Nigel said. 'Not "we". Why not you and Becky on your own?' He looked at his watch. 'And now we'd better get off to Brampton or it'll be too busy to move. Straight to "Mums and Kids", do you reckon?'

'I've no plans to go anywhere else,' Venus told him.

*   *   *

172

The prams, cots, car seats, baby chairs were all in the basement, as if segregated from the rest of life. 'How stupid!' Venus said. 'Just the area you wouldn't want to come to if you were very pregnant, or carting a baby or a toddler.'

'I suppose they have their reasons,' Nigel said. 'Large stores usually do, and it's probably most interested in what sells fastest.'

What 'Mums and Kids' did have was a large selection of equipment of all kinds, including prams—which Venus quickly found out were no longer called prams, but had various other names, and in the case of the twin conveyance they were looking for it was pushchairs. The selection of pushchairs for two babies was naturally smaller than that for one child.

'What we want,' Venus said as they looked around, 'is one where both the babies can fit in from birth. Some of these, you see, take a young baby in the back and a toddler in the front, which is no good to us.' In the end they found what they wanted, a pram which would take the twins side by side. 'Which will be nicer for them,' Venus observed, 'but not so easy to get through doorways. Still, we'll manage somehow!'

They checked through the details: ' "Suitable from birth, raincover, five-position seats, sun visor, twelve-month guarantee." There's nothing they haven't thought of,' Venus said, 'but the price is a bit steep. More than two hundred pounds. What will your mother say to that?'

'She'll be happy enough,' Nigel said. 'After all, it is for her grandchildren.'

'Then we should get them to take it off the stand so that we can see what it's like when it comes to pushing it.'

'Oh, I don't think we need bother about that,' Nigel said. 'It'll be all right.'

'Nigel Baines,' Venus said firmly, 'would you buy a car without having a test drive? No, you would not! Nor are we going to buy this without seeing how it runs. And I do mean both of us.'

The assistant lifted it down from the stand and, though not without difficulty because the place was crowded, cleared a space where they could push it. 'It's fine!' Nigel said quickly. 'Absolutely fine!'

'I agree,' Venus said. It felt wonderful. She imagined herself pushing it around the village, the babies tucked into it sleeping, or awake and smiling; everyone in Thurston stopping her to have a look at them. And then she and Nigel—it was particularly good to Nigel's mind—found that if they paid for it, or paid a large deposit on it, 'Mums and Kids' would store it for them until nearer the time.

'Perfect,' Nigel said, writing out a cheque.

'Perhaps,' Venus ventured, 'we could look at cots and baby chairs and so on while we're here?'

'Definitely not!' Nigel said. 'This is quite enough for one day.'

*   *   *

They rang Nigel's mother that afternoon. Venus gave her a detailed description of the purchase.

'It sounds wonderful,' Mrs Baines said. 'And a sun visor, no less! The things they think of!'

Venus told her the cost. 'I'm afraid it *is* rather expensive,' she said. 'And I have to admit there were cheaper ones, but nothing quite as good as this.'

'Oh, don't you be worrying about the cost!' Mrs Baines said. 'Don't I want the very best for my grandsons? I'll be putting a cheque in the post tomorrow.'

* * *

That afternoon Venus went round to see her mother.

'I rang you this morning,' her mother said, 'but I didn't get any reply.'

'Did you leave a message on the phone?'

'Oh no,' Mrs Foster said. 'I don't bother with those things. I thought I'd catch you later—and here you are.'

'Nigel and I went to Brampton,' Venus told her. She explained why.

Her mother seemed a little taken aback. 'Oh!' she said. 'Oh really! Well that's something your Dad and I had it in mind to do. He'll be disappointed.'

It was clear to Venus that her mother was.

'Well, that's very kind of you and Dad, but there's still a lot of things we're going to need. Cots and chairs and car seats. There seems to be no end to the expense. Not that we begrudge a penny of it, of course.'

'I should think not!' Mrs Foster was indignant. 'So before we go any further you can put your Dad and me down for the cots. You'll be needing two, won't you? You're not contemplating both babies sharing a cot?'

'Oh no,' Venus said. 'And thank you very much. Perhaps when you're feeling up to it you'd like to go to "Mums and Kids" with me. They seemed to have a good selection of everything.'

*   *   *

The next morning, in the intercessions at the Eucharist, she prayed for George Phillipson and for those who mourned him. Connie, who, unusually, was in church, certainly needed prayers. And then at the end of the service, when Venus gave out the notices, she informed the congregation that they now had a new Treasurer to succeed George. 'David Wainright has agreed to take on this important job,' she announced. 'Most of you will know David. He has been a valued member of the Parochial Church Council for some time now and I am sure he will serve us well as Treasurer. We are very fortunate to have him. We will remember him in our prayers and we wish him well.' She meant every word she said, but she wished she felt happier about it in her heart.

'And I have one more notice,' she said. She smiled, and spoke pleasantly. She was not sure how this was going to be received. 'As you know, the PCC recently decided that the church should now be kept locked at all times, except when there are services or when there is an authorised person here to look after it. For my part, and I think you know this, I would like to think that the church was kept open as much as possible for those who, for whatever reason, have need of it. I have never thought that the church was only for Sunday, or only for set services, and for that reason I have decided that I shall bring as much of my work as I can and do it in the church. So, if you need to see

176

me, or to talk to me, this is where I shall often be—except when my job takes me out and about in the parish. And, as always, if you need me for something urgent, please don't hesitate to ring me on my mobile. The number is in the parish magazine.'

There was a slight stir in the congregation, which she had expected. It was, after all, apparent that she was publicly going against the wishes of the PCC. It was not a usual happening in St Mary's, but there were those who didn't mind in the least. It added a bit of spice to the usual non-controversial Sunday morning notices.

*   *   *

At coffee, in the parish hall after the service, Venus sat for a few minutes with Carla Brown, her husband Walter, Trudy Santer, who still ran the Sunday School in spite of having told Venus on the latter's very first Sunday in the parish that she wanted to give it up, and Elsie Jones, who was still running the Brownies. How loyal they have all been to me, Venus thought as she joined them at the table. And would she ever forget that very first Sunday when she had sat at this table with much the same people, but in addition then there'd been the Honourable Miss Amelia Frazer, and little Thora Bateman, Miss Frazer's satellite. Miss Frazer had thoroughly trounced her, standing up and delivering her tirade against women priests. Well, she had experienced Miss Frazer recently, though probably no-one around the table knew about that encounter. Thora Bateman, she was sorry to say, she never saw now, not even in the village. Perhaps she ought to call on her, risk the embarrassment of not being made welcome.

It was Carla Brown who had confessed, on that first Sunday, that she seldom came to church, but she'd been curious to see what the new Vicar was like. Now she was here every Sunday, and always at the forefront in offering to do practical jobs, giving out the service sheets, taking the collection. Or, to be more accurate, offering her husband to do them—which she demonstrated at this precise moment. 'Walter,' she ordered, 'get the Vicar's coffee. White. No sugar.'

'I know,' Walter said as he dutifully went off.

'I was interested to hear you say you're going to be a one-woman church minder,' Carla said.

'When I can,' Venus said. 'Which won't be every day, I suppose.'

'But is it safe?' Elsie Jones asked. 'I mean . . . on your own . . .' It was what Miss Tordoff had asked, and Venus had not allowed herself to think too much along those lines.

'Oh, I think so,' Venus said. 'Reasonably so.'

'If you want someone to be with you, I wouldn't mind,' Carla said. 'Not every day, of course, but quite often. Or Walter would,' she added.

'That's very kind of you,' Venus said. 'I'll see how it works out.' She specifically did not want Carla to sit with her, kind woman though she was. How would she ever get any work done? And how would she have her quiet times, which meant so much to her? Walter would be different from Carla, but what would they find to talk about at all? He was so much an echo of his wife. 'Perhaps, Carla,' she ventured, 'you might like to do it from time to time when I'm not able to be there?'

178

Carla made a non-committal murmur. It was not at all what she had in mind. She liked a good chat. She was happy to work at the same time, do something useful like cleaning the brass or dusting the pews, but solitary confinement was not her thing.

'Anyway,' Venus said, 'we'll think about it. In the meantime, I have to be off. I'm cooking the lunch and, it being Sunday, my parents are coming.'

'If I may say so,' Carla said, 'your mother doesn't look all that well. I've thought so for a week or two.'

'She's not totally fit at the moment,' Venus said. 'She has trouble with her hip.'

There followed a conversation about hips, not that anyone present had such trouble, they were mostly too young, but they knew those who had: those who had had the operation, and who had performed it, how well it had gone, those who were still waiting and how long they had waited. The waiting time, they all agreed, was a disgrace and something should be done about it. Amongst all the talk, Venus's departure was hardly noticed.

*   *   *

Wednesday's Chapter meeting came all too soon for Venus. On the other hand, she tried to console herself as she got into the car to drive herself to the next parish where it was to take place, sooner come, sooner over. In spite of wearing her cassock she was aware that her pregnancy would show. She was, after all, carrying twins—very different from a single baby. And even if it didn't show she had little doubt that most of them would by now know about

179

it. Word would have spread around the Deanery; indeed the Bishop, or perhaps the Archdeacon, might well have informed the Rural Dean. She wasn't worried about the Rural Dean. He was a pleasant man, married, and with three children of his own. It was the older ones, to whom the very thought of women in the priesthood was anathema, something they had never thought would happen in their lifetime, if ever, and to some extent the younger ones, especially the single ones. It was as if theirs was an exclusive men's club, with its own rules, which they did not wish to change. And then she chided herself. Young or old, they were *not* all like that. Some were quite pleasant. But probably none, she thought, and certainly not in this diocese, had had to deal with a pregnant priest before.

It was in the quietest possible time, in the middle of silent prayer when a dropped pin would have clanged on the floor, that it happened. She felt—it came without any warning—a sudden movement, a lurching, almost a thumping in her body. She knew what it was. Though it was a long time since, when she'd been pregnant with Becky, she'd experienced it. It was unmistakeable. This was the quickening, the first felt movements of the baby, or in this case probably both babies at once. And although she knew what it was, and it was welcome as a sure and certain sign of vigorous life, at that precise moment it was so unexpected, so physically startling, that, without realising it, though there was no way she could have kept it back, she gave a small, sharp cry—which in the prayerful silence of the room came out as a loud yell.

Heads shot up and without exception were turned in her direction as she sat there, still clutching her stomach. The Rural Dean was the first to speak.

'Are you all right, my dear?' he asked gently.

'Yes,' she said hesitantly. 'Yes, I'm all right. I'm sorry!' But was she all right, or would it happen again any minute? She couldn't be sure.

'Don't apologise, my dear,' the Rural Dean said. Then he spoke to a young man sitting at the front. Venus didn't know him. He must be the new curate, in his first job at St Matthias at the other end of the Deanery.

'Jeffrey,' he said, 'get Venus a drink of water.'

'I'm all right, really I am,' Venus protested. 'It was just . . .'

The Rural Dean smiled at her. 'Of course!' he said. 'But a drink of water . . . And if you would like to go home, we've almost finished, feel free to do so.'

'Oh no,' Venus said. 'I don't want to leave. I'm perfectly all right!' She spoke with more confidence than she felt, but she wasn't going to give in. 'I'm sorry I interrupted the meeting.'

'Don't worry,' the Rural Dean said.

What a nice man he is, Venus thought.

*　　　*　　　*

Back in her car, before she set off for home, she rang Nigel from her mobile and told him what had happened.

'That's wonderful!' he said. 'You must tell me all about it later. At the moment I'm with a patient.'

CHAPTER THIRTEEN

From time to time, since Nigel had spoken about her relationship with Becky, his words had come into Venus's mind. She had not quite believed him, she wasn't sure she did even now, but there was a space between herself and Becky for which she couldn't quite see the explanation, and perhaps Nigel's was the correct one. It was not that there were specific disagreements between the two of them, it was more that Becky was disinterested. She was keeping herself to herself, which was unlike her. She had always been one for pouring out whatever came into her mind. Also, Venus noted it specifically, Becky never started a conversation about the babies; it was as if they didn't exist.

They certainly did exist. Since the day of the Chapter meeting they had kicked at her every day, often more than once a day. Once, at a moment when they were being unusually lively, she told Becky about it. 'And if you put your hand just here,' she said, indicating a spot on her abdomen, 'you can feel them!'

'Thank you,' Becky said, 'but no thank you!' It was the look on her face which said everything.

Venus spoke to Nigel about it that evening, after Becky had gone to bed. 'You were right,' she said. 'I was quite shaken—and I have to do something about it. What shall I do?'

'That's for you to decide,' Nigel said firmly. 'It wouldn't be the same if the idea came from me. Moreover, it has to come from the heart. Believe

182

me, Becky will know if it doesn't!'

Venus lay awake a long time, thinking about it, but nothing came to her and she fell asleep still worried. Then when she wakened in the morning it came to her at once; she knew exactly what she would do, and she wouldn't even tell Nigel until she'd suggested it to Becky. There was no time to mention it before school so, during the day, on and off, she checked times and trains, places and programmes, and had it all worked out by the time Becky came home.

'I've had an idea,' she said. 'There's something I'd very much like to do. And I'd especially like to do it with you. You'd be the perfect person.'

She noted the wary look on Becky's face. She reckons I'm going to involve her in buying something for the babies, she thought.

'What is it?' Becky asked in a cool voice.

'I thought we might go to the ballet. I've never been to the ballet, though I've always wanted to. And nor have you. I thought we might both enjoy it. They're doing "Sleeping Beauty".'

'I didn't know the ballet came to Brampton,' Becky said. She was giving nothing away.

'Oh, I don't mean Brampton!' Venus waved away the idea. 'It's in London, at Covent Garden. The real thing! We'd have to go up by train.'

Becky began to look slightly interested.

'And we could go for a meal afterwards,' Venus added, though taking care not to sound over-eager.

While Becky pondered, Venus held her breath.

'Could Anna go, too?' Becky asked.

'Well,' Venus said, 'I had thought just you and me . . .'

'I would like Anna to go,' Becky said firmly.

183

We are bargaining, Venus thought. And what's more, my daughter is going to get the best of the bargain because I don't want to lose this one.

'Well, I suppose she could,' she agreed. 'We'd have to see what her mother said.'

'Oh, she'd say yes,' Becky said confidently. 'Shall I ring and ask her?'

'Are you quite sure you want to go?' Venus said.

'Oh yes!' Becky said. 'If Anna can come. She's never been to the ballet, either!'

'All right then,' Venus agreed. 'Shall I ring Anna's mother?'

'I'd like to tell Anna myself,' Becky said.

Venus listened while her daughter telephoned, and was delighted to hear the enthusiasm in Becky's voice. Until this moment she had kept it well hidden. At least, she thought, I've won a few points, even if she's not going to say so out loud.

'Anna's mother wants to speak to you,' Becky said presently, handing over the phone.

'Is this true?' Sally Brent said.

'Absolutely!' Venus confirmed. She would not say that she had planned to have her daughter to herself.

'Well, it's mighty kind of you,' Sally said.

'I thought Saturday week,' Venus said, 'if I can get seats. And we'll stay in town for a meal.

'Well, that's that!' she said a minute later to Becky. 'I'll try to get seats in the dress circle. You can see everything from there.'

'What shall I wear?' Becky said, with a complete change of tone. 'Oh, Mummy, do you think I could possibly have a new dress?'

Venus looked at her daughter's shining face. 'I think that could be managed,' she said. 'We'll go

184

and look for one after school tomorrow. Just you and me.' She knew Anna had a music lesson immediately after school the next day. These days she knew Anna's timetable almost as well as Becky's.

'Well done,' Nigel said when she told him about the arrangements, later that evening. 'And you'll get extra points for inviting Anna.'

'Are you sure you wouldn't like to come with us, I mean if I could get another ticket?'

'Quite sure,' Nigel said. 'It would lose the point. You'll be all girls together. In any case, I'm not mad on ballet. Give me a nice, juicy crime any day!'

A little later Venus's mother telephoned.

'I've got an appointment with the consultant,' she said. 'Next Friday, ten a.m.'

'You know I'll take you,' Venus offered immediately.

'Oh, there's no need, love,' Mrs Foster said. 'I told you your Dad'll do that.'

'But I'd like to,' Venus persisted. What was happening? First Becky was distant, and now her mother.

'Well, all right, then,' Mrs Foster said, with a change of tone. 'In fact, it would be nice. I'd prefer it. I don't think Dad likes doctors' waiting rooms. Men don't, do they?'

*   *   *

The next morning Venus decided that this would be one of the days when she took her work into the church. She had plenty of paperwork to catch up with; it was something she disliked doing so it was neglected, and piled up. She would also say her

Office in church, and if there was time she would do some reading. She read not only to keep up with what was happening in the church outside her own parish and diocese, but what the thinking was, where it was going. She supposed most people believed that what there was to say about the Christian church had long ago been said—and it was there anyway, in the Bible and in the Prayer Book—but they were wrong, at least to an extent. Every month, every week almost, though the basic tenets held, there were new insights, new ideas, new ways to be explored. Some of them were barmy, some of them seemed impossible, none of them were without interest. And some of them were to be thrown out, discarded. Almost every day she read or heard somewhere that the church was dying. It was not her own experience, but it had to be thought about, it couldn't be ignored. And as well as the writings on the Christian faith there were other faiths which she knew she should give heed to. They were there, they were possibly in her own parish; she needed, as well as wanted, to know about them.

So, she thought, gathering her books and papers together, if she took a sandwich for lunch she could easily and happily spend the entire day in the church. Not that that was possible. There were other things to be done. One of them was to phone Connie Phillipson, which she decided she would do before she left home.

The phone was answered immediately, as if Connie was right there beside it, waiting for it to ring. Did many people call her? Venus wondered. Probably not.

'It's Venus,' she said. 'I'm just ringing to ask how

186

you are.'

'Oh, thank you!' Connie said. 'I'm all right . . . I suppose.' Her voice sounded flat.

'What are you going to do today?' Venus asked.

'I don't know,' Connie answered. 'A bit of housework, I suppose—though the house doesn't seem to get untidy these days. I expect you have a busy day in front of you?' She sounded envious.

'I'm going to take some work into the church,' Venus said. 'So that I can keep it open. I have plenty to keep me occupied . . .' She knew as soon as she had said the words that they were the wrong ones. 'But do drop in if you want to,' she added. She half hoped that Connie would not do so, and was immediately ashamed of herself for the thought. Connie Phillipson was more important, at the moment, than any amount of paperwork. And where was the point of reading about the Christian life while at the same time baulking at living it at the point where it was needed, however unappealing that might be at this moment? 'I shall be there at least all morning,' she said to Connie, hoping that she sounded welcoming.

*   *   *

It was cool in the church, and Venus particularly wished to leave the door ajar—what was the point, otherwise? So far, it had been thought too extravagant to put on the heating, though before long, she thought, it would have to go on for Sundays. The ancient church walls were thick, which meant that to a certain extent they kept out the cold, but at the same time they did not allow the summer's heat to penetrate and collect, so it

187

was never anything other than cool inside. Venus, though being pregnant somehow kept her warmer than was normal for her, was glad she had had the forethought to put on a cardigan under her cassock.

She settled herself down in a pew halfway down the nave, sitting well towards the wall end of the pew so that without turning round she could see who came and went. For the best part of an hour no-one at all came in, and then one elderly man entered. He walked around, looking at everything, studying the inscriptions beneath the stained glass windows, stopping to examine the pulpit. He walked up to the altar and took a close look at that, then he turned round and made his way back down the nave, wishing Venus good-morning, but not stopping—and was gone. A few minutes after that, Connie Phillipson came in, and sat by Venus. 'You said it would be all right if I came,' she said nervously.

'Of course!' Venus said, putting away the sheaf of papers she was studying.

'Am I interrupting you?' Connie asked—and then said, 'That's a silly question, isn't it? I can see I am. Well, I won't stay long.'

'Stay as long as you like,' Venus said. 'The church is here for you as well as for services. I don't think enough people realise that. So what have you been doing with yourself the last few days?'

'Not a lot,' Connie admitted. 'But I've got all George's clothes together. And a few other things. His bowls. He was a keen bowler.'

'Yes,' Venus said. 'My father had got to know him. Dad's a bowler, too. He says George will be much missed.'

'So do you think if I went to the Hospice shop in Brampton they would take all these things? They're in good condition.'

'I'm sure they'd be glad of them,' Venus said.

A few minutes later David Wainright came in. He said nothing about the church being open, he didn't need to, he could have come in anyway. He had his own key, which he had not had to use and was still in his hand.

'Good-morning, Vicar,' he said. He had never called her Venus. She thought he might prefer to call her Mrs Baines rather than Vicar, but he was a correct man. He smiled at Connie.

'You know Mrs Phillipson, don't you?' Venus said. 'But what a silly question! Of course you do!'

'Of course!' he said. 'How are you getting on?' he asked Connie.

'All right, I suppose,' she said.

'It isn't easy,' he said. 'I know that from experience.'

Connie looked at Venus. She clearly didn't know what he was talking about.

'David's' (she deliberately called him David) 'wife died just before he came to live in Thurston,' Venus explained.

'Oh! I'm sorry! I didn't know,' Connie said.

'Connie has just been through the experience of sorting out George's clothes and so on—and you know how distressing that can be.' So do I, she thought. She remembered clearly having to do it after Philip had died but she said nothing of that now. It was possible that David Wainright, at any rate, didn't even know that she had been widowed.

'We were talking about taking George's things to the Hospice shop in Brampton,' she said.

189

'Oh, that would be quite the best thing to do,' David said. 'I took all my wife's things there. They were pleased to have them. In fact nowadays I take anything I don't need, whether it's clothes or something else, to the Hospice shop. I'm quite a supporter of theirs in more ways than one. The Hospice can do with all the support it can get.'

There was a short silence and then Connie Phillipson said, 'Well, I'd better be going. I must let Venus get on with her work.'

'And I just came in to check a few things,' David said. 'I'm not yet familiar with everything, and I must make myself so.' He turned to Connie. 'I have a hard task before me, Mrs Phillipson, following in your husband's footsteps. We all know how efficient he was!'

Eventually, he too left, presumably having done what he wanted to do, into which Venus did not enquire too closely. After that, she completed a certain amount of paperwork, which left no time for reading. Even so, she sat for a while, doing nothing, simply looking around her. It *was* a lovely church, with its beautiful windows, its pillars, the pictures on the wall and the statue of the Virgin and Child. But it was not all these things which made it seem special, she knew that. Perhaps, she thought, it was that people had prayed and worshipped in this sacred space for centuries. But did it then follow that a new church, possibly quite bare, functional, and almost certainly different, a church set in a harsh urban landscape instead of in a beautiful village, could not be as holy? She couldn't believe that. But she could be thankful, and she was, that life had brought her to Thurston and St Mary's, and most of all to Nigel.

She looked at her watch. It was half-past two and she had things to do at home. She left reluctantly, locking the door behind her. Joe Hargreaves was tidying the beds which bordered the main path.

'Hello, Joe,' she said. 'How's everything? Has there been any further sign of the tramp? I'm sure you would know if anyone did.'

'Not that I've seen,' Joe said. 'But I hold out no hope that he won't come back. They usually do.'

She walked home, dropping in at Gander's for a loaf of bread. Her nostrils were assailed by the aroma of the second baking of the day and her eyes by the display of cream cakes, for which Gander's was famous.

'It's no use, Daisy,' she said. 'I've got to have some cream cakes. I can't resist them!'

'Got a craving for them, have you?' Daisy asked. 'It's funny what pregnant women go for. With me it was pickled onions. I couldn't resist them, never mind the indigestion. Arnold said if I didn't give them up he wouldn't sleep with me!'

'Oh, it's not being pregnant,' Venus said. 'I could eat your cream cakes any time. I'll take two chocolate éclairs and two coffee.' She was so hungry that she could have eaten them on the spot. As it was, the minute she was back in the Vicarage she made a pot of tea and immediately ate a chocolate one followed by half a coffee one. That left one-and-a-half for Becky and one for Nigel, who was not as keen on cream cakes as were the females in his family.

Sitting there, eating the cakes, drinking her tea, she fell to wondering what, if anything, she had achieved by keeping the church open for a few hours today. Would she have accomplished as much, or even more, by staying at home, or by walking around the parish? How could she know? What she did know was that she was bone tired. The pews were not made for pregnant women. Next time, and even in the face of her doubts she was determined there would be a next time, she would take a cushion.

*   *   *

On Friday morning Venus took her mother to Brampton to see Mr Conway, the consultant surgeon whom Sonia had recommended as being the very best person possible for what ailed Mrs Foster. A charming secretary showed the two women into the waiting room.

'Mr Conway won't keep you more than a few minutes,' she said.

'Will I be allowed to go in with my mother?' Venus asked. 'I would like to.'

'Oh, I'd think so,' the secretary said. 'I'll ask.'

When she had left, Mrs Foster surveyed her surroundings. 'This is really very pleasant,' she said. 'Just like a drawing room in a private house—I mean the flowers and pictures and so on. Do you suppose he lives here?'

'Oh, I wouldn't think so,' Venus said. Pleasant and well-furnished though the room was, there was nothing personal about it. It was totally tidy, the glossy magazines were neatly displayed, not a thing was out of place. Even the flower arrangements were symmetrical.

They waited less than ten minutes before the secretary returned, and showed them both to Mr Conway's consulting room. He rose from his desk,

192

all six-foot-three of him, topped by a thick mane of silver-white hair, shook hands with Mrs Foster, then turned to Venus. 'And you are Mrs Foster's daughter?'

'My daughter's the Vicar of Thurston,' Mrs Foster said.

Sonia Leyton had mentioned that the patient was the mother of the local vicar, but not that the vicar was a woman, and pregnant—and right now not wearing a dog collar—so for a brief moment he was slightly confused.

'Venus Baines. My mother's happy for me to be with her. I hope that's all right with you?'

'Perfectly!' he said.

He asked several questions, looked closely at the X-rays, and then made what seemed a surprisingly quick physical examination.

'Well, I don't think there's any doubt, Mrs Foster, that you need a hip replacement. It's quite clear in the X-rays, and in your movements. You must have been in quite a bit of pain.'

'Well . . .' Mrs Foster began.

Venus chipped in. 'My mother will play it light,' she said, 'but she has been in considerable pain for quite some time.'

'That doesn't surprise me,' Mr Conway said. 'So now, Mrs Foster, I think you should let me do something about it. I can assure you, you'll feel much better afterwards. I can recommend you to Brampton General hospital—I do also operate there—but there's a long wait . . .'

'Oh, that's all right!' Mrs Foster interrupted. 'I've got health insurance. And I'd like to get it over with.'

'Very sensible!' he said. 'So you could go into

193

The Larches at any time, could you?'

She knew The Larches was the local private hospital, though she had never been there. After all, she'd never been ill, not what you'd call ill. Flu, coughs and colds, the occasional stomach upset; nothing more. People said The Larches was quite posh.

'Yes, I could,' she said. 'And the sooner, the better!'

'Well then,' Mr Conway said, 'my secretary will be in touch with The Larches and we'll contact you, possibly tomorrow.'

'What a very nice man,' Mrs Foster said on the way home.

'Yes,' Venus agreed. 'I liked him.'

'I don't know what your Dad will do while I'm in hospital,' Mrs Foster said.

'Oh, he'll be all right,' Venus said. 'In any case, I'll keep an eye on him. He can eat at the Vicarage whenever he wants to.'

In her opinion her father could very well look after himself. It was just that he had been cosseted by his wife—well, they had cosseted each other, which, when one came to think of it, was rather nice after all those years of marriage.

*　　　*　　　*

Next day, in the middle of the morning, the phone rang just as Venus was leaving the Vicarage. She turned back to answer it. It was her mother.

'You'll never believe,' Mrs Foster said, 'I've already had a call from Mr Conway's secretary! That's quick, isn't it?'

'And?' Venus said.

'I can go in on Monday week. In the afternoon. I must say, I'm very pleased about that.'

'So am I,' Venus agreed.

'Should I let Doctor Sonia know?' Mrs Foster asked.

'Oh, I think so. But you could ring her. I don't suppose you need go to the surgery. Would you like me to pop around and see you later? It would have to be after lunch. I'm just off to have a meeting with my churchwardens.' And my new Treasurer, she thought. She had insisted—it was perhaps not very nice of her—that the meeting should be in the church, so that the building could be open, though Henry had pointed out that they could hardly sit in the pews to have it. That was all right, she'd told him. They would have it in the parish office, and if she left the door open she'd be able to see who came in and out of the church.

*   *   *

Saturday week came, and with it the trip to London. All went smoothly. Becky wore her new dress, chosen in Brampton entirely according to her wishes. It was in a fine material with a silky finish, navy, with touches of red—apparently a very sophisticated choice of colours for those in the know. It had the merest vestige of sleeves, and in Venus's opinion the neck was cut a little too low, but since, as yet, Becky's bosom was far from burgeoning (from time to time she mentioned that several of the girls in her class already had bras, and why couldn't she?) that didn't matter too much. Halfway through the conversation with Becky about bras Venus recalled that she herself

195

hadn't had the slightest vestige of a bosom until she was almost fourteen, and that she and her friend Freda, anxiously inspecting each other, decided that in any case until you could shake yourself and your breasts moved independently of each other it couldn't rightly be called a bosom. Well, Venus thought, girls don't have to wait that long nowadays. They all grow up faster.

Little was said during the performance. It was too entrancing for words. In the interval the girls came down to earth long enough to eat ice cream, and immediately afterwards they were back in the dream world.

'Mummy,' Becky said on the way home, replete with a high tea which had been full of fats and calories and probably totally unhealthy, but delicious. 'Mummy, do you think I'm too old to train as a ballet dancer?'

'Probably, dear!' Venus said.

All afternoon not a word had been said about babies until, on the train on the way home, Becky herself brought up the subject.

'Mummy,' she said, 'if the boys wanted to be ballet dancers—I mean when they were older— they'd have to start when they were very small, wouldn't they?'

Venus tipped her head back against the seat and closed her eyes. 'Yes, dear, they would,' she agreed.

As far as she was concerned, and feeling the *pas de deux* which was at that moment going on inside her, they were already in training.

196

CHAPTER FOURTEEN

On Sunday morning Venus stood at the small wooden altar she had commissioned as her wedding gift to St Mary's. She had chosen its size and design deliberately and the PCC had agreed to it, though some of them reluctantly. What was wrong with the old altar? Now, the new one fitted into the chancel arch, and as far forward as it could be without falling down the chancel steps. She could see two thirds of the congregation, and they her, but there was still a significant group of worshippers in the south aisle who, because of the sturdy pillars which divided them from the nave, were lost to her, and she to them. Becky, since she was nowhere to be seen, must be among them: she was not sitting with her grandparents in their usual pew halfway down the left-hand side of the nave. Her excuse would be that this morning Anna, perhaps as a thank you for having been taken to the ballet yesterday, had decided to make a rare visit to church, and she had chosen where they would sit. More likely, though, it was Becky's declaration of independence. At any rate, both girls had achieved their object. They were invisible.

If it's the last thing I do, Venus thought, not for the first time, one day I will get this church turned around so that we can all see each other. At the moment, that south aisle group of people were no more than disembodied voices to her, as she was to them, united only by the organist and the last two lines of the hymn:

'Thus provided, pardoned, guided,
Nothing can our peace destroy.'

When it was over she took her place behind the crucifer with the cross, and the two young servers, and walked down the aisle and out of the building, then stood in her usual place outside the door to bid farewell to everyone.

It had been a good service, she thought, even though it was the third time in five weeks they had sung 'Love Divine All Loves Excelling'. Not that it wasn't a lovely hymn, one of Charles Wesley's finest, and it had been sung, probably in this very church as well as world-wide, for more than two hundred years. But three times in five weeks? She must have a word with Jim. He was a good organist but his repertoire was not wide. Or, as she knew was more likely, he didn't care for the new hymns she sometimes liked to introduce. And it was true what he said, they didn't always go well with the organ. She had still not achieved her ambition of having a music group: different instruments, two or three good singers. It would not be in opposition to Jim, that was never in her mind, but sometimes it would be the group, sometimes the organ. Something for everyone.

'Are you going in to coffee?' she asked her parents as they came out of church. Her mother was leaning heavily on a stick.

'Oh, yes!' her mother said. 'After all, it's going to be a few weeks before I get to church again.'

'I shall bring you your communion,' Venus said. 'You know I will.'

'I do know, love,' her mother said. 'But it's not the same, is it?'

198

It was not the time or place to argue about the validity of that, Venus thought. There was also a chilly wind blowing down the back of her neck. In another week or two she would have to stand inside after the service.

'I'll see you in the hall,' she said. 'If you don't want to stay long, Becky will be back at home.' Her parents were lunching at the Vicarage. The girls had already fled at the speed of light, tearing down the church path as if released from prison.

'We'll wait for you,' her mother said. 'There's one or two people I want to speak to.'

By the time Venus went into the parish hall her mother was at the centre of a group of six people, sitting at a table. She was clearly holding the attention of all of them with the news of her impending hip replacement.

'You'll be fine in The Larches,' Venus heard someone saying as she passed on her way to join another group of parishioners. 'My sister-in-law said it was like a five-star hotel!'

Her mother was still holding court—her father sitting quietly by—when Venus left twenty minutes later. But I'm so pleased she's settled here, and made friends, Venus thought. The same applied to her father, though his friends were mostly on the golf course. Neither of them seemed to miss their previous home in Clipton, where they had lived so long.

*   *   *

The next afternoon she helped her mother to pack her small case, and then drove her to the hospital, where they were taken at once to the room which

199

would be Mrs Foster's for the rest of her ten-day stay at The Larches.

'This all looks very nice,' Mrs Foster said when the nurse had left them, promising to be back in fifteen minutes. She peered into the bathroom, turned the shower on and off; came back into the main room, opened and closed drawers, checked the television. Venus helped her to unpack and hang her clothes in the wardrobe. There was a comfortable armchair and two smaller chairs for visitors, pretty curtains at the window, which looked out on to green lawns. On the wall opposite to the bed there was a framed print of something Mediterranean—France, Italy, who could say? White buildings, blue skies, red-sailed boats on the water, sunshine.

'That's nice, too,' Mrs Foster said. 'Quite cheerful!'

'This is a particularly pleasant room,' Venus said. She had been to The Larches from time to time, visiting parishioners, so she knew something of the layout. 'You're happy with everything, are you?'

'Oh yes!' Mrs Foster said. 'So far, so good.'

'Happy' was not the word she would have chosen, but she was not going to say so. Inside she was a quivering jelly, but she would keep that to herself. The only time in her life she had ever been in hospital before—and it was not really a hospital, it was a maternity home—was when she had had Venus. That was half a lifetime ago. It had been all right, and in the end, with Venus in the small cot beside her bed, it was well worth the pain, and the long wait she had had before conceiving Venus. But things would be very different now, more up-to-date, she told herself, though with not much conviction. And she had sensed this morning that Ernest was even more nervous than she was, so she had sent him off to his golf, saying that she would be happier to have Venus take her in.

'Now, are you sure you have everything you need?' Venus asked. 'If you haven't, please ring me. You have your own telephone, right beside you.'

'Oh, I will! I will!' her mother assured her.

Not long afterwards a different nurse came in. 'I don't want to rush you, Mrs Foster,' she said, 'but there are a few questions I need to ask you, and one or two small tests . . .'

Venus broke in. 'I'm just going!' She turned to her mother. 'I'll give you a ring this evening.'

'Fine!' Mrs Foster said.

She watched as her daughter left the room. Suddenly, she didn't want to see her go.

*   *   *

'How was she?' Nigel asked Venus that evening.

'All right, I suppose,' Venus said. 'Or at least she was trying to be. But you know my mother, she's not going to give anything away.'

'She'll be fine, love,' Nigel said. 'Don't worry! It's a straightforward operation, and Mr Conway is easily the best.'

'I suppose so,' Venus said. 'I'm just not used to anything being wrong with my mother. She's never ill.'

'Strictly speaking,' Nigel said, 'she's not ill now. She doesn't have any disease. She's a healthy woman.'

Venus nodded. 'I know. That's what I keep

201

telling myself. It's just that she's *my mother*!'

*   *   *

A little later that evening the Blessed Henry telephoned. 'I've been having a word with David Wainright,' he said. 'Going over a few figures. Most of them are new to him. He thinks we need to look at the budget. So we should meet with you, and of course with Edward, before next week's PCC meeting. I suggest the sooner the better. Let's get it out of the way.'

'Anything serious?' Venus enquired.

'Not really,' Henry replied, 'but we need to make sure we're all on the same wavelength. How about tomorrow? Shall we come to you?'

'That would be best,' Venus agreed. 'Nigel might well be on call and I wouldn't want to leave Becky. Also, my mother has her operation tomorrow. I'd like to be at home if I can. Shall we say eight o'clock?'

*   *   *

Tuesday morning brought the usual ten o'clock Eucharist. Venus was pleased that it coincided with the day of her mother's surgery. Though there were only the usual six people present—all sitting at a distance from each other—and possibly only two of them knew her mother, because the others were not Sunday attenders, she nevertheless felt better that she had this group of people around her. 'I'm particularly glad to see you here this morning,' she said to them before starting the service. 'My mother is in hospital. She will be having surgery on

202

her hip this afternoon. So the intention of this Eucharist is for her, and for all who are in our local hospitals. I know you will pray for her. And for them.'

When it was over she was pleased that, though usually they scurried away like mice who were afraid of being caught by the cat, this morning four out of six hovered. Two smiled, nodded and left, but the other four stopped to speak. They commiserated with her, and sent good wishes to her mother. 'Such a nice, cheerful lady!' one of the Sunday worshippers said. 'I'll send her a card.'

'She'd like that, Mrs Newboult,' Venus said. 'She's in The Larches.'

'Well, if you have to be in hospital,' Mrs Newboult replied, 'The Larches is the best place.'

'So everyone says.' And maybe, Venus thought, I could nip up there now and see her for a few minutes. She didn't know whether visitors would be welcomed in the middle of the morning, but it was surprising how easy access was to such places when one was wearing a clerical collar. On the other hand, she thought, it will be a busy time, I might be in the way. It would be better to phone her mother, which she would do on her mobile while she was still in church.

'I'm fine!' Mrs Foster said. 'I've certainly had lots of attention. There's someone here every ten minutes doing something or other, asking questions, writing things down. I go down to the theatre at three o'clock. Funny, calling it a theatre! Where are you now?'

'In church,' Venus said. 'The Eucharist was for you. People sent their best wishes, Mrs Newboult particularly. Do you know her?'

'Oh yes,' Mrs Foster said. 'I sometimes sit with her at coffee. That was nice of her. Oh! here comes Nurse again!'

'I'll ring off,' Venus said. 'Lots of love, darling. I'll phone this evening, see how it's all gone, and I'll be in to see you tomorrow.'

* * *

Edward Mason, David Wainright and the Blessed Henry arrived promptly at eight o'clock.

'What's the news of your mother?' Henry asked at once.

'She's OK,' Venus said. 'It went well. I phoned an hour ago. She'll be in the High Dependency Unit overnight but she should be back in her own room tomorrow.'

'Good!' Henry said. 'Molly sends love to her. We'll pop in and see her in a day or two.'

Venus took the men into her study, asked them if they'd like coffee, which they all refused. 'We'll get straight down to business,' Henry said. 'It shouldn't take long. David has been looking through the accounts, so we'll let him speak first, shall we?'

Venus nodded assent. Apart from their greetings on arriving neither of the other two men had said anything. David Wainright looked grim, but then, Venus thought, he was not one of the world's smilers and in the time he had been on the PCC he had seldom had much to say.

'Well,' he said now, 'I have to admit that our finances are not in a healthy state—in fact I was rather taken aback, as I've already told these two gentlemen. There's more money going out than

204

there is coming in and—I'm sorry, but I have to be blunt—that won't do! It's the start of the slippery slope. I've gone back over the books and it seems that a little over a year ago everything was all right. There was a small surplus. Now that's no longer the case.'

Henry looked uncomfortably at Venus; Edward looked down at his papers. He had only been churchwarden since Richard Proctor had left Thurston but he had been on the PCC before that. He must have known the reason why there was less money coming in, Venus thought. Why had neither of her churchwardens put the new Treasurer in the picture? The only reason, she knew, was to save her pain.

'Ah!' she said now. 'That was when Miss Frazer left us. It was just before you came to live here. She was a tremendous source of income to St Mary's.'

'So she's left the area?' David Wainright said. 'That's a pity.'

'No, she hasn't left the area,' Venus said evenly. 'She still lives in the parish. She has simply left the church and withdrawn all her financial support.'

There was a short silence, then the Treasurer said, 'Why? Why did she leave?'

'I'm afraid because of me,' Venus said. 'Because I was both a woman and a priest. It was something she couldn't take.'

Henry spoke up. 'She gave Venus a hard time, a very hard time, both privately and publicly. The things she did were totally unacceptable, including seeking out the Bishop and asking him to remove Venus from her post. Of course he wouldn't do that. No way!'

'So you see,' Venus said, 'it's my fault we're so

205

short of money.'

'It's not your fault at all,' Henry protested. 'Miss Frazer was totally out of order!'

David Wainright gave Venus a long look. She wondered what he was thinking.

'Yes, I do see,' he said eventually. 'But is there no way of patching this up? Mending fences? Turning the other cheek?'

Venus took a deep breath. 'On Miss Frazer's side I would say none whatever. On my side, of course, there must be. She is, after all, a parishioner. I am her priest. She is in my care. I would . . .' She hesitated, then said, 'Well, perhaps "welcome" is too strong a word, but I would do my best, though the money would not be my motive.'

'You actually mean you would forgive her?' Henry sounded astonished.

'I hope so,' Venus said. 'Though whether seventy times seven I'm not sure. But for practical purposes it makes no difference. She will never come back while I'm here. She hates me. And I have no intention of leaving.'

'Nor should you!' Henry spoke forcefully, and Edward nodded in agreement.

'I see!' David Wainright said. 'Well, be that as it may, and it is regrettable, one thing is certain, we'll have to cut down somewhere, and quite a lot. But I haven't been wasting my time over the last few days, I've been considering what we can do.'

'So what have you thought of?' Venus asked. She wasn't sure she wanted to hear.

'Lots of small areas,' the Treasurer said. 'For a start, we could do away with having new service sheets every Sunday in the year. All that paper. Hymns printed afresh every week! We could go back to hymn books. I remember that's what you used to use. When my wife was alive we came here from time to time. I expect you still have them. And then the news sheet—very nice, of course, but not strictly necessary. There's nothing in that that can't be given out in the notices.'

'I couldn't agree to either of those measures,' Venus said quickly. 'The cost of paper is negligible, and we print them ourselves on the photocopier.'

The Treasurer shook his head. His face was set like concrete. 'No cost is negligible when we're so short of money,' he said. 'As for the photocopier—well, it's on hire, isn't it? So we have to pay that, and the materials, and the servicing. Churches have existed hundreds of years without photocopiers!'

'Churches have existed hundreds of years without electric light, or heating, or a lavatory on the premises,' Venus said shortly. 'How far back into the Dark Ages do you want us to go?'

'I was just suggesting—' he began.

Venus didn't allow him to continue.

'I can tell you for certain,' she said, 'that I will not give up the weekly service sheets. Those sheets allow me to use variations in the services, all of which are allowable. New forms of prayers, or I can revive some of the really ancient ones which have been neglected. I can introduce new hymns—there are scores of wonderful new hymns—and at the same time, of course, keep many of the old ones. As we do. And the sheets are much easier to handle than fiddling around between hymn book and Prayer Book. Strangers to the church have more than once complimented us on the service sheets. In fact'—she felt the blood rising in her cheeks—'rather than give up the service sheets I would pay for the paper out of my own pocket!'

There was dead silence. She and David Wainright glared at each other. Then she felt the tears pricking at her eyes. Oh dear, she thought, I can't bear it if I'm going to cry! She was not a person who readily did so, but these days she was not always in control of her emotions.

'There are, surely,' the Treasurer said in a firm voice, 'plenty of prayers to be found in the Book of Common Prayer? It has served well for hundreds of years. People are familiar with it.'

'My point precisely,' Venus said. 'So familiar that they don't always listen.'

'But we *know* the prayers!' He spoke patiently, as if to an awkward child.

'*You* do,' Venus said. 'And I do. And I'm not dismissing them wholesale. I always use some of them. But new people don't know them, especially young people. Sometimes they don't even understand the language. Language changes all the time.' She recalled vividly how, when she was young, she had been puzzled by 'rightly and indifferently administer justice'. Was God indifferent, then? she'd wondered. Didn't he care?

'The Book of Common Prayer will last for all time,' the Treasurer said.

'I daresay,' Venus said. 'And I for one am not calling for its abolition. But if parts of it aren't understood, where does that leave us? If church attendance is in decline could it partly be that not everyone, especially young people, understand what we're saying? And what I'm saying is that the weekly service sheets, as well as allowing me to mix the old with the new, give me the freedom to use language which is relevant to ordinary people. To keep in touch, in fact.'

David Wainright shook his head slowly from side to side, as if sorrowing.

'This is a matter of money,' he said. 'Money we don't have. And small economies add up.' He smiled at Venus. 'I'm sure you ladies find that in your housekeeping. It was something I used to remind my wife about. "You worry your pretty head about the little things and I'll take care of the important ones," I used to tell her. Dear Rita! She was a wonderful wife but she had no head for money!'

Venus opened her mouth, but the words wouldn't come. So it was all down to the shortcomings of women, was it? Why doesn't Henry say something, she thought angrily? All right, so it was she who had introduced the service sheets, soon after she'd arrived. He'd never made a murmur then. Nor, as far as she knew, had anyone else. Certainly not in her hearing.

'And while we're on the subject,' she said, 'all the labour in producing the service sheets, and the news sheets, is given freely and voluntarily.'

'Very well,' the Treasurer said. 'We'll leave that for the moment . . .'

In my book we will leave it for good, Venus thought.

'. . . and we will come on to other economies we might make,' he continued. 'I'm sure none of you will deny that they have to be made. Now, I note that at this time last year, and indeed in previous years, a substantial sum of money was expended in financing a trip to the pantomime for the children.'

'That is something we've done for many years,' Henry put in. 'It used to be financed by Miss

Frazer.'

'I see,' the Treasurer said. 'Well I'm afraid we can't possibly do that this year, nice though it would be. We just don't have the money.'

'Miss Frazer didn't finance it last year,' Venus said. 'She had already withdrawn her support. We paid for it ourselves. We raised the money, in quite a short time, in several small ways. We can do that again.'

David Wainright sighed.

'Vicar,' he said, 'when I look at these accounts I know that we need all the money that can be raised, by whatever means, to keep the church going. Lighting, heating, repairs.'

'You will find that people will work much more readily to send the children to the pantomime,' Venus said.

'Oh, I know!' David Wainright agreed. 'But they must be made to see—'

Edward Mason spoke up for the first time.

'Why can't we keep the children out of this? Why couldn't we have a special meeting to tell our own churchgoers that we need each and every one of them to give a little more money than they are doing at present? Lay the cards on the table; give them the figures. Ask them to pledge the money so that we know where we are?'

'I think that is a sound idea,' Venus said, not giving the Treasurer time to speak. 'I suggest we put that to the PCC on Thursday. In the meantime, *I* will undertake to raise the money for the pantomime. It's almost time we were booking it.' She had no idea how she would do it, but somehow she would.

'So thank you all, gentlemen,' she said.

There was no doubt that the meeting was at an end. Who had won, and, more important, who would win in the end, she wasn't sure. She hated battles.

When she had seen the men out she went into the sitting room. Nigel was sprawled on the sofa, catching up with the morning paper, gin-and-tonic in hand. One way and another—she had been occupied most of the day, he had had two busy surgeries and some visits—they had not seen each other since breakfast.

'Hello, my love!' he said. 'Come and sit by me. What sort of a day have you had? Would you like a drink?'

'Half a glass of red wine,' Venus said. 'The way I feel I could drink half a bottle, but I must remember the babes. I read this week that in the womb they have periods of waking and periods of sleeping. All I can say is that these two are both insomniacs!'

'And you reckon half a glass of red wine might send them to sleep?' Nigel asked.

'I hope so.'

He went into the kitchen to pour her wine. When he came back they sat on the sofa together. He put his arm around her and she leaned her head on his shoulder.

'How was the financial meeting?' Nigel enquired.

'Don't ask me!' Venus said.

'Consider yourself unasked,' he said.

'Would you like to sponsor a child, or preferably two, to go to the pantomime?' Venus asked.

'Gladly!' Nigel said. 'I remember what a happy time it was last year.'

211

CHAPTER FIFTEEN

The PCC meeting on Thursday evening was much as Venus, from the session at the Vicarage on Tuesday, had expected. David Wainright, with all the gravitas of a new Chancellor of the Exchequer presenting his first budget, gave the state of the church's finances, but, unlike most Chancellors, was not optimistic. There was no talk of how much better everything would be in the coming year under his command. His forecast was gloom now and more gloom to follow. He was, though, Venus thought, a surprisingly eloquent speaker with all the dire facts at his fingertips.

'So there is no doubt,' he summed up, 'that we have to raise more money and spend less.'

He then lost no time in putting forward the idea of a direct appeal to the entire congregation to give more cash, and give it directly. 'It's the simplest and most effective way,' he said.

Of course it was, Venus agreed with that in her heart, but how many people would go for it? People did not like putting their hands in their pockets and dishing out hard cash. They would rather work ceaselessly in a dozen different ways to earn the money which they would then hand over. Their time, it seemed, was of much less value than the few extra pounds they might contribute as a result of their labours.

It was not that the churchgoers of Thurston were particularly impoverished, she thought, though a few pensioners, living alone, might well be. On the whole they were middle-class people with middle incomes. They—especially the women—and it was true that they were always the chief fundraisers—would apparently rather spend several hours knitting woolly jumpers for African babies than send the cost of the wool in cash to whichever organisation would know best how to use it. Though, if consulted, they might, in some cases, say 'Send us the woolly jumpers.'

In the end it was agreed by a small margin that the Treasurer should mount a demonstration, with as many visual aids as he could muster, on finance, and that this would incorporate a plea for increased direct giving. Also, that it should be given on the earliest possible Sunday in place of the sermon.

The latter did not please Venus. She supposed she could have stopped it but before she could do so it was pointed out that it would be ideal as the Treasurer would have a captive audience.

'People won't come to a meeting on a weekday evening just to be asked to give money,' someone said, 'they'll stay away in droves.'

The Treasurer nodded his head in agreement.

'Precisely my point!' he said. 'And in addition I have put forward one or two schemes to *save* money. For instance . . .' He glanced at Venus. He would leave her to outline the proposals, and also her disagreement with them, thus absolving him.

'Our Treasurer,' Venus said, 'has suggested, as one way of saving money, that we should do away with the service sheets and the weekly news sheet.' And then, not allowing time for any reaction, she said, 'And also that we should not give our children their usual Christmas visit to the pantomime in Brampton. I am not in favour of either of those proposals.'

'Of course not!' Miss Tordoff interrupted quickly. 'We couldn't possibly give up the pantomime. The dear children look forward to it so much!'

'Thank you, Miss Tordoff,' Venus said. 'I feel the same way. And as far as that's concerned I have already decided that I will raise the money myself. And bearing in mind our Treasurer's words about asking directly I shall ask people to sponsor a child from our Sunday School, or more than one if they so wish. And I don't propose to ask the parents to do this. It's something St Mary's has always done for the children. So I intend to contact the theatre in the next day or two and see what sort of discount we might get for a block booking, and then I shall be asking you all, as well as other members of the congregation, to help.'

Her suggestions gave rise to so much discussion, ranging from what the pantomime was to be, where they might sit, and would there be enough money for a bag of sweets, or ice cream in the interval, that the subject of service sheets was somehow lost until it was too late in the evening to debate it.

*　　　*　　　*

'So what was it like?' Nigel asked later. He knew she hadn't been looking forward to the meeting.

'I skated on some thin ice,' Venus said, 'but I didn't quite fall in the water.' Though she yet might, she thought. She would have to tread carefully.

'I don't like meetings, as you know,' she said, 'but if you're a parish priest they come with the job.'

'And I suppose if you go up higher you don't get rid of meetings,' Nigel said. 'I suppose if you were a bishop you'd have just as many. Would you like to be a bishop?'

'That's a fruitless question,' Venus said. 'I couldn't be. It's the natural progression, if he is so called, for a priest to become a bishop—as long as he's a man. But not if the priest is a woman. As things stand, it would be against the law. But if we were in what some call the real world, that wouldn't be allowed, would it? It would be sex discrimination. Isn't it strange that the Church is allowed to practise sex discrimination?'

'But if you *could* be . . . ?'

'No!' Venus said. 'I'm happy in a parish. I'm happy here in Thurston, in spite of the pinpricks.'

'That's good,' Nigel said. 'I wouldn't want to be married to a bishop!'

'But I would fight for other women to become bishops,' Venus added. 'And some of them would be good ones. In the same way, ten years ago when women were asking for ordination, lots of women who had no such desires nevertheless joined in the fight. As, to be fair, did some men.'

'I remember that,' Nigel said.

'And how about you?' Venus asked him. 'Wouldn't you like to be a consultant, specialising in some rare condition that most people had never heard of? Or the head of a great hospital?'

'Not a bit,' Nigel said. 'I'm happy to be a GP as you are to be a parish priest. And as a bonus to be the husband of a parish priest and the father of twin boys!'

'Oh, Nigel, I do love you!' Venus said.

215

On Friday afternoon Venus went to see her mother in hospital. She had popped in each day of course, but today, if her mother felt like it, she would stay longer. Becky would be going to Anna's to tea and Nigel had a surgery, so there was no rush to get back.

She nodded at the two women on the reception desk as she went past to take the lift to her mother's room. They knew her by now, she had no need to identify herself. Room twenty-three, her mother's room, was on the second floor. She gave a token knock on the door and walked in. To her surprise, the room was empty. Not only was it empty, but the bed was stripped. For a moment, she felt as if her heart stopped beating. She stood completely still, then looked around. There was no sign of occupancy; nothing on the dressing table or the windowsill; no glasses, cups, magazines, newspapers. She opened a drawer and found it empty. There were no clothes hanging in the wardrobe. She immediately left the room and made straight for the nurses' station at the far end of the corridor.

'My mother!' she said. 'Mrs Foster. She was in room twenty-three. She's not there!'

'Perhaps she's gone for some treatment or other.' The nurse spoke in a soothing tone. 'I've just come on duty, but I'll find out for you.'

'I don't just mean she isn't in her room,' Venus said. 'There's nothing else in the room. It's totally empty. Where is she?'

The nurse looked puzzled, picked up the

216

telephone, and spoke. 'Mrs Foster. She was in room twenty-three. She doesn't appear to be there now.' Clearly, Venus thought, she has no idea where my mother is!

'It's not that she doesn't *appear* to be there,' she said. 'She *isn't* there. There's no sign of her.'

The nurse put down the phone. 'It's all right,' she said, 'your mother's been moved to room thirty-one. Go to the end of the corridor and take a left.'

'Why has she been moved?' Venus enquired.

'I'm afraid I don't know,' the nurse said.

Venus found room thirty-one, and tapped on the door. To her great relief, her mother's voice, sounding completely normal, almost hale and hearty, called out at once. 'Come in!' she said. When Venus entered she was sitting up in bed, enjoying her afternoon tea.

'Mother, whatever are you doing here?' Venus asked. She would not tell her mother all the stupid things which had gone through her mind—she recognised now that they were stupid.

'It's a long story!' Mrs Foster said.

'I have plenty of time,' Venus said, 'so tell me.'

'Well,' Mrs Foster said, with some relish, 'I was wakened this morning by a nurse tapping at the door and saying, "Are you ready for your breakfast, Mrs Foster?" We order it the night before, you see—the breakfasts here are very good—but they always ask you if you're ready in case you're in the middle of something else—in the bathroom or something of that nature . . .'

Venus settled back in her chair. There was no way her mother was going to give a quick answer. It was to be from thread to needle. But it didn't

217

matter because she was obviously all right.

'. . . so I said, "Not until you've straightened me up. I've tossed and turned all night and my bed's like a battlefield!" "OK," she says. "Then I'll just get another nurse to give me a hand," and off she goes. She hadn't actually come into the room, not then. Presently, she comes back with the second nurse and the minute they both step near the bed she—that's the second one—says, "Good heavens! The carpet's all wet!" And then the first one says, "Oh dear, Mrs Foster, your catheter must have slipped out!"'

'Mother! How awful for you!' Venus interrupted.

'I know!' her mother agreed. 'I was so embarrassed! Then one of the nurses says, "Well, the carpet's wet all the way to the window"—which as you will remember, Venus, is as much as two square yards. So I thought, that can't be me! Not two square yards of soaking carpet! "I'll just check," one of the nurses says. So she does. "That's all right," she says. "Everything's in place there!"

'By this time,' Mrs Foster continued, 'the other nurse has gone into the bathroom. "Oh my goodness!" she calls out, "it's a real flood in here! There's a pipe dripping under the washbasin! I can see it!" So of course they had to move me, as quickly as possible, and that's why I'm here. I was very late getting my breakfast.'

'Well, as long as you're all right,' Venus said. 'It's quite a nice room, isn't it?'

'Well, yes,' her mother answered, 'but if you go into the bathroom you'll see there isn't a walk-in shower, just one over the bath, and there's no way I can get into the bath. So what am I going to do?'

'But this is ridiculous,' Venus said. 'I'll go and

218

sort this out right away.' She stood up to leave the room.

'And I don't know where they've put all my bits and pieces—I mean my nightdresses, my toilet things. They just brought them in in a heap.'

'Don't worry about that,' Venus said. 'I'll sort that out as well.'

She was gone fifteen minutes. When she returned she was accompanied by two nurses.

'You're to move to another room, *with* a shower,' Venus said.

'The third room in twenty-four hours!' Mrs Foster said. 'That must be a record!'

'I'll see to your clothes and so on,' Venus said. 'Don't you bother about anything!'

'You needn't get out of bed, Mrs Foster,' one of the nurses said. 'We'll wheel your bed, it's only down the corridor, but a nicer view than this one.'

'Never mind the view,' Mrs Foster said. 'It's the shower I'm after.'

Venus sorted out her mother's belongings, then sat down in the chair at the side of the bed.

'Now,' she said, 'tell me how you've been, aside from all your adventures.'

'Quite good,' her mother acknowledged. 'I can get myself out of bed, and to the bathroom, with the Zimmer frame. I don't know who invented them, but he was a clever person.'

'He was probably a man named Zimmer,' Venus said.

'Would you like a cup of tea, love?' her mother asked. 'They'll bring you one if you would.'

'No, I'm fine, thank you,' Venus said.

'So tell me how Becky's getting on. And Nigel. And how's everyone in the church?' Mrs Foster leaned back against her pillow and settled down for a nice long gossip. 'And how is Miss Jowett?' she added.

'I haven't seen her for a little while,' Venus admitted. 'I must pay her a visit.'

'Well, when you do, tell her how much your Dad and I are enjoying living in what was her house.'

'I'm not sure I shall do that,' Venus said. 'The last time I saw her she was missing her old home.'

They chatted away and the time passed quickly. Venus was amazed by the improvement in her mother even over a few days, especially in her spirits. In the last three days, though physically restricted, she had almost been back to her usual cheerful self, the self she hadn't been for some months now.

'I could have had it done six months ago,' she said when Venus remarked on this. 'That's what's so stupid. I could have, there was nothing to stop me. I didn't have to go on a long waiting list.'

'Never mind,' Venus said. 'It's over now. But don't think you're going to skip around like a two-year-old as soon as you get home. You'll have to take things easy for a while.'

Mrs Foster waved away the idea. 'I'll be fine,' she said. 'I don't want to be coddled! Anyway, I've got your Dad, bless him! There's not much your Dad can't do if he sets his mind to it. He'll be in to see me this evening.'

'Even so,' Venus persisted, 'I think you should have Ethel Leigh in more often. Certainly for the first few weeks.'

'I'll see,' Mrs Foster said. 'As you know, I like to look after my own house. And *you're* the one who shouldn't be doing too much,' Mrs Foster said.

'Never mind me. You're the one who should be taking more rest instead of being here, there and everywhere, at everyone's beck and call.'

'Oh, Mum, I've never felt better!' Venus protested. 'And it's my job to be at everyone's beck and call, as you describe it. It's the way I want it.' But, though she wouldn't admit it to her mother, sometimes she did feel quite tired, especially towards the end of the day.

It had now been arranged, thanks to the kindness of the Bishop, that someone—quite who had not been specified—should come into the parish to help her in the last month of her pregnancy and for a month or so after the birth. It might be a retired priest, if one could be found, or it might be a young man who didn't yet have his own living to look after. But if he wasn't yet priested, then he wouldn't be able to celebrate the Eucharist, would he, she thought. One thing was certain, it wouldn't be a female member of the clergy. There wasn't one to be had. But never mind, somehow it would work out. She wouldn't let the fact that she was going to have two babies keep her out of circulation a day longer than was necessary.

'I'd better be off,' she said presently. 'I have a bit of shopping to do in the village.'

* * *

Back at home, her conscience having been pricked by her mother's enquiries about the lady, she decided she would visit Bertha Jowett the very next day. Moreover, she would go in the afternoon and allow herself enough time to have a game of

Scrabble with her. She wished she could think of someone else who could do this regularly; it would be so good for Bertha. But it was not easy. Aside from her being good at Scrabble, so that any opponent would have to be somewhere near her standard or it wouldn't work, she was also not the easiest person in the world with whom to have a conversation. Connie Phillipson came to mind as a woman who must now have more time on her hands than she knew what to do with, only to be quickly dismissed. Quite apart from the game, she wouldn't fill the bill at all. Bertha Jowett would eat her alive.

That evening, over supper, she put the problem to Nigel.

'I don't see an easy answer,' he said. 'I don't know Miss Jowett, she's a name on a list to me. It was Sonia she saw, and that very seldom. But if she's as you've described her I don't think she'd take kindly to you arranging her life. I reckon you'll just have to give her what time you can, and when you can, and perhaps tell her you'd like it to be more but you can't always manage it.'

'I suppose you're right,' Venus agreed reluctantly.

'And when we have the babies, you'll have even less time—and not only for Miss Jowett. That's something a male priest wouldn't have to contend with.'

'Too true!' Venus agreed. 'It's my intention to take them with me wherever I can, though I suppose some places might be ruled out.'

*   *   *

Next day she took her work with her into church and stayed there most of the morning. One woman came in, walked around looking at things, sat in a pew in the side aisle a few minutes, then left—all without saying a word. Do I look too busy to interrupt? Venus asked herself. Or have they nothing to say to me anyway? On the way out she saw Joe Hargreaves working in the churchyard.

'He's back again!' he said. 'I saw him in the High Street.'

'The tramp?' Venus asked.

'That's right. I've seen no signs of him in the churchyard, but we will. You mark my words!'

'It's getting rather cold to be sleeping rough,' Venus said.

'Oh, these people don't feel the cold,' Joe said.

After lunch—it was an unusually free day, no funerals, no bereavement or sick visits—she went to see Bertha Jowett. Bertha was in bed, not up and dressed, sitting in the armchair, as she usually was. She called out, though in a husky voice, the moment Venus stepped into the room.

'Oh, it's you! I thought you must have left the country.'

'Oh dear!' Venus said. 'Is it so long since I was here? I am sorry!'

'I'm sure you've had better things to do,' Bertha Jowett said.

'Not at all,' Venus said. 'Not necessarily better, but I have been a bit busy.' It was unlike Bertha Jowett to sound so affronted, but, from the sound of her voice, she wasn't herself.

'Are you not well?' Venus asked.

'A stupid cold. On my chest. They insisted on calling the doctor though I told them it was quite unnecessary. She said I had to stay in bed for a couple of days. Your Doctor Sonia, that was. I'd have thought she'd have had more sense.'

'I expect it's just a precaution,' Venus said. 'Perhaps you won't be in bed for long.'

Bertha gave her a disgusted look. 'I should hope not. Anyway, that's enough about me. Where have you been all this time? And I hope now that you are here you can stay longer than five minutes.'

Oh dear, she is disgruntled, Venus thought. 'As a matter of fact,' she said, 'I can stay long enough to have a game of Scrabble. That's if you're up to it, of course, but if you'd rather not . . .'

'Of course I'm up to it,' Bertha Jowett interrupted. 'There's nothing wrong with me except a bit of a sore chest. So let's get on with it!'

Venus fetched the box from the cupboard and laid out the board on the bed table. 'Are you sure you're well enough?' she asked.

'I've told you I am,' Bertha Jowett said impatiently.

But she was not quite up to it, Venus soon discovered. She was not her usual brilliant self at the game. She missed several chances although, it came to light afterwards, she had the necessary tiles in her hand. Even so, she won the game, though by a much smaller margin than usual, and was clearly triumphant at doing so.

'Why do you always win?' Venus complained.

'Because I'm a better player than you are,' her opponent said, grinning.

'Shall we have another?' Venus offered.

To her great surprise, Bertha shook her head. 'Not at the moment,' she said. 'I'm a bit tired.'

'Shall I leave you to have a nap?' Venus asked.

'No! No!' Bertha Jowett was emphatic. 'I've got all the time in the world for napping. Tell me what's been happening in the village, or even in the church. I don't hear a thing, stuck in here.'

'Well, we've got a new Treasurer,' Venus said. 'You did know about George Phillipson, of course.'

Bertha nodded. 'So what's the new one like?'

'I'm sure he'll be very competent,' Venus said. 'He's done the job before, in his previous parish.'

'But? There's a "but" in your voice. You don't like him, do you?'

Venus hesitated, but not for long. Bertha Jowett was a woman who somehow got the truth out of one, possibly because she asked direct questions. 'Not a lot,' she said.

'There you are,' Bertha Jowett said. 'That's what the church is like. It always was. A load of Christians, supposed to love one another, and they can't even like each other!'

'I hope that's not totally true,' Venus said. 'But in any case I learnt a long time ago that it's easier to love than to like.'

There was a brief silence, then Bertha Jowett said, 'Yes, I think I can see that!'

'We're bidden to love one another,' Venus said. 'I don't recall anywhere where we're bidden to like. Just as well!

'My mother's in hospital,' she added, changing the subject. 'In The Larches. She's had a hip replacement.'

Bertha Jowett was all apologies.

'Oh, my dear,' she said. 'I'm sorry! No wonder you haven't had time to visit me! So how is she?'

'She's doing very well,' Venus said. 'She asked me to give you her best wishes.' She would

225

definitely not say how pleased her mother was to be living in Bertha's old house, certainly not in Bertha's present state of mind.

'Give her mine,' Bertha Jowett said. 'And to your father.'

'I will,' Venus promised. There was a pause, and then she said, 'There is another thing . . .' She was not sure Bertha Jowett was in a suitable mood to be asked, but she was going to do it anyway. She was going to ask everyone she could possibly think of. 'I wonder if I could ask you a favour?' she said.

Bertha Jowett raised her unkempt eyebrows. 'It's not often anyone asks a favour of me,' she said. 'So what is it?'

'Well,' Venus said, 'the church usually takes all the children to the pantomime in Brampton every year. It's our treat and we pay for them. This year we're very short of money so I've undertaken to raise enough to cover the outing. If I don't, then they won't be able to go. I'm asking everyone of good will whom I know to sponsor a child. I know it's a cheek to ask you when I know your view about the church, but I'm doing so all the same!'

Bertha Jowett frowned. She's going to send me away with a flea in my ear, Venus thought. Serve me right for asking.

'I might not hold with the church,' Bertha Jowett said, 'indeed you know very well I don't—but that doesn't mean I'd take it out on the children. Of course I'll sponsor one! How much will it cost?'

'I don't yet know. Possibly about twelve pounds at a matinee, including the bus or coach fare, and possibly an ice cream. Or it could be a bit more. I'll let you know.'

'In that case,' Bertha Jowett said, 'I'll sponsor

226

two children. I'll give you thirty pounds.'

'Oh, Miss Jowett, that's most generous of you!' Venus said. 'Thank you very much.'

'You needn't thank me,' Bertha Jowett said. 'And you might as well call me Bertha. There's no-one left who calls me Bertha. I reckon a visit to the pantomime will do the children more good than going to church! It'll certainly give them more pleasure. My parents used to take me every year when I was little. Aladdin, I liked best.'

A sudden thought came to Venus.

'Bertha,' she said, 'would you like to go with us? There'll be several adults going—paying for themselves, of course. It would be no trouble getting you there and back and you'd be very welcome!'

'Oh, I don't know about that,' Bertha said. 'I daresay I'm a bit too old for pantomimes.'

'No-one is too old for the pantomime,' Venus said. 'Think about it, and let me know. I'll drop in again in a week or so.'

CHAPTER SIXTEEN

'What are your plans for today?' Nigel asked Venus at breakfast. 'Or don't you have anything special?'

'I have quite a busy day,' Venus said. 'I plan to catch up on my sick visits. I've fallen behind on them, both house ones and visits to the hospital. I don't like to do that. And then later this afternoon I shall pop in to see Mum, since she's going home tomorrow. Pack up her things, and so on.'

'She's done well, hasn't she?' Nigel said.

'She has,' Venus agreed. 'And she hasn't seemed to mind being in hospital, except for a few minor ups and downs. I expect Dad will be pleased to have her home.'

'And it's fortunate for her she has him,' Nigel observed.

The morning went much as Venus had expected. She had three house visits and two hospital visits, both of the latter at the NHS hospital in Brampton. When she had been the curate to Father Humphrey at Holy Trinity in Clipton she had done almost all of the sick visiting, especially of the elderly or chronic sick. Father Humphrey had saved himself for what he saw as the more important patients.

Of the two patients, both of them women, she was visiting at Brampton General the only one she knew reasonably well was Thora Bateman. The other one, Agnes Moore, had been the name on a piece of paper which someone had thrust at her on Sunday, two minutes before she was about to celebrate the Eucharist—not an ideal time to conduct a conversation—with a suggestion that she might like to be visited.

Venus knew nothing of Agnes Moore, or why she was in hospital, but of course she would visit her. She checked with the hospital and found that Agnes Moore was having a scan, so she would have to visit her another day. She could then spend however much time was needed with her. Thora Bateman she had always thought of as Miss Frazer's satellite. She was there to fetch and carry, obey commands, and generally worship at Miss Frazer's feet—if a satellite could be said to worship. It had therefore been inevitable that when

Miss Frazer had made her very public exit from St Mary's Thora Bateman would follow after her like a small devoted puppy, and this she had done, though whether she was devoted or merely frightened was open to doubt. Venus was pretty sure she had not wanted to defect. And now, a member of the congregation had informed Venus, Thora was very ill. She had cancer. Venus's hope and prayer as she went into the hospital was that she would not meet Miss Frazer at the bedside. That would be very difficult for Thora.

Venus's prayers were answered. It was well outside visiting hours and the only person not in bed in the ward, apart from two elderly ladies wandering around in dressing gowns, was a nurse, who was writing up notes at the desk. She looked up when Venus arrived, and was about to say something about these not being visiting hours when she noticed the clerical collar.

'I came to see Miss Thora Bateman,' Venus said. 'Would that be possible?'

'Oh yes! Yes, of course,' the nurse said. 'She is awake, but it would be better not to stay too long. She's really quite ill.' She escorted Venus to a bed around which the curtains were almost, but not quite completely, drawn.

'Thora,' she said. 'A visitor for you!'

Without raising her head from the pillow, Thora turned her head until her eyes met Venus's.

'Oh, Vicar!' she said. 'How nice!' Her voice was barely audible. Why wasn't I told before that she was so ill? Venus asked herself. If Thora had still been coming to St Mary's she would have been alerted by her absence from the services, but as it was she had had no idea. How quickly, she thought, people could be overlooked or forgotten if they dropped out of the usual routine.

'Hello, Thora,' Venus said. 'How are you?'

'Not very well at the moment,' Thora said. She tried to smile but it came out as a grimace. 'Who told you I was here?'

'Carla Brown,' Venus said.

Thora's eyes flickered and Venus smiled at her. They were both aware that if anyone knew who was where and what they were doing it would be Carla Brown, though in this case Carla had obviously not known how ill Thora was.

'I'm glad she did,' Venus added. 'And if I'd known earlier I'd have been here before this.'

'Thank you. I didn't like . . .' Thora's voice trailed away.

'Are you being well looked after?' Venus asked.

Thora's nod this time was almost imperceptible. She was too tired, Venus realised.

'I've brought Holy Communion with me,' she said tentatively. 'If you would like . . . But if not . . .'

She didn't know what the answer would be. Thora had, like Miss Frazer, left the church because she didn't approve of women priests, but whether that was her own opinion or Miss Frazer's Venus had never quite known.

'Yes please,' Thora said.

'Then I'll just tell the nurse, so that we won't be disturbed,' Venus said.

She did so. The nurse came and drew the curtains completely. Venus took out the small silver box with the consecrated wafers, and began the prayers.

'The bread of life,' she said. She put the wafer into Thora's mouth, judging that she would not

230

easily be able to raise her hands to her lips. Then she did what she had to do, and after that she gave a blessing. Thora, she thought, was conscious, but now perhaps only just. It was as if she had kept going just long enough for this. Venus said a final prayer and left quietly. 'I'll come and see you tomorrow,' she whispered. It seemed to her, though, that Thora's tomorrow would not be in Brampton hospital.

She went home saddened. She had never been able to take such visits as routine, to be dealt with then put aside when the next job came up. It was the same with funerals. With each one she felt as if she herself died a little, even though knowing that she would be resurrected. But why shouldn't I feel these things? she thought. Am I of more use if I stand outside them? She thought not. So back at home, for a quick lunch, her thoughts were very much with Thora. She would, as she had promised, call the hospital tomorrow and see what the situation was, though she felt she already knew.

In the afternoon she went to see her mother. It was a very different atmosphere there from Brampton General, not in any way that one hospital was better or more efficient than the other, she doubted that, but that her mother was up and dressed and full of cheer at the thought of going home on the next day.

'How have you been?' Venus enquired.

'I've been all right,' Mrs Foster said. 'I had a little altercation with the night nurse over my elastic sock, but I soon sorted that out.'

'Elastic sock? What in the world was that about?' Venus asked.

'Well, as you know, I have to wear them all the

231

time and if there's one thing I can't do it's see to my socks. I shall have to depend on you or Dad for a week or two for that.'

'Of course,' Venus said. 'So what happened?' Drama was not the first thing one thought of in connection with a sock.

'Well,' her mother said, 'the routine is that when the nurse changes them, each day, she washes out the dirty ones and hangs them in the bathroom to dry. This nurse couldn't find them, nor was I wearing any, and I knew I should be. "What have you done with them?" she asked me. She's a very bossy nurse, that one! "How could *I* have done anything?" I asked her. "I can't deal with them. I never touch them. So you'll have to get me another pair from somewhere, won't you?" And then what do you think she said to me?'

'I can't imagine,' Venus said. It was obviously of great importance. 'Do tell me.'

'She stood there, as bold as brass, and she said, "If I have to issue you with another pair of socks, Mrs Foster, you will have to pay for them. They will have to go on your bill."

'Well, you can imagine how I felt about that!' Mrs Foster said. 'When I think what it's costing to stay here! So I said, "You can charge me all you like, Nurse, but there's no way I'll pay! I wasn't the one who lost the socks!" So she stormed out. And I still had no socks on. Mr Conway wouldn't have been pleased! So you can be sure I'll scrutinise the account very carefully! Paying extra for socks someone else has lost! I never heard of such a thing! It's not what you'd expect in The Larches, is it?'

'Well, you can't say nothing ever happens,'

232

Venus said. 'But well done you! And now I'm going to help you to pack whatever you won't need between now and tomorrow afternoon. It will save time when I come to collect you. By the way, I had a word with Ethel Leigh and she said she'd be pleased to come in an extra two mornings a week until you get back on your feet.'

'I'm not sure I need her,' Mrs Foster said. 'I expect I can manage.'

'Well, I didn't make it definite,' Venus said. 'It's your house, after all. But Dad thought it was a good idea. Anyway, she'll drop in to see you. She could do your shopping, that might be useful. You know that's not Dad's favourite occupation. And the ironing. You'll find it difficult to do that.'

'Well, we'll see,' Mrs Foster said reluctantly.

*   *   *

When Venus arrived back at the Vicarage Becky was already home from school. She had lately, following an incident when she'd arrived home to a locked door and had, much to her disgust, had to wait around for fifteen minutes, been given her own key. Even so, Venus continued to make an effort to be at home when Becky arrived. It had always meant a lot to her that when she had been Becky's age her mother had made a point of being in when she came home from school. Times were different, of course. Not so many of her mother's generation had gone out to work, certainly not full time. 'Everyone in my class has their own key,' Becky had complained. 'All except me! And I *am* eleven! I'm not an infant.'

It was true, Venus thought. Her daughter was

233

growing up fast, though it seemed no time at all since she was a small girl. Now she was almost as tall as Venus herself. Next year she would be going to a new school, almost certainly travelling to Brampton. There would probably be lots of after-school activities and who knew what sorts of times she would arrive home. So she had been duly presented with a newly cut key, on a snazzy keyring.

'There was a phone call for you,' she said as Venus came in. 'It was from the *Brampton Echo*. What do you suppose they'd want?'

'I've no idea,' Venus said.

'I've written the number down,' Becky told her. 'The man said would you ring him back. His name is Tony Smithers.'

Venus took off her jacket, put the kettle on, and dialled the number.

'I'm the Vicar of St Mary's church in Thurston,' she said. 'Tony Smithers left a message to call him.'

She was put through at once.

'Thank you for calling back so promptly,' he said.

'What can I do for you?' Venus asked.

'I was ringing to ask if you'd let us come and interview you,' Tony Smithers told her. 'We like to interview people who live and work in the area. I don't think we've had the pleasure of speaking with you?'

'No,' Venus agreed. 'Do you often interview the clergy?'

'From time to time,' he said, 'but we've never had the opportunity of interviewing a woman vicar before.'

She had guessed, before the words were out of

234

his mouth, what they would be.

'I sometimes feel like some rare specimen in the zoo,' she said to Nigel later that evening.

'But you agreed to it?' Nigel asked.

'Oh yes!' she said. 'All for the good of the cause, one hopes! And I can more or less guess what he'll ask me. Why would I, a married woman, with a child, want to do such a job? And when he sees I'm pregnant, which he can't fail to see, he'll find it even odder.'

'But you don't mind?'

'Not a bit,' Venus said. 'Not if it gives me a chance to tell him why anyone, man or woman, would choose to be a priest.'

*   *   *

Next morning, not long after Nigel had left the house, Venus had a phone call from Sonia.

'Thora Bateman . . .' Sonia began.

'I saw her yesterday afternoon,' Venus said.

'The hospital phoned me,' Sonia continued. 'She died early this morning. They called me because she's down as having no next-of-kin and they knew I was her doctor. But I don't know any more than they do. I wondered if you might. She was one of yours, wasn't she?'

'Once she was,' Venus said. 'But not any longer. She left St Mary's. Poor Thora! No next-of-kin. No-one to mourn her. Doesn't it sound terrible?'

'I agree,' Sonia said. 'She never mentioned anyone to me—but then, people don't necessarily talk to their GPs about their family.'

'Especially if they don't have one,' Venus said. 'I suppose she must have a solicitor. Henry Nugent might know. Should I ask him?'

'Would you?' Sonia said.

Miss Frazer would be the one who would know, Venus thought when she had rung off, but it would be useless for her to try to get anything out of Miss Frazer. Henry might do so, or know who would. She rang him at once.

'He's taken the dog for a walk,' his wife said. 'He usually does at this time of day. Shall I ask him to phone you? He shouldn't be long.'

'Yes please,' Venus said.

She put the phone down. She was so glad she had seen Thora yesterday. She might well have put it off for another day or so, she hadn't known it was critical, and perhaps it hadn't been at the time she'd been informed. She hoped she had brought her some comfort.

Ten minutes later Henry phoned. 'Molly said you wanted me.'

'That's right,' Venus said. She gave him the news. 'You've known Thora much longer than I have. Do you know anything about her affairs?'

'Very little,' Henry said. 'She never talked much about herself. But it so happens that I do know her next-door neighbour, Brian Carter. Perhaps you and I could go around and have a word with him?'

'Good!' Venus said. 'I'll pick you up in five minutes.'

Mr Carter, and also his wife, did indeed know Thora Bateman very well. They had been neighbours for twenty-five years. He was aware, he said, that she had no relatives. Hers had been a small family of which she and a cousin, Ivy, had been the last survivors, and Ivy had died two years ago. She had left Thora her house, and a small

236

legacy, so Thora had consulted him about seeing a solicitor.

'I recommended Fairmile & Fairmile,' he said. 'They're my solicitors. I know they looked after her because she told me so, thanked me. Shall I give Charlie Fairmile a ring? He'll know what to do.'

Henry looked at Venus.

'Yes, I think so,' she said. 'Who else is there? There'll be procedures to be gone through and they'll know what they are.'

Fairmile & Fairmile were very helpful.

'Oh yes,' Charlie Fairmile said. 'She left everything in order—a will, and a letter with her wishes. She made us executors.'

What Thora Bateman's letter said, among other things, was that she wished to be buried in St Mary's churchyard, and what her will said was that she wished her money to go to St Mary's church. It was a useful sum, several thousand pounds.

'The thing is,' Venus said to Henry, 'she wrote that letter and made that will before I came to Thurston. Would she still want her money to go to St Mary's? She had left the church.'

'It's all legal and binding,' the solicitor said. 'She made no later will and she never rescinded the letter. Perhaps it remained exactly what she wanted to do.'

'You know, Venus,' Henry said, 'I don't truly think Thora Bateman had a thing against you; nothing at all. She was influenced by Miss Frazer to leave St Mary's, it wasn't really you. You must know that.'

In her heart, Venus thought she did. Thora had never been rude to her. On the few occasions they had met by chance in the village since, she had been embarrassed, but never unpleasant. And yesterday, she thought, she had seemed pleased to see her and she had had no compunction about taking Holy Communion from her.

'So we'll do whatever's necessary,' Charlie Fairmile said. 'I'm sorry to hear about Miss Bateman. She was a nice lady.'

When they left the solicitor's office Henry said, 'Will you come back and have a cup of coffee with Molly and me? You look as though you could do with it.'

'I'd like to,' Venus said. 'I'd very much like to, but I can't. I have a reporter coming from the *Brampton Echo* to interview me.'

'Fame at last!' Henry said.

* * *

Tony Smithers was tall and thin, with ill-assorted features which nevertheless combined in such a way as to make him attractive. He had a shock of unruly sandy-coloured hair and he looked very young indeed.

'Please come in,' Venus said.

She showed him into her study, a small room which faced the street. The back of the house, facing on to the garden, was the private part, for family and friends. In any case, the study seemed the most appropriate place if he was going to ask her about her work—which she assumed he was. She could think of nothing else to talk to him about which would be of interest to the readers of the *Brampton Echo*, nor was there anything else in her life which need concern them. It was not that she was hostile, she wasn't in the least, but she did want

238

the interview to be on her terms.

He seemed very shy. They exchanged pleasantries about the weather, which was fine, though, they agreed, it looked as though it might rain later. He admired the room, told her that he didn't know Thurston as well as perhaps he ought to, and then, since he seemed not to know quite how to start the interview, she did it for him.

'And how long have you lived in this area, Mr Smithers?' she asked. 'I mean, you say you don't really know Thurston.'

'That's quite true,' he said. 'And I've not been around here long. In fact,' he confided, 'I'm fairly new to the job.'

I could have guessed that, Venus thought.

'Have you been in Thurston long, Mrs Baines?' he asked.

'Not really,' Venus said. 'About eighteen months. I came here from Clipton. I was the Curate at Holy Trinity there, under Father Humphrey. Do you know it?'

He shook his head. 'I'm afraid I don't go to church,' he said—then quickly added, 'not that I've anything against it, of course.'

'If that's an apology, please don't,' Venus said, smiling. 'And if I had a fiver for every person who's apologised to me for not going to church I'd be able to take a world cruise.'

Her words, as she'd intended, seemed to break the ice. 'So what do you want to know?' she asked.

'Well,' Smithers said, 'almost anything you're willing to tell me. About your family; about your work, why you wanted to be a priest. Whatever.'

How could I explain to this young man why anyone wants to be a priest, Venus thought, let

239

alone why nothing else in the world will do? How could he understand the persistent calling, the compulsion—and sometimes, in bad moments, the running away from—which comes before taking the final step and perhaps right up to the moment of taking the final step? And in the end, when it's happened, the knowledge that you now are where you were meant to be.

'I just knew,' she said in the end. 'Did you always want to be a reporter?'

'I always wanted to work on a newspaper, but I want to be an editor,' he said. 'I don't want to stay a reporter.'

'Well, there you go,' she said. 'But I'm happy to stay as a parish priest. I don't want to be a bishop, even if I could be.'

'So what about your family?' he asked eventually.

'I'm married to a doctor,' Venus said. 'He shares a practice in the village. I have an eleven-year-old daughter, Becky, who goes to the local primary school. She is my daughter by my first husband, who died.' She knew he had noticed that she was pregnant, so she put him out of his misery: 'And yes, my husband and I are expecting a baby, in fact we're expecting twins, in the New Year.'

'Congratulations,' he said. 'Can I quote that?'

'I don't see why not,' she told him. 'I don't think it's any longer a secret—and certainly it couldn't be for long. And that's all I can tell you about my family, unless you'd like to know that my parents now live in Thurston. So shall we move back to my job?'

'Certainly!' he said. 'And you'll excuse me, won't you, if I write all this down.'

'Of course!'

'So what exactly do you do, Mrs Baines? I know you must take services on Sundays, but what else? For instance, apart from me taking up your time, what else will you do today—or any other day?'

'As a matter of fact,' Venus said, 'most people think that taking the Sunday services, and the odd wedding or funeral as required, is the sum total of what a parish priest does, but it's actually not like that at all. Of course, presiding at the Eucharist on Sundays—and other days—is at the heart of what I do, but there's a lot flows out from that.'

'Such as what?' Smithers asked. 'You must excuse my ignorance but I really know nothing about it.'

'Did your heart sink when your boss asked you to interview me?' Venus asked.

'As a matter of fact, it did,' he admitted.

'Poor old you!' she said. 'Well, I'll try to make it easy. Ask me whatever you like and I'll try to answer. And I'll kick off, as you suggested, by telling you what I did yesterday, and this morning, and what I'm likely to do the rest of the week.'

In the end he said, 'Why do you do all this for people who don't necessarily come to church?'

'Because anyone who lives in St Mary's parish, which covers the whole of Thurston, is in my care. Every single person,' Venus answered. 'They might not want me, of course—probably many of them don't and never will, except when it comes to weddings and baptisms and funerals—but I'm here for them whatever it is and whoever they are. They don't have to be Christians, or indeed of any faith. I daresay most of them aren't. I meet people where they are. They don't have to adapt to me. I expect

241

you have to do the same in your job?'

He looked pleasantly surprised at that. 'As a matter of fact, I do,' he admitted. 'But then, I don't have to give people advice—and I'm sure you must be expected to do that.'

'I say whatever seems right, and the truth, at the moment, and for them. Often I can only talk about practical things because that's what they need.'

He wrote it all down, asked several more questions, all of which she answered as well as she could. 'Though I certainly don't have the answer to all things,' she said. He was a nice young man, she thought, and obviously trying to do a good job.

'Would you be agreeable to me sending a photographer around to take some pictures?' he asked. 'We usually do that.'

'Of me, if you must,' Venus said. 'Though not of my family. You must respect their privacy.'

'Oh I will, Mrs Baines,' he assured her. 'Could the photographer come tomorrow?'

'He could come in the morning,' Venus said. 'In the afternoon I'm bringing my mother home from hospital.'

'I'll speak to him as soon as I get back and ring you with a time,' Smithers said. 'And thank you very much for your time today.'

'So it wasn't too bad, was it?' Venus said.

'No,' Smithers said. 'It was easy. And I learnt a few things.'

CHAPTER SEVENTEEN

The photographer, name of Rodney Marsh, rang later that day and made an appointment for nine-thirty the following morning. He was on the Vicarage doorstep on the dot. Venus wished she'd had time to have her hair done, then told herself not to be silly. She wasn't meant to be glamorous; it didn't go with the job.

She quickly lost count of how many photographs he took: standing by the sink; sitting at her desk in the study; at least half-a-dozen in the garden, which to her chagrin was not at its best. Then he said, 'I'd like to take one with the church as a background. That would seem appropriate. Would you mind if we walked up to the church?'

'Of course not! I was going to do so as soon as you'd left,' Venus said, 'so it would fit in perfectly well.'

Joe Hargreaves broke off his work and watched with interest as Venus and the photographer walked towards him up the church path.

'Good-morning, Joe,' Venus said. 'This is Mr Marsh. If you hang around long enough you might get your photograph taken for the *Brampton Echo*.'

'Well now,' Joe said, 'that would be something!'

'Then perhaps I'll take one of you on the way out, talking to the Vicar,' the photographer said.

He posed Venus in front of the church door, which at the moment was locked. 'Wait a minute,' Venus said. 'Let me open the door. A church door closed gives the wrong message.'

She unlocked it, opened it wide, then stood in

the doorway, as requested.

'Perfect!' Rodney Marsh said. 'You're a natural.'

'It would be nice if you *would* take one of me talking to Joe,' she said. 'It would make his day.'

'No problem,' he said.

It was clear to Venus when they joined Joe that he had been tidying himself up. His trousers were hitched up, his jacket was fastened. She could have sworn that he had combed his hair.

'Right!' the photographer said after he had taken at least half-a-dozen snaps of the two of them supposedly discussing the length of the grass. 'That's all fine! Thank you very much.' Then he called back as he was leaving, 'The article should be in the paper the weekend after next. You'll be sent a copy, Mrs Baines.'

'I shall order one from Bob Chester,' Joe said to Venus. 'He might sell out in the circumstances.'

'Well, yes,' Venus agreed. 'I expect all your fans will want to buy one!'

She went back into the church and sat in a pew. She had hardly started on the work she had brought with her, which on this occasion was notes for next Sunday's sermon, when Connie Phillipson came in.

'Good-morning, Vicar,' she said. 'I thought I might find you here.'

'I'm often here,' Venus said. 'Did you want me for something special?' Connie, she thought, didn't look her usual self, not by a long way. She had never known her all that well but whenever she had met her with George she had been nicely dressed, though not in the height of fashion. She had been a neat and tidy woman whose appearance said she looked after herself. Today she was not at all like

244

that. Her hair was a mess, her suit crumpled. Her face was pale and she wore no make-up.

'Not really special,' Connie said. 'I just had to get out of the house. I was dealing with George's clothes—he had such a lot, he was rather a dressy man.'

He was a bit of a dandy, really, Venus thought.

'He was fussy about what he wore. Everything had to match,' Connie said. And then she was silent, as if she'd run out of things to say.

'Did you want to ask me something?' Venus prompted.

'No. I mean . . . I don't know. I was just dealing with his clothes. Not only his suits. His shirts, his socks, shoes . . . and his pipes. He had a lot of pipes. He knew he shouldn't smoke, but he did. It was the smell of his pipes! I used to like the smell of his tobacco in the evening. He always had a smoke after supper.' She ran out of words.

'I know what you mean,' Venus said. She did too. After Philip had died it had been the little things which had upset her; coming across them suddenly, face to face with the memories they brought.

'I couldn't go on sorting things,' Connie said. 'I just couldn't. I had to get out of the house. You must think I'm stupid.'

'Not stupid at all,' Venus said. 'It's normal.'

'But I have to get on with it because David Wainright has offered to take me down to the Hospice shop tomorrow. Day after day I've been putting it off, and now I can't any longer.' Her voice rose. Tears filled her eyes.

'Would you like me to give you a hand?' Venus asked.

Connie gave her a blank look.

'I mean with sorting things. Folding them, packing them. I know what's to be done. Then you'd have them all ready when David came.'

'You mean you'd come and do it?' Connie asked.

'No, I won't do it,' Venus said. 'That's to say, I won't do it on my own. We'll do it together. You wouldn't feel right afterwards if you'd left it all to me. I could come today early after lunch. It will have to be early because I have to collect my mother from the hospital later.'

'Oh, Vicar!' Connie said. 'It's so good of you!'

'Shall we say two o'clock then? And George always called me Venus.'

When Connie left, Venus stayed in church until it was time to go home and grab a sandwich. No-one else had come into the church but she told herself that that was to be expected. The summer weather was over so there were fewer visitors about. Some might say she had been wasting her time, but on the other hand there had been Connie, and that was important. She didn't think Connie would have made her way around to the Vicarage.

As she was locking up it occurred to her that she would take a look around the back of the church. She hadn't done so for several days. She walked up the side of the church, in between the gravestones since there was no path, then, the moment she turned the corner to the back of the church it was clear that the tramp had been again. Here was the usual detritus. Food wrappings, tissues, a cardboard soup carton she recognised as having come from the new delicatessen in the village. Not cheap. A newspaper with yesterday's date, an empty beer can, cigarette ends. Gingerly, she picked them up one by one and, holding them at arm's length, took them to the dustbin.

When she went back down the church path Joe was still at work.

'The tramp *is* back,' she said. 'I've just been around the back of the church. The usual rubbish, and he's obviously slept there. Did you know?'

'I told you he'd been seen in the village,' Joe admitted. 'I didn't know he'd been in the churchyard. I don't have the time to go round the back all that much.'

Well, she thought, it was a welcome variation on only having one pair of hands. And to be fair, it was probably true.

'It must be uncomfortably chilly,' she said, 'sleeping rough at this time of the year. And we've not come to the really cold weather yet. There ought to be somewhere better for him to spend his nights.'

'Oh, as I've told you before, Vicar, his sort don't feel the cold,' Joe said.

She walked home wondering what could possibly be done, but came to no conclusion.

*   *   *

After her sandwich she drove around to the Phillipsons' house. Normally she walked everywhere in the parish, partly for the exercise but much more because that was one of the ways she met people. It was important to be seen around, to pass the time of day, to be available—but today she was in a hurry. She planned to go straight from Connie's to The Larches. Her mother was due to leave at four-thirty and it would be unkind to keep her waiting even five minutes beyond that. She was so anxious to be back in her own home. Of course her father would willingly have done the job. He had offered, but Venus had said, 'No! You make sure you're back from your golf and that the heating's turned up. It's like a hothouse in The Larches and Mum'll feel it if the house is cold. And you can be ready with a cup of tea the minute we get in.'

'It will be lovely to have Mavis back,' her father had said. 'I have missed her.'

*   *   *

By the time Venus had parked her car outside the Phillipsons' house, Connie was opening the door. She looked as pale and drawn as ever. Venus, offering up a short, silent prayer, prepared herself for an uncomfortable visit.

'Have you had some lunch?' she asked Connie as she stepped into the hall.

'I had some soup,' Connie said.

'Good!' Venus said. 'Then shall we make a start? Where would you like to begin?'

'I think with the wardrobe in the bedroom,' Connie said. 'That's where I'd got to when I decided I couldn't do any more. You see, George and I had separate wardrobes. I wouldn't share his because I said it always smelled of tobacco and it would make my clothes smell. I wish now I hadn't said it!'

'It was a perfectly reasonable thing to say,' Venus told her. And when Connie slid back the doors of George's wardrobe and the smell of tobacco hit them like a thick cloud, she thought it

248

was even more justified. 'Are there any of these things you would like to keep?' she asked.

'Not really,' Connie said. 'Not his clothes. I expect some of them will need cleaning.'

'I think you'll find the Hospice shop does that before they put them on sale,' Venus said. 'Shall we start at one side and work through to the other? Perhaps if you were to lay a clean sheet over the bed we could put them straight on to that, then sort them out and fold them.'

They worked together, Venus trying to keep up some sort of a conversation but Connie hardly speaking, until the wardrobe rails were emptied except for a few odds and ends, which they both agreed would be better to go to a jumble sale than to the Hospice shop. 'But there's not a lot for the jumble,' Venus said. 'George had some nice clothes.'

'He was always well turned out,' Connie said. 'It was one of the things which attracted me when we were young.'

When it was done, Connie fetched two large suitcases down from the attic and between them they packed everything into them. 'There you are!' Venus said. 'All David Wainright has to do now is pick them up and take them to the shop. Remind him you want the suitcases back.'

'I don't suppose I shall have much use for them now,' Connie said. 'We used to enjoy our holidays.'

There was no easy answer to that, Venus thought. No-one had been able to give her one at the time she needed it. It had only been when her mother had pointed out that Becky could do with a holiday that she had made a move.

'I expect we could both do with a cup of tea,' she

said now. 'I know I'd like one before I have to go to The Larches.'

'Oh, yes, of course!' Connie said. 'I should have thought of it! I'll make one right away.'

'And in the meantime,' Venus said, 'I'll take these suitcases down into the hall.' She particularly didn't want them to stay in the bedroom all night, a reminder that George was, so to speak, finally leaving.

*   *   *

Her mother was ready and waiting, sitting in her hat and coat although there was no way she was going to walk even a yard out of doors. Her holdall was on the floor beside her chair, her handbag clasped tightly in her hands.

'I'm not late, am I?' Venus asked.

'Not at all, love,' Mrs Foster said. 'But you know me. I like to be on time; I don't like to keep anyone waiting. "Punctuality is the politeness of kings!" my Dad used to say. And the ambulance will be here in fifteen minutes.'

She'd been surprised when they'd said she'd have to travel home lying in an ambulance. She'd been walking quite well in her room and along the corridors. But, they said, it was too soon for her to be travelling in a car. They would take her on a stretcher and a nurse would travel with her in addition to the ambulance driver. At first, she hadn't liked the idea, but when she'd come to think about it it had seemed quite a splendid way to arrive home, descending from an ambulance and with a nurse in attendance.

'I'll take your bits and pieces,' Venus said. 'And

250

once you're in the ambulance, I'll set off in my car. I'll be home before you, but in any case Dad will be there. He's so looking forward to having you back.'

'I'm looking forward to it,' Mrs Foster said. ' "No Place Like Home", as the song says.'

'Have you done everything you're supposed to do?' Venus asked. 'Signed everything you're supposed to sign?'

'I've done all that,' her mother said. 'I asked to look at the bill—they'll send it on in a day or two. I wanted to check that they hadn't charged me for those socks.'

'And had they?' Venus asked.

'No. And if they had, I'd have had something to say! As a matter of fact, I've never set eyes on that nurse since. I think she's been keeping away from me.'

*   *   *

Everything was in order for the homecoming. The heating had been turned up, the gas fire had been switched on for extra warmth, the tray was laid for tea. Ernest Foster was at the window, watching out for the ambulance. The minute it was in sight he rushed to the door, and when his wife came in, walking with her elbow crutches, as well as he could, he gave her a hug.

'Oh, Mavis love!' he said, 'it's lovely to have you home.'

'It's lovely to be home, Ernest,' his wife said. She looked around the room with approval. Everything looked clean and shining, though she suspected that was Ethel Leigh's work rather than her husband's. Nevertheless, let him take the credit if

251

he wanted to.

'I'll switch the kettle on,' he said. 'You'll be ready for a cup of tea. What about you, Venus? Have you time to stop for one?'

'Yes please,' Venus said. 'And I'd like to ring Becky, make sure she's home. She won't have gone to Anna's because Anna had an appointment with the dentist.'

'Ask Becky to come round here,' Mrs Foster said. 'Tell her her grandma would like to see her.'

Becky was there within ten minutes.

'It's lovely to see you,' her grandmother said. 'You're looking very bonny.'

'Thank you!' Becky said. 'It's nice to see you. I came top in maths today.'

'Well then, you must take after your Grandad,' Mrs Foster said. 'He was always good at figures.'

'Can I have a go with your crutches?' Becky asked.

'Why not?' her grandmother said. 'I was going to say they'd be too tall for you but I'm not sure about that. I've got short legs and I'm sure you've grown while I've been in hospital.'

Becky took the crutches from where they were lying against her grandmother's chair, swung skilfully around the room with them and into the hall, then came back with one leg tucked up against her as if she had lost the use of it.

'Super!' she said. 'Can I go outside with them? Just for a bit.'

'Certainly not!' Venus said. 'They're not toys! And they don't belong to Grandma; they have to be given back.'

After tea, which Becky drank while manoeuvring the crutches, Venus said, 'Well if there's nothing

252

more you want me to do right now, Becky and I had better be going. Nigel will be back from his visits—and he doesn't have a surgery this evening. Will you be all right, Mum?'

'Of course I will,' her mother said. 'I've got Dad, haven't I?'

Since Venus had the car, they were home in little more than five minutes. Missie barked loudly at the sound of them, a bark half welcoming and half reproachful. Becky ran from the car and let herself in with her own key. Missie was jumping up at her even before she was over the threshold.

'Poor Missie!' Becky said. 'She's been on her own for hours!'

'Oh, no, she hasn't,' Venus contradicted. 'I gave her a very quick walk at lunchtime and Nigel said he would stop off in between his visits and let her into the garden. I'm sure he'll have done so.'

'Well, yes,' Becky conceded. 'Nigel *always* keeps his promises.'

Quite what that meant, Venus wasn't sure, and decided not to ask.

'I should have taken her with me to Gran's,' Becky said.

'I don't think Gran's quite ready for a boisterous dog,' Venus said. 'Give her another day or two.'

'If I were to break my leg,' Becky asked, 'would I have to have crutches like Gran's?'

'I daresay you would,' Venus said. 'But would it be worth it?'

'I was only saying *if*!' Becky said. 'Shall I take Missie out for a walk now?'

'Well, all right,' Venus said. 'But only a short one. And not on the Downs. Keep to the village.'

Becky had been gone no more than ten minutes

when Nigel arrived home.

'Hello, darling! You're nice and early,' Venus said. 'Have you had a good day?'

'Busy,' Nigel said. 'But that's not unusual, is it? What about you?'

'Also quite busy,' Venus said. 'I went to collect Mum this afternoon. She was glad to be home. I don't think The Larches was her favourite place in the world, at least not in the last week. But she's OK.'

'You look tired,' Nigel said.

'I am tired,' Venus admitted. She patted her stomach. 'These two are getting quite heavy,' she said. 'I'll be glad when they're out in the real wide world.'

'Sit down,' Nigel ordered. 'Would you like a cup of tea?'

'No, thank you,' Venus said. 'I feel as though I'm swimming in tea. But if the doctor would allow me a small glass of wine, I'd very much like that.'

'A very small one, then,' Nigel said. He poured her a half glass of red wine and handed it to her. 'And since I'm not pregnant,' he said, 'I'll join you.' He sat down in the armchair opposite to her and stretched out his long legs in front of him. 'Bliss!' he said.

'Make the most of it,' Venus said. 'If Becky isn't back with Missie in a quarter of an hour or so it might be a good idea to go and meet her. I told her to keep to the village. I'll make the meal as soon as she's back.'

'I'll tell you what,' Nigel said. 'Why don't we treat ourselves, go out for a meal, the three of us? We could go to the Chinese—or wherever.'

'That sounds a wonderful idea,' Venus said.

'I'm on call, of course,' Nigel said. 'But the Chinese is quite near.' It was not unusual when either he or Sonia had not taken the evening surgery that they would then be on call afterwards. It seemed to work well between them.

Fifteen minutes later, as Nigel was about to set off to meet her, Becky arrived.

'Hi!' he said. 'We were just talking about going out for a Chinese meal—but I daresay you'd rather stay at home with Missie?'

Her face fell. 'You wouldn't leave me behind?' she said. 'You wouldn't! You know I just love Chinese!'

'Of course we wouldn't!' Venus said. 'You know he's teasing. So now that Missie's had her walk, why don't you give her her supper, then we'll go.'

It being a week night, the restaurant was not busy, though several tables were occupied. It was a popular place, sometimes too popular for Nigel because he was recognised, and there were always those who would treat any place where they happened to come across him as an extension to his surgery. Venus did not suffer to the same extent because, although by now she was well known, no-one seemed to want to bring spiritual problems to her in a restaurant. Church, or the privacy of one's own home, was the place for that. Nigel, recognising one or two people, smiled and nodded, and made for a table as isolated as possible. It was not that they were not perfectly nice people; he just didn't want to know about their ailments this evening.

The three of them each studied their menu intently, Becky especially. She read every item, though what she would choose in the end, all three of them knew, would be what she always chose.

'I would like . . .' she said eventually, 'spare ribs, and then crispy duck. With noodles, please. And after that apple fritters, or perhaps pineapple fritters, I can't decide which.'

'You could have one of each,' the waitress suggested.

'Wait until you've eaten your duck,' Nigel said, 'and then decide. You might not want anything else.'

'Oh, yes, I will!' Becky said. 'I'm not going to miss anything.'

'Spoken like a true daughter of your mother!' Nigel said. 'What are you going to have, darling?' he asked Venus.

'I've not decided,' Venus said. 'There's such a choice.'

In the end, they decided, and were served. The conversation at the table was not about medicine and patients or church and congregations, but teachers and pupils of St Mary's Primary School came into it a great deal. Thankfully, Venus thought, Becky now seemed happy there. She had long got over the handicap of being the Vicar's daughter.

'Another two terms,' Venus said, 'and you'll have to move on to Brampton Grammar—or wherever. What will you think about that?'

'Oh, that'll be all right!' Becky said. 'A whole lot of us will be going. And Anna will be. They do all sorts of things there. Sometimes they go to the theatre—or even to London.'

'Sounds a doddle to me,' Nigel said.

They were halfway through their main course when his mobile rang. He took it out of his pocket,

256

and listened.

'I see!' he said. 'Yes, of course I'll come. Tell Adrian I'm on my way.' He turned to Venus. 'I'm sorry, love,' he said. 'I must go. I'll see you back at home, but don't wait up for me. I don't know how long I'll be.'

'Very well,' Venus said. She knew better than to ask him for any details.

He kissed Becky, saying, 'Enjoy your meal. You could have ice cream with your fritters if you wanted to.' And then he was gone.

Venus did wait up for him, in spite of what he had said. She could see that he was troubled and she wanted to be there when he came in. It was after midnight. Used though he was to crises, to being called out at any time, he looked unusually sad and troubled.

'Coffee?' she asked. 'Or would you like some soup? You missed your supper.'

'Coffee would be fine,' he said. 'I'm not hungry.'

She made coffee for both of them. They sat opposite each other, he on the sofa, she in her usual armchair, neither of them speaking. Eventually, Venus said, 'Was it bad?'

He paused, as if he couldn't find the words. Then he said. 'He died. Adrian died. In the end there was nothing I could do for him.'

'Except be there,' Venus said. 'Do I know Adrian?'

'He's the boy I told you about. He had leukaemia. In his case it was inevitable. He was an only son.'

'The boy you didn't want to tell?' she asked.

He nodded. 'His parents knew. They couldn't bear to tell him. They couldn't give up hope. But

257

he wanted to know. In the end he asked me. And I told him. It was strange that he seemed to take some comfort from knowing, from not being kept in the dark.'

Venus rose from her chair and went to sit beside her husband. She took her hand in his, held it tightly. For a while they didn't speak, then he said, 'I don't understand why terrible things happen to people, people who don't deserve them—and don't happen to others.'

'Nor do I,' Venus admitted. 'And I'm expected to. But I don't.'

CHAPTER EIGHTEEN

Tuesday morning, and the ten o'clock Eucharist. The sky was like lead and the rain was falling in torrents. Would anyone turn up? Then Venus chided herself for even having had the thought. Of course they would. It was a remarkable thing about St Mary's that whatever the weather the numbers of the congregation remained the same, and that applied as much to the small weekday services as it did to the ten o'clock on Sunday mornings. She put on her raincoat, grabbed her umbrella from the stand in the hall, and set off.

Arriving at the church, she unlocked the door, shook the rain from her umbrella before parking it in the porch, then went into the vestry and shed her raincoat. She was in good time; she always tried to make sure of that because she liked to have a few minutes in hand to say her own prayers. At five minutes to ten the faithful few appeared. They were the same as always, no fewer, no more. They came in, plastic rainhoods on their heads, dripping umbrellas in their hands, quietly moaning about the weather. Mrs Prendergast, as always, was the last to arrive. She moaned louder than anyone else, as if the driving rain was a personal insult to her.

Venus wondered, not for the first time, why, though they remained so devoted to the Tuesday Eucharist, members of this congregation seldom set foot in church on Sundays, except on special occasions like Easter or Christmas. Today, as always, they would sit in exactly the same seats in the side aisle as they always occupied. This was the reason why, on weekdays, she celebrated at the small altar. It was more intimate: they were not lost in the size of the nave.

When she had vested—it was still the green stole of Ordinary Time, but in a few weeks now that would give way to the purple stole of Advent—she walked at an even pace to take her place before the altar.

'The Lord be with you!' she said.

Six separate voices from five separate pews—only two of the women ever sat together—answered, 'And also with you!' It was a short service, there was no sermon and to give communion to six people took very little time, but still she enjoyed it. It was somehow calming. As usual, little Miss Broome scuttled away as if she had a train to catch. The others bade Venus good-morning and said a few nasty words about the weather. Mrs Prendergast looked her up and down and said, in a jokey voice, 'I see you're carrying all before you, Vicar! Bearing your burden!'

My goodness, Venus thought, if it shows when

I'm wearing vestments what must I look like in ordinary clothes? And still four-and-a-half months to go!

'That's right, Mrs Prendergast,' she said, smiling amiably.

When they had braved the weather and left she went into the vestry and made herself a cup of coffee, which she drank before going back into the church and sitting in a pew halfway down the nave to do the work she had brought with her. This morning it was largely reading, which came in ever-increasing amounts from the Diocesan Office and other places and was not, on the whole, the least bit interesting, though it had to be read and, if necessary, replied to.

The rain was coming down harder than ever now, beating against the windows on the southwest side. It was the kind of rain which, when it came on a Sunday morning, was audible above the singing of the congregation and caused people's thoughts to stray to how they would get home afterwards without being drenched. Perhaps it didn't make sense, Venus thought as she sat there, to keep the church open on a morning like this. Was it worthwhile or sensible to be here just to give people shelter from the rain?

And then she heard someone enter. Her back was to him—she knew it was a man by the heaviness of his footsteps—but as he came closer it was the smell of him rather than the sound which assailed her. A sour, heavy smell, compounded, she reckoned, by his wet clothes.

His shuffling footsteps stopped short of her. For one moment—it was the fact that the footsteps had stopped—she recalled Miss Tordoff's warning words, 'Will you be safe, Vicar?' She turned around to speak to him.

'Good-morning!' she said. 'Not a very nice one, is it?'

The man raised his hand and pulled off a green-and-white knitted cap, with ear flaps, revealing thick, dark, curly hair—none too clean.

'Good-morning, Reverend!' he said.

His voice had the husky roughness of a man who caught one cold after another without ever being totally clear of them in between, but his accent was nowhere near rough. It was almost educated. As for his age, he might have been in his fifties, or it could have been his lifestyle—if his appearance was anything to go by—which had aged him prematurely, Venus thought. At the sight and sound of him all fear left her.

'My goodness, you are wet!' she said.

He wore a thin, beige jacket which had probably once been clean, and dark blue, baggy jeans. On his feet he wore sandals, not shoes. It was a long time since the sandals had seen better days, and now they were clearly leaking. There was a long trail of wet, muddy footmarks on the aisle, all the way from the door to where he now stood, dripping. She guessed at once who he was. He must be the tramp who dossed down behind the church.

'I am wet,' he said. 'I'm sorry about the footmarks.'

'That's all right,' Venus said. She wasn't sure that Amy Sedgwick, who made it her voluntary duty to keep the church floor clean, would see it quite like that. 'Are you the person who sleeps behind the church?' she asked.

'Sometimes I do,' he said cautiously. 'But not

261

always. I'm not always in Thurston.'

'But you have been here before?' she said.

'From time to time,' he admitted. 'I'm not one for going into churches, though they're all right when the weather's bad.'

'Yes, and I'm sure you're not the only one who thinks that way,' Venus said.

'No offence, Reverend,' he said. 'And it's a very nice church. I have been in here before because it used to be kept open during the day. I've sometimes, if it's been a bit cold out, had a bit of shut-eye in the back pew. I hope you don't mind.'

'Not at all,' Venus said.

'I was wondering . . .' He sounded suddenly nervous.

'Yes?'

'Do you think I could take my jacket off and hang it over the pipes to dry?'

'You can,' Venus said, 'but I shan't be here much more than an hour, and when I go I have to lock the church.'

'It didn't used to be locked,' he said.

'I know,' Venus told him. 'But we had things stolen.' She looked him straight in the eye. 'A pair of valuable candlesticks, for instance. Taken from the altar.'

For a moment he looked frightened. 'I didn't do it!' he protested. 'It was nothing to do with me! What would I want with candlesticks?'

'The feeling was that whoever had taken them would make a nice bit of money by selling them,' Venus said, watching his face as she spoke.

'Well it wasn't me, Reverend,' he assured her. 'I wouldn't steal from a church. I wouldn't dare to steal from a church. Bad luck, that would be!'

262

'What's your name?' Venus asked him.

'Lester,' he said.

'Is that your first name or your last?'

'My first name,' he said, without offering her his surname.

It was an upmarket name, she thought, for a tramp. 'Well, Lester,' she said, 'since you can't stay here for more than an hour or so, perhaps you'd better take your jacket off right away. It might get a little bit drier.' The pipes, she knew, were not all that hot, but there was a little residual heat left in them from the weekend.

He did as she suggested. The moment the wet jacket hit the warm pipes it gave off an even stronger smell. She held her breath for a second, then said, 'What about your shoes? They don't look all that good.'

He looked down at them ruefully. 'They're not,' he agreed. 'I don't suppose you'd have an old newspaper anywhere, would you?'

Venus struggled with her conscience. She had brought with her the portion of that day's *Times* which contained the crossword with the intention, when she took a break to eat the sandwiches which she had also brought, of trying to do the puzzle. It was something she attempted every day. Sometimes she completed it, sometimes she didn't, but the effort was as powerful as a drug.

'As it happens . . .' she said—then she paused, strengthened her resolve, and went on again '. . . I do have part of *The Times* with me. You can have that.' She handed it over to him and he went and sat in the front pew, where he took off his wet sandals.

She watched him from a distance taking off his

263

footwear, trying to dry it out as best as he could with the newspaper, then carefully crumpling up what was left and stuffing it down into the toes. She was pleased that he had put a distance between them. She had to stay in church, that was her bargain for keeping it open, but there were circumstances, and this was one of them, when she needed space between herself and a less hygienic visitor. Even if it wasn't his fault. It was at this point that she decided what she would do.

'As I said,' she told him, 'we shall both have to leave here soon after midday, I have a visit to make, but if you'd like to come back here at two o'clock, I might be able to do something about your shoes. What size do you take?'

'Size ten,' he said.

Damn! That was the first part of her plan gone awry. She had hoped to find him an old pair of Nigel's—the two men were of a similar height and weight, and might well take the same size in shoes, she had thought—but now that wouldn't do. Nigel took a smallish nine. Never mind, she would think of something else.

Still sitting at a distance from Lester, she called Nigel on her mobile, and explained the situation. 'Could you spare that awful old green anorak of yours?' she asked him. 'I've been telling you for ages it was time you threw it out.'

'I like it,' he protested. 'But all right, go on then. But don't you go raiding the rest of my things!'

* * *

At noon she opened her packet of sandwiches, took out half of them and took the rest to Lester. She felt the loss of the sandwiches much less deeply than she'd felt the loss of *The Times*. He ate them hungrily and then, when he heard her gathering her papers together, he put on his half-dry jacket.

The rain was falling less fiercely as they left. It had settled into a steady drizzle. The tramp, pulling on his woolly cap, seemed unabashed by it.

'Well then,' Venus said, 'I'll see you back here, just after two.' When she left him at the lych gate she wondered what he would do with himself in the interim, where he would go. She herself made her way to the shoe shop in the village.

'I want to buy a pair of good, strong boots, Mr Corson,' she said. 'Waterproof. Size ten.'

He gave her a strange look. He knew she took a six; he knew the sizes of all his regular customers.

'Men's,' she said.

He also knew Doctor Baines took a size nine.

'Don't ask me, Mr Corson!' Venus said. 'Just don't ask me! Not unless you want to get me into trouble!' She doubted that what she was about to do would be approved of.

'I wouldn't want to do that,' Mr Corson said. 'Not at any price. Black or brown?'

'Doesn't matter,' Venus said. 'Strong, watertight, comfortable.'

He went into the back room and came out carrying a pair of brown leather boots.

'You're lucky, Vicar,' he said. 'This pair was about to go into my next sale—thirty per cent off!'

She didn't believe him for a minute. The season for strong, waterproof boots was right now. 'That's very kind of you, Mr Corson,' she said. 'And while I'm at it I'd better take a couple of pairs of thick socks.' Heaven knew what state Lester's socks were

265

in.

Then as she was leaving the shop, she turned back.

'Mr Corson,' she said, 'this purchase is strictly between you and me!'

'Of course it is,' he said solemnly. 'Why would I want to tell anyone that the Vicar bought a pair of men's shoes in a size not her husband's?'

'I knew you'd understand,' Venus said. 'Thank you.'

He watched her as she walked away up the High Street. He wasn't a churchgoer himself, never went near the place, but he reckoned that in spite of the mixed feelings when she'd first come here—and of course he'd heard all about them, who hadn't?—she was one of the best things that had happened to Thurston.

Next, she hurried back to the Vicarage, collected Nigel's old anorak, then decided, since she was running out of time, to drive to her sick visit. Mrs Raby lived a mile or so outside the parish but when she was well she came regularly to the Sunday Eucharist. Mrs Raby, Venus had been told, would be on her own. She was to ring the bell, and walk in. Venus found her in a downstairs room, sitting up in a narrow bed.

'How nice to see you, Vicar!' she said. 'And only this morning your husband called! What a kind couple you are. Do you ever both turn up at the same place at the same time?'

'Never, so far!' Venus said. 'In fact it's seldom either of us knows who the other might be visiting.' She had known Mrs Raby was one of Nigel's patients, but no more than that.

'I'm especially pleased to see you,' Mrs Raby

266

said, 'because I don't know when I'll get to church. It's my heart, you see. Doctor Baines says I have to have a nice rest. I'm sitting up like this because it makes it easier to breathe.'

'Then you must do as the doctor tells you,' Venus said.

'Do you?' Mrs Raby enquired.

'He's not my doctor,' Venus said. 'Doctor Sonia looks after me. Not that I'm ever ill.'

'But now that you're pregnant?' Mrs Raby began.

'Doctor Sonia is looking after me very well,' Venus said.

'It will be nice having babies at the Vicarage,' Mrs Raby mused. 'We've never had that before. The old Vicar didn't even have grandchildren. And then there's your daughter. She's growing, isn't she?'

She chattered away. Venus felt sure she shouldn't be talking so much—she was clearly breathless—but nothing seemed to stop her. In the end—she had not intended to stay so long—she said, 'Well, I'll leave you to get some rest now. And I'll mention your progress in "This Week". People like to know. Let's hope you'll be back with us quite soon.'

'Oh, I'll be fine!' Mrs Raby said.

The words were brave, Venus thought as she left, but Mrs Raby looked ill and exhausted.

*   *   *

By the time she reached the church the rain had stopped. The tramp was waiting for her at the door. She unlocked it, and the two of them went in.

'Here you are,' Venus said. 'I've brought you an anorak which belonged to my husband. It's not new, but I reckon it's waterproof. And there's some boots, a sweater and a couple of pairs of socks. If I were you I'd change into them right now.'

'You're very kind, Reverend,' the tramp said. 'I didn't expect any of this.'

'That's all right,' Venus said. 'And another thing, Lester . . .' His face lightened as she addressed him by his name. '. . . I've phoned and booked you in the night shelter in Brampton for tonight. You'll get a good meal there and I reckon you could do with a good night's sleep in a dry bed—not to mention a hot shower! I've made the necessary arrangements, so you won't have anything to pay.'

'I'm very grateful,' Lester said. 'I don't know what I can do to thank you!'

'I do,' Venus said. 'Next time you sleep around the back of my church, you can clear up after yourself. That's something I don't enjoy.'

'I will! I will!' he promised.

'Well, God bless you!' she said.

He left shortly afterwards. She wondered where he would go, though she didn't ask him and he offered no information. She wondered what had brought him to this kind of life. He seemed reasonably intelligent, he was well-spoken and, if he was tidied up a bit, and decently dressed, he would be more than presentable. She watched him walk away down the path. When he got to the lych gate he turned around and waved, and she waved back at him. She felt sure that he would return at some time in the future, perhaps sooner rather than later.

Fifteen minutes later—she was ready to leave—

Connie Phillipson came into the church.

'I noticed the door was open so I thought you must be here,' she said.

'You've just caught me,' Venus told her. 'I was about to leave.'

'Oh, I'm sorry,' Connie said.

'No, don't be,' Venus said. 'I'm pleased to see you. How's everything?'

'I suppose I should say not too bad,' Connie said. 'It takes some getting used to. One minute someone is there, with you. The next he isn't and never will be. But you know the feeling. You were a widow when you first came here.'

Venus nodded. 'Yes. And in a way I felt terrible that I'd perhaps left Philip behind me by moving from Clipton and starting a new life here. But that particular feeling didn't last long. I knew he, of all people, would understand.'

'And then of course you met Doctor Baines,' Connie said. 'No disrespect, but I don't think I could do that. I couldn't put anyone else in George's place.'

'Oh, but one doesn't!' Venus said. 'It's not like that at all. Philip had his own place with me, and always will have. Nigel has another.'

'And you have Becky from your first marriage,' Connie said. 'George and I would have liked children, but it never happened.'

There was a short, though not uncomfortable, silence between them, then Connie said, 'Well, I won't keep you. I expect you're always busy.' She sounded envious. 'I just wanted to tell you that I'd taken all George's things to the Hospice shop. Or at least, David Wainright took me. It was very kind of him. He introduced me to the woman who runs it and she said she'd always be glad of help in the shop if I liked to give a hand, part-time of course.'

'That would be quite a good idea,' Venus said. What a pity, she thought, that she hadn't encountered Lester before Connie had taken all those clothes to the Hospice shop. He could certainly have made use of some of them.

'Yes,' Connie said. 'I shall consider it.'

They left the church together, then parted, Connie to Winterton's, to buy some tomatoes, Venus back to the Vicarage. It had started to rain again.

As she let herself into the warmth of her house she couldn't help thinking about Lester. Well, at least he would have a warm, dry place to spend this night. She was glad she had been able to provide him with some dry clothes. And then, as she went into the kitchen and put on the kettle to make a cup of tea, a thought came to her. She would phone Carla Brown.

Carla, though still passing herself off as nothing more than a reluctant churchgoer, had more or less put herself in charge of various bits of fundraising, one of which was running the annual jumble sale. Venus did not like jumble sales but, as several people had pointed out, they did raise money, and money was very much needed.

'Hi Carla,' Venus said. 'This is a cry for help, though not a very loud one.'

'Fire away,' Carla said. 'What can I do for you?'

'Jumble sale stuff. Clothes, footwear and so on. You do keep what's left over from one sale to the next, don't you?'

'My attic is full of it,' Carla confirmed. 'Can't move for it. Walter gets quite cross. Why? Are you hoping to replenish your wardrobe?'

'Not mine!' Venus assured her. 'I just wondered if you had any men's clothes. And footwear.'

'Don't tell me Doctor Nigel is on his beam ends, can't afford a new coat!' Carla said. 'I always thought doctors were well off.'

'Most people do,' Venus said. 'It's not true. But it isn't Nigel I have in mind. In fact, I don't have anyone special in mind, but it struck me that it wouldn't be a bad idea to keep back a jacket or two, a raincoat, a pair of wellies. I mean just in case someone were to come along who needed them.'

'Vicar,' Carla said, 'I can read you like a book! Moreover, I know just what you've been up to but I promise not to tell. I saw him—the tramp—walking down the High Street in a very untramp-like jacket and a pair of new boots. I didn't suspect you, I must say. I thought he must have robbed a bank.'

'So do you have anything suitable?' Venus asked. 'I don't mean just for him. I mean should the occasion arise.'

'And if he tells his friends there'll be a queue at the church door,' Carla said. 'Before we know where we are we'll be doling out bowls of hot soup. But actually, we get very few men's clothes. I think they refuse to part with them. It's the same with Walter; it's like trying to get blood from a stone.'

'But have you anything?' Venus persisted.

'One or two bits,' Carla confessed. 'And yes, you can have them. Where are you going to keep them?'

'At the Vicarage, I suppose,' Venus said. She hadn't thought so far.

'Then if some stray turns up,' Carla said, 'you're to phone me at once. You're not to see him on your

271

own. In fact it might be better if I were to keep them and you send him around to me.'

'If you say so,' Venus said. 'And if Walter agrees, of course.'

'Oh, Walter will agree,' Carla said confidently, 'as long as I promise not to give away anything of his. Not that I wouldn't like to do so. Some of his things are beyond the pale. Why do men cling to old clothes?'

'Goodness knows!' Venus said. 'Oh, and while we're on the phone, the pantomime tickets have been booked. Thanks for raising the money, Carla. I don't know how you do it!'

'Better not ask,' Carla said. 'Not that I've done anything illegal, of course. And it's always easier to raise money to give children a treat.'

The Sunday School's children's yearly pantomime visit went back a long way and had always been paid for by Miss Frazer—and before that by her father—as indeed they had always paid for the summer outing to Eastbourne. Those treats had been cut off abruptly as yet another protest at having a woman priest in St Mary's, and the money had had to be raised by other means. But raised it had been.

'I'm looking forward to *Aladdin*. I've never seen it. Have you?'

'Ages ago,' Venus said. 'It's wonderful, especially the bit where it goes into Aladdin's cave. All those treasures!' But *Cinderella* would be forever her favourite pantomime. It was the one they had taken the Sunday School children to last year, shortly after she and Nigel had become engaged, when they'd been so eagerly looking forward to the Bishop giving Venus final permission to marry. She had sat in the dress circle, Nigel on one side of her, Becky on the other, surrounded by children and friends. The whole evening had been pure bliss.

They chatted a little longer—Carla always had plenty to say—and then Venus heard Becky's key in the lock. 'Goodness!' she said. 'Is that the time already?'

'And I must go,' Carla said. 'There isn't much Walter won't do, but he doesn't like making his own tea.'

CHAPTER NINETEEN

October was not the ideal month for a holiday, Venus thought as she carried her suitcase down from the attic. It was three days before they were due to leave, on Saturday morning, but she liked to pack a bit at a time, throwing things into the case as they came to mind. Well-organised people, she was sure, made a neat packing list, laid out everything on the bed an hour beforehand, beautifully folded and in the right order, and ticked them off as they were put in the case. They never found themselves in a foreign country minus a toothbrush, or not knowing the Spanish for 'hair rollers'. They never took the wrong shoes.

She would have to take warm things, even for Devon. No point in taking a bikini at this time of the year. But of course, in her condition, she thought, catching sight of herself in the full-length mirror on the wardrobe door, there was no chance of wearing her bikini whatever the temperature. She sighed at her reflection. Would she ever regain

273

her figure? It had taken her some time to do so after Becky's birth; then she had put on more weight beforehand than she had wanted to, and with twins it was bound to take longer. But never mind all that, she was looking forward to them with growing excitement and love. If only she were not so tired, so much of the time!

It was because she was so consistently tired that Sonia had told Nigel he should take a few days off—he had days owing to him—and give Venus a holiday. 'For your own sake also,' she'd said. 'Believe you me, you'll need all your strength and energy once you're a father of two boys! And neither of you have had so much as a weekend away since your honeymoon.'

'But are you sure you can manage?' he'd asked.

'Absolutely!' Sonia had said. 'And if things get hectic I'll find a locum. Why don't you leave on Saturday—in any case it's my weekend on call—and come back the following Saturday?' So Nigel had discussed it with Venus and Venus had discussed it with the Blessed Henry, and he had said, 'Do go, my dear!' So everything had been arranged. That nice man, the Rural Dean, had found cover for her for the Sunday, and for both weekday Eucharists, and the churchwardens would take care of the rest. 'I suddenly feel as free as air!' Venus said to Nigel.

Devon had not been their first choice. They had wanted to go to Ireland, to Nigel's family, and his mother was dying to see them. 'She would look after you, spoil you rotten!' Nigel said to Venus. 'And Aunt Veronica would love us to be there.' But of course that had been impossible; Venus was too far into her pregnancy to fly. So Devon had seemed the next best choice. Nigel would drive. He had been there before, and had loved it; Venus had never been but she was sure she would, too.

Becky was not happy that she couldn't go with Venus and Nigel but, as Venus pointed out, there was no question of that; it was term time. Venus's parents were to stay at the Vicarage with Becky. Mrs Foster had recovered fully from her hip replacement. 'And even if I hadn't quite,' she'd said, 'there's your Dad. He'll help. You know how much we love looking after Becky. And being in the Vicarage will be like a little holiday for us.'

'And better for Missie,' Becky said, slightly cheered at the prospect of being spoilt by her grandparents.

She waved off Venus and Nigel early on Saturday morning and a little later, as a consolation, Mrs Foster took Becky and Anna Brent by taxi to Brampton to look at the shops and get rid of their pocket money. 'And we'll have a bit of lunch in Brampton, and get a taxi back!' Mrs Foster said. 'Spoil ourselves!'

'You do that, Mavis love,' Ernest said. 'And I'll take Missie for a long walk over the Downs. She'll like that!' And so would he, he thought. It was a beautiful day for the time of the year. And after his walk he would drop in at the Ewe Lamb and have a pint and a pie.

*   *   *

When Sunday morning came Becky said, 'Do I have to go to church, Gran? After all, I could have a bit of a holiday even if I can't go to Devon.'

'Indeed you do, young madam!' her

275

grandmother said. 'What would I say to your mother if you didn't go?'

'You could tell her I was very tired,' Becky suggested. 'It would be quite true. I'm always tired on Sunday mornings. If I rested more on Sunday I'd be fitter. No wonder I'm always too tired for school on Monday morning. It's all this churchgoing!'

'A good try, love,' Mrs Foster said. 'But it won't work. We shall go to church as usual, you, me and Grandpa.'

*   *   *

Worshippers at the ten o'clock Eucharist on Sunday were surprised, as they walked into church, to find a priest who was unknown to them. The Reverend Giles Smithers, who had moved into the area on his retirement, helped out (and thereby augmented his inadequate pension) by stepping into other pulpits and celebrating at other altars in times of need. He was a short, round, smiling man, but to a few, though by now it was only a very few of St Mary's congregation, whose opinions would never change, at least he *was* a man. He himself was surprised at the numbers turning up for the service. He couldn't flatter himself that they had come to see and hear him (though he had been a powerful preacher in his time) because they couldn't have known; he was there at short notice. They came in confidently, with the air of regulars, and, he also noticed, there was a good mix of ages, even one or two babies.

Henry, in his capacity as churchwarden, stood nearby, explaining, when it seemed necessary, that

276

Venus was taking a short holiday. 'Much overdue,' he said. 'She'll be back with us next Sunday.' Venus would have been chuffed, he thought, by the concern with which so many people asked after her.

The last notes of the church bell died away, the two young servers and the crucifer were waiting, the visiting priest looked at his watch. 'I'd better go in,' he said. Henry nodded assent. He would stay here for a few minutes, mopping up the latecomers. The short procession had just begun its walk down the aisle when a woman walked up the church path and into the building.

'Why, Miss Frazer!' Henry said. 'Good-morning to you!'

She ignored his greeting and went into the church, walking—Henry reckoned deliberately—just a yard or two behind the priest, as if she was an essential part of the procession. She wore a long velvet skirt, a short fur jacket and an important hat. As the procession climbed the three steps to the chancel she turned to the right and sat in the front pew. It was the place, as those who knew her of old were aware, where she had always sat, and reputedly her father before her. It was the place she had so conspicuously vacated soon after Venus had been appointed to the living. From the moment, in fact, when the Bishop had made it quite clear that the woman priest was here to stay and there was nothing Miss Frazer could do about it.

Insofar as it was polite, and amongst those who knew her, necks craned to look at her. Why had she come? Would there be another scene? She remained outwardly unmoved, singing the hymns and responses in her high, thin, elderly voice.

Henry Nugent knew exactly why she had come. It was because she had heard—the grapevine in Thurston was particularly efficient—that Venus was away. Well, he thought, Miss Frazer had better behave herself. He wasn't going to stand for any nonsense, particularly in front of a visiting clergyman.

She did behave herself. She stood and knelt in the right places—no-one knew better than she which these were—and joined the queue to take communion in an orderly manner, nothing untoward at all. But then, when she had taken the wafer, sipped the wine, instead of going back to her pew she marched purposefully, with measured tread and head held high, down the length of the aisle and out through the door, not waiting for the service to end. 'She's made her point,' Henry whispered to his wife.

'I'm glad Venus wasn't here,' Molly replied under cover of 'Praise God, From Whom All Blessings Flow'.

'Don't be silly, love!' Henry whispered back. 'If Venus was here, Miss Frazer wouldn't be! That's the whole idea!' He hoped no-one would take the trouble to inform Venus that Miss Frazer had been, but it was too much to hope for. She had also, he found out later, put a fifty-pound note in the plate, exactly as she had done on a similar occasion. It was a 'See what you're missing' gesture. Well, Venus didn't need to know about that, either.

There was plenty of talk about it at coffee after the service. 'What a cheek!' Carla Brown said. 'I'd like to have put my foot out and tripped her up! I could have too; I don't know why I didn't.' Connie

Phillipson explained to David Wainright—they both happened to be sitting at the same table— what Carla meant. He hadn't been there in Miss Frazer's time. His view, as Treasurer, though he didn't voice it, partly because Venus's parents were within earshot, was that it was a pity the Vicar had antagonised someone who gave so generously to the church.

Miss Frazer came again; in fact, she came to both the weekday Eucharists. So did Henry, though he didn't normally attend them—he was there this week in case the Reverend Giles Smithers should need him—and he was pretty sure Miss Frazer hadn't done so when she'd been part of St Mary's. She didn't approve of weekday services. She had been heard to say, more than once, that Sunday was the day for church, no need to go overboard, attending during the week. Also she did not approve of Holy Communion being available three times a week. It smacked of Rome.

On the Tuesday and the Thursday Henry kept an eye on her, but she behaved reasonably and, as at the weekday Eucharists no collection was ever taken, there were no more fifty-pound notes.

*   *   *

On the Thursday morning Henry had been about to leave for home after the service when, the door being open, the tramp came in. Henry had never spoken to him, but he had seen him in the village and now he guessed, both by his appearance and by the description other people had given him, who he was.

'Good-morning, sir,' Lester said politely.

279

'Good-morning,' Henry said. He was as surprised by Lester's voice and accent as Venus had been. 'I'm afraid I was just about to lock up.'

'I came to see the lady, the one whose church this is,' Lester said.

'You mean the Vicar,' Henry said. 'I'm afraid she's not here at the moment.' No way was he going to say that she was away from home. That was an open invitation to rob the Vicarage. 'Can I help?' he asked.

Lester shook his head. 'I just wanted to say Hello, and to thank her. She's a very kind lady.'

'She is,' Henry agreed. What had she been doing? he asked himself. What had she been up to?

'Well, I'll see her some other time,' Lester said. He raised his hand to his woolly cap in a sort of salute, and left. When he was out of sight, Henry locked up and also left. Walking down the path he encountered Joe Hargreaves.

'I see the tramp's back!' Joe said.

'Yes. I've just spoken to him,' Henry said. 'He seems a decent fellow.'

Joe shook his head. 'He needs watching!' he warned. 'You can't trust these people.'

*   *   *

Henry Nugent and Joe Hargreaves were not the only ones who saw Lester. Mr Corson, rearranging his shop window, also saw him. Not that he recognised Lester, as such; as far as he knew he had never set eyes on him before, but he recognised the boots he was wearing. They were one of his few mistakes, a line which had not sold well. In any case he tended to recognise the footwear he had sold. There was a lot of it about in Thurston. And the circumstances of the sale had been unusual, the Vicar buying a pair of men's boots in a rather mysterious fashion. It was easily remembered. All in all, including the assistant at Gander's where the customer she recognised as the tramp bought a Cornish pasty, and a man just leaving the Ewe Lamb who saw this fellow wearing the sweater his wife had given to the jumble sale, there were several people who were to remember that the tramp had been in Thurston that week.

*   *   *

On Wednesday evening, in Devon, after yet another delicious meal in the hotel, Venus said, 'I'd like to ring home. I haven't done so since the night we arrived.'

'Is that really necessary, darling?' Nigel protested. 'You've already let them know we're here, safe and sound. What more do they need to know? We shall be home the day after tomorrow. If there was anything your Mum and Dad couldn't deal with—which I very much doubt—they'd soon get in touch, as would Henry if there was anything in the church.'

'I'm not the least bit worried about the church,' Venus said. 'Henry's quite capable of looking after that. And I've met Giles Smithers. He's fine! In fact, people might even enjoy a change for the odd Sunday. Who knows? But I would quite like a word with Becky.'

Nigel shrugged. 'Then it's up to you, my love. Go ahead—though I expect she's having a whale of a time. She won't be expecting to hear from you.'

'I daresay she is having a wonderful time,' Venus said, at the same time dialling Reception for an outside line.

Her father answered the phone. 'Hello, love,' he said. 'Is everything all right? We weren't expecting to hear from you.'

'That's what Nigel said,' Venus admitted. 'And yes, everything's fine. We're having a lovely holiday. Nice hotel, good weather. We've had a few outings. Is Becky there?'

'I'm sorry, she's not,' her father said. 'There's only me. They've gone to the cinema. A Harry Potter film. Not in my line.'

'Oh good! I mean good that they've gone to the cinema.' Venus tried not to sound disappointed. 'Is she all right?'

'Absolutely fine. Becky and your mother are having a high old time. Their feet don't seem to touch the ground.'

'Well that's good,' Venus repeated. 'Any other news? Anything interesting happened?'

'Nothing at all,' her father said.

'Well, give them both my love, and love to you, Dad. And Nigel's. We'll see you Saturday evening.'

Later, she couldn't resist giving Henry a quick ring. 'Is everything all right with St Mary's?' she asked.

'Fine!' Henry said.

'Nothing to report?'

'Nothing at all,' he said; 'Everything's under control.'

There was no way he was going to recount the Miss Frazer episode. Of course, ten minutes after Venus was back in Thurston someone would probably tell her every detail, even though it wouldn't necessarily be from malice. It would be from thoughtlessness, or the desire to be a bringer of news, but there was no need for her to know about it while she was on holiday. She deserved this break. She had worked very hard and done a great deal of good in the parish in the short time she'd been there. He hadn't been madly keen on having a woman priest; he'd been, to say the least, dubious about it. But now he'd admit he'd been wrong. Except for a few ups and downs—and there'd be those with any vicar—it had worked out well. 'Edward Mason and I have been going down to the church in turn, checking things out,' he said.

'Everything seems to be OK,' she told Nigel when she had put the phone down. 'Both my churchwardens are keeping an eye on things. I *am* lucky.'

'I won't say "I told you so",' Nigel said. 'Though I did! All right to go to bed now?'

'Of course,' Venus said.

*   *   *

Thurston, though fortunate in that several shops sold cartons of milk, was doubly fortunate in that Downlands Dairies, for those who preferred it, delivered milk to their doorsteps daily, along with cream, potatoes, sliced bread, plastic-wrapped cheese and sundry other foodstuffs. Whether this was their reply to all the other shops in the village which sold milk, or the reply of the village shops to Downlands for selling groceries, no-one seemed to remember. It had been going on for a long time. Ron Pearson, who delivered the milk at a very early hour, swore that Downlands had been doing it long

283

before any of the shops started up, which was not quite true since the Gander family had been baking and selling bread for two hundred years or more. But Ron could be said to be biased, since it was his living.

He had a set routine. He delivered first to the outskirts of Thurston, sometimes tipping over into the next village of Henston, where he had a few customers. After that he attended to the housing estate on the edge of Thurston, though most people on the estate bought from the supermarkets in Brampton, saying it was cheaper there. His reply to that was that it might be a penny a pint cheaper but it was neither as fresh nor as creamy. And who knew where it came from? Whereas with Downlands Dairies you only had to look up and you could see the cows grazing on the tops of the Downs.

Later, he delivered in the village, which he usually reached around three-thirty in the morning. A few insomniacs, or mothers kept awake by teething babies, might hear the high-pitched whine of his milk float, but few of the householders ever saw Ron, except when he did his special round, once a week, to collect the money from those who chose not to leave it in an envelope on the doorstep.

Though chilly, it was a beautiful night, with a full moon. It was wonderful for October. He was not looking forward to November, with its rain, damp fog, long nights, and fallen leaves making the paths slippery. At least December, though nippier, brought Christmas, with a few welcome monetary appreciations of his services throughout the past year. But no way could he grumble about these

284

present early-morning hours.

He didn't have many customers in the High Street because the shopkeepers naturally bought from each other. 'You buy my carrots and I'll buy your milk.' It was fair enough. Everything was eerily quiet as he drove up the High Street. Under the moon it was a different country from daytime. In fact, he didn't see a single soul, unless you could count a tabby cat, and at one point a dog fox on his rounds, nor did he expect to.

He delivered to the Vicarage. An extra pint, and half-a-dozen large-sized eggs—they must have someone staying—and then drove on to the church, at which, naturally, he didn't normally stop.

But now he did. It was not, at first, what he saw. It was the smell. It hit him fair and square in the face. At first he couldn't identify it; it was like no other smell he'd ever known. Acrid, pungent. A foul stink, in fact. And then, as a small cloud which had momentarily hidden the moon drifted away, he saw the smoke: thick, dense, rising from the church roof and then, even as he watched it, suddenly billowing out, blacker than the sky. The church was on fire!

He jumped down from his float and began to run towards the church, and then realised that that was a futile move. There was nothing he could do. He couldn't even get in.

He turned and ran back to the float, took out his mobile from the side pocket and dialled 999, shouting down the phone as if that would somehow make them hear better in Brampton Fire Station, and get here sooner.

'Fire! In Thurston. The church is on fire! You'd better hurry!'

285

Was there anyone in the building, they wanted to know.

'I wouldn't think so,' he said. 'Not at this time of day.' But who was to know?

He was asked where he was ringing from and gave them his mobile number. Then he ran as fast as he could to the Vicarage.

He kept his finger on the bell, letting it ring continuously while he waited impatiently for it to be answered. What was taking so long, for goodness' sake? In the end, an elderly man in a dressing gown opened the door. He looked flustered, still half asleep.

'What in the world—' he began.

'The Vicar! Where's the Vicar?' Ron said. 'The church is on fire!'

'The Vicar's away,' Ernest Foster said automatically—and then, pulling himself together, 'The church is on fire? Are you sure? How do I know who . . .' But now, wide awake, he didn't need to ask for the man's credentials. He could smell the smoke.

Ron waited impatiently, his hand outstretched, while Ernest fetched the keys.

'I'll ring the churchwarden at once,' Ernest said. 'Then I'll get dressed and be right down there.'

His words floated away on the air. Ron was already on his way, running faster than he'd ever thought he could.

Ernest dressed quickly, informed Mavis briefly and said, 'You're to keep away. Is that clear? You can't do anything; you'd be in the way. In any case, you mustn't leave Becky. I'll be back whenever.'

'For goodness' sake, Ernest, take care!' his wife called out as he ran down the stairs. 'You're not a young man, remember!'

He didn't answer. He was already halfway out of the door.

Becky, when her grandmother crept into the bedroom to look at her, was still sound asleep.

CHAPTER TWENTY

The fire appliances, two of them because it was a church and who knew what was involved, except that it was likely to be expensive, irreplaceable, historic and possibly extremely flammable, arrived from Brampton within ten minutes; a crew of five in the first appliance and four in the second. The station manager in his car, blue light flashing, was a matter of yards behind them. Inevitably, in Thurston's quiet High Street, in the dead of the night, the noise of the fire engines wakened all but the deepest sleepers. If the noise had died away as the appliances went through the village and out on the other side, on their way to somewhere else, then most of those who had been disturbed would have turned over in bed and dozed off again. It was the fact that the vehicles stopped, and their alarms ceased suddenly, which finally got people out of their beds, drawing back the curtains, peering through the windows. It was not long before a small crowd, who had sussed out the site of the fire, gathered around the church.

Ron Pearson, Edward Mason and Henry Nugent were all three there to meet the Fire Service: Henry only by the skin of his teeth since he had wakened reluctantly from a profound sleep. He and Molly had been out to a family dinner and had dined and wined well. The three men were frustrated by the fact that, for the moment, they could do nothing to help. Henry it was who decreed that he should not unlock and open the door in case that was the wrong thing to do. 'We must leave that to the firemen!' he ordered. The words were hardly out of his mouth when the fire engines arrived.

'Is there anyone inside?' was the first question he was asked.

'I wouldn't think so,' Henry answered. 'I always look around before I lock up.' He was uneasily aware, though, that his inspection earlier in the day had been a mite cursory. He had been in a hurry to get away and had simply cast his eyes around the pews. He could have missed someone. 'Not unless someone was locked in there,' he added now. 'And if he was, he wouldn't be able to get out without a key. There's a deadlock on the door. But in any case, who would want to stay in the church?'

Even as he said the words, he thought of the tramp. If he'd had a mind to, the tramp could have sneaked in while I was in the vestry, putting things away, he thought. There were lots of places in which a man could hide if he was determined to do so. But before he could say anything of this, the fire officer spoke.

'Someone wanting shelter,' he said. 'It's been known. So we'll need to search, first thing. If anyone was in here after you left, he still will be.' But in what state? he asked himself. Possibly asphyxiated by smoke.

The fire crews, wearing breathing apparatus, were inside the building within seconds, Henry moving quickly to one side as they hurried past him. He would have followed after them, so desperate was he to see exactly what was happening, and where, but once he had unlocked the door and let the firemen in he was told in no uncertain terms that he must go back outside and remain there. It was immediately obvious though, in the short time he did see anything, and even through the thick, black smoke which was being sucked up to the high roof space and out through whatever gaps it could find, that the fire itself was at the east end of the church, in the chancel, not far from the altar and even closer to the organ. The flames were leaping with tremendous energy, in several directions, from one spot to another. He had never thought of flames as being full of energy and greed, but that was how it seemed to him now. They were living things: avaricious, rapacious.

He could not remember, in all his life, having felt such desolation as he did at this moment. Nor had he ever felt so helpless, so impotent. It was his church, the church he had known and loved for so very long; for most of his life, in fact. As a small boy he had sung in the choir here, right at the spot—though the choir stalls had been moved out several years ago—where it was being destroyed before his eyes. And he could do nothing.

'I'm sorry, sir, you must leave the premises,' the officer in charge said firmly, and for what Henry realised from the tone of the man's voice was not for the first time. He took a last look at the chancel, noted the thick foam pouring out from the firemen's hoses, and briefly wondered why it wasn't water—did they not use water these days? And then, at a nudge from the officer, he turned and left. It seemed to him as he came out of the church that half the village was there. They had obviously not been allowed to come anywhere close to the building and were congregated on the pavement at the far side of the road, which was where he was directed to go. It was common sense, of course. Allowed to stand where they liked, they would have been in the way of the fire crews, not to mention in possible danger. But for him it was the fact of having to stand there, watching the smoke still pouring out through the roof and unable to do anything about it—except to watch others deal with it—which upset him. 'If there was just *something* we could do!' he said to no-one in particular.

There was general agreement with this. It was their church, in their village, and all they could do was watch. They plied Henry for information. He, after all, had had a glimpse inside, he had spoken with the firemen. 'So what started it?' they asked. 'Was it done deliberately? Who could have done it?' 'The tramp's been around a lot lately,' someone said. 'He's been seen by plenty in these last few days!'

Henry shook his head. 'I don't see that it can have been the tramp,' he said. 'He's not been found in there. It was the first thing the men looked for. And he couldn't have got out without a key because I'd locked the door.'

There was plenty of muttering about that. Tramps, the general feeling was, could get in and out of anywhere they chose to.

'Just where was the fire?' he was asked. 'Which bit of the church? How far had it spread?' Had it reached the pulpit, they wondered: that famous, intricately carved pulpit which, though the regular congregation were used to it, almost every visitor stopped to examine with awe. That pulpit from which, over several centuries, not only sermons but news which affected the whole village had been given out: Times of war. Declarations of peace. Exhortations. Joyful celebrations. Sad tidings. The pulpit, or whoever had stood in it over all the years, had delivered them all.

Henry told them what little he had observed in the short time he'd been allowed to stay there. Ron, the milkman, was still hovering. He also, savouring his moment of importance because he had discovered the fire, had told his story several times over, to anyone who was interested, but now he was worried about his round. 'There'll be hell to pay if people don't get their milk, fire or no fire,' he said.

'Then you'd better check that it's all right for you to leave,' Henry said. 'I expect it will be. Would you like me to find out for you?' He would be glad of the excuse to do so; anything to be back on the scene, to find out what was going on.

'I'd be glad of that,' Ron said.

Henry returned within a very few minutes. He had still not been allowed to go even one step inside the church door, but he had managed a word with the station manager, who said yes, Ron could carry on with his round, provided he left his name and address.

'How's it all going?' Henry had asked. 'I'm sorry to pester you, but as churchwarden, and in the Vicar's absence, I feel responsible.'

'It's being dealt with,' the station manager said. 'And you did everything you could. Don't worry!'

'How long do you reckon it had been burning

before the milkman discovered it?' Henry asked.

'That's something we'll hope to find out,' the station manager said. 'Possibly it wasn't long. A fire can develop very quickly, especially if there's plenty of inflammable material around, which there often is in a church. You'd be surprised how far it can spread, even in ten minutes!'

I would have been once, Henry thought, but not now. Not since I caught sight of those ravenous flames. 'And you don't know what caused it?' he said, yet again.

'That's something we hope and expect to find out,' the station manager said patiently. 'But first we have to deal with putting it out.' His tone now was politely but firmly dismissive. He had other things to do.

Henry went back to the other side of the road and informed Ron that he was free to go.

It was a pity, Ron thought as he went back to his round, that it was still too early for his customers to be up and about. He would have had a right tale to tell them.

Everyone wanted to know if Henry had learnt any more. 'I gather it's under control,' he said. 'More than that I wasn't told. They're too busy to bother with the likes of me. And now I must phone the Vicar. She's on holiday.'

*   *   *

The telephone rang in Venus's and Nigel's bedroom at four-thirty on Friday morning. Nigel, not quite believing his ears, hardly knowing where he was, answered it.

'Doctor Baines?' the night porter asked.

292

'Yes. What on earth . . . ?'

'I'm sorry, sir. The caller insists on being put through. It's Mrs Baines he wants to speak to.'

'Can't I take a message?' Nigel said. 'She's asleep.'

He realised as he said it how stupid that was. No-one was going to ring in the middle of the night unless it was important. Then, even while the porter was speaking, Venus wakened.

'What? Who . . . ?' she began.

'Someone to speak to you—'

He got no further. 'Becky!' she cried. 'What's happened to her?' She snatched the phone from Nigel's hand. 'What's happened? It's Becky, isn't it?'

'No, Becky's all right. Everyone's all right!' the voice at the other end said. 'It's Henry. Henry Nugent.'

'Henry?' She looked at the clock on the bedside table. 'Henry, it's half-past four. Why are you ringing me at half-past four in the morning if everything's all right? Tell me the truth! At once!'

He told her.

'Oh no! No! I don't believe it! When? How?' She was shouting now.

'What's happening?' Nigel demanded.

She waved him away.

'Yes! Yes, of course,' she said. 'We'll leave right away. Are you sure you're all right? You would tell me, wouldn't you? Yes, we'll get back as soon as we can. I'll hand you over to Nigel.'

She gave the phone to Nigel. He listened while Henry gave him the news.

'Yes, of course!' he said. 'We'll be back as quickly as possible. In the meantime—'

293

'In the meantime,' Henry broke in, 'I'll just do as I'm told. I can't do anything else, more's the pity. I'll see you when I see you. Drive carefully!'

*   *   *

The drive was more than six long hours of torture for Venus. It would have been in any case, but her pregnancy made it worse. It was difficult for her to remain comfortable in the same position for long. Nigel was also anxious that they should stop to eat, and that she should walk about.

She protested. 'I want to get on,' she insisted.

'First things first!' Nigel said, pulling into a service station.

As soon as they had eaten they got back into the car and set off on the road again, Venus still panicking about what might be happening in Thurston. 'You can't do anything about the fire,' Nigel said. 'Leave that to the experts. But *you* have to think about the babies. So try to keep calm.'

'How can I possibly keep calm?' Venus demanded. 'My church is burning down! I know I'm not popular, or at least I wasn't when I first came, but I never thought someone would set fire to my church!'

For a split second Nigel took his eyes off the road and stared at her in disbelief.

'What in the world are you saying?'

'I'm saying it could have been deliberate,' Venus said. 'You know it could!'

'I know nothing of the kind,' Nigel said. 'And nor do you. That's about the most stupid thing I've ever heard you say!'

'It could be true!' she insisted. 'Some people will

stop at nothing!'

'And you could be talking a load of rubbish!' Nigel said. 'Which you undoubtedly are.'

'How will we know?' she persisted. 'Will we ever know?'

'We will know, eventually,' Nigel said as patiently as he could, 'we will know because the Fire Service and/or the police will find out. It's part of their job. So please, my love, stop being silly. It's not like you.'

'Perhaps it *is* like me when I hear my church is burning down!' Venus said. 'Oh Nigel! It's so awful!' The tears rolled down her face; she buried her head in her hands.

He drove for several minutes, letting her cry, and then eventually he pulled on to the hard shoulder, turned off the engine, and held her close. 'I know it's a nasty shock, my darling,' he said. 'It's awful. But perhaps it's not as awful as either of us thinks. It could be a relatively small fire. It could be out, even as we speak. And we're getting there as fast as we can.'

'Henry didn't give the impression it was a small fire,' Venus said.

'True,' Nigel acknowledged, 'but he was speaking in a rush. Come to that, he didn't really give us *any* details. So why don't we just get there as fast as we can and try not to solve the problem until we know what it is.'

'We do know,' Venus said. 'The church is on fire!'

'And might already have been put out,' Nigel said yet again. 'In any case, we're more than a couple of hundred miles away even now, so all we can do is press on. And at this moment I'm more concerned about you than I am about the fire. So I suggest we set off again, and you lie back and try to get some sleep. I'll put some music on.'

Music, Venus thought, was the last thing she was concerned about. But nevertheless . . . 'All right,' she said. 'I'll try.'

In the end, she did sleep, and for more than an hour, making up for some of what she had lost in the night. When she wakened, the whole thing hit her again but somehow she was calmer. Now it was Nigel she worried about. 'I think we should stop again at the next service station,' she said. 'You must be tired out. We could have a hot drink and then perhaps you could snatch some sleep while I drive.'

'No,' Nigel said. 'You're not going to drive. But I will stop at the next place, and after that we'll pull up somewhere and I'll snatch forty winks. I'll be all right, love. Doctors are used to disturbed sleep.'

*   *   *

It was mid-afternoon when they reached Thurston. They had made good time on the motorway, but once away from it they had run into heavy traffic in several places. They drove straight to the Vicarage, partly to get the whole story before going to the church, but partly because Venus, though she knew it was ridiculous, wanted to set eyes on Becky. The moment when she had heard the telephone and thought that something had happened to Becky was still there at the back of her mind. She knew it was all right now, but she wanted to see her. In the end, as she could have worked out if she'd had her wits about her, Becky was still at school.

296

Mavis Foster was in. 'Oh, Venus love, you look awful! Sit down. The kettle's on. I'll have you a cup of tea in a minute.'

'No, Mother,' Venus said. 'I must get straight round to the church. Where's Dad?'

'He's taken Missie for a walk,' her mother said. 'Your Dad's a bit frustrated because they won't let him do anything. But I told him, it stands to reason they won't. They're the experts.'

'The fire isn't still burning, surely?' Venus asked.

'Oh no! They've put it out, though I believe not long ago. Henry's been keeping us informed as far as he could. But of course they're still in there— and the police with them now. They won't let anyone else in.'

'I think they'll have to let me in,' Venus said. 'I need to know everything there is to know.'

'I'll go with you,' Nigel said.

There was a policeman on duty at the church door, which was firmly closed to the general public.

'I'm the Vicar,' Venus said. 'And this is my husband, Doctor Baines.'

'Have you any identification, madam?' the policeman asked politely. He was, after all, confronted by a heavily pregnant woman, not wearing a single sign of clerical clothing and also looking rather dishevelled. He himself was a stranger to the area, having only recently been posted. Indeed, it was the first day he had ever set foot in Thurston.

'As a matter of fact, no,' Venus said. 'I didn't expect to need any to get into my own church! We were on holiday. We came back at once.'

'With respect, madam,' the policeman said, 'I don't actually know you. You will need to be

297

vouched for before I can let you in, and I'm afraid your husband can't be the one to vouch for you.'

'The constable is quite right, Venus,' Nigel said. 'We could be anyone.'

'This is ridiculous!' Venus protested.

'But it so happens,' the policeman said, 'that one of the churchwardens is here. I'm sure he'll be able to identify you. If you are the Vicar,' he added, though still politely.

'Henry!' Venus said. 'Thank goodness!'

'A Mr Nugent,' the policeman said.

'Then will you get him, please? And I assure you he'll tell you I am exactly who I say I am!'

'Certainly, madam!' the policeman said. He opened the door a crack. The smell, overpowering, revolting, hit Venus in the face. She had never experienced anything like it. She put her hand over her nose and mouth, trying to shut it out. The policeman stepped inside briefly, called out to someone else, not visible to Venus. 'Can you get Mr Nugent, please. He's probably with the Inspector.' Having done that he came back and waited with Venus and Nigel.

Henry appeared within a few minutes. He was very pale, still clearly shocked.

'Venus!' he said. 'Thank heaven you're here! This is a terrible do!'

'Oh, Henry!' Venus said. 'What in the world happened? How bad is it? What started it?'

'Quite bad,' Henry said. 'We don't know what started it. That's why the police are here.' He turned to the man who had accompanied him into the porch. 'This is Inspector Chapman,' he said. 'He's in charge.'

'All we can say at present is that the fire was

what we describe as "of doubtful origin",' the Inspector said. 'That's why, as soon as the fire was put out, we were called in. It's now a police enquiry.'

Venus swiftly turned to Nigel. 'There you are!' she said. 'It could have been started by anyone! Anyone who had a grudge. You wouldn't set fire to a church for profit, would you? What would you get out of it?'

'That's not quite what I meant, Vicar!' the Inspector interrupted. 'So far we've found no proof that it was started by any human agency. Nor, of course, that it wasn't. It's just that it's not clear how it did start. That's what we have to find out.'

'Then if I may I'd like to come in and look at my church,' Venus said.

'Of course,' the Inspector said.

'Be prepared for a shock, Venus,' Henry warned her.

In spite of his warning, she was not prepared for what faced her as she followed Henry and Inspector Chapman back into the church, the draught from the roof still drawing the smoke upwards. The fire had been put out, so there were no more flames, but everything in their wake was charred and, wherever the smoke had reached, blackened. Only a few tattered remains of the altar frontal hung from the blackened wood beneath it. Underneath the foam, some of which still clung to it, the crimson of the chancel carpet showed through in a few isolated patches. Further forward, the lectern, and the large Bible which normally stood on it, had been burnt until it had tipped over and was now lying on the floor.

'But the pulpit!' Venus cried. 'Oh, Nigel! The

pulpit!' No-one would preach from that pulpit again, not unless a miracle were to take place. The steps curving up to it, being of stone, were undamaged, though scorch-marked. She had a sudden, vivid memory of her first Sunday in St Mary's when she had climbed those steps, in fear and trembling, to preach her first sermon here. Her family, sitting in the front pew below her, had been there to support her. Now that pew, and at least three behind it, were partly burnt.

'It's old wood, you see, and very dry,' Inspector Chapman said. 'It could all have been infinitely worse if the milkman hadn't happened to be doing his rounds when he did.'

'Did the fire people have an idea where it started?' Nigel asked. By now Venus was too shocked to speak. She was shaking from top to toe.

'It wasn't difficult to know *where* it started,' Inspector Chapman said. 'The Fire Investigation Officer was pretty sure about that. Apparently it began in the old vestry.'

'Where is the Fire Investigation Officer now?' Nigel asked.

'He was called away,' Inspector Chapman said. 'He'll be back. It seems the vestry was packed with all manner of things, as if it was used as a storeroom and perhaps not often gone into.'

'That's true,' Venus said. 'It was packed. I never finished discovering what was actually in there. There was never time.'

'But it looks as though most of it was flammable,' the Inspector said. 'The fire started in there, caught hold rapidly, then burst through the door and out into the chancel. After that, it could go where it wanted! Yes, it was apparently easy to

300

see where it started, but that's not the same as knowing how and why it started. Did anyone ever go in there?'

Henry Nugent answered. 'Hardly ever! And I can vouch that there was a lot of—well, not exactly rubbish, but things put aside, I suppose, until someone had time to deal with them. Old choir robes, files, hymn books we'd stopped using a few years ago and no-one else wanted.'

The Inspector nodded. 'The very stuff for a bonfire! Was the door kept locked?'

Henry shook his head. 'There was nothing of any great value in it.'

'Which leaves us with just what did start it,' the Inspector said.

'Or who!' Venus said.

The Inspector gave her a sharp look. 'Have you any reason for saying that?' he asked.

Venus hesitated—then said, 'No. Not really.'

'Well, we shall find out. We usually do. The Fire Investigation Officer will be back first thing in the morning and possibly a forensic scientist, if that's deemed necessary. He would have to come from London. There's not much more we can do right now. It's already getting dark. The electrics might be dicey, and we'll need good light to work by. So I suggest we all go home and get some sleep!'

He looked sympathetically at Venus. She looked all in—and she was obviously in no state to be here at all. He wondered when the baby was due.

'Will there be someone here during the night?' she asked.

'Oh, we'll be keeping an eye on things!' the Inspector assured her. 'Don't you worry about that, Vicar. Best if you get some sleep.'

How will I ever sleep? Venus asked herself. Yet she was quite desperately tired.

*   *   *

They were all there the next morning: the Fire Investigation Officer with two assistants, Venus, Henry, and Edward Mason. The churchwardens were accompanied by a Mr Perkins, a representative of the insurance company. Henry had got in touch with them quickly and Mr Perkins was here not only to assess, as far as he could at present, the damage, but to ensure that no further damage would arise if that could be prevented. 'We might have to shore up some windows, possibly doors also,' Mr Perkins said. He was a gloomy-looking man, with a grave voice. But no wonder, Henry thought, since he must spend his working life viewing dire results and having in mind worse ones to come.

It had been decided, because St Mary's was a historic church and there might be more than usual loss involved, that the forensic scientist should be called in, and he was expected to arrive from London in the course of the morning. In the meantime two men from the Fire Department arrived with a sniffer dog, a beautiful black labrador.

'Bruce is trained to sniff out petrol, or any other kind of fuel,' he explained to Venus. 'He's extremely good at it.'

'You mean in case someone deliberately started the fire?' Venus asked.

'In case it was arson, yes,' the dog handler said. 'Or in case there was fuel of some sort around for another reason. Not necessarily arson.'

He took the dog into what was left of the old vestry, where the Fire Investigation people were working, down on their knees, sifting patiently through debris and ashes. The dog obligingly sniffed everywhere, but in the end sat back, having found nothing of interest to him. His handler rewarded him, then took him away. In the meantime, the Investigation men, heads down, plodded on. It looked, Venus thought, as if it would all come to nothing, nothing would be discovered, and then, suddenly, there was a cry from one of the men.

'Got it! Come and look at this!'

His colleague joined him as, immediately, did the churchwardens, the insurance assessor, and Venus, all of them gathering around him as he knelt there.

'Look at that!' he said, pointing to two burnt ends of wires. 'The electrical arcing—two conductors touched and started the fire.'

'But why?' Venus asked. 'Do we know why?'

'Almost certainly mice,' the man said. 'The mouse has chewed through the wire.' He was sure of it.

'But how—' Venus began.

'I'm not sure you'd want to know, madam,' the man said.

'Oh, yes, I do!' Venus said. 'I want to know everything!'

'Well then, if you must . . . The mouse chews through the wire and he electrocutes himself. But that doesn't mean he just drops dead, as I expect you'd imagine. It means that he catches fire himself. He's a whole ball of fire, and in a place like this it's no time at all before everything else is. It all follows from there. The fire burst the door down, it would more or less blast it down, and the flames rushed out into the church. It's a matter of a very few minutes.'

The insurance assessor nodded in agreement. 'Not the first time a mouse has burnt down a building. And of course if it's in a room full of stuff easy to catch fire, and they're undisturbed . . . I daresay there was at least one mouse nest in a place like this,' he said. Then he looked around lugubriously and said, 'Well there won't be now, will there?'

Henry looked decidedly uncomfortable, though he said nothing. Was it all going to come down to some sort of negligence on the part of the church? He was sure they were under-insured anyway. He'd been saying so for years. But people—and PCCs were no exception—didn't like paying out good money to insure against something which might never happen. They preferred to trust to luck.

Well at least, Venus thought, she need no longer tell herself that someone had done it deliberately, or against her. One poor little mouse would seem to have proved that.

CHAPTER TWENTY-ONE

On Saturday evenings, now, Venus had to go to the parish hall to prepare for the next day's services. This had been the case since the fire had happened, and who knew how many more weeks it would go on? So much of the east end of the church was still sheeted off, out of bounds for safety reasons. At the same time the parish hall was now being used for non-church events—events which would have taken place in the village hall had there still been one. That hall had had to be abandoned as it was not up to safety standard until money could be raised to refurbish or—more likely—rebuild it. In the meantime these events now took place in the parish hall, the organisations involved paying a modest fee. This was a useful financial advantage for St Mary's. A nice little earner.

On this particular Saturday afternoon there had been dancing displays—ballet, tap, the lot, by the several children's dancing schools which thrived in Thurston and the surrounding areas. All who used the parish hall were supposed to clear up after themselves, to leave the premises as clean and tidy as they had (hopefully) found them, but this did not always work. In any case, now chairs had to be arranged for the church congregation, an altar set up, and so on, for the early Sunday service and for the ten o'clock Eucharist which would follow it. And then afterwards it had to be dismantled and put away.

There was no dearth of helpers willing to do this, but being willing and being able were two different things, so coordination between one group and another, and sometimes between one person and another, tended to be lacking. Also, to augment the chairs available in the hall, eight pews had been brought from the back of the church into the parish hall, and whether, when the 'church in the hall' was arranged, these should go at the front, or the back, or down the sides of the hall chairs, was a matter for debate. It was still not settled. Much depended on who, physically, was doing the moving.

The altar was easier. As Venus pointed out, the basis of an altar was nothing more than a table. Any table would do. A card table would do: a packing case would do. It was what went on at it which made it different from all other tables. The cross from the church altar had not been irrevocably damaged. It had been salvaged, cleaned up and could be used again, possibly for ever. Candlesticks, which had in any case been replacement candlesticks for the ones which had been stolen earlier, were replaced without difficulty, and since the supply of altar linen had always been kept in a chest at the back of the church, and the chalice and so on were kept in the safe, there was no difficulty about those items. Seventy-two hours after the fire had raged, the Sunday services had gone ahead in the church hall, and were still doing so.

Surprisingly, the attendance since then had been even better than usual, perhaps from a feeling of curiosity as to how it was all working out, but more, Venus hoped and believed, from people's loyalty and solidarity, even from those in Thurston who, in the normal course of events, never came to church. It was their church and their village. They would stand by it in hard times.

When the service was over it was a matter of minutes to move the chairs to the other end of the hall where the coffee was served. This had the positive and, Venus reckoned, welcome effect that most of those who would not have dreamt of going across to the hall for coffee after the service in church now appeared to find no difficulty in moving a few yards along the room. Thus it seemed that new acquaintances were being made, and possibly—who knew?—new friendships started, out of horrible circumstances. Also, she observed, people were more cheerful, almost in a determined sort of way.

'It reminds me of the War!' Mrs Firth, an elderly widow, said. If Mrs Firth was known for anything, which was doubtful, it was for *not* fraternising. She had always kept herself to herself, hurrying away after the service ended. Until now, that was.

'My mother was a child in World War Two,' Venus said. 'She remembers lots of things about it. I must introduce you.'

'I was a bride,' Mrs Firth said.

Venus felt a sudden sadness; no way could she picture Mrs Firth as a bride. Looking at her she saw a woman who was thin, saggy, old. Her hair was white and wispy, her hands knobbly, the backs blue-veined. And yet, Venus chided herself, that's arrogance on my part. Mrs Firth had possibly been a beautiful bride, even though there were few signs of it left.

'It didn't last long, our marriage,' Mrs Firth said. 'We got married by special licence when Norman was on leave. And he was killed within days of going back.'

'That's very sad,' Venus said.

If the church hadn't been half burnt down, if we hadn't been driven to using this not very suitable hall, Venus thought, I might never have heard Mrs Firth's story. It was another war story, probably not unusual, but for Mrs Firth it had no doubt changed her life from everything she had expected it to be. Venus looked again at the woman standing there,

307

holding her coffee cup, and searched for signs of what she might once have been like when she was young, in love, newly married. All she could find now was in her eyebrows—still black, and beautifully arched, owing nothing to an eyebrow pencil—above rheumy eyes which, though purple-shadowed beneath, were circled with lustrous, black lashes, again without any trace of mascara.

'My mother's here now,' she said. 'Why don't I take you along and introduce you?'

*　　　*　　　*

'I'm pleased to meet you,' Mrs Foster said. 'Do sit down for a minute.' She indicated a vacant chair on her left. 'And this is my husband, Ernest,' she said. 'He'll fetch you a fresh cup of coffee.'

'I'll leave you both to it,' Venus said. 'See you next week, Mrs Firth. And see you later, Mum!'

'We usually go to the Vicarage for Sunday dinner,' Mrs Foster explained. 'I think I've seen you in church—do you sit down the far side, near the back?—but I haven't seen you at coffee before, have I?'

'Probably not,' Mrs Firth said. 'It's not something I've done.' She didn't give the reason, which was simply that she didn't like breaking into anything new on her own. She was almost incapable of it. That was why she kept herself to herself. If the truth were to be known, she envied people who could do what she couldn't; find something to say, make friends quickly. Or even just acquaintances.

'So what made you decide to come today?' Mrs Foster enquired. She had no inhibitions about

308

asking questions.

'Well . . .' Mrs Firth spoke hesitantly. 'It was really because I felt so sorry about what had happened. I mean the fire, and so sorry for the Vicar that—well, I'd been thinking I ought to. I mean for support. She's been doing a good job. Not that *I* can really do anything, of course.'

'Oh, but it's support for Venus just for people to be here,' Mrs Foster assured her. 'And here's Ernest with your coffee. That was quick, love,' she said to him.

'If you don't mind,' Ernest Foster said, 'I'll be off now. I want to take Missie for a walk before dinner. And Becky.'

'All right, love,' Mavis Foster said. 'But don't be late back. It's beef today. I can't keep the Yorkshire puddings waiting.'

'I wouldn't dare be late where Yorkshire puddings were concerned,' Ernest said. 'I know my place!' He smiled at Mrs Firth. 'I expect you're the same as my wife when it comes to Yorkshire puddings.'

'I'm afraid I've never been much good at them,' Mrs Firth confessed. 'Mine never rise the way they should.'

'Now I can probably tell you what to do about that,' Mavis Foster intervened. 'For a start, you must leave the batter to stand for at least an hour after it's made. And the fat—beef dripping if you can get it—must be very hot, likewise the oven . . . and then . . .'

Ernest Foster escaped while his wife was still in full flow. He had heard it all before. In fact, without ever having done it—he seldom ventured into the kitchen, unless to make a cup of tea—he was sure he could do the Yorkshire pudding bit himself. On the other hand, his wife's veins were filled with unadulterated Yorkshire blood, which seemed to be a requisite, while his were filled with what his wife saw as the weaker mixture of the Home Counties.

*   *   *

'I thought she was a very nice woman, Mrs Firth,' Mavis Foster said as they sat around the table later. 'Of course she needs to pull herself together a bit, be a bit more assertive, but she's very pleasant. I reckon half the problem is that she doesn't have anyone to cook for. I suppose it's easy to fall behind if you don't have anyone else to please.'

'Well, love,' Ernest said, 'I'll do my best to keep you up to scratch, if that's what you want.'

'You can jest, Ernest,' Mavis said. 'But there's a lot of truth in that.' Part of the joy of cooking a meal, she thought, was to see the pleasure, as they ate it, of the person for whom you'd cooked. Who wanted to take time over a meal and then sit down to it alone?

They were reaching the end of the pudding course—apple crumble with custard and/or, at Ernest's special request, rice pudding, creamy in the middle, with a crispy brown skin on top and around the edges of the dish—when the phone rang. Venus went to answer it and returned looking unusually distressed.

'I'm sorry,' she said. 'I have to go.'

Nigel followed her out into the hall.

'What is it, love? Anything I can do?'

'I think not,' Venus said. 'Sonia is already there.

310

It's Mrs Carter. She's had her baby. Stillborn.'

'Oh, my God!' Nigel exclaimed. 'That's terrible! You won't know this, but her last pregnancy ended in miscarriage.'

'I had heard,' Venus said. 'She comes to church, not regularly, but from time to time. Oh Nigel, it's so cruel.'

'I know,' he said.

It was at that moment Venus felt the babies she was carrying, one of them or both, she wasn't sure, move in her womb. They had been doing a lot of that lately. Had that been the case with Fiona Carter? Had she been filled with joy at the thought of, at last, having a baby? What in the world can I say to her? she thought. Especially looking the way I do? How can I be the right person to intrude? And yet, Sonia had said on the phone, Fiona had asked for her.

Fiona Carter had, by her own choice, had the baby at home. There had been no reason at all not to. She lived in a spacious, semi-detached house in Thurston, set in a pleasant, well-cared for garden. When Venus rang the bell the door was opened by a middle-aged woman who introduced herself as Mrs James, Fiona's mother. Sonia was also in the hall.

'I thought I would stay until you came,' Sonia said. 'I'm not sure a visit from you is the best thing for either of you, but it's what she wanted. Are you all right?'

'Of course!' Venus said.

'Then I'll leave you to it,' Sonia said. 'I've given Fiona a sedative, so she might be a bit sleepy. I hope she is.'

Mrs James took Venus upstairs to the bedroom.

311

Fiona was lying on the bed, facing towards the wall. Between the bed and the wall was a small crib, new, and beautifully covered in crisp white cotton, with frills and flounces. It was on the crib or, rather, on the small mound in the centre of it, covered by a white sheet, that Fiona's eyes were fixed. She did not look up when Venus came into the room. Venus went round to that side of the bed and sat on the edge of it. She took Fiona's hand, which was as cold as ice, in her own.

'I'll leave you,' Mrs James said.

'I'm so sorry, Fiona!' Venus said. 'So very sorry!'

For what seemed a long time, Fiona said nothing and Venus said nothing more, though by now they were holding each other's hands, Fiona gripping so tightly that Venus had to steel herself not to make a sound as the pain of it shot up her arm.

In the end, it was Fiona who spoke first.

'I want to hold her,' she said. 'Please let me hold her! My mother says no.'

'I'll let you hold her,' Venus said. 'But I think you must sit up. You do that, and I'll give her to you.'

Fiona did as she was told. Her face was like chalk, her eyes were black pools. Venus went to the crib and picked up the baby. She was so light; she was as light as a doll. Her pretty face, eyes closed, a tiny snub nose, a rosebud of a mouth, was as white as the gown she had been put into.

'She's beautiful!' Venus said. 'She's so beautiful!'

Fiona held out her arms and Venus placed the baby in them. Fiona held the baby to her breast. 'Her name is Helen,' she said.

'It's a beautiful name,' Venus said.

Nothing more was said for a few minutes while

Fiona cradled her baby and Venus watched. What is there to say? Venus asked herself. Finally, Fiona broke the silence. She lifted her head and looked Venus straight in the face.

'Why?' she asked. 'Why?'

'I don't know,' Venus said. 'I don't know!'

'The nurse said . . .' Fiona struggled to get the words out. 'The nurse said . . . she was such a beautiful baby that God wanted her for himself. He took her back to be with Him in heaven! That's what the nurse said.'

Venus felt a surge of anger. She wanted to take hold of the nurse, whoever she was, and shake her till her teeth rattled. How dare she! How dare she? But that, she recognised, wouldn't help Fiona.

'I couldn't believe in a God who gave you a beautiful child and then decided to take her back,' she said firmly. 'I don't know what the answer is—perhaps Doctor Sonia might know something in the end, some medical reason—but no way do I believe God did it.' But how easy for me to say that, she thought, even though I do believe it. What could Fiona believe, holding her dead baby in her arms?

And then she felt a sudden rush of love in her own body, love for the two boys she was carrying. She felt it would set her on fire, but she could say nothing.

'Can I hold her a bit longer?' Fiona begged. 'You won't take her away just yet, will you?'

'No,' Venus said. 'You can hold her a bit longer. Until you're tired. I'll stay with you and then I'll put her back in her lovely crib. If you want to, we'll say a prayer.'

'Will she go to heaven?' Fiona asked. She

313

sounded like a small child, seeking assurance.

'I think her soul is in heaven already,' Venus said. 'I really and truly believe that, with all my heart.'

She sat quietly by the bedside for almost an hour. In the end it was obvious that the sedative Sonia had given Fiona was working. If she didn't give up the baby there was a danger it might roll away from her.

'You're very tired, Fiona,' she said. 'Let me put Helen back in the crib and you can have a sleep.'

Fiona kissed the baby, and handed her back. Venus placed her in the crib, and said a short prayer.

'Will you come again tomorrow?' Fiona asked sleepily.

'Of course I will!' Venus said. 'I'll come as often as you want me to!' And then she sat in the chair and stayed until Fiona had fallen asleep.

On the way out she spoke to Mrs James. 'You'll need to see Cliff Preston,' she said. 'You might know him, or more likely not. He's our funeral director. He'll take care of everything. Would you like me to tell him?'

'Yes please,' Mrs James said. 'I don't know him.'

'Then I'll do so now, on my way home,' Venus promised. 'And if there's anything else . . . But I'll be in to see Fiona tomorrow. I told her I would.'

*　　　*　　　*

On the way back to the Vicarage Venus stopped off to see Cliff Preston. It being Sunday, the funeral parlour was closed, but, as everyone in Thurston knew, Cliff lived in the house next door. Venus rang the bell and the door was opened by his wife, a small, plump, pleasant-looking woman. She was her husband's right hand in the business since she had exactly the right personality for it: caring, compassionate, yet businesslike. In fact she had worked for Cliff almost from leaving school, and in the end had married the boss. She still worked for him. What would he do without her? he often asked. There were tasks in his profession which it was seemly for only a woman to do, and these she carried out meticulously and with dignity.

'He's not in, Vicar!' she said now. 'Is it urgent? If it is, I can get him on his mobile. Otherwise I reckon he'll be back within the hour.'

'An hour's fine,' Venus said. 'Will you ask him to give me a ring, Betty?'

'Certainly,' Betty Preston said. She looked more closely at Venus. 'Are you all right, love?' she asked. 'You look a bit peaky, if you don't mind me saying so.'

'I'm all right,' Venus said. 'A bit tired.' She didn't want to go into details. All she wanted now was to be at home with Nigel. She needed him, she needed his reassurance. She was used, by now, to dealing with the sick and the dying, even, sometimes, children; but never before with a stillborn baby and a stricken mother. And the consciousness of her own babies, so close to her, waiting to be born into the world, had made everything so much worse.

Nigel must have been watching out for her. When she reached the front door it was already open and he was standing there. She stepped into the hall, closed the door behind her, and was at once in his arms, shaking and trembling from head

315

to foot. She laid her head on his shoulder and he stroked her hair.

'I'm so sorry, sweetheart,' he said. 'Was it awful?'

'It was rather,' she said. 'But ten thousand times worse for Fiona. She's devastated.'

She told Nigel how Fiona had wanted to hold the baby, and how she had helped her to do so. 'It seemed the right thing,' she said. 'I couldn't have refused her.'

'It was the right thing,' Nigel said.

'She was so tiny,' Venus said. 'She seemed almost weightless. And I felt terrible when I had to take her back again, take her away from her mother. Terrible for Fiona, I mean.'

She had been standing in the hall all the time she'd told the story. Now Nigel led her into the living room and sat her down on a chair. 'I'm going to pour you a drink,' he said.

'No!' Venus said. 'You know I'm not drinking.'

'This won't hurt you,' he said, pouring a glass of sherry. 'Or the babies. Come on! Doctor's orders!'

She took it from him and sipped it.

'I kept thinking . . .' She hesitated. 'I kept thinking . . . what if . . . ?'

'I know what you were thinking,' Nigel spoke sternly. 'And you are not to do so. It's not going to happen to us. You had better put that right out of your mind, my love! You still have the funeral to go through. Unless . . .' A thought occurred to him. '. . . Unless you'd like the Rural Dean to ask Smithers to do that. I'm sure he would, in the circumstances.'

'Oh, no!' Venus said quickly. 'No, I wouldn't do that. It's the one thing I can do for Fiona. I wouldn't for the world opt out of it.'

'That's my girl!' Nigel said. 'And you're quite right.'

They sat quietly for a while, and then Venus said, 'Where's Becky?'

'She went home with your Mum and Dad,' Nigel said. 'It seemed a good idea. Your Dad will bring her back at bedtime.'

A few minutes later Cliff Preston phoned. Venus gave him the news.

'That's terrible!' he said. 'Poor Fiona! I've known her all her life. Did you know her husband's in the Army? He's overseas.'

'I did know, vaguely,' Venus said. 'Will he get leave, do you think?'

'I would expect so,' Cliff answered. 'He's not in a war zone.'

*　　　*　　　*

Sergeant Geoffrey Carter was given leave, and flown home, arriving on the evening before the funeral. He was a tall, well-made young man, but now, in spite of his size, looked pinched and diminished. He insisted that he should carry the small, white coffin on his shoulder all the way from Cliff Preston's premises to the churchyard. Fiona, moving as if in a dream, walked beside him. From the moment Cliff had taken her baby away she had spent most of her waking hours at his premises, sitting by the small coffin in the back room which Cliff had set aside for her. Betty Preston brought her endless cups of tea, mugs of soup and occasional sandwiches (which were never eaten).

Now, when the simple funeral was over—it had rained gently throughout the burial but no-one appeared to have noticed it—she allowed her husband to lead her back home.

*　　　*　　　*

Venus had been back at the Vicarage no more than twenty minutes when the telephone rang. It was the insurance assessor, wishing to take yet another look at the fire damage in the church. He had already made several visits. There were a few things, he said, which he needed to verify. Somehow, awful though it was, the state of the church seemed as nothing compared to the sadness of the day so far. Nevertheless, she would have to deal with it. It was almost certain that the money from the insurance would nowhere near cover the cost of the work which would have to be done to put the church to rights, if indeed that could ever be done completely.

'Very well, Mr Perkins,' she said. 'I'll give both my churchwardens a ring and we'll meet you at the church at two o'clock.'

She rang Henry Nugent, who said he would let Edward Mason know. 'He'll not be any happier than I am,' Henry said. 'Every time the insurance bloke sets foot, the picture gets gloomier. I don't know what we're going to do!'

'Cheer up, Henry!' Venus said, though feeling far from optimistic herself. 'He might have a bit of good news! Who knows?'

'Now you don't believe that, Venus, and nor do I,' Henry said. 'Anyway, we'll both be there at two o'clock.'

No sooner had she put the phone down than Nigel came in. 'I've finished surgery,' he said. 'I

318

thought I'd pop in before I start the visits. You've got to eat some lunch, and I'm here to see that you do. Was it awful?'

'Yes,' Venus said. 'I don't think I'll ever forget the sight of Fiona, walking by her husband while he carried the coffin.'

'You must still eat some lunch,' Nigel said.

'I know, and I will,' she promised. She knew she must. She had her babies to consider.

CHAPTER TWENTY-TWO

Although the cause of the fire had been ascertained by the Fire Investigation team as the work of mice, with which neither the insurance assessor nor Venus had any difficulty in agreeing— she had talked to the Investigating Officer and his view was that it was a clear-cut case—and in spite of the fact that this information had been given to the congregation, spread through the village and published in the *Brampton Echo*, the rumour that it was the work of the tramp was still rife in Thurston. It was too good a story to throw out easily. That the tramp had not been seen since the week of the fire made no difference. On the contrary, for most people it confirmed their suspicions. 'No more than you'd expect,' they said. 'He got out quick!'

Nor was the rumour kept alive only in the village. Members of St Mary's congregation were not guiltless, even to Venus's face. Pushing her shopping trolley around the nearby supermarket for all the items she couldn't find in Thurston because there was no longer a grocer, she was stopped by Mrs Ackroyd, an occasional member of her congregation, and a man whom Venus took to be Mr Ackroyd, since he was pushing the trolley.

'I'm so sorry about the fire, Vicar,' Mrs Ackroyd said. 'I hope they catch the man.'

'What man?' Venus asked the question though she knew what the reply would be. She simply wanted to squash it.

'The one who started the fire,' Mrs Ackroyd said. 'The tramp.'

'Oh, Mrs Ackroyd, hadn't you heard?' Venus said pleasantly. 'It wasn't the tramp. No way! It was the mice—or even just one mouse. Would you credit it!'

Mrs Ackroyd shook her head, more in sorrow than in anger. 'No, I wouldn't, dear. He was seen around, you know. It's especially awful because I heard you'd been so kind to him . . .' (How does she know that? Venus asked herself) '. . . but there it is. Believe me, you can't trust these people. They should be locked up! That's what I say!'

Mr Ackroyd, if that was who he was, did not join in. He was probably used to keeping quiet, Venus thought.

'I've had enough of this,' she said to Nigel that evening. 'I'm going to speak from the pulpit on Sunday. Put an end to it.' In any case, she didn't want to believe, she really couldn't believe, that Lester would do such a thing, either deliberately or carelessly.

*　　　*　　　*

'There are no real grounds for this rumour,' she

said the following Sunday. (Mrs Ackroyd, she noted, was not in the hall.) 'It is quite wrong to form opinions—especially on serious matters, which this is—simply on prejudice. We've had the result of a most thorough investigation, and that we should accept. So let's all put an end to the rumours.'

'Not that you ever will,' Nigel said when she told him what she had done. 'A great many years from now, when someone writes yet another history of St Mary's, it will probably say, "Early in the twenty-first century a serious fire, thought to be the work of a tramp, caused extensive damage to the church."'

Venus sighed. 'I daresay you're right,' she conceded. 'But I had to speak out.'

Of course she had not actually spoken from the pulpit because they no longer had one. It would be a long time before the old pulpit could be restored, if indeed it could be done at all. In the meantime St Patrick's had lent a high, narrow desk at which Venus could stand to deliver the sermon. In fact, the Catholic church in Thurston had been most helpful. In addition to the substitute pulpit they had also lent a small oak table which could be used as a lectern. Unfortunately, they could not supply a replacement for the large Bible which had been on the lectern longer than anyone in St Mary's could remember, and now was so charred as to be useless. For the moment, a smaller Bible had to suffice for the reading of the lessons.

'It's no use,' Connie Phillipson said one Sunday at coffee. 'This Bible we're making do with is so small that whoever's reading can't see the print without getting his head practically inside it, and then we can't hear what he says because his face is hidden. He might as well be talking to himself. So, I've made a decision!' She paused for a second or two so that everyone at the table would pay attention and hear what she had to say. 'I've decided that I would like to give a new Bible; something more suitable in every way, something around the size of the old one. And I would like to give it in memory of my George!'

There were murmurs of approval from all sides. 'That's very generous of you,' Venus said.

'It's no more than George himself would have done if he'd been here,' Connie said. 'I'm sure you all know that. But of course I shall need guidance on what to buy and where to find it. I don't know much about these things.'

'I'll gladly advise you on that,' Venus said. 'But I don't think you'll get one in Brampton. I think you might have to go to London.'

David Wainright spoke up.

'As Venus says, as we all agree . . .' he looked round the table for assent, '. . . it's a very generous gesture on your part, Connie. And if it would be of any help I'd be pleased to accompany you to London, or wherever the search might take us.' He sounded as though he would be ready to traverse the world if need be. 'Two heads might be better than one,' he added. 'Not to mention carrying a heavy Bible back with you!'

Connie smiled at him. She had a lovely smile, though it had not been seen as frequently since her husband's untimely death. David was so kind. He'd been wonderful to her recently. Look at the way he'd helped her when she'd been sorting out George's clothes by taking her to deliver them to

322

the Hospice shop in Brampton. And that had had a good outcome. She'd eventually volunteered to help in the shop and now she went there every Friday. She was getting to be quite good at it; she met lots of people—she'd been surprised at who bought clothes from the Hospice shop—and it had made her feel useful. It had given her a purpose in life, at least on Fridays.

'Thank you very much, David,' she said. 'That would be a great help. I've never been one for going to London on my own.'

'Then we'll fix a day,' David said.

'And, of course,' Connie said, turning to Venus, 'I would like something written in the Bible, an inscription of some kind to say that it's in memory of George, and that he was Treasurer here for so many years. He would have liked that, too.'

'That can certainly be arranged,' Venus said. 'And when the time comes we could dedicate it.'

'And, who knows,' David said, 'such a gift might encourage others to give. We're going to need a great many things and a large amount of money. The insurance won't cover everything, not by a long chalk.'

There speaks a treasurer, Venus thought. George would have said exactly the same. Not that he wasn't right. Of course he was.

Next day, Venus decided to call on Bertha Jowett; really, she could put it off no longer. It was not a chore, she enjoyed Bertha's company, including the home truths which that lady dispensed without fear or favour. It was a visit long overdue, but there had been so much happening of late that Bertha, though not forgotten, had been pushed to the back. So, early in the afternoon, she set off for The Beeches.

'Well, I never!' Bertha cried out as Venus was shown into the room. 'So you *are* still in the land of the living? I was beginning to wonder!'

She was sitting in her usual armchair, though she didn't look at all comfortable. She was twisting her body around; slowly, awkwardly, as if she was trying, but failing, to find a comfortable position. She had also clearly lost weight. She was normally a comfortably plump person with a rounded face, but now her features were sharper, there were loose folds of skin around her neck, and her mauve knitted jumper—a colour which didn't suit her anyway—hung on her. Her skin was pale and her eyes dark-rimmed. She has gone downhill, Venus thought. But it couldn't be all that long since she had seen her, could it?

'I'm sorry,' Venus said. 'I suppose it has been too long since I visited. So much has been happening, especially the fire. That's taken all our attention.'

'Oh yes,' Bertha said. 'I heard all about that. Who didn't? It kept us going for several days here—though whether what I heard was the truth, who knows? There were a lot of contrary descriptions, all told as absolute fact. According to some, the church had practically been burnt to the ground; if you listened to someone else there'd been very little damage at all. And then, the fire had been started by hooligans, or, alternatively, by one person with a grievance. Paraffin—or possibly petrol—had been used—'

Venus interrupted. 'Not so! The fire was started by mice, biting through a cable. As for the damage, yes, there was a great deal, mostly at the front of the church: the organ, the altar, the lectern and several pews. The trouble is that for the most part people only know what they've been told by someone else—someone who doesn't necessarily know the facts—or what they've read in the *Brampton Echo*, which I reckon does tend to exaggerate if it makes for a better story. There's no end of guesswork around.'

'People do exaggerate,' Bertha agreed. 'And then they're contradicted by someone who doesn't know the truth themselves. That's how it goes. And I heard you were missing. No-one knew where you were. I certainly had no idea.' She sounded peeved.

'I was *not* missing,' Venus said. 'I was away with my husband on a very short holiday. And several people knew where I was: both churchwardens, my parents, my daughter—lots of people. They got in touch with me and Nigel and I drove home at once.'

'Oh, I'm sure you did,' Bertha said testily. 'But I didn't know, did I? You don't in here. It's another world.'

It was unusual, Venus thought, for Bertha to be sorry for herself. She wasn't made like that. She was her own woman, usually defiant rather than sorry. 'Oh dear!' she apologised. 'I should have come to see you sooner. I am sorry!'

Bertha dismissed the apology with a wave of her hand. 'You're here now,' she said, and then, after a short pause, added, 'but I don't suppose, since you're so busy with more important affairs, you'll have time for a game of Scrabble? They say there's a way of playing Scrabble on one's own, but I've never managed to work it out. And what's the point if you don't have an opponent? There's no victory

325

in that, is there?'

'I'd love to have a game with you,' Venus said. 'It would have to be a short one on this occasion because I have to be home to give Becky her tea. She has a music lesson straight afterwards. She's learning the violin. Or we could wait just a day or two and have a proper game.'

Bertha brightened up at that. 'I'll hold you to it!' she said. 'So we won't bother with one today. I'm rather tired. Anyway, tell me a bit more about the fire. Now you *can* speak with authority. You can give me the truth. I'm not unsympathetic, you know, just because I think your beliefs are rubbish. In any case, it's a beautiful building and I respect good buildings. Oh yes, I've been in several times—though never when there was a service going on.'

'There's not much more to tell,' Venus said. She related what the firemen had done, how the investigations had been carried out, about the sniffer dog. 'A black labrador,' she said.

'Now, *that's* interesting,' Bertha said. 'My father kept black labradors. So does the Queen, of course. Lovely creatures, they are—though I'd have thought German Shepherds would have been used for sniffing things out.'

'So would I,' Venus said. 'But apparently the black labrador is the chosen breed. The church was under-insured, of course. What isn't? And goodness knows when we'll be able to hold services in it again, so we're having to use the parish hall. We do our best, but it's not the same.'

Bertha broke in quickly.

'Oh, but it should be!' There was a note of triumph in her voice. 'That's where you're wrong! It should be the same, whether it's in a cathedral or in a tent in the garden.'

Venus was quiet for a moment. Then she said, 'Yes, you're right of course. It should be, but it doesn't feel so.'

'There weren't always church buildings,' Bertha said. 'If my memory serves me rightly—which I'm pleased to say it still does—the Israelites were wandering tribes; driven out, seeking another place. They pitched their tents and worshipped God wherever they happened to be. Even far from home, in a foreign land. Even in exile. They took the Ark of the Covenant with them as they travelled. God went with them.'

Venus nodded. 'Again, you are quite right. But it isn't the same today, is it? People's expectations are so different.'

'Here, in this country, maybe,' Bertha agreed. 'Not so everywhere. And the basics *are* the same. You can worship God wherever you are—if you're so inclined, that is.' She waved her hand as if pushing something away which, though she was informed about it, was really of no interest to her. End of conversation, so to speak. Suddenly she looked weary, leaning her head against the back of her chair, closing her eyes as if her strength had left her.

'I must go,' Venus said. 'I'll see you one day next week for Scrabble. I'll give you a ring beforehand.'

How is it, she asked herself as she walked home, that this old woman, who denies everything I believe in, can still point me back to the absolute truths?

*   *   *

327

When Venus reached home there was a message on her answerphone. It was from Henry Nugent. 'Ring me back, Venus,' he said. He gave no explanation, which was unlike him, as to what it was about. It could be anything, she thought, and most likely to do with the clearing-up work in the church. That was going at a snail's pace and was as yet nowhere near being completed. But the call couldn't be urgent, she reckoned, or he would have said so. She switched on the kettle; she would have a cup of tea first, and she might snatch ten minutes with her feet up before Becky came in from school.

She was sound asleep when Becky arrived, announcing her presence by banging the front door shut, dropping her schoolbag in the hall and calling out, 'Mum! Where are you?'

Venus awoke with a start and found Becky already in the room. 'Hello, darling,' Venus said. 'I must have dropped off. Would you like some tea? I daresay it's still hot.'

'I'd rather have a coke,' Becky said.

Becky drinks too much coke, Venus thought, and perhaps that's my fault for buying it in weak moments and having it in the fridge. She knew she ought to protest, maybe suggest a glass of milk, but at the moment she was too tired to argue. The longer her pregnancy went on—and sometimes she felt as if she'd been pregnant for ever—the more easily and deeply she was fatigued. But in any case Becky was already opening the can, pouring the contents down her throat.

'How was school?' Venus asked. 'Did you have a good day?'

Becky pulled a face. 'Tests!' she said. 'It's always tests!'

Before Venus could agree with her, which she might well have done, the phone rang. It was Henry. 'I left a message,' he said. He sounded accusing, as if she had had no business to be out of the house when he wished to speak with her. He was not at all his genial self.

'I know,' Venus said. 'I'm sorry I didn't ring you back straight away. I fell asleep. Was it urgent?'

'You could say that. You certainly could!'

'What—'

He interrupted her. 'I've had a letter from Miss Frazer!' he announced.

Venus, who had been lounging back in her chair, sat upright. '*What?* Miss Frazer? What on earth . . . ?'

'I think I'd better bring it round,' Henry said. 'Now, if that's convenient.'

'Of course!'

What in the world could it be, Venus asked herself. There had been neither sight nor sound of Miss Frazer for several months, not even in the village—or if she has been around, Venus thought, I've been lucky enough to miss her. She didn't have long to wait for Henry. He arrived ten minutes later; unsmiling, totally serious. He refused a cup of tea.

'You're not going to like this,' he said as he sat down. 'Well, certainly not parts of it.'

'I wouldn't expect to,' Venus replied. 'There's very little Miss Frazer says which I like, and none of it is likely to surprise me.'

'I think this might,' Henry said as he handed over the letter. Then he watched, without speaking, while Venus read it.

Dear Mr Nugent,

I have heard, naturally, with the greatest regret, about the fire in St Mary's and of the great damage it has done. I cannot say I am totally surprised by the incident. One cannot expect to desecrate the House of God in the way St Mary's has been desecrated in the last year without Divine retribution. GOD IS NOT MOCKED!

It grieves me deeply to see what my family, over many generations, has built up and cherished so wantonly destroyed. So much so that I cannot let it go by, even though I myself have been driven out of the church where I have worshipped all my life. I have therefore, for this reason, made the decision to do whatever I can, financially, to ensure that the church upon which, I repeat, I and my family have lavished endless care can be restored to its former state. So that it can become once more the church so many of the good people of Thurston have known and loved over so many years.

THIS MUST BE DONE!

I expect you are under-insured. It is part and parcel of the carelessness of these modern times and something my father would never have allowed to happen.

Naturally, there is no way I can ever attend St Mary's while the so-called woman priest is its Vicar—that would be AN OFFENCE AGAINST GOD—but after careful thought I have decided that I will do what I can, and use all means, to restore the church to its former glory. It is what my dear father would have

330

wished. Please get in touch with me at your earliest convenience.

Yours truly,
Amelia Frazer

Venus handed the letter back to Henry without speaking, taking herself firmly in hand so that she would not show the rage boiling inside her, which had nothing to do with Miss Frazer's personal remarks about her.

'Well?' Henry said.

'I think not well at all,' Venus said. 'You see what this means, don't you?'

He did see, but he didn't want to face it. His tone was cautious. 'She is a very rich woman, and we are woefully short of money.'

'True,' Venus said. 'Quite true. But don't you see the truth of what she's saying?'

'What are you getting at?' Henry asked.

'You know perfectly well what I'm getting at, Henry! You must know! Surely you see that if she provides the money she'll want to do every single thing her way? It's as plain as the nose on your face! If we take the money there's no way we'll be able to use it as we like. Everything will have to be according to Miss Frazer's taste.'

'We don't know that,' Henry said.

'Oh, come on, Henry!' Venus said. 'Don't be so naïve! Of course it will be. You know it will be. "Restored to its former state." What do you think that means? You know what it means, and so do I. It means everything will end up an exact replica of what it was.'

'Is that so bad?' Henry asked.

Venus gave him a long look. Then she said, 'I

don't believe I'm hearing this. You're snatching at the easy way out. I didn't want any part of the church to go up in flames. I would far rather it hadn't happened. But it has, and that being the case, and recognising that parts of it will have to be rebuilt before it can be used again, it would be madness not to ask ourselves, seriously, whether we want it exactly as it was in the past, or are there things we can now do to make it more suitable for today's needs.'

'We seem to have managed well enough up to now—I mean until the fire,' Henry said.

'Managed?' Venus said. 'Oh, yes, we've managed. We've managed in a church where the altar is so far distant from the people that a great deal of the time the priest can't see them, nor they him. "Managed" is not good enough.'

'So what are you saying?' Henry asked.

'For one thing, I'm saying we shouldn't rush into this. We should give ourselves time to think and discuss. But I am saying, for my part, that as the altar and the front part of the church—the pulpit, the lectern, the pews and so on—are so badly damaged that they'll probably never be able to be used again, and certainly the space will have to be cleared—that this is our chance to make changes for the better. For a start, to bring everything forward so that we can all see what's going on. But that's not the only thing; there's a lot to think about. That's why I say we shouldn't rush into anything.'

'But we don't want to stay in the parish hall for ever and a day,' Henry demurred.

'Of course not,' Venus agreed. 'But if Miss Frazer gets her way, if she pays for the restoration,

332

everything will be rushed through and will end up exactly as it always was—though never quite what it was because it will be an imitation of another age. It will have nothing to do with the times we live in. You know that, Henry.'

'Some people might like that,' Henry said. 'In fact I'm sure they will!'

'And some people might like what I've suggested,' Venus said. 'It's not that radical, after all. If I had my way completely, which I know I won't get, I'd change the interior of the church completely. I'd make it more functional. For a start I'd make it so that the congregation weren't just looking at the backs of people's heads. I'd turn it around on its axis.'

'Well one thing's certain,' Henry said: 'you'd not get that past Miss Frazer!'

'I, personally, will never get anything past Miss Frazer,' Venus said. 'We all know that. But there might be others who would agree with some of my ideas—and also put forward ideas of their own. We don't know, do we? It's not a situation St Mary's has ever been in before. It must be discussed. We should listen to everyone.'

Henry shook his head. 'It's a bad do,' he said. 'It's going to cause a lot of dissension, a big upset, whatever we do. But Miss Frazer's letter will have to go before the PCC, of course. And in the meantime I'll have to reply to her—and consult Edward, and David Wainright, of course.'

'We must all consult,' Venus said. David Wainright, she thought, will jump at Miss Frazer's offer. Probably any treasurer would. She wasn't sure about her other churchwardens and she was a little surprised, and inwardly considerably upset, by

Henry's seeming immediate leaning towards Miss Frazer's offer.

'It's quite easy what you reply to Miss Frazer initially,' she said to Henry. 'You tell her what you've just told me, that her letter will be put to the next PCC meeting.'

'She should have addressed this letter to you,' Henry said.

'Of course she should,' Venus agreed. 'But that was never on the cards, was it?'

CHAPTER TWENTY-THREE

Henry Nugent, at Venus's request, had drafted a reply to Miss Frazer's letter, and also at her request they were to meet with Edward. 'I think both churchwardens should see this,' Henry said to her. 'Not just me. In fact I think David Wainright should be in the picture too. After all, it's money, and he is the Treasurer.' Though he would have to be part of it at a later stage, and certainly at the PCC, Venus would rather not have had David Wainright yet. She felt certain he would come down on the side of Miss Frazer, what treasurer wouldn't? He had never met Miss Frazer, had no idea what she was like, but then, Venus thought, money talks! All the same, Henry was right. David should be invited, and allowed to see both Miss Frazer's letter and Henry's suggested reply to it. The meeting was fixed for two o'clock on Wednesday afternoon.

It came as a pleasant surprise to Venus, therefore, when on Wednesday morning, shortly after nine o'clock, the Bishop telephoned.

'Venus,' he said. 'I'm so sorry I haven't been to St Mary's. Unfortunately I was on holiday, and straight after that I had confirmations to do. You've kindly kept my office in touch but now I want to come down and see the damage for myself.'

'I'd like that,' Venus said. 'When would you come?'

'Well, there again I have to apologise, but I would actually like to come this afternoon if that would be convenient to you? I'm sorry it's such short notice. Would it be possible?'

'Absolutely!' Venus said. 'In fact it couldn't be better. Both my churchwardens will be here this afternoon, and our Treasurer. They're coming to discuss a letter we've had from Miss Frazer.'

'Miss Frazer has written to *you*?' the Bishop asked.

'Oh no! Not to me!' Venus said. 'She wouldn't do that. No, she has bypassed me and written to my senior churchwarden. But never mind.'

'And what was the subject of her letter?'

'She offered financial help in restoring the church,' Venus said. 'Though it's not as simple as that sounds. Restoring the church to its former state, as it once was, is what she has in mind. In other words, she wants control.'

'Then you must not let her have it,' the Bishop said firmly. 'And we must discuss this further. So, my dear, I'm particularly pleased I'm coming to see you today. We can examine the state of the damage, you and your churchwardens can tell me what you're proposing to do about that, and then we'll discuss Miss Frazer's letter.'

'I look forward to it,' Venus said. At least the

Bishop would be disposed to be on her side. He had had his own altercation with Miss Frazer when she had demanded Venus's removal from her post on the grounds that, being a woman, her Orders were not valid. The Bishop had put a stop to that idea. He could be friendly and charming, but he was no pussycat. He had seen off Miss Frazer all right.

'But the Miss Frazers of this world,' he said now, as if he could read Venus's mind, 'always continue to bob up again. They prowl about like lions, seeking whom they might devour. One must be ready—and wary. And we must make plans for you, my dear,' he added. 'We must sort out what we're going to do in the last few weeks before you have your babies, and then after they're born. You are keeping well, I hope?'

'Very well,' Venus replied. It was true. There was nothing wrong with her, it was only that she was sometimes uncomfortable, and always so very tired.

She felt so much happier as she put down the phone. She hadn't won—the battle was hardly engaged—but now she had support on her side. She felt sure she was going to need it.

*　　*　　*

The Bishop arrived on the dot of two and the others, having been informed about his visit, were there to welcome him. Neither Edward nor David had met him before. Edward had been churchwarden less than a year, David Treasurer for an even shorter time. Venus was amused, watching their faces as they were introduced to him. Clearly, he came over as a benign, well-mannered cleric;

336

easy-going, nothing to worry about. He might be all those things, Venus thought, but he was a great deal more besides. He was as sharp as a needle; he was nobody's fool.

'Well then,' the Bishop said the moment the introductions were over, 'shall we take a look at the church first? Consider the moves to be made there, and then perhaps return to the Vicarage to discuss Miss Frazer's letter? Among other things, of course!' He spoke as though the letter was no great matter, but Venus—and indeed Henry, who had met with him two or three times since he had replaced the former bishop—knew better.

* * *

Henry unlocked the church door and the five of them stepped inside. The Bishop's gasp as he viewed the scene before him was audible to all.

'Dear me!' he said. 'This is awful!'

'It is indeed,' Henry said, 'but it's better than it was. As soon as we were allowed to we concentrated on clearing up some of the mess, at least at ground level, though even then, there's still a lot to do. And nothing, as yet, has been done about the roof. That will take both time and money. Even after it's been repaired, every inch of it will have to be cleaned and repainted.'

Again, they tilted back their heads and looked at the roof. What had once been white-painted between the oak beams was now filthy black with smoke damage. 'It can't be other than very costly to deal with it,' Henry said. 'To begin with, we'll have to put up very high scaffolding, and that's never cheap.'

337

'Yes, I do see that,' the Bishop said. 'But as long as the roof is safe, as long as nothing is going to fall down and hit someone on the head, then one could put up with the appearance for a while. I am more concerned that you're still not able to hold services in the church. The parish hall, I'm sure, is adequate as a make-do, and I'm sure everyone is pulling together on that, but I would like to see the congregation back where they belong.'

What would Bertha Jowett say to that? Venus wondered.

'So what comes next?' the Bishop asked.

'What I aim for,' Venus said, 'is to be able to be back in the church for the Christmas services. It would make such a difference.'

'What we propose,' Henry said, 'as a temporary measure of course, is to move as much as possible of the damaged furniture—pulpit, pews . . .'

'And I'm afraid the Bishop's chair,' Venus put in. 'That didn't escape.'

'. . . to the east end, and then to screen it off for the time being. We would need to have screens which were purpose-built to cut off that area, and hopefully they wouldn't be too unsightly.'

'And then,' Venus said, 'we would clear the space at the front of the nave where the pews were damaged and we would build as large a platform as the space would take—a sort of stage, perhaps a foot high with two steps up to it. This would house the altar, the lectern table and the desk which we are using as a pulpit. Our good friends in St Patrick's have been very kind in lending us these.'

'What about the altar rail?' It was the first time David had spoken.

'There won't be an altar rail,' Venus said. 'There

338

won't actually be enough room for people to kneel. I would come down the two steps from the altar, I would stand at the front of the nave, and people would walk up to take the wafers from me. Then they would move a step or two to the chalice bearer, who would administer the wine. Very much as it's done now when we have a larger congregation, at Easter or Christmas, but no kneeling at an altar rail.'

David shook his head.

'People won't like not kneeling to receive communion.' His voice was full of doubt.

'Some won't,' Venus agreed, 'but they'll get used to it. It's already done in a great many churches. And I daresay the people who find kneeling difficult might be quite glad of it. Some of them already have to stand at the altar.'

'In fact,' Henry said, 'it's what we're doing in the parish hall now. We don't have an altar rail there.'

'Ah, but that's different,' Edward said. 'What we're doing in the parish hall is—well, it's a sort of makeshift, isn't it?'

'I strongly deny—' Venus began—but was interrupted by Henry.

'We have a reasonably wide centre aisle in the nave here,' he said. 'People could go up to the priest on the left-hand side and come back down the other. There'd be no congestion. I think it might work quite well. In any case, it's the only solution we have space for at the moment.'

'Well,' said the Bishop, 'that seems a satisfactory solution for the present, no matter what you come up with in the future. And you could surely put it into effect quite quickly? Screen off the east end, build the platform—which will only be temporary.

Yes, I think you have it!'

'If we made a start soon, we could certainly put it all in place before Christmas,' Venus said.

'Let us remind ourselves,' Henry said, 'that it can only be a temporary arrangement. To do anything permanent we would have to go through the Diocese, consult the architects and all that.'

'And no-one knows better than I do how long that takes,' the Bishop said. 'It can be enormously long-drawn-out and frustrating.' He looked at his watch. 'And now,' he said, 'I think we must go back to the Vicarage and consider the other matter which I know is of concern to you at the moment.'

*   *   *

Back in the Vicarage, Henry handed Miss Frazer's letter to the Bishop, who read it in silence. Then he looked up, glanced around at the others, and said: 'I take it you are all aware of the contents of this letter?'

They nodded.

'This is the first time I have read it,' the Bishop said. 'Though Venus has apprised me of the contents. So what are your thoughts on it?'

David Wainright, taking advantage of the fact that there seemed to be some hesitation on the part of the others to speak, weighed in. 'It's a wonderfully generous offer,' he said. 'Goodness knows we need the money!'

'Beware of the Greeks when they come bearing gifts,' the Bishop said, though almost to himself. If anyone heard it, they made no reply. And then he said: 'How many of you know Miss Frazer?'

'I have never had that pleasure, but she is

340

obviously a most generous lady,' David said.

'David has not long been in the parish,' Venus said, trying to keep an even tone.

'Nor do *I* know Miss Frazer,' Edward spoke up. 'I've not been churchwarden all that long and I've only met her on the odd occasion, superficially, so to speak. I'm not aware that she comes to St Mary's now. I would want to know more of the background to this extraordinarily generous offer.'

The Bishop nodded approval. 'Quite right! And so you should. Always look at the motives behind such gifts, and particularly as to what conditions might be attached.'

'She doesn't say anything about conditions,' David said.

'Oh, but I think she does, if you read carefully what she says,' the Bishop said. 'Implicit in the wording of her letter is the condition that the church shall be restored *exactly as it was* before the fire occurred.'

David looked at him as if he were speaking a foreign language. 'But isn't that exactly what we want?' he queried.

'It might be or it might not,' the Bishop said. 'That is a matter for discussion with your PCC, and perhaps even with all the members of your congregation who might have their own points of view. Miss Frazer, as one of you said, is not a member of St Mary's congregation any longer, and that is by her own choice.'

'Does that matter?' David said. 'I mean, does the fact that she doesn't go to church mean that she shouldn't leave money to it?'

'It's not a matter that she doesn't go to church,' the Bishop said. 'It's much more that she will not,

341

ever, attend St Mary's again. She might be attending some other church in the diocese, but St Mary's, never!'

David looked bemused. 'Why not?' he asked.

'Because she does not approve of your vicar,' the Bishop said. 'Not of your vicar as a person, but because she is a woman. Miss Frazer hates women priests. I can't put that too strongly. After causing a great deal of trouble in St Mary's, over several weeks, she demanded of me that Venus should be sacked from her job on those grounds alone. Now I am rather afraid she is seeking further revenge. She is seeking the power to do everything in St Mary's as she wants it to be done.'

'If I may say so, Bishop, that observation seems a bit strong!' David said.

'Oh, it is,' the Bishop agreed. 'Nevertheless I believe it's true. I have dealt with Miss Frazer. I know what I'm talking about. Miss Frazer seeks to have the say over whatever is done in the restoration, but whatever the temptation, no church, no Christian organisation, should allow itself to be held in thrall to someone who seeks power. Power is one of the temptations of the devil—as you all know from your readings of the gospel. Matthew four, Luke four,' he added automatically.

David looked to Henry, as if he needed confirmation of what the Bishop had said about Miss Frazer.

Henry said: 'What the Bishop says about Miss Frazer is quite true. On the other hand, I'm not sure that this should prevent us talking to her. There might be some compromise we could make.' In his heart he didn't believe it. 'But it is true what

342

David has said, we are going to need a great deal of money which we simply haven't got—and Miss Frazer has.'

'Money should not be your first objective,' the Bishop said firmly.

'We could raise the money,' Venus said. 'A bit at a time, maybe; not all at once, but I'm sure if we worked hard we could raise it.'

The Bishop intervened. 'Now, all this is a matter for those of you here and for your PCC, so I leave it to you. But please bear in mind what I have said. I do know what I'm talking about. Keep me closely in touch and let me know if I can be of any help whatsoever.'

It was clearly the end of the discussion as far as he was concerned. 'And now,' he said, 'we must discuss what sort of help we can provide for Venus for the last few weeks before she has her babies, and indeed for the first month or so after they are born. I've given it some thought,' he said, smiling at Venus. 'It's not a matter I've had to deal with before, as you can imagine. I've not so far had a prospective father needing to be looked after because his wife is having a baby . . .'

'I'm sorry if I'm causing a problem,' Venus interrupted. 'And I'm sure I can carry on almost to the end. Other women do.'

The Bishop waved away her apology. 'You're not causing a problem, Venus. And I'm sure you're not the first woman incumbent to have a baby. It's just that it hasn't happened in this diocese since I came here, nor did it in my last. It's something to be sorted out as well as we can, both for you and for the parish. And we must bear in mind, my wife tells me, that twins often come early, so we must have

343

all the arrangements in place in good time. But you don't mind, do you, that I talk about this while your churchwardens and Treasurer are here?'

'I don't mind in the least,' Venus said. 'They'll need to know about the arrangements.'

'Well,' said the Bishop, 'I do have a young priest in mind. He is at work in the diocese, but he has not yet had a parish of his own. I don't think a parish is what he aspires to. What he more likely has in mind is the world of education, or even the monastic life, in an Order. And it might well be that that is his true vocation. Who knows? But it is my strong view—I could be wrong, but nevertheless it is my view—that first of all he should have some experience of life in what we are sometimes pleased to call the real world. And that is not to say that what he has in mind is not the real world— simply that I think it would be better all round if he had experience of more sides of life.'

'But would he want to come here?' Venus questioned.

'Oh, he would go where he was directed,' the Bishop said. 'Obedience needs to be in his nature if he is ever to contemplate being in an Order. But even apart from that, I think he would fit in. He comes from a large, not very affluent, family, of which he is the eldest son, so he's to a certain extent used to the rough and tumble of life. And if he were to come to St Mary's it would be up to you to ensure that he gets the experience he needs.'

'I see,' Venus said. 'And he would know that I would be here most of the time?'

'Oh yes!' the Bishop said. 'You would be in charge. He would do as you decided. But then, except for just a short time you would be here physically, wouldn't you?'

'Of course,' Venus agreed. 'I'm booked into hospital for the birth, but they only keep you a few days. Apart from that I'll be at home, in the Vicarage.'

The Bishop nodded agreement. 'That's what I expected,' he said. 'So what do you think?'

'It sounds fine to me!' Venus admitted.

The Bishop looked at the churchwardens. 'Do you agree? He would also have to work with you.'

'First-rate!' Henry said.

'I agree,' Edward said. 'How long would he be here?'

'Perhaps six weeks before the birth and maybe a month afterwards.' He turned to Venus. 'What do you say?'

'That sounds about right to me,' she said.

David Wainright had taken no part in the discussion. It didn't seem to pertain to him.

'Well then,' the Bishop said, 'I shall put that into motion, and I shall do it through the Rural Dean, of course, so he will phone you with a date.'

'Where will he live?' Edward asked.

'You must sort that out,' the Bishop said. 'I would advise not at the Vicarage. Both he and Venus will need space. Perhaps you could think of somewhere suitable in the parish; preferably with someone who will take good care of him.'

'I'm sure we can do that,' Henry said.

'What's his name?' Venus asked.

'Tim Crawford,' the Bishop said. 'And now I must rush off. Let me know how things go with St Mary's, and don't hesitate to call me if I can be of any help. In particular, keep me in touch about Miss Frazer. If you need help in that direction,

345

don't hesitate to ask me.'

Five minutes later he was gone, driving off in his red sports car at a speed, Venus thought as she watched him zoom away, not consistent with a village and certainly not with her idea of a bishop.

Having seen off the Bishop, the three of them went back into the house.

'He certainly expressed his opinions!' David said.

'Of course he does,' Venus said. 'Especially when he knows what he's talking about.'

They all knew, without her say-so, that they were talking about Miss Frazer.

'Anyway,' Henry intervened. 'I shall send off my reply. He seemed to think that that was uncontroversial enough. And then the rest can wait until the PCC meeting.' He was trying to be even-handed, though the truth was that he was not totally sure where he himself stood in the matter. He could see both sides.

'Quite right,' Venus said. 'And in the meantime we mustn't be deflected from what's particularly urgent. We must now make a quick start on putting the church to rights—by which I mean at least so that we can use it. We can't afford to hang about. So I reckon that we should get together a working party who will start by cleaning things up, moving things around. Get the screen and the platform built.'

'I'm not at all sure about the platform,' David demurred. 'Not in the church. It sounds a bit theatrical.'

'Not at all!' Venus objected. 'Few things are more truly dramatic than the Mass itself. It's a production we go through every time we perform

346

it. It is a drama. We show it forth to the people—the ritual, the ceremony—and we all become part of it. I mean that in the best possible way. We partake. We should always make it the real and living happening that it is.'

David looked unconvinced. It was the kind of talk he didn't quite understand. Sometimes, he thought, Venus went a bit over the top.

'So I shall mention all this at Sunday's Eucharist,' Venus said. 'And in the parish magazine. I shall ask for help in clearing things away, making space. And we must look around for a carpenter who will build the screens and the platform without too much delay, and preferably at the lowest possible cost, providing it's done well.

'And in the parish magazine I shall mention the Bishop's visit—that will encourage people—but I shall not mention Miss Frazer's letter. That must go to the PCC before the rest of the congregation—let alone those outside the church who read the parish magazine. I shall stick to the church building, etc.'

She was as good as her word, and the response was exactly as she had expected. Almost everyone at the service volunteered to give whatever help they could and, when the appeal for help went into the parish magazine, which by great good fortune came out only a day or two later, there were even more offers, some of them from those who seemed to have no connection whatever with St Mary's. So it was decided that anyone who was willing to help should turn up in the parish hall at half-past nine on the next-but-one Saturday morning, and that Henry, since he knew everyone in the church and most of the people in the village, should sort out

347

who would do what.

Carla Brown turned out to have a brother-in-law—Walter's brother, in fact—who was a good joiner and carpenter and who, she was sure, would give a hand at a fair price. 'He'll not cheat you, not our Cyril,' she said. She also volunteered her husband. 'Walter will give a hand with anything you like,' she said.

Elsie Jones, who ran the Brownies, also offered their services. 'There might be *something* they could do,' she said. 'And if there is, I'm sure they'd be delighted. You know the motto "Lend a hand".'

'Well,' Venus said, 'certainly I will bear it in mind.' She couldn't, offhand, think what a group of little girls could do in the middle of all that mess, but maybe she would think of something. Perhaps they might bring round cups of tea, or cold drinks?

'I shall be pleased to involve them,' Venus said. 'We must involve everyone we can—not only for the help they'll give, but because it's important that it's seen as a village affair. It's everybody's church.'

CHAPTER TWENTY-FOUR

On the Thursday morning before the Saturday on which everyone was going to help in the church, Venus was walking up the High Street on her way back from Winterton's, the greengrocer where she had been buying salad greens, when she ran into Mark Dover.

'Venus!' he cried. 'How are you? It's been ages! I must say, you look blooming.'

It was his choice of the word as well as his swift

glance which told her that he had taken in her enhanced shape and size. 'Enhanced', she thought, was a nicer word than, for instance, 'bulky'. Though perhaps less accurate.

'Oh, I am!' she said. 'And how about you?'

He looked the same as ever: lean figure, crisp dark hair, slightly longer than was fashionable but suitable for an artist. She suspected he had it cut in London. He was dressed in the latest, though casual, fashion. Expensive. He was undoubtedly a most attractive man.

'I'm well,' he said. 'I've been away. I've been in the Canaries.'

'Painting?' she asked.

'Of course. And if I'd had any sense I'd have stayed there—except of course that I'd have missed you! I'd forgotten how miserable England could be in November.'

'We manage,' Venus said.

'So why don't we brighten up the day by me taking you to Gander's for a pot of tea and some of their wonderful cream cakes? I won't let you turn me down again!'

'I suppose you didn't get cream cakes in the Canaries?'

'We didn't,' he admitted. 'And it's ages since you and I did that. Do you remember?'

'I do,' Venus said.

'Well then?'

'I was just on my way home,' Venus demurred.

'Which means you've finished your shopping. So come along!'

She gave in. It was ages since she'd been into Gander's, except to buy a loaf of bread. It would be a pleasant change—apart from the fact that she would enjoy one of their chocolate éclairs, the kind of thing she'd been denying herself in the battle not to put on weight while she was pregnant.

'Well, thank you,' she said. 'That would be pleasant.'

He took her shopping bags from her and they crossed the road to Gander's and went through to the back of the shop, where the café was. As she'd expected—it was a popular place—most of the tables were taken, several by people who knew her and called out to her as she and Mark wove their way through them.

'Vicars,' she said to Mark as they seated themselves, 'especially lady vicars, are not supposed to have tea and cakes with members of the opposite sex! Unless related to them.'

'In that case,' Mark said, 'how interesting for these people. They will probably all decide to have another cake so as to stay and watch, and you'll be doing Gander's a favour. Now tell me about the church. I only returned four days ago but I've heard several theories as to how it caught fire. A tramp, a militant atheist . . .'

'Neither,' Venus said. 'Not true—unless it was a militant atheist mouse!'

'A mouse?'

'Truly!' Venus assured him. 'There's no doubt about it. One small mouse did an enormous amount of damage. And we now have a huge task, putting it right.'

'I read that in the parish magazine,' Mark said. 'Oh yes! I do read the parish magazine. I find it quite amusing.'

'There was nothing amusing about this,' Venus said crisply.

350

'Of course not, and I'm sorry,' Mark said. 'In fact I had thought I might answer the call for helpers. Is there anything I could do?'

'Undoubtedly,' Venus said. 'As long as you are prepared to roll your sleeves up and get stuck in. Get your hands dirty.'

'Anything for you!' he said.

'Not for me. For the church,' Venus told him.

He shrugged his shoulders. 'I never did anything for the last vicar. He didn't inspire me. Whereas you . . .'

They chatted for a little longer, then Venus said, 'I must be going.'

'You're running away from me,' he accused her. 'Besides, you've only eaten one cream cake!'

'I have lots to do,' she said, rising from her seat. 'I'm a busy parish priest. And one éclair is my ration.'

'If you must,' Mark said. 'Then I'll see you to the Vicarage.'

'No,' Venus said. 'I'll leave on my own. And thank you very much.'

'Then I'll be in church on Saturday morning,' Mark said.

She didn't believe him.

*   *   *

'I had tea with Mark Dover, in Gander's,' Venus said to Nigel that evening. Nigel was eating a late supper. He had had a long evening surgery, it was Sonia's day off, and after that he'd had two visits which couldn't be put off until next day, patients he was anxious about. Venus and Becky had eaten together earlier and now Becky was in her own room, watching television.

'Mark,' Nigel said. 'I haven't seen him for ages.'

'He's been abroad again,' Venus told him. 'Painting.'

Nigel sighed in envy. 'Why wasn't I a painter?' he demanded.

'Could it be because you haven't the talent, sweetheart?' Venus suggested.

'Who knows whether I have or not?' Nigel demanded. 'But I wouldn't need to be a portrait painter, would I? I could paint abstract paintings in primary colours—great splashes of red, blue, yellow—on very large canvases. A half-open eye in a large triangle, right next to the back wheel of a bicycle.'

'Why would you want to be anything other than a doctor?' Venus asked him. 'It's a wonderful job and you do it so well. All those patients you cure.'

'The ones I remember best are the ones I couldn't cure,' Nigel said. 'So how was Mark?'

'As usual,' Venus said.

'You mean flirting with you?'

'As usual,' Venus repeated.

'I think he's in love with you,' Nigel said.

'What rubbish!' Venus replied.

'Oh, but people do fall in love with priests. At least, women do with male priests. I see it all the time in my church and I expect you do in yours. Adolescent girls. Middle-aged women.'

'Well yes,' Venus agreed. 'As the same women do with their doctors?'

Nigel grinned. 'Touché!' he said. 'But seriously, do you think men fall in love with women priests?'

'I wouldn't think so,' Venus said.

Nigel ate the last morsel of his meal and pushed

his plate away. 'I know one who did,' he said.

'Oh really? Who was that?'

'Me, of course, you idiot!'

She came and stood behind him, putting her hands on his shoulders. He reached back, caught hold of her hand and kissed it.

'Still am. In love with you, I mean. I'll sock that Mark Dover if he pesters you!'

'Don't worry,' Venus said. 'I'll sock him myself!'

*   *   *

On Friday afternoon, as Venus was about to leave the Vicarage, the telephone rang. She turned back to answer it.

'St Mary's Vicarage,' she said. 'Venus Baines.'

'Good afternoon,' a deep voice said. 'You won't know me, but I'm Tim Crawford. The Bishop asked me to get in touch with you.'

My goodness, Venus thought, the Bishop certainly doesn't let the grass grow under his feet. The Rural Dean had phoned her about the appointment the very next day. 'Oh good!' she said. 'I was expecting to hear from you, but perhaps not so soon. However, it's a very welcome call.'

'The Bishop thought I should come down and meet you, see the parish and so on. I'd be very pleased to do that whenever it would suit you. When would you like me to come? I'm free from today on, and any day next week would be fine.'

'Well now,' Venus said. 'Let's see! Not tomorrow. Tomorrow a whole lot of us are meeting in the church to try to clear it up. I expect the Bishop told you about our fire?'

'He did,' Tim Crawford said. 'It sounds awful.'

353

'It was,' Venus confirmed. 'It still is. Such a mess!'

'Then why don't I come tomorrow,' he suggested. 'I could give a hand. And it would be a great opportunity to meet your parishioners.'

'It certainly would,' Venus said. 'And not only parishioners. I'm expecting people from the village to pop in and help. So you would kill two birds with one stone. But are you sure? It seems quite a tough introduction.'

'I'm quite sure,' he said. 'What time do you kick off?'

'Ten o'clock,' Venus said.

'Then I'll be at your Vicarage about nine-thirty. I know where Brampton is, so if you'd just give me the directions from there to Thurston—I'll be driving.'

Venus did so. He sounded very businesslike and capable. 'I'll see you then,' she said. 'I look forward to it.'

'So do I,' he said. 'Good-bye for now.'

She phoned Henry Nugent. 'I've just had Tim Crawford on the phone—' she said, 'you remember, the young priest who's coming to help out later on.'

'I remember,' Henry said.

'Apparently the Bishop suggested he should come here fairly soon, just to meet us. So he's coming tomorrow!'

'Tomorrow!' Henry said. 'But we'll all be slaving away in church! Up to the eyes in muck and mess!'

'I told him so,' Venus said. 'He thought he could help, and at the same time meet people.'

'Well, that does sound promising,' Henry said. 'Just the sort of chap we want. We'll find him plenty

354

to do, I'm sure.'

'He'll be here at the Vicarage around half-past nine, so if you and Edward want to meet him first I suggest you come here. Otherwise we'll meet you at the church.'

'Oh, I think we'll come to you,' Henry said. 'Do you want me to ring Edward?'

'I'd be grateful if you would,' Venus said. 'I was just going into Brampton. I have some shopping which won't wait—things I can't get in the village.'

'OK,' Henry said. 'See you tomorrow morning! Is everything else all right?'

'As far as I know,' Venus said.

*   *   *

Tim Crawford arrived at the Vicarage just before nine-thirty, driving a Mercedes silver coupé. Seeing this elegant car stop outside her house was the first surprise to Venus. She was immediately green with envy. Who ever heard of a young priest driving a Mercedes? Especially a priest whose intention was to give up his worldly possessions and embrace an austere life of poverty and obedience, owning nothing. How will he ever give up *that* particular passion? she asked herself.

But she must be wrong! This was probably not Tim Crawford at all. It was probably a visitor to someone else in the road who had stopped outside the wrong house. But while she watched, the driver emerged from his car and he was definitely a clergyman—or at least he was wearing a clerical collar, which went oddly with his blue jeans and heavy sweater.

Out of the car, he unfolded himself to his full

355

height, which was all of six-foot-three. Then he turned and looked at the house and she dodged out of sight—she didn't want to be seen watching him—but by the time he reached the door she was there to open it to him on the first ring.

'Tim Crawford,' he said. 'Good-morning!'

'Venus Baines,' she said. 'Do come in. Obviously you found your way all right.'

'Your instructions were very clear,' he said as he followed her into the sitting room. He had a pleasant voice; clearer, more lively than it had sounded on the telephone.

'Both my churchwardens will be here in a minute or two,' Venus said. 'They'd like to meet you before we set off for church. But the coffee's on and we have time for a cup if you'd like one.'

'That would be great,' he said.

He followed her into the kitchen. 'This seems like a nice vicarage,' he said.

'It is,' Venus agreed. 'Nigel and I are both pleased with it. Nigel's my husband. He's the local doctor. He has a hopefully brief surgery this morning; emergencies only, it being a Saturday. Then he'll join us in church to give a hand. In fact he's hoping to bring two or three people with him from his church.'

Tim looked puzzled.

'Nigel's a Catholic,' Venus explained. 'He worships at St Patrick's. You would have passed it before you turned into the High Street.' She handed him a mug of coffee.

'That's very ecumenical,' Tim said. 'I mean the two churches helping each other out.'

'Oh,' Venus said, 'St Mary's has a very good relationship with St Patrick's.'

There was a ring at the door. 'That will be my churchwardens,' Venus said. She left Tim and went to let them in.

Tim looked around him. He liked kitchens, and this one, not too tidy, with its cushioned chairs around a big square table, its prints on the walls and a shelf full of cookery books, had a warm feel about it.

Henry Nugent and Edward Mason arrived in the next few minutes, were introduced, and accepted mugs of coffee. Soon afterwards Venus said, 'I think we should leave. There'll be people waiting.'

She was right about that. There were several people standing around the church door by the time the party from the Vicarage arrived, all of them waiting for someone with a key who would let them in.

'For safety reasons, only authorised people have been allowed into the church since the fire,' Venus explained to Tim Crawford as they walked up the path behind the two churchwardens. 'They're going to get a nasty shock when they do go in!'

'They look ready for the job,' Tim said. They did, too. Between them they were carrying an assortment of buckets, baskets, mops, step-ladders, long-handled feather dusters and who knew what else. They mostly wore jeans and several of the women had their hair tied up in headscarves. Brown Owl was there, flanked by a team of excited Brownies in full uniform, with badges.

'Oh yes,' Venus said. 'They're a good lot. I don't doubt they'll turn their hands to anything. The trickiest thing will be organising them into who does what, instead of everyone going off and doing what takes their fancy.'

357

'Don't worry, Venus!' Henry said. 'I'll sort all that out.'

'It's a job you're welcome to!' Venus said. She had fond memories of her last church, Holy Trinity in Clipton, where she had had to learn who cleaned the brass candlesticks but was not let loose on the cross. Who had the honour of doing the altar flowers and just who had done the arrangement in the porch from time immemorial, and chose her own deputy on the rare occasions when she went on holiday (which she preferred to take in Lent, the season of no church flowers).

'Right!' Henry said, walking to the front of the small crowd, key in hand. 'First of all let me tell you you're going to get a big shock when you walk in, and then let me advise you to be very careful where you tread. There's a lot of debris and such around. We don't want anyone falling—we don't have time to be giving First Aid!' His smile took the edge off his words.

It was as Henry was speaking that she saw Nigel with a small group of friends from St Patrick's walking up the path, but that was not what astonished her. What did was the sight of Mark Dover, strolling up behind them. He caught her eye, smiled and nodded at her, then joined the group at the door, following them when Henry opened up.

Nothing could have stopped the gasps of shock and horror from everyone at the sight before them as they entered. For a long moment there was dead silence, and then the talk broke out.

'Oh, my goodness!'

'I don't believe it!'

'Where *is* everything? Where's the altar?'

358

'Under the dust sheets,' Henry said grimly. 'With a lot of other things.'

Venus felt she had to say something to counteract the shock everyone seemed to be feeling. They all had to get in the mood to work, and work hard. She attempted to stand on a pew halfway down the nave but, being so pregnant, she couldn't quite make it. So she said, 'Will the rest of you sit down in the pews, just for a minute. I want to be able to see you, and you me. The pews in this bit of the church are quite safe, even if a bit dirty.'

They found themselves places, and sat down.

'As I told you all earlier,' she said, 'I want us to make the church suitable for us to, once more, have our services here. You have been wonderful in supporting St Mary's while we've been using the parish hall, but I do want us to be back in church, certainly for Christmas, as I'm sure you all do.'

There were nods, and murmurs of agreement all round.

'And we can do it,' she said. 'I know we can. But before we begin I'll tell you what we envisage— what I hope we'll be able to do in what is only a very few weeks. The work falls into several categories and there'll be jobs for everyone. Tell Henry Nugent what you think you can do and what you'd like to do, and he will sort that out. If you have a special skill, please own up to it. Don't hide your light under a bushel. But bear in mind that Henry will be the gaffer and he will co-ordinate everything.'

She went on to tell them more or less what she and the churchwardens had discussed with the Bishop.

'First of all,' she said, 'we shall screen off the

359

east end and the chancel where the greatest damage is. We will need a few strong men to move everything which is badly damaged back into that area: altar, pulpit, lectern; the damaged pews from the front of the nave. We can't move the organ, which is now totally unusable, so that will have somehow to be curtained off. Then when we've moved everything else back into that space the idea is that we will close it off by building a temporary wooden screen. We shall leave access to that back space and, of course, enough room for people to work, eventually, on what's stored in there. Walter Brown's brother, Cyril, has offered to build the screen at the lowest possible cost. He'll need help in building it, of course, so consider if that's something you could do. Any questions so far? But keep them to the area I've just mentioned.'

'If we don't have an organ, what are we going to do about music?' The question came from Jim Carstairs, the organist.

'I'm not sure, Jim,' Venus confessed. 'The obvious thing would be to have a piano but they cost a great deal of money to hire and we certainly can't afford to buy one. Obviously at the moment we have to look twice at every penny.'

'We have the piano in the parish hall,' someone suggested.

'That's true,' Venus said. 'But the hall is let fairly regularly to groups who need the piano—the children's dancing classes for instance. They can't do without a piano, and we earn money from the rent on these groups. If we didn't have a piano they'd all move to somewhere else.'

'Perhaps someone in the congregation has a keyboard—and they could at least play the hymns,' someone said. 'Or a guitar?' Jim Carstairs winced as if in pain at these suggestions.

'If all else fails,' Venus said, 'if we have no-one to accompany us, we'll all have to sing that bit louder! It's not beyond us to sing the hymns most of us know without any accompaniment. But the music is one of several things we have to bear in mind, and we'll come back to it at a later stage.' Thus she brought that particular bit of discussion to a close.

'And then the next thing we propose to do is . . .' She paused. She felt fairly certain that this was not going to be popular. Then she took a breath and went on.

'We propose to build a platform in the space at the front of the nave from which we've moved the damaged pews. The pulpit, etc. It will be big enough to hold the altar—'

'We haven't got an altar!' a woman called out. 'It's damaged beyond repair!'

'True!' Venus said. 'Perhaps not totally beyond repair, but certainly not fit to use. But an altar is easily replaced. Cyril Brown would be able to build us a new, simple altar, but in the meantime, if any one of you has a firm table of a suitable size that you could lend, please do let Henry know. Once we put our own altar frontals and covers on it—which mercifully were not in the damaged end of the church—it will serve its purpose as well as any other altar.'

A hand immediately shot up. Surprisingly, to Venus, it was her mother's hand. 'We have a spare table, Venus,' she said. 'It's up in the spare bedroom. You know the one.'

'Thank you, Mother,' Venus said. 'I'd forgotten that.' It was one at which she used to do her homework when she was a schoolgirl.

'I'd quite like to think of that old table being an altar,' Mrs Foster said, turning to her husband.

'Right,' Venus said. 'Let's move on. The platform would be built higher than floor level in the nave and there would be two or three steps up to it. Oh yes, and we shall need at least three chairs—one for the priest and two for servers. So if anyone has nice spare chairs we could use until we decide on new ones, please let me know.

'The service would be exactly as it is now,' she went on, 'but after the consecration, I would come down and give communion at the front of the nave, and you would form a procession to partake of the sacrament.' She waited for objections about the absence of an altar rail and not being able to kneel to receive, but, surprisingly, there were none. It seemed, for the moment, as if everyone was caught up in the desire to make things happen, to do whatever was possible for the common good. She felt very close to tears of gratitude to these good people in front of her. She drew in her breath.

'Right!' she said as briskly as she could. 'Then let's make a start!'

They needed no further encouragement. Henry was besieged by men and women queuing up to offer their services and to be given their orders. Brown Owl took the Brownies off to the parish hall, where they would make the drinks. There was a certain amount of discussion as to whether the workers should take a break and go across to the hall for their drinks, or whether cups should be brought to them on the job. Henry settled it. 'Those who want to go across to the hall can do so—but no more than fifteen minutes at the outside, mind! Those who want it brought to them, just say so!'

'Can I suggest,' Carla Brown said—though she usually ordered, not suggested, 'that if we're here for the next few Saturdays, which I expect we will be . . .' (there were sounds of agreement) '. . . either we bring sandwiches, or we'll bring the stuff to make them and I'll organise a few people to do it in the hall. Of course,' she added kindly, 'we shall still look to our Brownies to make the drinks!'

'A good idea, Carla,' Henry said. He was not usually enamoured of Carla Brown, she had too much to say for herself, but on this occasion it made sense. There was always the possibility that if people went home for lunch, or even went into the Ewe Lamb for a pint and a pie, they wouldn't be inclined to come back in the afternoon.

It was not long before they were all at work. Venus went around and spoke to everyone in turn. It was surprising just who was there. Until now she had not quite taken it in. Sally Brent had come with Anna, and was keeping an eye on Becky; Trudy Santer was there with two or three of the children from the Sunday School; so was Joe Hargreaves, who usually refused to be involved in anything outside his job as gardener. Evelyn Sharp, headmistress of the Primary School, was there with her husband, Colin. So was Bob Chester, the newsagent. 'I've left the wife in charge for an hour or two,' he said, 'otherwise she'd have been here.' A couple whom Venus had recently married in St Mary's, and the father and godparent of a baby she had recently baptised, turned up at the last minute.

For a brief moment, Venus stood apart, simply looking at everyone. There they were, up to their

363

eyes in the dirt and mess and as cheerful as if they were at a party. God's people—and under God, her people too. She felt a powerful rush of love for all of them.

She moved to the east end, where she knew Nigel had gone, and to her surprise found him helping Mark Dover to move what was left of the historic pulpit. Of course they knew each other. Mark had been at the first dinner she had been invited to, soon after she had come to Thurston. It had been given by Sonia, Nigel's partner in the practice, and Nigel, tall, thin, red-haired, and with a soft Irish voice, whom she had met at the surgery only a few days before, had been a guest. Looking back, as she sometimes did, she thought she had probably fallen in love with him at that dinner party.

'How's it going?' she asked. They both grunted, too breathless to speak. She had been amazed to see Mark Dover clad in paint-stained jeans. Not for one moment had she believed him when he'd said he'd come.

Now they lifted the pulpit against the back wall and lowered it carefully. 'Such a shame,' Mark said. 'A beautiful piece of work!'

'I'll leave you both to it,' she said. She moved over to where Cyril Brown was making some preliminary measurements for the screen he would erect. 'Everything all right?' she asked. 'Fine, Vicar!' he said. 'I'll work it out at home during this week and check with you. Then I'll order the wood. Next Saturday we'll make a proper start. Walter will give a hand.'

Everything was going to be all right, she thought as she moved away. She had hardly thought about

364

Miss Frazer all day, and when she did, seeing all these people here, she felt optimistic about the outcome even of that. Perhaps foolishly so.

As she reached the door two Brownies were coming in. 'Brown Owl says the tea is ready for those who want to come, and we're to take orders for those who want it brought into church.'

'Good,' Venus said. 'I'll get everyone to be quiet and then you two can make the announcement yourselves.'

CHAPTER TWENTY-FIVE

The work in the church continued at a good pace and not only on Saturdays, as Venus had expected. On several weekdays small groups, or even a couple working away on their own, were to be found. (Venus and the churchwardens had stipulated that no-one should be allowed to work entirely alone, except for Cyril Brown, who was a professional, and in any case usually had an assistant with him.) Nor did the numbers on Saturdays fall off as she had expected. One or two helpers had other commitments, but their numbers were made up by new people joining in. Irene Chester told Bob, on the second Saturday, that he could look after the shop while she took a turn at working in the church. 'Not that I mind being in the shop,' she confided to Venus, when she turned up wearing a wraparound overall and carrying rubber gloves, 'but I wanted to know what was going on. Everyone's talking about it!'

Tim Crawford came again on the second

Saturday (bringing greetings from the Bishop) but couldn't make any promises to come regularly after that since there were things he had to do in the diocese. And to Venus's surprise Mark Dover also turned up. 'How could I keep away?' he asked, looking her straight in the eye. Once again, he worked mostly with Nigel and Cyril Brown. Cyril's assistant played football on Saturday mornings and even the thought of overtime pay didn't tempt him away from that. The three of them worked on the new screen, and on the blocking off of the organ to protect it as far as possible from the dust in the atmosphere. Venus swore she could still smell the smoke and charred wood every time she entered the church.

Connie Phillipson was there quite a lot. She had made it her mission to clean as many of the pews as she could. 'They've not been properly cleaned, not what I'd call properly cleaned, in years,' she said, 'never mind the fire, and now they're all filthy from the smoke!' And then on the second Saturday she came bearing a batch of freshly baked scones she'd got up early that morning to make, plus a jar of her own strawberry jam, which, she told Venus, always sold well at the bring-and-buys. 'I thought they'd go nicely with our tea,' she said. 'Of course, I know Carla was going to do it, but since she's gone down with tonsillitis—there's a lot of it about, so you should be careful in your condition—if you like, Venus, once I've broken the back of the pews, so to speak, I wouldn't mind taking on the catering while I'm here!'

'Catering?' Venus queried.

'Oh, nothing fancy!' Connie said. 'Sandwiches, pizzas. And something in the tin for those who come in and work during the week.'

'That sounds wonderful!' Venus said. 'Are you sure it won't be too much for you?'

'Quite sure!' Connie said firmly. 'To tell you the truth, it's something I miss. George was a hearty eater, both savoury and sweet. Now, if I bake a cake it never gets finished. I found one last week, gone green mouldy in the tin.'

'Well if you're sure,' Venus said.

'You'd be doing me a favour,' Connie told her.

So Venus, who popped into church at some time each day, and frequently more than once in the day, often came across Connie Phillipson doing something or other. And at the same time, David Wainright would be there since, as he pointed out, someone with a key had to let Connie in, and being there he might as well stay and work with her, or do his own thing or maybe just poke around on his own. It didn't much matter what.

'You know very well Venus won't let you work in the church on your own,' he told Connie, 'and I wouldn't want you to. In any case someone has to be here to lock up when you go.'

*   *   *

It was towards the end of the second Saturday's work—Nigel had already left to visit a patient—that Mark Dover, as he was about to go, came to Venus with a proposition.

'I don't know whether you have anything in mind about the screen,' he said. 'I mean once it's in place, which it almost is.'

'Not really,' Venus said. 'I hadn't thought that far. I just wanted everything to look decent and tidy

367

so that we could start our services again.'

'Oh, I think we could do better than neat and tidy,' Mark said. 'Neat and tidy doesn't sound very interesting, does it?'

'Perhaps not,' Venus said. 'Though it would be a pleasant change. So what do you suggest?'

'I thought we might paint the screen—' Mark began the sentence but Venus quickly interrupted him.

'Oh yes! I always thought we'd do that. A nice neutral colour. Something which wouldn't attract attention—in fact would take away attention from that end of the church.'

Mark shook his head. 'Now, I thought quite differently,' he said. 'I thought, why don't I paint a mural on the screen, something to integrate it with the rest of the church? It has, after all, always been an important area. Even I know that. One wouldn't want it to look abandoned, even for a short time.'

Venus stared at him. For some reason or another, perhaps because he had never shown the slightest interest in St Mary's, it was about the last thing she would have expected him to suggest. For Mark Dover to involve himself even in the clearing up had been a total surprise, but for him actually to suggest using his not inconsiderable painting skills was something else.

'But that sounds great!' she said. 'I'd never thought of such a thing. What would you paint?'

'I don't know,' Mark confessed. 'I've not had time to think about it. It's only the germ of an idea so far; we'd have to discuss it. An abstract, or a scene perhaps. But don't ask me to paint angels! I'm not into angels.'

'Nor me!' Venus admitted. 'And now that I come

to think of it, I'd like some colour. Would you?'

Mark nodded. 'Then why don't we give it some thought?' he suggested. 'You and I.'

'Sure!' Venus agreed. 'But I'd need to take it a bit further than that. We have a PCC meeting next Monday and I'd like to put your offer to them. I'm sure they'll be delighted to accept it, and there might be some ideas around.'

Mark looked slightly dubious. 'We don't want a competition, do we? We can pool whatever ideas there are, of course, but in the end . . .'

'. . . it must be something you'll be happy to paint,' Venus said. 'I do understand. And, of course, there is another thing. Whatever you do, it will have to be seen in the first place as temporary. For anything permanent we'd have to go through the hoop and wait ages for agreement.'

'That's no problem,' Mark said. 'If the people at the top decide they don't like it, you can always paint over it.'

*　　　　*　　　　*

On Monday evening, Venus left the Vicarage to go to the PCC meeting. To say she was not looking forward to it was an understatement. She seldom enjoyed meetings which were about finance, and this one, when Miss Frazer's offer would figure prominently on the agenda, promised to be more contentious than most.

'Will you be late back?' Nigel asked as she was leaving.

'I'm afraid so,' she answered. 'I can't see it being anything other than long, and some of it might well be unpleasant.'

369

When she had first wanted to be a priest, longed to be, in fact, meetings—and financial ones in particular—were not on her horizon; or when they did appear she had tended to push them aside. They were something which had to be endured, not her main purpose in life. That was still true, though she had learnt that some meetings were essential, they were necessary to the orderly running of the church, and also that the actual happening was seldom as tedious as she'd expected. More often than not they went well: most people taking part were reasonable and well-disposed; but she would never learn to love them. She was not by nature a committee woman.

She had asked Rose Barker, the PCC Secretary, to put the discussion of Miss Frazer's offer last on the agenda. If it were to come early on it might well take up most of the evening, and however long or short its duration it would certainly not be without difficulties.

'I place my hope on the fact that whatever's happening in the whole wide world, we don't like to go on much after ten o'clock,' she said to Nigel.

There were, thankfully, a number of less controversial matters to discuss—for instance, the annual visit to the pantomime; and then the progress of the church which, on this occasion, would include Mark Dover's offer to paint the screen. There might be differing opinions about that but she hardly thought it would raise the temperature of the meeting. It seemed such a good idea.

'Item number one,' she said, when they had settled down, she had said the opening prayer, they had gone through the Minutes of the last meeting

370

and the matters arising from them, 'is the visit to the pantomime. As you all know, Trudy has been dealing with this, so we'll hear what she has to say.' It had seemed natural that Trudy Santer would deal with it since, in spite of the fact that when Venus first came to St Mary's she had tried to unload it on to her, she still ran the Sunday School, and the Sunday School was largely the reason for the pantomime visit.

'I'm pleased to say it's all taken care of,' Trudy said. 'I've booked the seats, *and* the coach, though I'm still waiting for one or two people to pay me, and if that applies to any of you here I'd be glad to see the colour of your money.' She said it with a smile. She was not a person who would wish to offend anyone. At the same time, she had laid out the money from her own purse and there were always two or three who were unwilling to cough up until the last minute. 'I think we shall enjoy it. It seems not many of us have seen *Aladdin* before.'

Mention of the pantomime brought back happy memories to Venus. Last year's visit had been the first occasion on which she'd gone to something in the parish publicly with Nigel. It had been a magical evening.

They moved swiftly through the next few items on the agenda and then they came to what had been done, and what was being done, in the church since the fire.

'As most of you here will know, because you've been part of it,' Venus said, 'the work has gone exceedingly well. And what is so good is that it hasn't all been done by those of us who worship at St Mary's, but also by several friends in the village.'

'It's just like the War!' Miss Tordoff interrupted

371

happily. 'Everyone set to and helped then. You didn't mind what you did!'

Dear Miss Tordoff, Venus thought. She was probably the only one there old enough to have done anything in World War Two. Rumour had it, though it seemed unlikely to Venus, that she had been high up in the Women's Air Force.

'Quite!' Venus said. 'A wonderful spirit! And now I can tell you that the screen at the east end will be up this week, and the protection for the organ will be in place. We would seem to be all set for having our Christmas services in our own church.'

There were general murmurs of approval about that.

'In fact,' Venus said, 'it seems possible to me that we might be able to move in for Advent Sunday, the first Sunday in December. And that would be particularly appropriate because it's the beginning of the church year and also a sort of new beginning for us.'

'Then we must do everything we can to make that possible,' Mrs Heaton spoke up. Mrs Heaton always sat at the back and was seldom heard to utter a word on any subject. Clearly, Venus thought, smiling at her, Mrs Heaton's time had come.

'And there is another bit of news about the screen which I'm sure you'll all be pleased to hear,' Venus said. She didn't for one moment think they'd all be pleased to hear it, but she had decided beforehand to take a positive line. 'Mr Mark Dover, who I expect you all know is a wonderful artist and lives in Thurston, has offered to paint a mural on the new screen. Mark Dover is an artist

372

much in demand and we're very fortunate that not only has he been helping to erect the screen, but he has made this offer to paint it.'

There was a less than enthusiastic reaction to her announcement. Not a hostile one, certainly not that, but on the other hand it was hardly rapturous. 'Dubious', was the word.

'I once went to an exhibition of his,' a man said. 'There were a lot of nude women. I mean in the paintings, of course.'

'Of course!' Venus said, 'but I'm sure he won't be painting nude women, Mr Fitch!' Mr Fitch was another member who usually said nothing. She would not have imagined him going to art exhibitions.

'Then what will he paint?' someone else asked.

'Perhaps he could paint Jesus, blessing the little children!' Miss Tordoff said. 'That would be lovely!'

Somehow, Venus didn't see Mark Dover doing that. 'We must discuss with him what he might do,' Venus said. 'If any of you have any ideas, let me know later and I'll put them to him.'

'Why can't we have just plain cream emulsion?' Mr Fitch asked.

'It's interesting you should say that,' Venus said pleasantly. 'It's what I'd thought of but Mark Dover said he thought that end of the church was very important and should have something better than a plain wall. However, as I said, we'll talk to him.' Though Mark Dover, she thought, was hardly a man one could order what to do.

But, inevitably, they moved on to the last item on the agenda, noted as 'The restoration of the church' (though it was fixed in Venus's mind as

'Miss Frazer's Offer').

'I will hand over to Henry Nugent to talk about this,' she said.

Henry read out Miss Frazer's letter, and his reply to it. 'But in fact I have had a further letter from Miss Frazer by today's post, which the Vicar, my fellow churchwarden and also the Treasurer have already seen. It's a long letter and I will give you the gist of it.' He had no intention of making public, unless he had to, the abuse of Venus which the letter contained. He had not liked showing it to Venus, and wouldn't have, had it not been necessary.

'The gist of what Miss Frazer says,' he went on, 'is that she would be willing to pay what she knows is likely to be a large sum of money for the restoration of the interior of the church, providing that it is restored exactly as it was before the fire "Restored in every detail to its former beauty",' he read out.

Venus looked around at the faces of the members of the PCC: surprise, approval, blank 'don't mind', pursing of lips, a frown here and there, one or two heads slightly nodding, an equal number shaking. It had clearly aroused interest, but it was not going to be a walkover, either way. Well, she was prepared for that.

'She goes on to say,' Henry continued, 'that she will naturally wish to be consulted at every point, but that the money will be there immediately the work is completed. By which,' he added, 'she means to her satisfaction.'

There was a silence for a moment, then someone said, 'It's a very generous offer!'

A few heads nodded, including David

Wainright's. 'Very generous,' he said.

Venus's face was expressionless, but Henry gave David a sharp glance.

'I have to tell you,' he said to the meeting, 'that after the first letter from Miss Frazer, the Bishop counselled us to be very careful. "No-one", he said, "must be allowed to impose their wishes on the strength of giving money. And that applies particularly to a Christian community."'

'But if it is what the community wants—' David began.

Henry held up his hand to silence him.

'And that is not all. The other condition Miss Frazer has made in this most recent letter is that she will deal and negotiate only with the churchwardens and the Treasurer—and, of course, with her solicitor and ours. By which she means that she will not deal with our Vicar. I deeply deplore that. It smacks of blackmail. And I am not sure, in fact, whether it would be allowed. Venus is, after all, the incumbent. She has the freehold of both the Vicarage, and everything pertaining to the church.'

There were one or two murmurs of assent, but what had obviously surprised the meeting was Henry's firmness, almost vehemence. Competent though he was as Senior Churchwarden, he was seldom known to be contentious. He usually made his point with great smoothness, but there was no smoothness in him now.

'All the same,' David Wainright persisted, 'we do have a big problem. St Mary's was under-insured—very much so.' He said it with the aplomb of one who was in no way to blame for that—he hadn't been in Thurston, let alone Treasurer, at the time.

'We simply won't have the money to do what needs to be done. I would say we can't turn down Miss Frazer's offer without a thought. It would mean saying no to many thousands of pounds.'

'No-one is suggesting that we don't give it a thought,' Edward Mason put in. 'But nor must we accept any part of it too hastily.'

'There's no question of accepting any part of it, taking our pick,' Henry Nugent said. 'It reads like a firm all or nothing to me. And for my part no way could I accept all of it.'

'There is another point,' Mr Fitch said (he was certainly opening up, Venus thought).

'Yes, Mr Fitch. Please make it,' she said, taking charge of the meeting again.

He stood up, the better to be seen and heard.

'Well, first of all,' he said, 'we haven't had any discussion at all as to what we *do* want in the restored church. There hasn't been time for that. We *might* want what we've always had, or we might want something different, or something additional. This is the time to keep our minds open to all the ideas that might come to us. Who knows what they might be?'

Venus could have kissed him, though he was a man she had hardly noticed before. He was a man who sat well back in church and kept to himself. She wondered how he had come to be on the PCC. How surprising people were!

'But there is still the question of money!' David Wainright said. 'Possibly Miss Frazer might listen to any proposals we put forward—who knows, might even agree with them.'

There was a deep silence. It took little Miss Tordoff to break it. Miss Tordoff, with her naïve habit of hitting the nail on the head. 'If I may say so, Mr Treasurer—and no offence meant, of course—you don't know Miss Frazer. Am I right in thinking you have never met her? I have known her all my life and she is a very determined woman. Oh! I don't mean that unkindly, but she does like to have her own way! And of course she usually gets it. She has the money, you see. Money and position. My father always said we must never allow money and position to influence us—and he was a very wise man, God rest his soul!'

Miss Tordoff is never quite as naïve as she sounds, Venus thought. She herself was keeping fairly quiet. She didn't want to play the heavy hand, though, as Vicar, she would if she had to.

No-one spoke for several seconds, then Edward Mason broke in.

'I know *I* haven't been in the parish all that long,' he said. 'But wouldn't it be better to sort out *exactly* what we want for St Mary's for the future before rushing into anything? We've heard Venus say that we're going to get the church right for holding services again. That might tell us, as time goes by, what we need, and what we'd like but don't actually need. And there would be nothing to prevent us doing some fundraising in the meantime.'

'Now that is a splendid idea!' Miss Tordoff said. 'So many ways! I shall start making my bags of pot-pourri again to do that!'

'And, you mean, turn down Miss Frazer's offer?' David Wainright said to Edward.

'No, not entirely,' Edward replied. 'I mean, why not write a polite letter saying we're not totally sure how we intend to go ahead, but we propose to start fundraising quite soon and we would certainly be

377

most grateful for any contribution that she might wish to make. But as the Bishop says, and he's a man of experience—we should make it quite clear that we want no strings attached.'

'And in the meantime,' he added, 'perhaps we should form a group from this meeting—with the Vicar, the churchwardens, the Treasurer and just one or two others—to sort out what we do want, and then come back to the PCC with our findings.'

'Quite right, Edward,' Venus said. 'All in favour of doing that . . .'

Almost, but not quite, every hand was raised. 'Then I suggest we do it right away,' Venus said. 'And in addition to the officers Edward has already mentioned, the churchwardens, the Treasurer and myself, I suggest we choose not more than three others. That will give us a group of seven, which is probably enough for our preliminary discussions.' Since there was no overt sign of dissension, she took it that that was agreeable. 'So would anyone like to make a proposal?' she asked.

'I suggest Mr Fitch,' someone said.

Venus was pleased about that. She would have liked to have put forward his name herself. He had shown a lot of interest and said some sensible things.

'And a second person?' she invited.

'What about Mrs Heaton?' someone suggested.

It was a surprise nomination. Several people at the front of the meeting turned around to look at Mrs Heaton. She was not on any of the subcommittees.

'Would you be willing?' Venus asked her.

'Well, yes,' she said. 'I suppose I would.'

'Good!' Venus said. 'And one more?'

There was no suggestion forthcoming, which suited Venus because she knew exactly who she wanted.

'No-one?' she asked. 'Then I would like to suggest Miss Tordoff.'

Miss Tordoff turned a rosy pink, looked around her, her eyes wide open in astonishment. 'Why me?' she asked, her voice high with incredulity. It was a look mirrored in not a few faces, Venus thought as she look around, and not least in David Wainright's. Rose Barker paused her minute-taking, and looked up, pen in hand. She was not totally sure whether this was a serious suggestion, worthy of going down in the minutes.

'Because I think you would be an asset, Miss Tordoff. You have worshipped in St Mary's for many years,' Venus said. 'Probably longer than most of us here.' Also, she thought, because, old though Miss Tordoff was, she seldom failed to go, instinctively, to the root of the matter, and she could hold her ground. Venus hoped she was not letting the fact that Miss Tordoff would seem to have Miss Frazer taped influence her. But even if that was so, she still thought Miss Tordoff was a good choice.

'I think Miss Tordoff would do a splendid job,' Henry Nugent said.

'Well then, are there any other nominations?' Venus asked. She was fairly certain there wouldn't be, if only because that would mean taking a vote and this PCC, she had discovered, did not like taking votes.

'In that case,' Venus said, 'Mr Fitch, Mrs Heaton and Miss Tordoff, together with the church-wardens, the Treasurer, and myself. But I should like us to have the freedom, if we should feel we needed it, to co-opt anyone else on a particular occasion if we felt they had specialised knowledge which would be helpful.' She turned to the Secretary. 'Will you add that to the minutes, Rose?'

'Certainly, Vicar,' Rose said.

Venus looked at her watch. 'Then as it's five past ten and we've come to the end of our business, we should call it a day. Shall we say the Grace together?'

CHAPTER TWENTY-SIX

When Venus reached home Nigel was watching television. When she came into the room he looked up and smiled at her. It was such bliss, she thought, to see him, especially after the long and frazzled day that hers had been. She went across to him and gave him a kiss. 'It's great, just coming home and seeing you there. It never palls!'

Nigel smiled. 'I know,' he said. 'It's the same when I work late and you're here to greet me. Shall I make you some supper or have you eaten?'

'I ate before I went to the meeting,' Venus said. 'But I could murder a cup of coffee and a ginger biscuit.'

'Right!' he said. 'Sit down and I'll get it for you.'

'No,' Venus said. 'I'll do it. I don't want to interrupt your programme.'

'It's a load of rubbish, anyway,' Nigel said. 'So do as I say and sit down.'

She was pleased to give in. She took the armchair opposite to Nigel, and kicked off her

380

shoes. 'I take it Becky's in bed. Was she all right?' she enquired.

'Perfectly,' Nigel assured her. 'I must say, my love, she's a much easier child than she was this time last year. Could it be my refining influence?'

'Possibly,' Venus said. 'Or perhaps it could be that, like me, she's just glad that you're here. But she's a happier child altogether, isn't she? Happier at home, happier at school. I hope it's the same when she has to move on to Brampton next year.'

'Next year's a long way off; at least, next September is. In any case, she'll have friends to go with,' Nigel pointed out.

He went to make the coffee. Next year, Venus thought, things will be different for all of us. We'll have the twins. Anthony and Colin. She said their names out loud. They sounded good. She wanted the time to pass quickly now. She was tired—which was partly due to the babies, but also because there seemed to be so much more to do in the parish than there had been at this time last year. The congregation had increased at all except the weekday services, so there were more people to look after, which in a way was great. She was amazed that the Tuesday and Thursday morning services had not folded altogether since they couldn't be held in the church. The parish hall was too large to be suitable, and in any case not quite right for the rather conservative weekday people; but to make it more intimate she had set up a small table in a corner of the hall and grouped a few chairs around it, and the same people still came.

And overall she had extra work simply because she had got to know her parishioners better, had spent time and made friends with more of them.

381

She felt herself more acceptable than she had in those early months. Though still not to everyone, she reminded herself. She knew there were still those who no longer came to St Mary's and probably never would. They could not come to terms with the fact that she was a woman, doing a priest's job.

'How did the meeting go?' Nigel asked, coming back into the room with a tray of coffee. 'I know you weren't looking forward to it.'

'I was not,' Venus admitted. 'But in fact it wasn't too bad. Of course not everything's solved. Far from it. The letter to Miss Frazer will be no more than a holding move. There are those on the PCC who would like simply to have stretched out their hands and taken the money. With a "Thank you kindly, Ma'am!"' Not all that many, perhaps, but some of them are powerful, David Wainright for one, she thought. Once he had all the facts to hand he would be able to quote figures which might well sway some people to take the easy route, especially those who would be happy to see the church become again exactly as it had always been: nothing changed. Not to mention all the money problems solved in an instant.

'Well, let's forget it for the moment,' Nigel said. 'Shall we listen to some music before we go to bed?'

'Why not?' Venus said. It was music which had brought them together in the early days—that concert in Brampton at which, sitting side by side, they had listened to Sibelius and Rachmaninov. And, as Nigel sometimes said, music never let one down. There was something for every mood and occasion.

382

'So you choose,' he said. 'What do you fancy?'

She thought for a moment, then said, 'We haven't listened to Schubert lately.'

'Fine by me,' Nigel said. 'Songs or symphony?'

'The Trout,' Venus said. 'Soothing! Were there any messages for me?'

'Heavens, yes! I almost forgot. Someone ringing on behalf of a Mrs Gresham. She's ill. A neighbour was making the call for her.'

'I don't know a Mrs Gresham,' Venus said. 'Do you?'

'The name doesn't ring a bell,' Nigel answered. He was sorting through the CDs. 'The neighbour said it wasn't an emergency, but would you call and see her when you could. She's at home but she can't get out. I wrote down the address. It's by the telephone.'

Sixteen, Richmond Road, Venus read. It was in her parish, but only just; in fact it was the last road in Thurston, at the foot of the hill on the other side of which Thurston gave way to the outskirts of Brampton. 'I'm ashamed to admit it,' she said, 'but I've not yet visited that bit of my parish. That's awful, isn't it? When I first came here it was my firm intention to visit every house in the parish . . .'

'Whether they liked it or not,' Nigel interrupted.

'Whether they liked it or not,' Venus agreed. 'And I'm not even halfway through.'

Nigel put on the disc and the first precise yet gentle notes of the quintet sang out.

'I haven't seen you sitting around nearly enough,' he said. 'It's been too busy for you. New parish, new people, new husband, new babies-to-be . . .'

'You mean "to-be-born",' Venus corrected him.

383

'They're in being all right. As you would know if you were me!'

'You know what I meant,' Nigel said, 'but are you impatient for them to be born? Do you ever feel resentful that you have to carry them, with all the discomfort and so on that goes with it? I don't know about that, you see.'

'Good heavens, no!' Venus said. 'What an idea! Of course I don't. Naturally, I get tired—and maybe I don't always feel fighting fit. But I think ...' She broke off. Suddenly, she couldn't go on.

'Yes? What do you think?'

She was hesitant to tell him. Would it sound fanciful? Or even irreligious?

'Go on!' Nigel said.

'I think about Mary ...'

'Mary? Mary who?'

'Mary, the mother of Jesus,' Venus said. 'I do sometimes wonder what it must have been like for her. An unmarried mother with a strange tale to tell. Who could possibly believe what she said? I mean, to say "And then an angel came ..."! It's a bit far-fetched.'

'I suppose so,' Nigel said.

'And then that awful journey when she was just about ready to give birth. But in spite of all that I've always thought she was blessed above everything and everyone. And that's pretty much how I feel now; incredibly blessed, even though I'm no-one in particular. Does that sound crazy? I'm not putting it very well.'

'Not a bit,' Nigel said. 'And, in fact, sometimes I also feel blessed. I'm not sure it's something I ever thought would happen to me.'

384

After breakfast next morning Venus phoned Henry
to ask if he knew anything about Mrs Gresham.

'Never heard of her,' he said. 'Though I reckon
people in Richmond Road, if they go to church at
all, go to All Souls', which is closer to Richmond
Road than St Mary's is.'

'Well, I shall go and see her,' Venus said. 'Right
away.'

*　　　*　　　*

Richmond Road was a long terrace of substantial
three-storey stone-built houses which had once,
perhaps a hundred and fifty years ago, been
beautiful to look at, with their satisfying
proportions, large, deep windows and substantial
front doors. They now had no more than a faded
beauty, Venus thought as she parked her car in
front of number sixteen. Almost all the houses, by
the variety of curtains at the various windows, and
the differing colours of the front doors, had been
divided into flats. When she reached number
sixteen, via a broken flagged path and a flight of
steps, this was confirmed by the list of names and
their flat numbers. Mrs Gresham lived on the first
floor.

Venus rang the bell, and waited. There was no
reply. She rang again, keeping her finger pressed
on the bellpush. Surely someone would hear it?
She was at the point of pushing a note through the
letter box, arranging to call another time, when the
door was answered by an elderly man who, since
his striped pyjamas were showing below his grey

385

flannel trousers, had possibly been dragged from his bed. His thick white hair was tousled.

'I'm sorry to disturb you,' Venus said. 'I've come to see a Mrs Gresham. According to the list on the front door she's on the first floor, but I can't get any answer.'

The man sighed. 'You wouldn't,' he said. 'She's bedfast most of the time. You more or less have to catch her when one of the nurses or carers is there.'

'She asked me to come,' Venus said. 'At least, someone left a message on my phone. I'm the Vicar of St Mary's, Thurston.'

He looked at her suspiciously. 'Begging your pardon,' he said, 'but you don't look much like a vicar.'

'Sorry about that,' Venus said, 'but I am. So how do I get to see Mrs Gresham?'

'If you'd like to wait a minute,' he said, 'I'll give her a ring and check it out, and if she gives me the OK I'll take you up. I have most people's keys, seeing as I'm on the ground floor. For such occasions as these,' he added.

He kept her waiting on the step while he went back into his flat, though leaving the door open a crack. A minute or two later he reappeared. 'That's all right!' he said. 'I'll take you up.' He isn't going to trust me on my own with the key, Venus thought. She followed him up the wide, uncarpeted staircase and stood beside him while he unlocked the door of Mrs Gresham's flat and called out, 'Mrs Gresham! Your visitor. The Vicar!'

'Please come in!'

'I'll leave you to it,' the man said.

The woman's voice came as a surprise to Venus. Even though it was weak, it was still mellifluous,

386

and from the three short words she had uttered it
was clearly an educated voice. But why should that
surprise me, Venus chided herself. She followed
the direction of the voice and found herself in a
room in which Mrs Gresham lay in bed. It was a
fair-sized room, high-ceilinged, with elaborate
plaster cornices. The bed in which the woman lay
had its head to the wall between two deep sash
windows. The windows were heavily curtained in
dark green velvet, bordered with gold-coloured
braid and drawn almost across. Added to that, the
fact that the windows were partly shuttered and the
occupant of the bed had her back to the light
meant that her face was in shadow.

'Please do sit down,' she said.

There was a chair against the wall. Venus moved
it nearer to the bed and seated herself. Closer to,
she was shocked by the woman's appearance. Her
face was the dull yellow of old parchment; the flesh
at the sides of her temples was hollowed, and below
that the skin stretched tightly over her cheekbones.
Her lips were thin and colourless, her eyes sunken
in her head and violet-shadowed beneath; but
when she smiled, as she now did at the sight of
Venus, her mouth curved and her eyes lit up. She
had been beautiful once, Venus thought. Indeed,
she was now, her bones were good, but it was a not-
of-this-world beauty.

'How are you, Mrs Gresham?' Venus enquired,
then immediately thought what a stupid thing to
say! Clearly, the woman was very ill.

'Please call me Doreen,' the woman said. 'And in
answer to your question, I'm dying. As you can
see.'

Her frankness was shocking, but there was no

arguing with it. It would be a platitudinous insult to try to do so and already Venus had sensed that the woman on the bed was not one to be cheered by platitudes. She was painfully direct. So she waited, simply laying her own hand on top of Doreen's claw-like hand as it grasped at the sheet.

'I'm sorry, I didn't mean to shock you. Very bad-mannered! It just happens to be the truth. I have cancer,' Doreen said. 'Very commonplace, these days, isn't it? The fashionable complaint. And in this case, inoperable.'

'Should you be in hospital?' Venus asked.

'I was once,' Doreen said. 'I was in Brampton General for a while, but it was a waste of my time and theirs. Not to mention a bed. They offered me the therapy but I'd seen my mother suffer from that, years ago. In any case it wouldn't cure me. They were frank about that. And why would I wish to prolong my life? I'm three-score-years-and-ten. It would be all downhill. So I thanked them very politely and they brought me home in an ambulance.'

It took her a long time to say all this. Venus waited while she struggled to find the breath and form the words, and in the pauses between the sentences lay back exhausted before summoning the strength to go on again. But in spite of this, and in spite of her words, there was no note of self-pity. I have been sorrier for myself with a bad headache, Venus thought. No, behind the woman's words, and somewhere in her manner, there was almost a grain of cheerfulness. But why did she ask to see me? she wondered.

'I expect you're wondering why I asked you to come,' Doreen said, 'and I'm not sure myself now. I

388

reckon I was bored. I don't get to talk to anyone who knows words of more than two syllables—and then they're all about illness. Have you noticed how people talk at length about illness—especially their own?'

'I have indeed!' Venus agreed.

'So I thought about it, and it seemed to me that the only person—aside from the doctor—to whom one can say "please come and see me" is the priest. One doesn't even have to list one's symptoms to get a visit. I heard on the grapevine, though that's not a source readily available to me, that you were a woman, and that's a plus as far as I'm concerned. I'm off men!'

Venus found herself laughing. But how can this woman, who is so close to death, and even now is exhausted from saying a few sentences, make me laugh? she asked herself. She wondered why she was off men.

'Are you in a lot of pain?' she enquired.

'On and off,' Mrs Gresham said. 'But it's being dealt with. And now shall we talk about something other than illness? And we can skip the weather, too. I don't see much of that, my bed being the way round it is.'

'That's fine by me,' Venus said. 'What would you like to talk about?'

Mrs Gresham thought for a minute. Then she said, 'I don't really know. You run out of things to think about, let alone talk about. I suppose *you'd* like to talk about the church, and God. All that stuff. I don't want to be rude—though come to think of it I'm damned rude—but I'm not sure that I want that either. It's a long time since I've seen the inside of a church.'

389

'That's OK,' Venus replied. It was something she had heard a hundred times. 'So—books, music, politics? Television, newspapers, fashion? Horses, cricket, football, deep-sea diving? Take your pick, though on several of those topics you'll have to take the lead. Especially deep-sea diving. I can't even swim!'

Mrs Gresham's laugh was sudden and unexpected, and it obviously shook her painfully. Venus waited without speaking until she had recovered. 'I didn't include family,' she said then. 'Do you have a family?'

Mrs Gresham was slow to reply. In the end she said, 'If you mean, do I have blood ties, yes I do. I have two brothers and a sister. I have a son who lives in Brampton. I never see him. My fault, I daresay. It goes back a long way.'

Perhaps not yet the right time to ask for details, Venus thought. 'And you're a widow?' she said.

'I'm pleased to say I am,' Doreen said. 'My husband died several years ago. I don't know whether to say "God rest his soul" or "May he burn in hell". I suppose, seeing you're here, I'd better say the first! Give him the benefit of the doubt.'

Venus nodded agreement. She wasn't going to ask for the story. It would come out if and when Doreen Gresham chose it to. For now she would change the subject. She felt already that this was not going to be her last visit to Richmond Road.

'Do you read much?' she asked.

'I used to,' Doreen said. 'At any rate more than I do now. Albert changes my library books—he's the man who let you in—but he doesn't manage to get me what I want and he doesn't go all that often. He's not a reader himself. I mustn't grumble,

390

though. He's very kind.'

'The question of books can be easily solved,' Venus said. 'I'm sure the library will do a housebound service—from Brampton if not from Thurston. Would you like me to ask?'

'I suppose that might be all right,' Doreen said, with not much enthusiasm. She is not an easy lady, Venus thought—but who would be in the circumstances?

'Then I'll call in at the library and ask them,' she promised.

'I like detective stories,' Doreen said. 'Not violence and all that, but good crime novels.'

'So do I,' Venus said. 'We must compare notes some time. Perhaps next time I come.'

'You mean you will actually come again?' Doreen asked.

'Of course I will!' Venus said. 'I won't stay long today because you seem tired, but I'll pop in some time next week. I can't say exactly when, I have to juggle my time a bit.' Tomorrow evening the group chosen from the PCC to discuss what might be wanted in the newly restored church was to meet at the Vicarage. Who knew what would arise from that?

'Oh, that's all right!' Doreen said. 'I can promise to be here all right! I shan't be out on the town.'

*   *   *

On the following evening—Nigel was at a meeting in St Patrick's, Becky was upstairs in her own room, watching television—the members of the new sub-committee turned up, all of them promptly; indeed, Miss Tordoff was ten minutes early. 'I hope you

391

don't mind,' she said to Venus. 'I always like to be in good time.'

'Not at all,' Venus said. 'In fact, you can grab yourself the most comfortable chair. Will you excuse me for a minute? I just want to check on the coffee.'

'Oh, please let me help you!' Miss Tordoff said.

'There's nothing much left to do,' Venus said. 'Just you pick a chair. I'll be back in a minute.'

'It's so good of you to have me on this committee,' Miss Tordoff said. 'I really look forward to it!'

'You will be an asset,' Venus told her. 'And you mustn't hesitate to speak up and give your views. They're every bit as important as everyone else's.'

A ring at the door drowned her reply. When Venus went to answer it the other members of the group were standing together on the doorstep, plus Rose Barker, the PCC Secretary. 'I'm glad you could come, Rose,' Venus said as they moved into the study. 'I think it's important we have this meeting minuted so that afterwards we can check back on any decisions we make. In the meantime, would you like to give me a hand with the coffee?'

Fifteen minutes later, with everyone drinking coffee except Miss Tordoff, who said would anyone mind if she didn't since it kept her awake all night, Venus said, 'Shall we make a start? And I'll begin by telling you where we are with the work in the church at the moment. I was down there this afternoon, so I know how everything's going.' In fact, both churchwardens, together with David Wainright, had been there, together with a few other people hard at work.

'As you know,' she said, 'the screen is completed

392

and the organ has been well covered to keep it from any further harm until we decide what's to be done about it. Cyril was working this afternoon on the new platform and he assured us it would be finished by Saturday week, which is the eve of Advent Sunday. I think we all agreed that Advent Sunday would be a wonderful day to be back in our own church, even if everything isn't quite ready.'

Everyone, it appeared, agreed with this. 'We must make every effort!' Edward Mason said.

David Wainright spoke up. 'I do know Connie has just about finished cleaning the pews,' he said.

'Indeed she has,' Venus agreed. 'They're absolutely sparkling clean. I doubt if they've looked so good since heaven knows when!' David looked as pleased by her approbation as if it had been directed at him—which in a small way it had, since most of the time Connie Phillipson had worked in the church he had been there also. Not cleaning pews, of course, but there had been other things he'd found to do.

'Does the platform have to be painted?' Mr Fitch asked.

'Not at this stage,' Venus said. 'Though it would be nice if we could find a bit of carpet or a rug or two, especially for the altar to stand on.'

Miss Tordoff spoke for the first time. 'Oh, I do so agree! I don't quite like the idea of the altar of the Lord standing on bare boards! And in fact I have quite a nice-sized rug I could lend for the time being. The only thing is . . .' She hesitated.

Venus looked at her. 'Yes? Is there a problem?'

'Well, it is Indian,' Miss Tordoff said. 'I mean, it's not quite Christian, is it? Would that be all right?'

Dear Miss Tordoff, Venus thought. 'Of course it would,' she assured her. 'I'm quite sure of that. The Christian faith is for all people. Whoever wishes to take it.' She was not at all sure in her own mind how this applied to an Indian rug, but Miss Tordoff seemed satisfied.

'Well, if you think so,' she said. 'I'll give it a good vacuum and get someone to bring it round to the church.'

'I'll do that for you!' Mr Fitch said. 'Whenever it's convenient to you.'

'So what I was thinking,' Venus continued, 'was that it might be a good idea to see how these new arrangements fitted in with what we want in the future for St Mary's. I know that one of my priorities is to be in a position where I can see everyone in the church, and they can see me, and know exactly what I'm doing. That's quite impossible as things have been so far.'

'It's no different from a lot of churches,' David Wainright put in.

'Quite!' Venus said. 'But that doesn't make it ideal, does it? I spent most of my time in church as a young person with a priest way at the top of the chancel, with his back to the congregation for most of the service. Certainly for the important parts. I used to think he was talking to himself.'

'Well, we don't want to go to the point where the priest is right down there, cheek by jowl with the congregation,' David Wainright said.

'Don't we?' Venus asked.

Mr Fitch interrupted with his question. 'What about the painting on the screen? Shouldn't we be discussing that? It needs to be something suitable.'

'But what *is* suitable?' Edward Mason asked.

'So why don't we suggest what we think is?' Venus suggested.

Most people had an opinion about that. They ranged from Jesus blessing the children (Miss Tordoff), via the Nativity, the Feeding of the Five Thousand, the Last Supper, to the Crucifixion and the Resurrection. Or, indeed, leaving it a plain cream emulsion. 'We could have the Blessed Virgin Mary?' someone suggested. That was dismissed as going too far towards Rome, but the rest continued to argue—Rose Barker's pen was flying over the notes for her minutes, trying to keep up—until Venus decided, as they were getting nowhere, to call a halt. Before she could do so Mrs Heaton, who so far had been silent, spoke up.

'This is too big a question for us to agree on in a hurry,' she said, taking the words out of Venus's mouth. 'And we also have to think about what Mark Dover would want to paint. You can't force an artist to do what he doesn't want to do. So why don't we ask him to paint a local scene—the Downs, meadows, sheep—whatever? It's going to be temporary anyway, and that couldn't be controversial. Could it?'

Everyone stared at her, in silence.

'I think that's a very sensible suggestion,' Henry said in the end. 'It will give us time to consider. And no-one could object to such a subject.'

Mark Dover might, Venus thought. It was hardly in the Leonardo da Vinci class. But she would put it to him.

'Well, thank you all very much,' she said. 'It's been a most useful meeting. Thank you for your time. And can I remind you that we meet in the church next Saturday to put everything into place

395

for the Advent Sunday Eucharist. All hands to the pump!'

CHAPTER TWENTY-SEVEN

On Saturday morning the usual group of helpers was in the church, working away at what were now possibly last-minute jobs. In fact, Venus thought, there were more people than ever, both from the village and from the church congregation, as if everyone wanted to be in at the finish. Tim Crawford had turned up and was helping Cyril Brown, David Wainright and Nigel with the final adjustments to the platform. David still made no secret of the fact that he didn't think much of the platform business, it was not what he was used to, but after an initial bout of grumbling he kept his thoughts to himself. In any case, he was in the minority; some of the others actually thought it was a good idea. 'And it will look even better when we put the carpet down,' Miss Tordoff said happily. 'I'm so glad it came in useful. And I think my father would have been pleased. The carpet was always in his study. He would never have dreamt it would end up in the Church of England. He was a Baptist, you see.'

Mark Dover had arrived, weighed down by painting tackle. Venus had spoken to him during the week and asked him about depicting some kind of country scene, local to the area. In the end he had agreed to do so, though reluctantly. 'It doesn't sound the least bit exciting,' he'd complained. 'I had hoped you might have liked something—

well—rather different.'

'I know,' Venus agreed. 'And I daresay some would, including me; but honestly, I think most people have had about as much change as they can cope with for the moment. It's going to be so different from the St Mary's they've always known.'

He'd sighed. 'Very well! You can twist me around your little finger, as you well know! I'll work something out and make a start on Saturday. You'll have it in time for Advent. And as you say, it's only temporary. They won't be bringing parties around to view it five hundred years from now.'

And now he was here. Venus went across to speak to him. 'Would you like someone to help you—I mean a sort of dogsbody?' she asked.

'Not really,' Mark said. 'I work best alone. Unless, of course, *you'd* like to help me! I'd go for that.'

'Sorry!' Venus said, smiling. 'You never give up, do you? But I'm needed elsewhere.'

When she rejoined the others, Connie Phillipson was busy taking orders for teas and coffees. 'And I've made some nice pizzas I'm going to heat up for lunchtime,' she said. 'Most people like pizzas, don't they? It was a good move when we put an oven in the parish hall kitchen.'

'Pizzas will be great,' Venus said. 'Have you got all the help you need?'

'Oh yes!' Connie said. 'There's always plenty of willing hands.'

As Connie moved away, Tim Crawford, released for the moment from whatever he was doing with the platform, came across to Venus. 'Everything seems to be going well,' he said. 'You must be pleased.'

'I am!' Venus said. 'They're a good lot, aren't they? But I'm not expecting it to be plain sailing. Not everyone will approve of everything, not by a long way.'

Tim nodded. 'And the ones who'll object will be the ones who haven't given so much as a hand, or put forward an idea. But you still haven't decided what you're going to do about the music—I mean the hymns, the chants.'

Venus shook her head. 'You're right,' she said. 'Jim Carstairs is still bereft of the organ but there's no telling when we can raise the money to replace *that*, and we can't afford to hire a piano. So it looks as if we'll have to sing unaccompanied—which, on the whole, I don't mind, but I don't think the congregation's going to like it.'

'Well,' Tim said, 'I do have a keyboard.'

'Oh, Jim Carstairs would never play a keyboard!' Venus said. 'I'm pretty certain about that.'

Tim laughed at the thought. 'But I could,' he offered. 'And at least I know most of the hymns. I daresay I could get permission to come over for the Sunday morning services until I start my full-time stint here.'

'You can play the keyboard?' Venus said. 'I can't imagine it!'

'Oh yes!' Tim said. 'In fact, I'd like to do it accompanied by drums—and I have a friend who'd bring his drums. What do you think?' He sounded eager.

'Personally,' Venus said, 'I think that would be absolutely great. But I think we'd better leave the drums until we've got used to you with a keyboard.'

'OK,' Tim agreed. 'Actually, I expect there's someone in the parish, if not in the congregation, who can play a recorder or a flute or whatever. That might fit in better. We could choose the hymns accordingly. Easy ones.'

'Fine!' Venus said. 'But I think we'd better both put the idea to Jim Carstairs. He's been organist here for a good many years, and he's a nice man. I wouldn't want to upset him.'

'Sure!' Tim agreed. 'Then we'll do that. Is he coming this morning?'

'Yes. He'll be in later,' Venus said.

Jim Carstairs arrived within ten minutes. 'What would you like me to do?' he said. 'I can stay until lunchtime if that's of any use.'

'Sure to be. There's still lots to be done,' Venus told him. 'But I'm so pleased you're here. Tim and I were just agreeing that we needed to talk to you.'

'What about?' Jim asked.

'About the singing,' Venus said. 'I mean the congregational singing.' She turned to Tim. 'Tell him what we'd thought.' She knew she was being a coward, handing it over like this.

Tim outlined what they had discussed. The organist's face remained impassive until drums were mentioned, at which the corners of his mouth turned down and his eyebrows almost disappeared into his hairline.

'Not drums!' he protested. 'Please, not drums! I don't think that's at all appropriate!'

Tim shrugged his shoulders. 'It was just a thought. But the keyboard . . .'

'If we must,' Jim conceded. 'These are unusual times and yes, I do see the need. There's nothing finer than unaccompanied singing, even if I, as an accompanist, do say so, but it has to be first-class singing. I don't think we've quite reached that standard here in St Mary's. On the other hand, I hope you don't mind if I say I'd rather someone else officiated at the keyboard. I don't think it would be quite my line. Would you believe that my ambition once was to play the organ in the Albert Hall. For the *Messiah*!' He gave a wintry smile at the thought of his presumption.

'Then I quite understand your feelings about the keyboard,' Tim said. 'But since I'm a million miles from that school of talent, I wouldn't really mind at all. I'd be happy to do it.'

'As a temporary measure,' Venus put in. In her heart, temporary, in this case, meant quite a long time, but she didn't want to depress Jim Carstairs more than she need. 'And of course, as always, Jim, we'd be most grateful for your advice in choosing the music,' she added.

'Make it something within my capabilities,' Tim said. 'And perhaps, Mr Carstairs, you might know someone in the congregation who would be able to add another instrument or two.'

'I might well,' Jim Carstairs agreed. 'As long as it isn't drums. In fact, as a young man I was reasonably proficient on the flute.'

'There you are then!' Venus said.

'Oh, I don't think I could do it now!' he said. 'I'm sure I couldn't. And of course none of this would be necessary, or at least only for a short time, if the organ had been separately insured, and for a sufficiently large sum.'

'Yes, well, we'll see how things go!' Venus said. The whole subject of the church's under-insurance had caused considerable heat already. She didn't want to fan it into life again. 'And to begin with perhaps the three of us might get together to

400

choose the hymns for Advent Sunday.'

'Make them something I can cope with,' Tim requested.

'Right! Then will you both excuse me for the moment,' Venus said. 'I spy Henry Nugent and I must have a word with him.'

Everything seemed to be going well, she thought a little later. She had spoken to just about everyone, encouraging them, which she saw as being more useful than taking on a specific job of her own, though when lunchtime came she did give Connie Phillipson a hand with serving the soup and the pizzas. 'You shouldn't be doing any of this,' Connie said. 'You should be at home with your feet up. You look tired out.'

'I am a bit weary,' Venus confessed. 'I had no idea twins were so much more difficult than one baby—well, I suppose I mean difficult to carry.'

'I don't doubt it'll be even more difficult afterwards,' Connie said. 'I mean, doing everything twice. Stands to reason, doesn't it? Why don't you sit down, have a piece of pizza and take the weight off your feet? Somebody else can serve it out.'

In the end, Venus did as Connie suggested. She was glad to sit down. Nigel left what he was doing and came to speak to her. 'I've been watching you, love,' he said. 'You look all in. I think you should take a break and go off home for an hour or two. Lie down and take it easy.'

It was the most tempting idea in the world, Venus thought. Just to lie down—or even sit in a comfortable chair with her feet up.

'Your husband's quite right,' Connie said.

'He usually is!' Venus said. 'If you really think . . .'

'Off you go!' Nigel ordered. 'Do you want me to

walk around to the Vicarage with you?'

'Of course not,' Venus said. 'But I will go. And I'll be back here before you've all finished.'

'Only if you feel like it,' Nigel said. 'Henry and Edward can take care of things here.'

*   *   *

The next day was the last Sunday in the parish hall. As soon as the service was over, and before people began to move to the coffee area, Venus said, 'And now I'd like to detain you a little longer. I have news to which I'm sure you've all been looking forward. From next Sunday we shall be back in our beloved church!'

She paused long enough to allow for the smiles, the nods, the exclamations of pleasure. Then she held up her hand for silence.

'I particularly wanted this to happen next Sunday,' she said, 'because it will be the first Sunday of Advent which, as you know, is the beginning of the church's year—and therefore a new beginning for us. So many people have worked very hard in all kinds of ways to bring this about and I'm extremely grateful to them, as I'm sure everyone will be when they see what's been achieved.

'But,' she continued, 'there is no way we must expect everything to be as it was. When you come into church next Sunday you are not going to see it as it once was. That would be unrealistic, as I'm sure you'll appreciate. Fire, in the wrong place, can be a cruel and devastating happening. It will take time for everything in St Mary's to be resolved, time we can't as yet even begin to measure, and some things will never be exactly as they were. Some things will have gone, some will be new.'

She told them, in as much detail as was possible, what they could expect, remembering that most of them had not seen the inside of the church for more than perhaps a few minutes since the fire had happened.

'There are areas of the church we can no longer use,' she said. 'And we don't know when, if ever, we might be able to use them. But we have done the best we can for the time being, and we will go on working at it, as long as it takes.'

She reminded them about the damage which had been done to the east end of the church, and that Mark Dover was doing everything he could to make that area more acceptable. 'He has told me that the screen painting will be finished before next Sunday, so we can look forward to that.' She told them about the platform, the replacement altar, the rearrangement of the pews: about the absence of the organ and the fact that Tim Crawford would substitute with a keyboard. 'So we must all sing our best!' she said.

'But the Eucharist,' she went on, 'will be the same Eucharist it has always been, the same which takes place whenever and wherever it is said or sung, and in whatever surroundings. Nothing changes that. It is the same—yesterday, today, tomorrow, always.

'And afterwards,' she said, 'when next week's Eucharist is over, we will come back here, to this room, for coffee. And then we can talk about what it was like, what we felt, what we might want to do for the future. From Advent Sunday's new beginning we will look forward to the future, and plan for it, while at the same time building on what we still have, and what we have inherited from the past.'

*   *   *

At Sunday lunch, the same day—Venus's parents were there as usual—Mavis Foster, passing the potatoes, said, 'I thought you spoke up very well, love. It was very encouraging. Has everyone had the horseradish sauce?'

'Thank you, Mother,' Venus said. 'Encouraging is what I want to be, though in spite of anything I say, some people are not going to like it. Even the ones who were helping didn't necessarily approve of what they were doing.'

'You know me and your father would have helped if you'd allowed us,' Mrs Foster said. 'Your Dad's very good with a hammer, or anything else in the building line.'

Venus smiled at her father. 'I know,' she said. 'Oh, Dad, how could I ever forget the Wendy house you made me in the garden? And there's lots you're good at, Mother. But we could never take as many helpers as we had volunteers to give us a hand. There just wasn't room to move, apart from the fact that some of the areas weren't entirely safe, especially in the beginning.'

'You did a good job, love,' Ernest Foster said. 'Everybody did.'

Mrs Foster turned to Nigel, who was sitting next to her. 'And I must say, it was really good of you, being there most of the time, Nigel—I mean coming from a different religion.'

'Mother!' Venus cried. 'What *do* you mean?

404

Nigel and I are not of different religions! We are both Christians. It's the same God we worship. It happens we go to different churches.'

'Well, if you worship the same God, why don't you go to the same church?' her mother demanded.

'And that, Mavis,' Nigel said, 'is a most profound question!'

'Profound? Me profound?' Mavis said. 'You're having me on!'

'People have been asking that question for hundreds of years,' Nigel said. 'And no-one's come up with an answer that suits everyone.'

'And will it ever change?' Ernest Foster asked.

'Who knows, Dad?' Venus said. 'Though I've often thought that if it was left to the laity things might change more quickly. They don't seem to put up so many barriers. They don't seem afraid to move—some of them, that is.'

'Well, of course,' Mavis said, clutching at an explanation, 'you *are* Venus's husband. I suppose that's why you helped.'

'Not at all,' Nigel contradicted her. 'There were usually two or three people there from St Patrick's helping, and for that matter there were people from the village who don't go to any church. Mark Dover, for example. He's doing a very good job.'

The look on Mavis's face said more about Mark Dover than her tongue ever would.

'But then,' she said, 'we're all God's children, aren't we? I don't let it bother me. Not,' she said, turning to Nigel again, 'that I could ever go to your church.'

'And why not?' He sounded indignant.

'Nothing personal,' Mavis said. 'It's the incense. I couldn't go where they had incense. It goes straight on my chest.'

Becky broke in. 'Oh, for goodness' sake can we stop talking about God and church and all that stuff. It's so *boring*! I wish I lived in a heathen family!'

* * *

'Tomorrow,' Venus said as they were clearing the table, 'I intend to do some sick visiting. I'm a bit worried about Mrs Gresham, and then there's Bertha Jowett. I haven't seen Bertha for far too long. I've been too immersed in the church building.'

'Well, love,' Mrs Foster said, 'they neither of them come to church, do they?'

'That's beside the point,' Venus told her. 'They're in my parish. I have responsibility for them. And I've put that badly—as if it was a chore, which it isn't.' It was sometimes, she thought, refreshing to talk to someone who didn't come to church. It made her think along different lines. And Bertha Jowett was always stimulating. It was just that there never seemed to be enough time for everything she had to do, or wanted to do. A wise priest had once told her that God had made plenty of time, but she'd said then, as she sometimes still thought, that in that case she wished God would give her a firm hand with arranging her schedules.

Mavis changed the subject. 'Will your mother and your aunt be coming over from Ireland for Christmas?' she asked Nigel.

'Not for Christmas,' he replied. 'I have invited them but they both said they'd wait until after the babies were born so that they could see them too.

Early March isn't all that long after Christmas. They'll be my mother's first grandchildren,' he reminded her.

His mother-in-law nodded. 'I know. And I know how that feels, don't I? It's a wonderful moment.'

* * *

On Monday morning Venus said to Nigel, 'I shall drop into church first, see what's going on, and then I'll go to see Bertha Jowett. After that I'll give Doreen Gresham a ring and ask if it's convenient for me to pop along and see her. I've no idea what her best time of day is.'

'All right,' Nigel said. 'Just don't get too tired. Try to take a rest this afternoon. That's doctor's orders!'

'I will,' Venus promised.

There were two or three people hard at it in the church, though since it was a working day for anyone who wasn't retired Venus hadn't expected to see more. Among them was Harry Carpenter, the village electrician, who now that the platform was in place was fixing the lighting for it. He was not a churchgoer but, like some of the other villagers, he was doing the work for free. 'You can pay for the materials,' he'd said. 'Cost price only. But I'll give my time.' Now he said, 'I'll finish this today, Vicar. If you're popping round late afternoon I'll show you the way of everything.'

'Wonderful!' Venus said. 'We'll probably have better lighting than we've ever had. And I do want it to look good. It will make such a difference!'

'Well, of course, it's my opinion the whole church needs rewiring,' Harry said. 'But I suppose

407

that's not on just yet?'

'Afraid not!' Venus said. 'We just can't run to it.'

'People always put off rewiring, I suppose because it doesn't show,' Harry said. 'It's a big mistake.'

*   *   *

Bertha, dressed, and sitting in her armchair, was just about to have her mid-morning coffee when Venus arrived. Bertha was not a woman given overmuch to smiling but at the sight of Venus, and in spite of herself, the corners of her mouth turned up and there was something of a shine in her eyes. Not that she was going to express her pleasure, at least not yet.

'Well, hello, stranger,' she said. 'So you are still in the land of the living?'

'I'm sorry!' Venus said. 'Is it really so long since I was here? I don't know where the time goes. But here I am and I've brought you some chocolate mints. A peace offering!'

'Thank you,' Bertha said. 'I daresay you'd like a cup of coffee.'

'I saw Matron on the way in,' Venus said. 'Someone's bringing me one.'

'Not that you could call it coffee,' Bertha said. 'What wouldn't I give for a cup of real coffee, not this instant stuff.'

Oh dear, Venus thought. We are in a grumbling mood today and no mistake. 'How have you been?' she asked.

'Same as ever,' Bertha said. 'Nothing changes much. I don't get up as much as I did. And I get even more bored. And I don't suppose for one minute that you've time for a game of Scrabble? Well, no, you won't have,' she said, answering her own question. 'Nobody has.'

'I haven't this morning,' Venus admitted, 'but I do promise I'll come in later in the week, perhaps Wednesday afternoon, and we'll have a game.'

'That will be something to look forward to,' Bertha acknowledged. 'I'm sorry I'm so cranky. I didn't sleep well. Not that that's any excuse for taking it out on you. Anyway, I haven't asked how you are.'

'I'm OK,' Venus said. 'Getting quite tired, but I suppose that's par for the course.'

'So they say,' Bertha said. 'I wouldn't know. But wouldn't you think God would have devised something less inconvenient?'

Eventually they settled down to some sort of an amicable conversation. Almost in spite of herself Bertha seemed actually interested in what was happening in the church, even in the small details, of which Venus related as many as she could.

'So we're going to take the plunge and be back in church for Advent Sunday,' she said. 'The first Sunday in Advent is a special time in the church—'

Bertha interrupted her. 'Are you telling me what Advent Sunday is about?' she asked. 'I've lived through more dreary Advents than I can possibly remember. The only good thing about Advent was that it led to Christmas, and Christmas presents. I used to count the days and then the hours. I suppose,' she added thoughtfully, 'I was a horrid child. My poor father certainly didn't know what to make of me. However,' she went on, 'it sounds as though the changes you're about to make will be to the good. Will your young priest with the keyboard

jazz up the hymns? Some of them could do with it.'
She fell silent for a few seconds, then said, 'Perhaps
the fire was a good thing!'

'Oh, I could never really say that,' Venus
answered. 'But perhaps some of the changes I've
had in mind for some time wouldn't have happened
so soon—if at all—without the fire happening. So,
yes, it has its good side, I suppose. I'm now
apprehensive, but optimistic.' It was not the time,
nor was Bertha the person, to talk about one of her
chief worries, which was what would Miss Frazer
do next? There had been no reply to Henry's letter
to her, but Miss Frazer was hardly the person to
give in. There had to be something afoot.

'No point in being apprehensive, not unless you
can do something about it,' Bertha said crisply.
'Waste of energy!'

Presently, Venus said, 'I'm sorry, Bertha, I must
go soon. I have to go to see someone else, a lady
I'm quite worried about. She's very ill indeed. Now,
if you were the praying sort I'd ask you to pray for
her! You've got the time to do that.' She was
smiling as she said the words to Bertha.

'Don't ask me to take part in that claptrap!'
Bertha said. 'You know my views!' There was a
pause, and then she said, 'But I could think about
her. What's your view on the power of positive
thought, then?'

'If it's positive for good, then I'd say it's quite
close to prayer,' Venus said.

'Rubbish!' Bertha said. 'But I'll do it anyway.
What's her name?'

'Doreen,' Venus told her. 'She lives alone and
she's bedfast. I don't think she's going to get
better.'

'Right!' Bertha said. 'You do it your way and I'll do it mine!'

CHAPTER TWENTY-EIGHT

Venus stayed with Bertha for the best part of an hour, leaving her, she hoped, rather more cheerful than she had found her.

'Don't forget about Wednesday!' Bertha called out after her.

'As if I would,' Venus said. 'I promised, didn't I? I'll be here around two o'clock.'

'Oh no!' Bertha protested. 'Two o'clock won't do! I like a little nap after lunch. Make it nearer four.'

'Then we'll settle on three,' Venus said.

Bertha Jowett looked a little less than pleased. She liked to set the rules, more and more so as she got older, and there was little she could do in that line, sitting here in her chair, or lying in bed, in this small room in The Beeches. Everything took place within strict timing, which was something she would never take to.

Leaving Bertha, Venus set off to walk back to the Vicarage, where she would pick up her car to go to visit Doreen Gresham. At work in her parish it was her custom, almost a rule, that she went everywhere on foot. Apart from the fact that the exercise was good for her health, it was one of the ways she met people, including people who were not from St Mary's congregation. By now, almost everyone in Thurston knew her, or at least recognised her, whether or not she wore her clerical collar. People who, as far as she knew, never set foot in church, and probably never would, spoke to her—these days often pausing to ask how she was. No excuse was needed: Thurston was a village. She was the Vicar, she belonged to them, and she was very obviously pregnant. Today was one of those days she felt very pregnant—and Richmond Road was too far to walk. Earlier in the day, stooping in the garden to pick a few late flowers to take to Doreen Gresham had been quite a chore. The garden, she had thought, was not at its best, it was the wrong time of the year, but she had worked hard on it as often as she could and it was certainly an improvement on this time last year. Some of that she owed to her Dad.

Passing the village pond she was pleased to see how full it was once again after the dry summer. The ducks, too, looked happier about that. In the height of the summer there had been scarcely enough water for them to swim in. The swifts, which flew into Thurston every summer—presumably from some distant land—had long gone. When the swifts massed together, manoeuvring like a regiment of soldiers training for battle before they took off, Venus knew that, whatever the calendar said, it was the end of summer. Blackbirds, thankfully, were still around, and would be throughout the winter. It was hardly possible to go out of the house without seeing a pair of blackbirds, the handsome male with his bright orange beak and his less flamboyant female.

Crates of beer were being delivered, noisily, to the Ewe Lamb. It was ages, she thought, since she had last been in there. Her father was a fairly regular visitor, though seldom for more than one

412

pint. Once or twice, in her early days in Thurston, and before she had really got to know Nigel, Mark Dover had taken her there for lunch. It was a pleasant place, friendly.

Reaching the Vicarage, though without going into the house, she unlocked her small car and eased herself into the driving seat—and wondered how long she would be able to do so. The seat wouldn't move back any further. She thought how much she would like, right now, to go into the house and sit down in a comfortable chair, or lie down on the sofa for half-an-hour with her feet up. No time at the moment. It would have to wait.

Reaching the house in Richmond Road, she rang the bell, and waited, as before. Albert answered the door. 'Good-morning, Vicar,' he said. 'I take it you've come to see Mrs Gresham? I don't think you'll find her very well today. I looked in earlier, took her a cup of tea and a slice of toast, though I doubt she's eaten it.' While he was talking she followed him up the narrow stairs. He tapped on Doreen Gresham's door and called out to her. 'The Vicar to see you! Are you decent?'

'Come in!' Her voice was faint, hardly audible.

Albert went in with Venus. 'I'll take your breakfast things away,' he said to Doreen. 'Though I see you haven't eaten so much as a bite of toast.'

'I'm sorry!' Doreen apologised. 'I can't get it down. Anyway, I don't need it, lying here doing nothing. Sit down, Vicar.'

'Of course you need it,' Albert said. 'You have to keep your strength up, don't you?'

'He's very kind,' Doreen said when he had left the room, 'but he doesn't understand. He's determined I'm going to get better.'

'How have you been?' Venus asked.

Doreen managed a smile. 'As you see,' she said. 'Slipping. A bit each day.'

That much was apparent, Venus thought. She could see a big difference though it was less than a week since she'd been here.

'I wish it would be a bit quicker,' Doreen said. 'I'm getting impatient. Anyway, they came from the library. A very kind lady brought me some books. I don't seem to be able to get into them, though. My fault, of course. I can't concentrate.' It was all said with a great deal of effort, as if it was beyond her strength to utter the words.

'Did you get in touch with your son?' Venus asked.

Doreen shook her head. 'No, I didn't. I don't think I'd know what to say, though I do long to see him.'

'Let me telephone for you,' Venus suggested. 'I do think he ought to know you're ill. I'm sure he'd want to know.'

'The thing is, I can't remember why we quarrelled,' Doreen said. 'Or even if we did quarrel—or just drifted apart.'

'It happens,' Venus said. And it did. But it was so wrong, mother and son, living within a few miles of each other, not communicating. What would he feel like when she died, which she was surely going to, and before long? 'Let me telephone for you,' she repeated. 'I'm sure he'd be very upset if he weren't to know.'

Doreen deliberated. 'All right then,' she said after a pause. 'I suppose it can't do any harm. But he probably won't come.'

'I'll bet you he will,' Venus said. By the time she

had said what she had to say to him she hoped he'd come running, though she mustn't be rude, or judgmental—or say anything which would put him off. She'd have to do it tactfully. 'Give me his telephone number,' she said. 'What's his name?'

'James.' Doreen indicated a small diary on the bedside table. 'His home number's in that,' she said. 'I don't know his work number. Or even if he's still in the same job. But you're not to tell him I asked for him to come because I'm not doing that. Just tell him I'm not well.'

How awful, how sad, Venus thought, that even at death's door this woman couldn't bring herself to ask her son to visit her.

She stayed a little longer, but she could see that Doreen was by now inordinately tired. 'I'll leave you now, Doreen,' she said presently. 'I might not be able to see you tomorrow but I will come for certain the day after. Would you like me to say a prayer? You don't have to say yes if you'd rather I didn't.'

'Oddly enough, I would quite like that,' Doreen said. 'Though it seems a bit of a cheek when I've ignored Him for years!'

'I don't think God counts time like we do,' Venus said.

'I remember that in a hymn,' Doreen said. ' "A thousand ages in Thy sight are like an evening gone"! Funny, it's years since I sang a hymn, but isn't it strange I remember that bit? "O God, our help in ages past". It wasn't even a favourite hymn.'

'There you go, then!' Venus said.

She said a short prayer, bent over and kissed Doreen—her face was as cold as ice—and left.

415

When Venus reached home she tried at once to contact James Gresham, but there was no reply. She left a message, simply giving her phone number and asking to be called back as soon as possible. After that she heated some soup, which she had with a slice of bread, and then, suddenly and terribly tired, she went upstairs, took off her shoes and lay on the bed, where she fell asleep at once. She was awakened only when she heard Becky's key in the lock, followed by her daughter bursting into the house and calling out, 'Mum! Where are you?'

'I'll be down in a minute!' she called back. She looked at the clock. Great heavens! She had slept for almost two hours. It was unheard of for her to do that in the daytime but, she realised, as she put her shoes on again and combed her hair, she felt better for it. And presumably the phone had not rung or surely it would have wakened her?

When she went downstairs Nigel was coming in at the door. 'Finished my visits,' he said. 'An hour-and-a-half free before I have to be back for the evening surgery. Is there any tea going?'

'There will be in a minute,' Venus said.

'Can I have lemonade?' Becky asked. 'You know I hate tea.'

'Fizzy lemonade will do your teeth no good,' Venus said. 'But all right, just this once!' She was too tired to argue.

'You look all in,' Nigel said. 'What sort of a day have you had?'

'The last two hours I've been asleep on the bed,' Venus told him. 'It was marvellous. I went out like

416

a light!'

'You should be doing that every afternoon,' Nigel said.

'I wish!' she answered.

'So have you had a busy morning? Did you go to see Bertha Jowett?' he asked.

'I did. I went into church first . . .' She suddenly gave a small cry. 'Oh damn! I promised to go around this afternoon and see Harry Carpenter about the electrics. Oh dear, I forgot all about it!' She looked at her watch. 'I expect he'll have left by now. I wonder if I should try?'

'And I say you won't!' Nigel was firm about it. 'When I go back to surgery I'll drop in, see if he's still there—which I doubt. If not, you can give him a ring later.'

'My head was full of Mrs Gresham,' Venus said. 'I went to see her straight after Bertha Jowett.'

'And?' Nigel questioned.

'Very poorly. I'd think certainly near to death— and she'd welcome it. The only thing is . . .'

She told him about Doreen Gresham's estrangement from her family. 'A brother, a sister and a son. She hasn't seen any of them for who knows how long, and doesn't expect to either. It's terrible what families do to each other. Even nice, respectable families.'

Nigel nodded. 'I know. I see a lot of it.'

'I persuaded her to give me the son's phone number so that I could tell him what the situation was. She wasn't prepared to do it herself. I rang him as soon as I got back. There was no reply but I left my number. Surely if he'd rung back this afternoon I couldn't have slept through it?'

'Of course you wouldn't,' Nigel assured her. 'I

expect he was at work.'

'I'll give it another try,' she said.

When Nigel had gone back to the surgery she rang James Gresham again. He answered the phone immediately.

'My name's Venus Baines,' she said. 'I'm the Vicar of St Mary's, Thurston.'

'Sorry! You've got the wrong number,' he said quickly—and rang off.

She rang back immediately.

'I didn't get the wrong number,' she said. 'I'm ringing about your mother, Doreen Gresham. She gave me your number.'

'Why would she do that?' he asked. 'Why would she ask you to ring me?' He had a deep, pleasant voice. She didn't know why that surprised her, but it did. It was probably inherited from his mother.

'She's very ill. Very ill indeed. She would like to see you. And I think you might want to see her.'

'Oh!' he said. 'Oh, I'm sorry! I've been a bit out of touch. I haven't seen her for some time. You know how it is?'

No, I don't, Venus thought. 'She needs to see you, and I'd say it's urgent,' she said.

'What's wrong with her?' he asked. 'She was never ill.'

'She is now,' Venus told him.

'Well of course I'll go to see her,' he said. 'If you think I'll be welcomed.'

'With open arms,' Venus said. She was not entirely sure of that. She hoped that Doreen would do her part.

'And I believe she has a sister and a brother with whom she's lost touch,' she said.

'Two brothers and a sister,' he corrected her.

418

'Uncle John, Aunty Jenny and Uncle Brian. I don't think she's seen them for a few years. I haven't myself.'

'Well,' Venus said, 'and I hope you'll excuse me for being so frank—but your mother is going to die, and soon—so they might like to hear about her while she's still alive. Do they live locally?'

'Not exactly locally,' James said. 'In fact Uncle John went to Australia. I've completely lost touch with him. But the others are not all that far away. Aunty Jenny lives in London—she's widowed—and Uncle Brian and his wife in Eastbourne. I do have their addresses.'

'Then if you agree, they should be informed,' Venus said. 'Would you like me to contact them or will you do it?'

'I'll do it,' James said. 'Thank you for letting me know.'

'I wouldn't leave it too long if I were you,' Venus said. 'And I'm sorry it isn't more cheerful news. Perhaps I'll meet with you on another occasion.' She most certainly would, she thought. Unless Doreen Gresham had a specific request for her funeral not to be in her own parish, then they would meet at the funeral—which would not be, she was sure, long hence. But thankfully, she thought, now a more bearable occasion than it might have been. James had sounded a nice, reasonable person. What had led him to be estranged from his mother for so long? She would probably never know.

Two days later, as promised, she visited Doreen Gresham again and found her, though physically she had undoubtedly deteriorated, in a happy mood.

'I've got wonderful news for you!' she said. 'James came to see me yesterday. I couldn't believe it when Albert came up and said there was this young man at the door, wanting to see me. "He says his name's James, and he's your son. Shall I bring him up?" he said. And James was just the same, lovely person he'd been when he was younger. I have you to thank for that, Venus. And I can never thank you enough.'

'Anyone might have done it,' Venus protested.

'Oh no!' Doreen was adamant. 'For some reason I don't seek to understand, you were there.'

'I was there because you sent for me,' Venus reminded her. 'Don't you remember—you were getting bored!'

'Whatever started it,' Doreen said, 'you came. And you did it. I'd like to think it was meant to be. I'm a very happy woman. And to add to that, my sister and my brother—or at any rate one of my brothers—might—just might—be coming to see me any day now. James is getting in touch with them. It's almost worth being poorly!'

'I'm really pleased for you,' Venus said. 'I'll pop in to see you tomorrow.' She felt now that she must be available every day, if need be. 'Is there anything you want?'

Doreen's smile lit up her face. 'Not now,' she said. 'I've been given it all!'

*   *   *

On most evenings, when Becky had finally gone to bed and they were alone, Venus and Nigel talked about the events of their respective days, about their own ups and downs. They never spoke of anything which was truly confidential to the people concerned—that was totally forbidden, an unwritten rule between them—but they discussed happenings in general, often, when it was necessary, without ever mentioning names.

'So did you see Mrs Gresham?' Nigel asked. 'And how was she?'

'I did,' Venus said. 'And she was very poorly. But there's great news on that front!' She told him about James's visit.

'You did a good job there,' Nigel said.

Venus shook her head. 'Nothing sensational. You would have done it; anyone would have done it, given the opportunity. In fact, it's a privilege of my job, and in a way of yours, that we do have the opportunity, that sometimes I can be side by side with people in their lives, especially in times of need.'

'I agree,' Nigel said. 'So you're never sorry that you chose to be a priest?'

'Never! In fact . . .' She hesitated.

'What?'

'I like to believe that God chose me. Is that big-headed? I would only say it to you.'

'Of course not,' Nigel said. 'And in my opinion he chose wisely.'

'I'm not at all good at some of it,' Venus said. 'As you know, I don't like the financial bits. Perhaps the fact that I'm not good at those helps to stop me being big-headed. Anyway, never mind about me! How many people have you cured today, darling?'

'Not as many as I'd like,' Nigel said. 'I could say that any day. I couldn't have done anything for your Mrs Gresham—but you could—and did.'

'Then we're a good team,' Venus said, smiling.

'I never doubted it,' he said.

*　　　*　　　*

It was Saturday afternoon, the eve of Advent Sunday, the very last opportunity to have everything ship-shape and ready for what was to be, for Venus, the great day. She was as nervous about it as if the fire, and the havoc it had caused, was her personal responsibility, as if she alone was the one who must make it right. She knew she was wrong on both counts, but it was a feeling difficult to shake off.

Looking around the church now was proof that she was far from alone. It had hummed and buzzed from early morning with people working at making everything special for the next day and now, between them, they had done all that could possibly be done. Mark Dover had finished the screen painting only yesterday afternoon, in the last of the light. In spite of his own misgivings it was exactly right for the place it was in and its fresh colouring lit up and brought light to the otherwise sad-looking area of devastation. It depicted, though not too exactly or too detailed—there was room for the viewer to add something of his own interpretation, to read into it what he saw, or imagined—the scenery which was familiar to the people of Thurston: the rolling Downs, the sheep, the sky and, above all, the clarity of the light. How Mark had achieved such clarity, Venus thought, was beyond her ken.

'Don't anyone dare to touch it!' he said. 'The paint isn't entirely dry.'

The platform had been completed, and painted

422

in a soft cream shade, two days earlier and this morning Miss Tordoff's Indian rug had been laid down. Mavis Foster's old table had been transformed into an altar by St Mary's own altar frontal, purple for Advent Sunday, and the small reading desk which had been lent by St Patrick's to be used as a lectern had been cleaned and polished within an inch of its life. Henry Nugent and his wife had lent nice-looking chairs for the priest and the servers. In front of and below the platform a chair had been set for Tim Crawford, and a table for his keyboard and music. 'I'm not sure I'll like being so much in view,' he said. 'But I'll put up with it. All for the good of the cause, I suppose.'

'It's great!' Venus enthused. 'Everyone's going to be closer to what's happening and I'll be able to see just about everyone.'

She went and stood at the back with her churchwardens and Treasurer, looking at it. 'I want to see how it all looks from here,' she said.

'I have to say, it looks good,' Henry said. 'And there were many times when I thought it wouldn't.'

'Now I never did think that way,' Edward Mason said. 'I quite looked forward to it. But perhaps that's because I haven't been here as long as you, Henry. I've less to miss.'

'It's certainly different,' David Wainright said. 'It'll take some getting used to, I suppose.' His tone said that he would never get used to it.

'At least, David,' Venus said, 'you must admit it hasn't cost much. A great deal of the labour has been free and most other things we've either been lent or given. Even the paint was a gift.'

'That's true!' Henry said. 'The traders in the village have come up trumps. We've hardly had to pay for anything. That should please you, David!'

Connie Phillipson came into the church and joined them as Henry was speaking to David.

'Oh, it will please him,' she said. 'That's a treasurer for you!'

'I have to watch the money,' David protested. 'It's my job. If I don't, who will?'

'I know all about that!' Connie said. 'Don't forget I was married to one for a good many years!' But she was smiling at him as she said it. 'Anyway, I've come in to tell you that the lunch is ready, and you're all to come and get it at once.'

It had been decided, largely by Connie, who had recruited a band of helpers, that a proper, sit-down lunch would be served to all those who had taken part in the work in the church. Whether or not they were regular churchgoers, or even if they were not at all, made no difference. All who had helped were invited, including Elsie Jones and her Brownies. Mark Dover had been in the church earlier but was sorry, he couldn't stay for lunch, he had to dash off to London. Venus didn't quite believe him, but no matter.

They left the church, locking it behind them—there were still tools and so on lying around—and went off to the parish hall, where those who hadn't worked in church on this particular morning were waiting. Several members of the PCC, including Miss Tordoff, were also there. To Venus's great surprise—she had known nothing of this—a table near the door was laid with glasses and bottles of wine, with Carla and Walter Brown standing behind it, ready to serve. Walter, Venus was quite sure, must have been ordered to do it by Carla, though he poured the wine with good grace, while

Cliff Preston and his wife, free from funerals for the moment, handed it around.

'I knew nothing of this!' David Wainright said to Connie.

'You didn't need to,' Connie replied. 'The church isn't paying for it!'

'Then who is?' he asked.

'An unknown, generous donor,' Connie said. He was not unknown to her. It was Mark Dover who had come to her earlier in the week and arranged to provide the wine, on the understanding that she told no-one. 'No-one at all, mind,' he'd said. 'Not even Venus. Especially not Venus!' Privately, Connie thought that was why he had opted out of being at the lunch. He didn't want anyone to guess.

When lunch was over those who still had things to attend to in the church went back—including Tim Crawford, who insisted that he must put in more practice on the hymns. He, Venus and Jim Carstairs had between them chosen the hymns for Advent Sunday and for the Sunday following. Tim, usually confident, was as nervous as a kitten. 'Hymns are not usually what I play,' he said for the umpteenth time.

'It was your idea—and I still think a good one—that you played the keyboard,' Venus pointed out.

'I just wish I had someone to play with me—some other instrument,' he said. Jim had firmly refused to brush up his prowess on the flute. 'It's all too long ago,' he'd said.

'If you're quite serious,' Venus said to Tim, 'I could put out a plea at tomorrow's service. There might be someone who could oblige. But you'd have to audition them first. We want the music to be good.'

'I wish you would,' Tim said.

'But don't worry, Tim!' Venus said. 'You'll be all right! I'm sure you will.'

She left him practising 'Hark, a Herald Voice is Calling'. It was an easy tune, though not one she particularly liked. Much as she liked the Advent season, she didn't care for some of its hymns. She was at the lectern, marking the places for tomorrow's readings, when the church door opened and a man entered. He was carrying a big bouquet of chrysanthemums with large heads of bronze, gold and yellow; at least a dozen of them.

'Is the Vicar here?' he called out.

Venus left what she was doing and went forward to meet him. 'I'm the Vicar,' she said.

'Oh!' He looked uncertain. 'Then in that case these are for you.'

He thrust them at her and left. There was a card, from a florist in Brampton, tucked into them. She took it out and read it.

'To Venus,' it said. 'Congratulations. Bertha Jowett.'

It was unbelievable! It was so completely out of character for Bertha. Venus had never known her pay a compliment. She hoped Bertha wasn't suddenly ill, or something. And then Nigel came.

'What wonderful flowers!' he said. 'Who sent them?' For a brief moment he suspected Mark Dover. It was the kind of extravagant thing he would do. Venus handed him the card.

'I can't believe it!' she said. 'Not Bertha! I must go round and see if she's all right.'

'Not now, you won't,' Nigel said. 'You look all in. You haven't had a minute's rest all day. I'm going to take you home.'

426

'All right,' she said. 'I am tired.' But she would not show anyone the card. And the minute she got home she would ring Bertha.

CHAPTER TWENTY-NINE

Advent Sunday was fine and sunny, and reasonably mild for the time of the year. Standing at the church door, it was clear that there were more people arriving than Venus had expected, certainly more than on a usual Sunday, and several of them were not regular churchgoers. Some, particularly from the village, she had seldom, if ever, seen there before. Cliff Preston and his wife came, so did Mr Winterton, the greengrocer. Venus had not seen him in church since the baptism of his baby granddaughter, several months ago. An assistant from Gander's bakery was there, as was Bob Chester's wife from the newsagent's. 'Bob would have been here,' Mrs Chester said, 'but Sunday morning is a busy time for newspapers.'

Sonia Leyton, Nigel's partner in the practice, who came to church spasmodically, arrived at the last minute. She looked tired, Venus thought—and wondered if she'd had a disturbed night. She and Nigel took it in turns and last night he'd not been on call.

'Lovely to see you,' Venus said. 'Did you have a busy night?'

'More or less usual,' Sonia said. 'Why are babies always born at night? But I did want to be here this morning. It is a bit special, isn't it?'

'I think so,' Venus said.

Evelyn Sharp, Becky's headmistress, also came. It was good to see her. She had proved such a friend when Becky had difficulties—thankfully now over—at school. 'We must get together soon,' Venus said.

When the very last straggler—it was Mr Fawcett, though he lived alone and had few responsibilities and could well have been the first—had arrived, Venus went in. Since the church was slightly more than half full, Venus thought, it couldn't be described as half empty—but then she remembered that there was far less room for the congregation than when they had had the full use of all the space in the church. But that in a way was all to the good. People were not nearly so spread out. Also, she realised with great satisfaction, for the very first time she could now see everyone, no matter where they were sitting.

She looked around. Her father and her mother, with Becky, were in the third row back, but of course no Nigel. He was in St Patrick's. It was so good that her parents had been able to come to live in Thurston, but it was a sadness, as always, that she and Nigel couldn't worship the same God in the same place.

Everything went well. It was almost, she thought, as if everyone was willing it to do so. Tim, sitting at a small table down in front of the platform, played well, though Venus sensed he was nervous. She was also well aware, as the service went on, that he would have been greatly helped by the presence of another instrument, or possibly two. But there were no hitches, either in the music or in the service. People processed to where she stood in front of the platform and took communion, standing, there

428

being no longer an altar rail at which to kneel. As far as she could see, it didn't seem to matter, though she was sure it would to some.

At the end of the service she thanked them all for coming, hoped they had liked what they saw, even though there was much more to be done when enough money had been raised, and invited everyone to coffee in the parish hall. Seconds before she was due to give out the notices a server had handed her a note from Tim. 'PLEASE, PLEASE don't forget to ask for another instrumentalist!'

She looked across, smiled at him, and did what he had asked. 'Don't be shy to come forward if you can help,' she said to the congregation. 'Tim has done a wonderful job this morning, but he would be very glad of help.'

*   *   *

In the parish hall Carla Brown came up to her.

'I might be able to help you,' she said. 'I mean about the music.'

'Really?' Venus said. 'I had no idea you played an instrument!'

'Oh I don't,' Carla said, 'though I used to be a dab hand with a comb and tissue paper. But it's my niece, Elisabeth. My sister's girl. She's doing very well on the flute. She's just passed her latest exam with distinction. She's twelve years old.'

'How interesting!' Venus said. 'Should I know her? Does she come to church?'

'I'm afraid not all that often,' Carla said. 'But she used to go to Sunday School. Trudy Santer will know her.'

'And would she be willing to help?' Venus asked.

'With a little encouragement.' Carla spoke with confidence. But then, Venus thought, she had seldom met anyone as clever as Carla at getting other people to do things.

'Then let's find Tim, and have a word with him,' she said. 'And with Jim Carstairs, of course.' They moved across the hall to where Tim was talking to a group of people.

'It sounds wonderful,' Tim said when Venus gave him the news. He called Jim across and they sorted out what they might do. It appeared that Tuesday evening would be convenient, and at the Vicarage, to meet up with Elisabeth. And if it wasn't totally convenient for Elisabeth, Venus thought, then her aunt would somehow see that it was. 'So seven o'clock, then,' Venus said. 'We don't want it to be too late for Elisabeth's sake.'

'I'll let her know,' Carla said, moving away. 'I'll ring you, Venus, and confirm it.' Venus had little doubt that it would be confirmed.

'I hope Elisabeth will be willing,' Tim said to Venus. 'If she is, and if she's competent, it could be marvellous.'

'Oh, I think Carla will see to it that she's willing,' Venus said. 'It might mean bribing her, but we can leave that to Carla.'

She moved around now, talking to people. There were quite a number of congratulations on the new state of the church. 'It seems to work well,' was what most people said. There were also a few who said, 'I suppose we'll have to get used to it,' some of them adding, 'until we get back to normal!' Whatever that will be, Venus thought to herself. But she reminded herself that there were members

430

of the congregation, and not a few, who had been coming to St Mary's for years—and, in many cases, their families before them. They couldn't be expected not to miss the way it had once been. Tim had been congratulated right and left on his playing, though again there were those who said, 'It's not like the organ, is it? I do miss the organ!'

Venus spoke to Jim again. 'You will be there on Tuesday evening, won't you?' she asked. 'You're the one who knows all about the music.'

'Oh, I'll be there,' Jim said.

Mavis Foster came up to them. 'I'm leaving now, Venus love,' she said. 'I'm making the lunch today,' she explained to the others. 'But don't be late for it,' she warned Venus.

Mavis had insisted that from now on she should take over the cooking of Sunday lunch. 'You need to rest, Venus,' she'd said. 'Especially after a busy morning. And I do know how to cook a good lunch. You won't get anything fancy, of course. I'm not into that. But though I says it as shouldn't, I can do a roast all right!'

*　　　*　　　*

After lunch Venus said, 'I'm going round to see Bertha Jowett now. I want to thank her for the flowers.'

'Must you?' Nigel said. 'I thought you'd already thanked her.'

'Only on the phone,' Venus said. 'It's not the same thing.'

'Well don't stay too long,' Nigel said. He himself had to make a hospital visit. 'I'll drop you off on my way,' he offered. 'Save you a walk, even if it's only a short one.'

Bertha was up and dressed, sitting at a small table by the bay window, the cards spread out before her in a game of patience.

'Oh, it's you!' she said. 'Well I'm pleased to see someone! I've played nearly a dozen games of patience and it's come out every time. It's so boring, getting it right every game.'

'Isn't that what you're supposed to do?' Venus asked, seating herself on a chair close to Bertha. 'I thought that was the object of the game?' Privately, she thought it more than likely that Bertha had cheated a bit, like shuffling the cards before she went through them again if the first time hadn't yielded anything. She had seen her do it. But as she was only cheating herself it probably didn't matter.

'I've brought you a Sunday paper,' she said.

'Oh good!' Bertha replied. 'I hope it's one of the scandal sheets! I could do with reading a good scandal or two. Political for preference, or the royal family of course. Now that's one thing you never do, Venus. You never bring me any really interesting gossip from the village. You must hear some!'

'From time to time,' Venus agreed. 'I suspect most of it's untrue. Anyway, I've brought you a scandal sheet today. And how are you?'

'Bored!' Bertha spat out the word. 'Bored with playing cards. Bored with looking out of the window.'

'But it's a very nice outlook,' Venus said.

The garden was spacious, with a large, well-

432

trimmed lawn in the centre, flower beds around it, and the whole surrounded by trees; some deciduous, which had already shed their leaves, rather more evergreen, holly and the like.

'It's not an *interesting* outlook,' Bertha said. 'Nothing happens. Have you ever tried to watch grass growing? And of course those bloody evergreens block off the view of the road. I'd like to take an axe to them. At least to watch people walking past would be something—or even to watch cars being driven up and down the road. It would be movement, wouldn't it?'

'My! We are in a bad mood today!' Venus said. 'We are so sorry for ourselves, aren't we?'

'Yes we are,' Bertha said firmly.

For a moment Venus wondered why she cared about this elderly woman who was so often bad-tempered, or even downright rude. She recognised, though, that Bertha's moods were born of frustration, about which little could be done. Even though Bertha Jowett could sometimes be more than a little annoying, Venus still felt sorry for her. And more than that, she actually liked her. Bertha was never dull. She said what she thought, she pulled no punches.

'I've brought you an apple pie,' Venus said now. 'My mother made it for you. She's good at apple pies.'

For the first time since Venus's arrival, Bertha's face showed pleasure, her eyes brightening. 'Now, that *is* good,' she said. 'I get sick of the food here. Oh! I know they do their best, but it's all pappy. Mashed potatoes, pureed parsnips, minced meat. The thing is, most of them haven't got many teeth left. But I have all mine. My father was rigorous

433

about teeth. A bit yellow mine are now, but I can chew most things. Celery I'm not good at.'

My mother, Venus thought, would not like the idea that her apple pie needed good, strong teeth to eat it.

'I've been thinking,' she said. 'Why don't I take you down to see what we've done in the church?'

Bertha stared at her. 'Why would I be interested to know what you've done in the church?' she demanded.

'You just might,' Venus said. 'And in any case it would be an outing, wouldn't it? We could put a wheelchair into my car boot—I presume they have a wheelchair or two here . . . ?'

'They have,' Bertha said. 'But if you think you're getting me into one, you're mistaken!'

'Why ever not?' Venus demanded.

'I don't want to be pushed around. I did it once,' Bertha said. 'I'd broken my leg. Do you know how people in wheelchairs are treated? If anyone wants to say anything to them, or ask a question, they do it through whoever's pushing! "What happened to her?" they ask. "Is she in a lot of pain?" You could be deaf and brainless from the way people talk to you—or rather, don't talk to you.'

'Good point. I've heard of that before and I'll bear it in mind,' Venus said. 'Though I hadn't thought of pushing you on display down the length of the High Street: simply putting you into the car and the wheelchair in the boot, so that I could take it out and push you up the church path, which is a bit steep, as far as the door. After that you could be on your own.'

'Well, I don't know . . .' Bertha began.

'Suit yourself,' Venus said. 'You said you were

434

bored, you said you didn't see enough of the world. Here's your chance.'

Bertha was silent for a minute or so, but she recognised an ultimatum when she saw one. In the end she said, 'Well, all right. I'll go! But just bear in mind I don't want to be involved in some service— or anything of that kind.'

'I can promise you won't be,' Venus said. 'In fact I can probably pick a time when you might not see another soul. How would that suit you?'

'Fine!' Bertha said. 'I don't want anyone to think I'm going soft in the head. On the other hand, if you think this is the thin edge of the wedge, then you're barking up the wrong tree, if you'll excuse my mixed metaphors.'

'Gladly, if you'll come,' Venus said.

'I just hope no-one would see me going in or coming out!' Bertha said.

'We could go at dead of night,' Venus said.

'And now you're being silly!' Bertha complained.

'So are you!' Venus retorted. 'Come on! Show your mettle! Do it for me. I do want to show you the church. Just this once.'

Bertha was silent for a while, then she said, 'All right then.'

'Then I'll come for you about ten o'clock in the morning,' Venus said.

*   *   *

This was not going to be easy, Venus thought as she turned into The Beeches. She half wished she hadn't suggested it. But even if Bertha didn't enjoy it, at least it would have taken her out of the house, broken her everyday routine. She half expected that Bertha would have changed her mind, but it was not so. She was ready and waiting, wearing her black winter coat with a fur collar and a black felt hat rather like an upturned flower pot. It was not in the least becoming. The paleness of her face and the slight redness of her over-large nose were not enhanced by the dead black of her outfit.

The wheelchair was in the hall, waiting. Matron herself helped to stow it in the boot, and then helped Bertha into the front passenger seat. 'How nice to see you taking a little trip, Miss Jowett!' she said. 'It will do you all the good in the world.'

'I can think of better places to take a trip to,' Bertha said ungraciously.

They met no-one while Venus parked the car and pushed Bertha up the church path in the wheelchair. As they went into the porch Venus said, 'Would you like me to push you around the church—though it won't all be easily accessible—or would you rather walk? Obviously there are plenty of seats if you get tired.'

'I want to walk, of course,' Bertha said. 'Why else would I bring my stick? You can give me a hand getting out of this contraption.'

Venus was surprised at how slow and hesitant Bertha's walking was, but then, she remembered, she had hardly seen it before, and certainly not since she had moved into The Beeches. They walked first of all up to the badly damaged part of the church and stood for a moment looking at it. 'Hm!' Bertha said. 'It is a bit of a mess, isn't it? But it was a good idea to put up the screen, and I like the painting. Much better than a bunch of anaemic-looking angels sitting around on clouds!'

'You and Mark Dover would have seen eye to

436

eye about that,' Venus said. 'He flatly refused to paint angels.'

Bertha nodded approval. 'Good for him!'

They moved on, slowly making their way around to the back of the church.

'This is the new arrangement,' Venus said. 'At least so far. It might only be temporary, we can't be sure, but it seemed to work all right on Sunday. We've a way to go and a great deal to decide about before the church is completely restored. But it will be in the end, I'm certain of it.'

'If you say so,' Bertha said.

'I certainly do,' Venus replied.

'If it were me,' Bertha said, 'I wouldn't have had all that fancy brocaded stuff draping the altar. It goes back to the year dot.'

'I know,' Venus said. 'That's exactly why a lot of people like it. In any case, it's only an old table underneath, one my mother lent us.'

'Well, all right,' Bertha said grudgingly. 'But I would think a nice, plain altar, in beautiful wood, no frilly bits, might be better.'

'You could be right,' Venus agreed. 'Not that we could afford it. And right now I'd rather not be deliberately contentious. Some people are having to put up with a lot they're not at all sure about. In any case, it's what goes on at the altar that matters, isn't it?'

'Oh, I know all about that!' Bertha said. 'Count me out!'

When they had looked at everything, in all of which Bertha seemed interested, Venus said, 'Now! How would you like to go down to Gander's and have coffee and a bun? That would make a change, wouldn't it?'

'It certainly would!' Bertha agreed. 'But not if it means being pushed there. I have my pride, but if you can park your car outside Gander's . . .'

'You know I can't do that,' Venus said. 'It's in the High Street and there's no parking except for deliveries. So it's the chair or nothing. But what makes you think everyone is going to look at you? There are plenty of other things going on in the High Street. You might not even be noticed.'

There was a lengthy silence. In the end, Bertha said, 'You are quite right, of course. Thank you for pointing it out. Why should anyone look at me? So we'll go, shall we?'

*   *   *

'Well!' Bertha said an hour or so later, 'I haven't enjoyed myself so much in quite a long time. And I'm sorry if I've been a bad-tempered old woman.'

*   *   *

Back at home, Venus rang Nigel at the surgery. 'I'm going to see Doreen Gresham this afternoon and I might not be home when Becky gets back from school,' she said. 'I don't know how I'm going to find things there. Is there any chance you might be home? She has her key, of course.'

'I daresay I can be there when she arrives,' Nigel said. 'I might not be able to stay. I'll have to see how it goes.'

'That should be OK,' Venus said. 'I might not be late, I just can't tell.'

'Are you all right?' Nigel asked.

'Fine! I've had an interesting morning with

438

Bertha Jowett. Tell you all about it when I see you.'

* * *

As usual, Albert opened the door to Venus. 'She's got visitors!' he announced. 'Her son, and two other people. They've been here since before dinnertime. You can find your own way up by now, can't you?'

When Venus rang the bell of Doreen Gresham's flat the door was opened by her son.

'Come in,' he said. 'I've been here most of the morning. I took a day off work. And now my aunt and uncle are here from Eastbourne.'

'Good!' Venus said. 'How is your mother?'

He shook his head. 'Not good. Not at all good. The doctor was here earlier. He gave her something for the pain, says he'll call tomorrow but I can ring him if I need him.'

'I won't stay long,' Venus says. 'I just wanted to see how she was.'

'She'll be pleased to see you,' James Gresham said. 'She keeps mentioning you.'

Venus followed him into the bedroom. Doreen was half lying, half sitting up, in bed. She looked ghastly, Venus thought. Certainly worse than she had yesterday. Her skin was a waxy yellow, her eyes more deeply hollowed than ever. And yet in spirits she seemed incredibly better. Her eyes were brighter than Venus had seen them in the few days she had known her, and there was a serenity about her which was new. She raised one hand in salute to Venus.

'This is turning out to be a great day,' she said. Her voice was weak, she found it difficult to say the

439

words. 'My son, my brother and his wife, and now you!' She smiled—a smile of great sweetness. If ever a woman so ill could be said to be happy, Venus thought, then Doreen Gresham was. She exuded happiness—even contentment.

'And my sister's coming from London,' Doreen said. 'When will Jenny be here, love?' she asked her son.

'Any time now, Mum,' he said. He leaned over her, speaking quietly. 'Shall I do your pillows?'

She nodded assent. 'He does my pillows better than any nurse!' she said. When he had arranged her pillows he sat by the bed and held her hand. The brother and his wife from Eastbourne spoke quietly to Venus, mostly about the weather, which they said was usually that bit better in Eastbourne than it was in Brampton, from what they read in the paper. Doreen listened, or didn't listen; it was difficult to tell and it didn't matter. She was all serenity, lying there, holding her son's hand.

A few minutes later, when her sister arrived, by taxi, from the station, Albert showed her upstairs and popped his head around the door to wave to Doreen. 'You're like the Queen!' he said. 'All these visitors!'

'I feel like the Queen!' she said.

The two sisters embraced lovingly. 'Oh, Doreen love, it's been too long!'

'Too long for all of us, Jenny,' Doreen said. 'But it doesn't matter now. Nothing matters now except that you're all here!'

This was one of those times, Venus thought, when she was not needed. Everything Doreen needed was there with her, in the room.

'I'll be making my way, Doreen,' she said. 'I can

see you're in good hands. I'll pop in again tomorrow. And I will pray for you all.'

She would have liked to have given Doreen the Last Rites. It seemed to her that the time was near. But somehow, she couldn't break into the atmosphere. Perhaps tomorrow she would broach it.

James Gresham saw her out of the room. 'Will you be here tomorrow?' she asked him.

'I'll be here every day,' he said. 'I'm sleeping here. I'll not leave her, I promise you.'

But very soon now, she will leave you, Venus thought as she drove away.

*   *   *

On her way home, on an impulse, Venus called in on her parents. Mavis was in but her father was out.

Venus put her arms around her mother and gave her a big kiss.

'I love you, Mum! I love you very much!' she said.

Mavis stepped back as if she had been assaulted. 'What's brought this on, love? Are you feeling all right?'

'Quite all right!' Venus said. 'I just suddenly wanted you to know. And Dad.'

'Well, I think I did know,' Mavis said. 'But I suppose it's nice to be told. Sit down for a minute, love, and I'll make you a nice cup of tea. You do look a bit tired. I daresay it's your condition.'

Dear Mum, Venus thought. She obviously thinks I'm ill, or off my head. How awful that we can't tell our nearest and dearest we care without embarrassing them.

CHAPTER THIRTY

It was Venus's firm intention, on Tuesday morning, to visit Doreen Gresham. She had wakened in the night, thinking about her. As soon as Becky had left for school, she decided, she would set off before anything else should happen to prevent her. She could have waited until after the ten o'clock Eucharist but somehow she didn't want to. As she went through the hall to the front door the post shuttered through the letter box on to the floor. It was late today. She picked it up. As usual, it was largely junk mail but on top of the pile was one letter. It was addressed, not to The Rev'd Venus Baines, but to Mrs Nigel Baines. She knew at once who the sender was. What gave it away was the handwriting on the envelope. Upright, written thickly, in black ink, as though force had been applied to every stroke. She had seen this writing before. It was Miss Frazer's.

For a second or two she debated whether or not she should open the envelope at once, then decided not to. She was on her way to see Doreen Gresham, and Doreen, today, was more important than a dozen letters from Miss Frazer. Nor did she wish to go to see Doreen with whatever Miss Frazer had to say uppermost in her mind. It would be nothing pleasant. She put the letter on the hall table, together with the rest of the mail, and left the house.

*   *   *

When she rang the bell in Richmond Road James Gresham himself answered the door. There was no need to ask how his mother was; the answer was in his face. 'Mum died an hour ago,' he said quietly. 'I was with her. I'd been with her all night. Aunty Jenny stayed over. I've phoned Eastbourne and they're on their way.'

She followed him up the stairs and into the room where Doreen lay on her bed.

'She died very peacefully,' James said.

'I can see that,' Venus said. 'So our prayers were answered.'

He gave her a sharp look. 'I don't see that,' he said. 'She died.'

'I didn't pray she wouldn't die,' Venus said. 'I knew she was going to die. She knew it, too. I prayed that she would be granted an easy and a happy death. With her family around her. And indeed she was given that. In her last few hours your mother was a very happy woman.'

'She'd have been happier if I'd been here sooner,' James said.

'I know,' Venus said. 'But please don't spend time reproaching yourself now. You were there at the most important time; when you were most needed. You looked after her and showed her love. And you also brought other members of her family here. You saw how happy that made her.'

There was a ring at the door. 'That will be my aunt and uncle from Eastbourne,' James said. 'Aunty Jenny's in the bathroom. I must let them in.'

'And I'd like to stay here for a few minutes with your mother, if I may,' Venus said.

443

When he had left the room she sat by the bedside and said her prayers for the dead. Then she sat on quietly, thinking about Doreen. After a while she joined the others in the living room.

'You have a lot of practical things to do now,' she said to James.

'I know,' he answered. 'But first there's one thing I'd like to ask you. A favour, actually.'

'Ask away,' Venus said. She had a good idea of what was coming.

'I don't know that my mother went to church much in the last few years, I was out of touch, and I don't know that she ever did all that much, but would you do her funeral? I mean give her a proper church funeral?'

'Of course I will,' Venus said. 'No problem! In fact, Richmond Road is in my parish. And I suggest you go to Cliff Preston, in Thurston. He's the best funeral director for miles around. Shall I give you his phone number? You'll find he'll take everything off your hands. You arrange the date and time with him and he'll liaise with me.'

She stood up to leave them.

'Thank you for everything,' James said.

'Not at all,' Venus said. 'It was a privilege knowing your mother, even if only for a short time. I wish I'd known her sooner. She taught me things, including how to die a good death.'

*　　　*　　　*

She went straight from Richmond Road to the church. There was no time to call in at the Vicarage first. She had told the very few people who came on Tuesdays that they would be back in

444

their own church by today, and there they were, all six of them. Miss Frazer had not been near since she had made one—and thankfully the last—of her dramatic public exits from a Sunday Eucharist. But it had been much more peaceful without her, Venus thought now, as, vested, she walked towards the altar, deliberately putting out of her mind what might be in the letter awaiting her on the hall table. Nothing pleasant, that was certain.

'The Lord be with you!' she said.

'And also with you,' six scarcely audible voices said.

'I have just come from the bed of a woman who died early this morning,' Venus said. 'You won't know her. Her name is Doreen. It doesn't matter that she didn't come to church, or that there are only a few of us here. I would like us to offer this Mass for Doreen, and for her family.'

Not thinking about it, she had used the word 'Mass' without the sky falling in on them. But then, she reasoned, it was probably as acceptable when thought of as a requiem as it was when describing the Midnight Mass at Christmas. And now, by name, she held Doreen and each one of her family before God. And afterwards, when the short service was over and she was back in the vestry saying her own prayers, she prayed for wisdom and strength to be given her when it came to reading Miss Frazer's letter.

*   *   *

Back at the Vicarage, she picked it up and went into the kitchen, where she sat down, then opened it and read it.

445

Dear Mrs Baines

I have heard about the mockery you made of the service you held in St Mary's on Advent Sunday. I am deeply shocked, but in no way surprised.

I use the word 'mockery' advisedly. As you well know, you are neither qualified nor indeed fitted to be a priest of God. No woman can be, yet you blatantly carry on with your blasphemous conduct!

As for your new arrangements in God's House—which I have seen with my own eyes since you persist in leaving the church unlocked so that thieves may break in and steal—I find it horrendous and offensive! Who are you to disturb what has stood for hundreds of years? My father would turn in his grave!

But GOD IS NOT MOCKED! Pride goeth before a fall, and you will be brought low! Nevertheless, in spite of your behaviour, and because of the long association of myself and my family with St Mary's, I renew my offer of financial help so that the church may be restored to what it once was.

I shall not hesitate to make my views known to the Bishop and I shall insist that he does his clear duty in this matter. None of this would have happened under the previous bishop!

Yours truly
Amelia Frazer

Venus moved straight to the phone and dialled

Henry Nugent.

'I've had a letter from Miss Frazer,' she said.

'So have I,' Henry said. 'By this morning's post. The woman is mad! Possibly mad, bad and dangerous! I phoned you earlier but you weren't in. I was going to come round and show it to you.'

'I haven't listened to my messages,' Venus said. 'Anyway, I'm here now.'

Fifteen minutes later Henry was at the Vicarage, handing over his letter to Venus. It said much the same as hers, vilifying her to the same degree and in addition calling him to account because he had not accepted her offer of financial assistance. 'You are neglecting your bounden duty,' she had written. 'I would not have thought it of a man of your standing! I'm afraid, unless I hear from you that you are re-thinking the matter, I must also report you to the Bishop!'

'The Bishop's going to have a high old time,' Henry said. 'He'll not be best pleased. He hates parochial upsets. But I'm sorry for you, Venus. You don't deserve it, and I really don't think there's anyone left in St Mary's who thinks the way this woman does.'

'If they do, they don't show it,' Venus said. She was well aware, though it had not been discussed, that there had been those who had left St Mary's and gone elsewhere because of her, and she had regretted it, but it had been balanced by new people who had come into the congregation over the last year. 'And what Miss Frazer says doesn't worry me,' she added. 'Or at least, not as long as she piles it on me. If she upsets any of the congregation I will be very angry. So I don't want anyone except you, Edward and David to know

447

about Miss Frazer's letter to me.'

'Not the PCC?' Henry queried.

'No. There's no need for it. If it went to the PCC it would be likely to spread further and I don't want the congregation to have to put up with it. They've had quite enough in the past few weeks, poor lambs! In any case, the letter is personal. It's me she's getting at, and I'll cope with it.'

'How?' Henry asked.

'Probably by ignoring it,' Venus said. 'The Bishop is going to be drawn into it, willy nilly— Miss Frazer will see to that—so I'll wait to hear what he says. I just hope he won't say we should accept her money towards the restoration.'

'I don't think he will,' Henry said. 'He's not a man to have conditions imposed on him.'

'I just hope you're right,' Venus said. She thought he would be. She had a good feeling about it. And in the meantime they could manage. They had already proved that.

* * *

Elisabeth, accompanied by Carla Brown, arrived at the Vicarage promptly at seven o'clock. 'I won't come in,' Carla said, standing on the doorstep. 'Things to do! I just wanted to introduce Elisabeth—and say would someone make sure she gets home safely afterwards. Her Mum isn't keen on her being out alone after dark.'

'Of course we will!' Venus said. 'Do come in, Elisabeth! Would you like to take your coat off, and then we'll join the others.'

Elisabeth put down her flute, in its case, then took off her coat and handed it to Venus. In her jeans and red tee-shirt, and without her grey tweed coat, she looked younger than her twelve years. She had a round, pretty face, small-featured, and blonde hair which would have fallen to her shoulders had it not been fastened back in an Alice band.

'The others are here,' Venus told her, taking her through to the sitting room, Elisabeth clinging to her flute as if it was a lifeline.

'Nice to meet you!' Tim said. Jim Carstairs smiled at her and shook her hand.

Venus explained the circumstances to her, and something of the service. She didn't think it necessary to go into too much detail. 'Between us,' she said, 'but it was mainly Mr Carstairs, he's the one who knows most about music, we've chosen the hymns for next Sunday's Eucharist. It's the second Sunday in Advent so we have to have some hymns suitable for the occasion. Do you know what Advent is?' she asked.

'No,' Elisabeth said. 'Not a bit. I'm sorry.'

'Oh, that's all right,' Venus said. 'It's about looking forward to Jesus coming at Christmas. So that's what some of the hymns are about. And the ones we've chosen have reasonably easy tunes.'

'In any case,' Jim Carstairs said, 'you'll be able to take the music home with you and practise it. But why don't you play us something of your own choice, Elisabeth? Anything. Something quite short will do.'

She played well, he thought, listening to her. It was a very mature performance for a girl of twelve. 'That's fine!' he said. 'Really good! Now here's the hymn music. Are you good at sight reading?'

'All right, I suppose,' Elisabeth said.

449

'Shall we have a go then?' he said. 'The first one is "On Jordan's Bank the Baptist's Cry".'

'We've chosen that because Sunday is John the Baptist's day,' Venus said.

It went well. 'That was fine,' Tim said. 'But next time you must take the lead, Elisabeth, and I will accompany you on the keyboard. That's the way it should be.'

'Tim is quite right,' Jim Carstairs agreed. 'And don't be nervous. You'll be all right!' She was quite remarkably accomplished for her age, he thought. And her sight reading was spot-on.

They practised another Advent hymn, 'Come Thou Long-expected Jesus', then Venus said, 'And I like the last hymn to be something with a swing. I like people to go out of church feeling cheerful. It's "Sing Hosanna!"—"Give me joy in my heart, keep me praising . . ." You might not know it.'

She didn't—but when they had gone through it she said, 'I liked that one!'

'I thought you would,' Venus said. 'And you played it very well indeed. But now I think Tim should take you home . . .'

'And you must take the music with you,' Jim Carstairs said, 'so that you can practise it.'

'Could you come on Saturday so that we can try it out in the church, get the feel of it?' Venus asked.

'Oh yes! I'd like to do that,' Elisabeth said.

'She was really remarkably good!' Jim Carstairs said to Venus when Tim had left with Elisabeth. 'Quite remarkable!' It was high praise from Jim, Venus thought, but well deserved.

*   *   *

450

Next day Henry phoned Venus. 'I've heard from the Bishop,' he said. 'He was pretty mad, I can tell you. His advice to me is to show my letter to Edward and David, then send a formal acknowledgement to Miss Frazer, saying more or less nothing, and that's all. He thinks you should do nothing at all. But he'll phone you later. He had to dash off to a Diocesan meeting.'

'What did the others say to that?' Venus asked.

'Edward thought it was sound advice. David's a bit unhappy because he sees Miss Frazer's money slipping further away. He was a bit surprised by her animosity to you but I said, "You don't have the pleasure of knowing Miss Frazer. She was before your time."'

Later in the day the Bishop telephoned Venus.

'My dear,' he said, 'I'm so sorry! That pesky woman! Who does she think she is?'

'What do you want me to do?' Venus asked. 'I had thought of doing nothing.'

'Quite right!' the Bishop said. 'I've spoken with Henry Nugent, as he's probably told you. I advised him simply to make a formal acknowledgement of the letter to him, more or less what he said after the last one, but I don't think you need do even that.'

'And you don't think there's any need for either of them to go to the PCC? I certainly wouldn't want them to see mine,' Venus said.

'There's no need for anyone to see yours, it was personal, but I'm pleased I did so. And Henry tells me that the next PCC meeting isn't due for another six weeks,' the Bishop said. 'It can be referred to then. I see no reason to call a special meeting. We mustn't let this woman rule us! And to change to a more pleasant subject, how are you, my dear?'

'I'm well, thank you,' Venus said. 'But rather tired. It's different from having one baby.'

'Of course!' he said. 'So I shall see to it that you can have Tim Crawford more often. How's he doing?'

'Very well indeed.' She described how Tim had helped on Advent Sunday. 'And he's well liked.'

'Good!' he said. 'Then keep him at it. I daresay you could have him most weekends until he comes to you full time.'

'That would be wonderful!' Venus said.

'Right! I'll see to it. Good-bye for now, and take care,' he said.

*　　　*　　　*

On Sunday everything went exceptionally well. After Saturday's rehearsal, at which everyone had worked hard, Elisabeth played like a dream. In addition, she looked so good, standing there in a pretty blue wool dress which Venus suspected had been bought for the occasion, her hair clean and shining, caught back in a silver-blue band to keep it away from her face. Saturday's rehearsal had greatly increased her confidence, and if she was nervous, all signs of it vanished once she started to play. Tim was a generous accompanist, leaving Elisabeth to take the lead but always supporting her. And to add to Elisabeth's pleasure her mother, who was never a churchgoer, was there in the pews, sitting next to Carla.

Venus looked around the church during the last hymn. 'Give me joy in my heart, keep me praising,' she sang with the rest—all of them going at it with

452

gusto, Tim and Elisabeth, with their instruments, almost swinging it. And I have so much to praise God for, she thought. If she had ever doubted why she had wanted to be a priest, the answer was plain, it was in front of her: it was in these dear people, each and every one of them. And each one precious in the sight of God. This was the true place for her to be. Nothing was more important than the people in the parish—in any parish, but these were her own—and no job in the church was more important than that of the parish priest. It came to her that even Miss Frazer must be precious in God's sight—though possibly only God could love Miss Frazer! She was so hard to bear. And then the same wise priest who had taught her so much came into her mind. 'The harder it is to do,' he had said, 'the more you must pray for that person!' But for the moment, as the hymn drew to an end she put Miss Frazer and everything to do with her out of her mind.

Afterwards, at coffee, praise for the music, and for Elisabeth in particular, flowed abundantly from all sides, though Venus did hear one person saying, 'She was very good, but you can't expect a little girl to be the same as the organ, can you?' There was always one, Venus thought.

'Perhaps, in time, we could get one or two more instrumentalists,' Tim Crawford said. 'Oboe, clarinet—who knows?'

'You're being a bit ambitious,' Venus said.

'Oh, I don't think so,' Tim disagreed. 'We can ask around. No harm in that.'

*   *   *

'Tomorrow,' she said to Nigel as they were preparing for bed, 'I have Doreen Gresham's funeral.' In the evenings neither she nor Nigel was in the habit of discussing their next day's work. It was an unwritten rule that, as far as possible, that time was for each other. Nigel looked at her in surprise.

'You're more than usually affected by this, aren't you, my love?'

'I am,' she admitted. 'I'm not sure why. It's at eleven in church, and afterwards at the crematorium. Spare a prayer for us then, love.'

'Of course I will,' Nigel promised. 'Now come to bed, my darling.'

CHAPTER THIRTY-ONE

For Venus, most of the weeks between Advent Sunday and Christmas flew by with the speed of light. Everything seemed to be happening at once; events jostled each other—though of course few of them were of any importance outside the world which was Thurston. Nothing made even the *Brampton Echo*, let alone *The Times* or the *Daily Mail*. Perhaps this was because so much was good news rather than bad? It was, Venus thought, as if the setbacks of the year, and especially of the last few months—the fire, and the destruction that had followed in its wake, Miss Frazer's nasty letters, and so on—had all been dealt with, and better things were taking their place.

The Sunday services were buzzing. The extra people who had come on Advent Sunday were still

454

coming. The music was improving all the time and there was now the possibility of a clarinettist joining Tim and Elisabeth. He was not a churchgoer, he was an older man who lived in the outskirts of Thurston and had heard of their need for another instrumentalist or two and had sought out Venus and offered to help. 'I've been playing in a band until recently,' he told her, 'but there's a lot of evening work and I don't want that any longer, though I'd still like to keep my hand in.'

Jim Carstairs had been dubious about a clarinettist playing the hymns, but then, he admitted, he had been dubious about the keyboard and the flute, especially the former, and they had worked well.

For much of the time most of this was exhilarating to Venus. Things were really moving. Christmas decorations for the church and for the parish hall—though two very different venues— were being discussed. Mr Winterton had promised to give not one, but two Christmas trees: a tall one for the outside of the church and a smaller one for the inside, where space was restricted. And since many of the decorations for the trees had been stored in the old vestry and had therefore gone up in flames, people offered to lend theirs.

'Though I'm not sure Christmas trees have much to do with the Christian faith,' Venus said to Nigel.

'You could hang small paper angels on them,' he said; 'that might ward off anything which was a bit dubious.'

But some of the time, though happy with the way things were going in the church, Venus was inordinately tired, especially in the evenings. There were times when she hardly knew where to put herself. All she wanted was to go to bed and sleep and sleep.

'It's no use,' Nigel said one evening when she had been too tired to eat any supper. 'You really will have to ease up! And I'm going to ask Sonia to take a look at you—whether you like it or not.'

*　　　*　　　*

Sonia was of the same mind as Nigel. 'Speaking as your doctor,' she said, 'I have to tell you that you must slow down. You must learn to leave things to other people—I'm sure you've got lots of capable people in the church—and you must take more rest.'

'But I'm not quite seven months pregnant,' Venus protested. 'I still have a while to go.'

'I know,' Sonia said. 'And I know it's a very busy time of the year for anyone. But please do slow down!'

'I'll try,' Venus promised.

*　　　*　　　*

That same evening, it being one of the rare evenings lately when neither Venus nor Nigel had commitments, Nigel insisted that he should cook the meal. Afterwards he cleared away, stacked the dishwasher, and made Venus sit down while he served her coffee.

'This is bliss!' Venus said. 'You are a love!'

'If I had my way,' he said, 'you wouldn't do another stroke until after you'd had the babies!'

'Fat chance!' Venus said. 'Anyway, I wouldn't like that. And speaking of the babies, don't you think

456

it's time we discussed godparents? We've done nothing about that yet. The Bishop, bless his heart, has said he'll do the baptism, but we haven't given a thought to godparents, have we?'

'Well, obviously Angus for one godfather,' Nigel said. 'He was after all my best man.'

'If he'll come down from Scotland,' Venus said.

'Of course he will!' Nigel told her.

'And I thought Sonia for one of the godmothers,' Venus said. 'She's close to both of us and she's really taking an interest in the babies.'

'You couldn't have made a better choice,' Nigel said. 'And the other godmother?'

'Well, I did wonder about Evelyn Sharp,' Venus said. 'She's been a good friend to me ever since I came here—and to Becky. She'd be a very conscientious godparent. But you've known Evelyn even longer than I have. What do you think?'

'I quite agree,' Nigel said. 'Let's ask her, and hope she'll agree. That just leaves one godfather still to select.'

That proved more difficult to choose than the other three godparents put together. 'The kind of person I would like,' Venus said, 'is someone like Henry Nugent. He's everything that one could want in a godfather—but, of course, he's too old. He's sixty-two. Or there's Tim Crawford perhaps—but no! He's too young, he probably doesn't know anything about children, and we don't know how long he's going to be around, do we?'

'He also mightn't want the responsibility,' Nigel said.

'Oh well,' Venus concluded, 'we'll just have to give it more thought. We have time to do that.'

'Not all that much,' Nigel said. 'Not for such an

important decision.'

She did try to slow down, but there were certain things—sick visiting, funerals, weddings, though there were fewer of the latter at this time of the year—which she would not let anyone else do, not even Tim Crawford. In the run-up to Christmas there was the end-of-term carol service for the school, and in the Sunday School there was the Christmas party. They were all things she loved to do and was not to be dissuaded from taking part. 'The only major event after Christmas, and it's not until the seventh of January,' she told Nigel, 'is the visit to the pantomime—and Trudy Santer has that all in hand. I know she's booked the coach. All you and I have to do is to turn up.'

'Then do that. And see you keep out of the rest of it!' Nigel cautioned.

*   *   *

In the week leading up to Christmas everyone was busy. Not since she had arrived at St Mary's had Venus seen so many people working together; more, even, than had turned up to help after the fire. There were small groups everywhere, inside the church, in the parish hall, and in the churchyard. The weather was fine: cold and frosty at night (though thankfully the heating was now working in the church) and, unusually for Thurston, there was no wind.

The front of the church was floodlit every day that week, from the moment darkness fell in the afternoon until midnight. It was a mellow light, accentuating, without glare, the shape of the centuries-old building against the darkness of the

458

December sky. The ancient stone took on a beauty of its own, as if it had been revitalised for the occasion. It was, Venus thought, pausing at the lych gate to gaze at it, heart-stopping.

But even more heart-stopping as the days went by were the people using their particular skills—and if they had no special skills, content to be dogsbodies—fetching and carrying, moving and clearing, doing whatever came to hand. Keith Chapman, husband of Jenny who had been coming to church (though always without him) ever since the fire, had fixed up lighting to illuminate Mark Dover's screen painting, in which the timeless fields and Downs—there were no buildings—looked for all the world as if they could have been the hills around Bethlehem. So skilled was Keith's work that only the painting showed, and the devastated area in front of it was in darkness. The sheep, of which there were no more than two or three, looked like very well-fed examples of local Southdown sheep. Nothing, Venus thought, like the specimens which might have grazed on Bethlehem's hills.

Outside on the lawn, in front of the church, a group of teenagers, recruited by Tony Franklin who taught Art at Brampton Art College (but who lived in Thurston), were constructing a nativity scene from who-knew-what materials—wood, cloth, bits of leather, papier mâché, modelling clay—and painting it. Only the baby in the crib had not been made by them, but borrowed from Molly Nugent's granddaughter on condition that it was returned to her every single night. Who would steal the Christ child? Venus asked herself. The answer, she knew, was that a great many people might. In the same way they would have to keep the closest watch they could on the nativity scene or it might well be defaced, even in Thurston.

Inside the church, early on Christmas Eve and on at least two occasions before that, Tim Crawford, Elisabeth and Ben Turner, the clarinettist, under Jim Carstairs, worked away at the Christmas music while the flower-arranging ladies were fixing and dressing the indoor Christmas tree and decorating the pew ends with greenery and berries.

* * *

The church was full for Midnight Mass, that is, the part of the church which was usable was full. Most of the people who had been helping earlier were there, with the exception of some of the children—and there were several strangers. That was par for the course on Christmas Eve. Henry and Edward fetched chairs from the parish hall and tucked them in wherever there was a space. Everything looked beautiful in the light from the dozens of candles and the lights from the Christmas trees. It was a brave, defiant beauty, as it might be of an old and damaged woman, bravely hiding her flaws and faults under pretty clothes and a mask of rejoicing—and in the soft light of the candles, it worked. There was a feeling in the air that everyone had given of their best to bring what had been a most difficult year to a better-than-ever conclusion.

Standing behind the altar, Venus viewed the sea of faces in front of her. So many of them were now good friends. And there were her mother and father with Becky, allowed to stay up for this special occasion, sitting between them. Not long now before Becky will have her two brothers and Nigel and I our two sons, she thought. Nine weeks. She said a silent prayer for Nigel, in St Patrick's.

Everything went smoothly. The music was splendid and Elisabeth, her hair tied back with sparkly gold ribbons, her eyes shining with excitement, looked so pretty. If Venus felt sorry for anyone it was for Jim Carstairs. As the congregation had streamed into the church before the service he had said, 'This is when I would have been playing the organ. The first Christmas in thirty years I haven't played here! I do so miss it.'

Afterwards, she stood at the door, receiving and giving Christmas wishes to a long queue of people. In the end it was Sonia who brought a chair, saying, 'You've just got to sit down, Venus. Doctor's orders!' And then in the end Sonia had said, 'I'm going to take you home. And please do try to rest over Christmas. Let everyone else do the work.'

'Oh, I will!' Venus promised. 'I don't think I'll be allowed to lift a finger once I've finished taking the sick communions.'

When Venus went into the Vicarage—Sonia had left her at the door—Nigel was already home, speaking on the phone to his mother in Quilty. He stretched out his hand and took hold of Venus's, and then in the end he handed the phone over to her. 'I hope you're looking after yourself,' Mrs Baines said. 'And those little grandsons of mine! We'll see you in early March, Veronica and myself. We'll get on a plane the minute Nigel tells us they've been born. Don't keep us waiting, will you, love?'

461

'I certainly hope not!' Venus said. 'Sonia says she doesn't think I'll go to full term. Anyway, outside Thurston, you'll be the first to hear.'

* * *

The rest of Christmas came and went. Venus's mother insisted on taking over most of the cooking on Christmas Day and Boxing Day, though she was assisted by Ann Stanton, who came to stay for three nights. 'I wouldn't want to miss seeing my granddaughter at Christmas, would I?' she said. 'Not to mention the rest of you!' And then on the Sunday after Christmas—everyone was now at coffee—a surprise came.

David Wainright, seated at Venus's table together with Henry and Molly Nugent and Connie Phillipson, suddenly rose to his feet. 'And now,' he said, 'I have an announcement to make!' Venus wondered what it could be. David had been reasonably calm and quiet for the last few weeks. There had been no further repercussions from Miss Frazer—though it was only a matter of time before there were, Venus thought. Miss Frazer was like a volcano, she could erupt at any time—and David had been well occupied trying to sort out the long-drawn-out insurance claims.

'I have an announcement to make!' he repeated. It was not in David to speak until he was sure he had a receptive audience, and in this case he had, since everyone went quiet. It was something in the tone of his voice.

'Connie,' he said, 'my dear Connie, has consented to be my wife! We are engaged to be married.' He took hold of Connie's hand and pulled her to her feet. She was smiling, blushing, and near to tears, all at the same time.

'Goodness, you're a dark horse!' Edward Mason said.

'Rubbish!' Molly Nugent whispered to Henry. 'Anyone who hasn't seen that coming must be half blind!'

Henry jumped to his feet and made a short, congratulatory speech. He frequently disagreed with David, but this was no time to think about that. 'And we all know Connie will make you a splendid wife!' he finished. 'After all, she knows what it's like to be married to a treasurer!'

Connie spoke up for the first time. 'I was very happily married to my first Treasurer,' she said. 'I shall never forget him. And for the future I shall be every bit as happy married to David. I'm a very lucky woman!' She sat down, blushing with dignified pleasure.

'Did you expect that?' Nigel asked Venus later, when they were back at the Vicarage.

'Yes and no,' Venus said. 'I've seen which way the wind was blowing for some time now, but I wasn't sure it would come to anything. Isn't it nice?'

'Will she keep him in order?' Nigel asked. 'Or will it be the other way round?'

'A bit of each, I guess,' Venus said. 'I'm sure Connie can hold her own.'

*   *   *

Sonia was proved right. On an evening in the first week of January—Becky was in bed, probably now fast asleep, and Nigel, who was on call, had been summoned to an emergency—Venus was watching television and thinking she would go to bed the minute he was back, when she felt the first contraction. There was no mistaking it, even though she had not experienced anything like it for more than eleven years, even though the babies were not due for another eight weeks. This was it! She felt, simultaneously, exhilaration—and a slight sense of fear. When the contraction was over she immediately phoned her mother.

'Can you come round at once?' she said. 'Nigel is out and I'm quite sure I've started labour.'

'I'll be round in a jiffy! Have you rung Sonia?'

'I will, right away,' Venus said.

Sonia arrived quickly, less than five minutes after Mavis. 'I've just put the kettle on for a cup of tea,' Mavis said.

'I don't think we'll wait for it,' Sonia said. 'We'll go straight to the hospital. I can't say this is unexpected, and twins can come quickly as well as early.'

'What about Nigel?' Venus asked. 'He wanted to be there.'

'And I expect he will be,' Sonia said. 'I'll ring him on his mobile as soon as we get to the hospital. I haven't any doubt he'll be there the first minute he can. Let's get you into the car.'

The second contraction came as Sonia drove into the hospital car park. She waited until it was over, before she took Venus to the Maternity block. In the few minutes they had to wait there for attention she dialled Nigel. 'Quite quickly, I would think,' she said to him. And then she handed the phone over to Venus.

'Oh, Nigel, it's happening!' Venus said. 'No, I

feel fine, honestly! Looking forward to seeing you. Love you!'

'I'll stay with you until Nigel arrives,' Sonia said. 'If I won't be in the way.'

'I'll soon tell you if you are,' the midwife said. 'For the moment you're fine.'

*   *   *

Nigel was there well before the first baby was born at two in the morning.

'Is he all right?' Venus asked anxiously. 'The baby?'

'That's what you mothers always say!' the midwife said. 'Of course he is! He's quite perfect! Now let's be having the next one.'

The second baby was born half-an-hour later. 'And he's perfect too!' the midwife said. 'He weighs in at four-and-a-half pounds—four ounces less than his elder brother! Congratulations to both of you.'

'They're so tiny—and so beautiful!' Venus said. 'Anthony and Colin. Our sons!'

There were tears running down Nigel's face. The midwife handed him a tissue. 'You dads are all alike,' she said. 'So which is Anthony and which is Colin?'

'The first one is Anthony and the second one Colin,' Venus said.

And then she was suddenly unbelievably tired. All she wanted was to go to sleep. 'Remember to phone your mother the minute you get home,' she said to Nigel. 'I promised she'd be one of the very first to know. And I'm sorry I'll miss the pantomime, but you must take Becky.' And then

465

she closed her eyes and slept.

*   *   *

A few days later the Bishop telephoned. 'I've had good reports from the new father,' he said. 'But I thought I'd like a word with you. How are you?'

'Absolutely fine!' Venus said. 'I'll be home in a few days.'

'And I understand the twins are the most beautiful babies in the world?'

'Naturally!' Venus agreed.

'Well, don't do anything much in the parish,' the Bishop said. 'Make as much use as you can of Tim Crawford. And do you still want the baptism in three weeks' time or is that too soon? Please do say.'

'I'm sure it will be fine,' Venus said. 'We're looking forward to it.'

After further thought she and Nigel had decided that Henry Nugent would be quite the best choice for Colin's godfather. He had, they agreed, every good quality they could ever want, except for his age. 'But sixty-two isn't old these days,' Nigel said. 'He's highly likely to be around all the time the boys are growing up—which is the most important time.'

Henry had been delighted to be asked. 'It's a wonderful compliment,' he said. 'And I'll do my best for the lad in every way.'

*   *   *

The baptism took place—it was how both Venus and Nigel wanted it—within the Sunday morning

466

Eucharist, in the presence of the whole congregation. She was reminded, by Mr Winterton himself, that the first time she had done that after coming to St Mary's was when she had baptised his granddaughter. 'I liked the way the whole congregation put the questions to the parents and godparents, and they answered to the congregation,' he said. 'It was as if everyone cared.'

Nigel's mother and his Aunt Veronica had, as promised, caught the first plane out from Shannon very soon after the birth, and had arranged to stay until after the baptism. It disappointed them a little that it was to be held in St Mary's rather than in St Patrick's, but they were pleased that Father Seamus had agreed to take part in the ceremony, as indeed he had done when Venus and Nigel had married there.

'People of God,' the Bishop said to the congregation, 'will you welcome Anthony and Colin, and will you uphold them in their new life in Christ?'

Nothing could have prevented the tears springing into Venus's eyes at the sound of the whole congregation saying, 'With the help of God, we will.' Nigel grabbed her hand and held it tightly. Only the sound of the babies crying lustily as the Bishop poured water over their heads in turn brought her back to near normal.

'There will be refreshments for everyone in the parish hall,' Henry Nugent announced at the end.

'And I must take these two off and give them their refreshment first,' Venus said to Nigel. Then she turned to Nigel's mother. 'And will their grandmother come with me and give me a hand?'